John Fletcher lives in a small coastal town south of Adelaide. He has lived and worked in Europe, Asia and Africa as well as Australia. An author and dramatist whose plays have been produced for radio and television by the BBC and the South African Broadcasting Corporation, his short stories have appeared in Australia and throughout the world. He writes a regular column for the *Straits Times* in Singapore.

John Fletcher is the author of four previous novels, all of which have received both critical and popular acclaim and earned him a wide audience and loyal following.

Claim the Kingdom and *The Burning Land*, both historical sagas set in Australia, were published by Arrow in 1996 and 1997.

A FAR COUNTRY

JOHN FLETCHER

ARROW

An Arrow book
published by
Random House Australia Pty Ltd
20 Alfred Street, Milsons Point, NSW 2061
http://www.randomhouse.com.au

Sydney   New York   Toronto
London   Auckland   Johannesburg

First published 2000
Copyright © John Fletcher 2000

National Library of Australia
Cataloguing-in-Publication Data
Fletcher, John, 1934–.
A Far Country.
ISBN 0 091 84195 X.
I. Title
A823.3

Typeset by Midland Typesetters, Maryborough, Victoria
Printed and bound by Griffin Press, Netley, South Australia

10 9 8 7 6 5 4 3 2 1

To Luke, who missed out last time, and to Stefan, who kindly gave me the use of his name

CONTENTS

PROLOGUE

I

I am in torment, therefore I shall go today to the place where it happened.

If Gavin knew he would prohibit it for fear it might upset me too much or—far worse—for fear it might not upset me at all.

He has always believed that he knows what is good for me, what is bad for me. He has always been sure of that, as of everything. At least he had been until now, until the death of Edward Erhart Matlock, our son, aged fourteen. I do not normally take issue with my husband but today is different. It is not every day, after all, that one mourns the loss of one's only child.

Gavin is afraid for me, what I may do or not do. I see it in his eyes. He no longer knows me. He is a big man, hard and on occasion pitiless, as he must be if he is to have any chance of subduing this hard and pitiless land. When he heard the news of our son's death he screamed his hurt like a baby, hands like hammers punishing the earth. He is incapable of understanding that my own sorrow is no less real for being hidden. Most women show their feelings and it offends his sense of propriety that I do not. I cannot do it. My grief is in my blood and marrow and bone, too deeply rooted to find expression in the tears and keening he expects. I see him watching my dry eyes, my face and voice without evidence of grief. He thinks I am cold.

I cannot help what he thinks.

All the same, it angers me. How can he think such things? He has known me seventeen years yet it is plain that he understands nothing of me, has never understood. This realisation shocks me. I am watching him—a person whom I thought as much a part of me as my breath and blood, a sharer in my fears, my joys, in eating and sleeping and loving—become a stranger before my eyes.

Death has taken more than the breath and bone and skin, the joy and hope that was our son. So be it. I have survived everything else that life has brought me. I shall survive this.

As soon as Gavin has left the house—it seems obscene that the daily work must continue despite death and grief, yet how can it be otherwise?—I shall go to the place where Edward died. I shall go alone. I shall say my farewells to my son in my own way. He will understand why my grief is hidden. He will not question it, he to whom all knowledge and all secrets are now revealed.

II

The peninsula runs from north-east to south-west. It is flat, featureless, a vast tongue of grass and scattered trees licking at the ocean. It is good country, or so Gavin believes: good for wheat, good for potatoes, good for sheep. When we first came to this continent ten years ago, with its heat and dust, its arid, enigmatic vastness, its scattering of white settlers and natives black as death, naked as air, he knew at once what he was going to do. From the moment he set eyes on this land he wanted it with an intensity that was, I now believe, closer to lust than love. He was determined to take it, by force if there were no other way; by force I would say was his preference: although why I should think such a thing I do not know. Certainly he has never used force with me, only kindness and consideration. From the first he made it easy for me to love him, this English giant who had himself been so strange to me when my father first took me from our home in western Norway to meet him.

My father was master of a barque trading between Britain and Norway. I was fifteen when I first accompanied him; eighteen when for the last time I travelled on his vessel to the sea town in north Yorkshire where I was to be married. It was strange to leave our wooden house at the head of the fjord where the still waters reflected the cliffs that rose vertically into the air for a thousand feet on either side, stranger still to come to this other land where the houses, the people, the very air were so different from everything I had known.

3

God knows what I would have thought had I realised that this preliminary foray into the world would be no more than the first step of a journey that four years later would bring me, no longer Asta Foldal but Asta Matlock, to a far country on the other side of the earth; a country so very different from the peat-dark waters, the mountains and white painted houses of home that it might have been in another universe. Not that it would have made any difference, whatever I had thought. In my father's house I did my father's bidding.

Things are not so different now, after all.

When we arrived in Australia my husband took a job with a surveying party at twenty-three shillings and sixpence a week: to spy out the land, as he put it. He spied to such good effect that within a year we had our own place on the outskirts of the city they called Adelaide, after an English queen. The land was fertile, although hot in summer, with flies and much dust. We grew wheat and ran sheep on the land we called ours but I knew from the first that we would not settle there. The presence of so many people a few miles down the road was a constant pressure in my husband's head as, indeed, it was in mine. In north Yorkshire, as in Norway, there are few people and no dust or flies to talk of. How I missed that clean northern stillness. I said nothing, however: there was no going back. Besides, I loved my husband. At that time I still believed that love made up for all else.

My husband also had a hunger for the north but not my north, with its stillness and clean cold air: the interior of this new land drew him like a lodestone. I was frightened by its harshness, the sense of alienation that I felt whenever I thought of it. I would be lonely there, as lonely as only a woman

4

can be in a strange land, pursuing a dream that is not, has never been, her own.

I would let no-one see my fear, neither Gavin nor my son Edward who had just turned fourteen and was as eager as his father to set out into the unknown. I would not let *myself* see it, burying it deep where I could deny its presence.

Ian Matlock saw it, for all my efforts. That man is a devil. Gavin's cousin, five years younger, with the same yellow hair and skin baked the colour of brick by the fierce southern sun. He joined us at Gavin's invitation two years after we first came out. I saw at once that he was as hungry for land as my husband, determined to seize whatever he could hold, whether he could put it to good use or not. He was acquisitive to the bone, and not only of land. I had met him only at my wedding; even then, I had felt the weight of his hungry eyes on me.

Like a fool I was relieved when, a year after my own wedding, he married Mary Hunter, daughter of a Whitby shopkeeper. I was even prepared to like him for a while until I realised that nothing, neither marriage nor anything else, would ever satisfy him.

We are as we are.

Here, in this southern land, his rapacious glare was a hundred times heavier than it had been in England. His eyes probed for the body beneath my clothes, pricing it by the quality of skin and flesh and hair.

Availability was irrelevant. It was not physical possession that interested him. He summed me up, knew and understood me, had me pinned like a specimen to a board. There were no secrets from those pale eyes. Being stripped naked would have felt less shameful.

I was helpless, of course. He had done nothing.

But I knew and he knew that I knew. That was the worst thing of all, the sense of violation compounded by helplessness.

A year after Edward's birth Mary had a daughter. They named her Alison after Ian's mother. By the time our two families moved north in 1846 she was twelve years old. In those years before the move, we had both had other children, I two, Mary one, but none had lived. No more of that.

On the day of our departure Ian sought me out, as I had known he would.

'An adventure,' he said, pale eyes smiling at me. 'Nothing to be afraid of.'

'Then it is fortunate that I am not afraid, is it not so?'

He knew the truth, of course, and made sure that I saw he knew, but said nothing. Just as he never mentioned how I had never learnt to speak his language as casually as my own, yet with him I was always conscious of it as I was with no-one else.

I have Gavin, I thought in self-defence. And Edward. But Edward, my joy and consolation, was too young to understand and Gavin, my protector and my husband, saw nothing.

We headed north up the eastern shore of the St Vincent Gulf. We passed many drays bringing ore south to Adelaide from the recently opened copper mine they called the Burra Burra. Each dray was drawn by a team of bullocks and guided by two drovers. The noise of their whips and voices filled the hot air as did the dust churned up by their passing. The sounds passed but the dust remained; a chalky film that covered our skins, irritated our eyes, filled our lungs. At times the sun itself was obscured, an orange disc peering through grey mist. Gavin was exasperated by the unexpected presence

6

of so many men. He craved solitude as much as space and as soon as we reached the head of the gulf we turned westwards across the range and so came into the land that we were to claim as our own.

Our company consisted of the two families, a forty-year-old farm supervisor named Hector Gallagher and his son Blake; and three shepherds, one black, two white. We brought cattle, sheep and horses and the guns and implements we would need to establish ourselves and survive in the wilderness.

There were no creeks, no surface water, but Gavin said nothing about turning back.

'Look at the grazing,' he said. 'Hundreds of miles of it. There must be water underneath the soil. Or a good rainfall.' And gazed speculatively at the cloud-free sky.

From time to time we saw parties of blacks, as remote and mysterious as the land through which we travelled. We made ready our guns but they did not trouble us, not then. It occurred to none of us that we were intruders in a land they considered their own, nor would it have made any difference had it done so. We were here to take the land and take it we would.

We settled at this place, a point rather more than halfway down the peninsula and close to its eastern shore, in a fold of land that we hoped would protect us from the worst of the hot north wind. There was enough timber to build a house for ourselves, another for Hector Gallagher and his son, and buildings for the animals. Ian Matlock and his wife and daughter took a property adjoining our southern boundary. Technically the flocks belonged half to Ian and half to ourselves but it was understood that they would graze in common over all the land. There were no neighbours, no fences, no lawyers to tell us where we might and might not go. Everything we saw was ours: by the power of our guns and of our will.

From the house the land falls away eastwards until it ends at the line of cliffs, a hundred feet in height, which border the gulf. The cliffs are sheer, affording no access to the water that creams rumbling at their feet. In the air beyond the cliff edge seabirds wheel and call, white plumage bright against the blue sea. The edge of the cliff might have been cut by a knife: a line dividing what is from what cannot be.

One day shortly after we arrived I took Edward for a walk towards the sea. I say I took Edward; in truth he took me. He had been there already, drawn by the sea, the cliffs, above all by the sense of danger that had attracted him since he first walked. I cautioned him: of course. He heard my warnings and ignored them: of course. He was not a boy to be held in a noose of words.

He pointed. 'There *is* a way down. See?'

I looked, my toes jutting over the edge. Growing up where I had, I had no fear of cliffs, of the unprotected and beckoning air. Sure enough, there was a cleft, steep—in places almost vertical and glassy with polished rock—and marked with a thin silt of dust and loose earth. It was a trail used by animals, I thought. It ran from the cliff top twenty yards to our left to—I had to crane my neck to see—a level patch of grass, ten yards or so wide, above a final section of cliff that plunged vertically into a small inlet a few yards across that I thought might be exposed at low tide. From here it was hard to tell how high the final step was, perhaps not more than five or six feet. Not that it mattered; neither Edward nor I was going down there to find out.

'Please,' Edward pleaded, reading my thoughts.

'It is too steep.'

At home I had clambered down steeper paths than that before I was his age.

'I can manage it.'

'No.'

The distant swathe of grass was cool and enticing but I would not allow myself to look at it. I turned my back, Edward following reluctantly at my heels, and walked slowly away along the edge of the cliffs, enjoying the salt breeze that cooled my face and moved the heavy weight of hair on my neck.

'I could manage it easily,' Edward complained.

I know now that I should have permitted him to use the path but I did not. We walked on until I wished to go no further then circled back inland until we reached the house: as though by avoiding further sight of the path I would somehow put it out of his mind.

When we reached home I put my hands on his shoulders and looked down at him. 'I want you to promise not to climb down there.' I shook him slightly to show how serious I was. 'It is too dangerous. Do you understand?'

He tried to avoid answering but I insisted. I should not have asked it; even as I spoke I knew that, given his nature, it was a promise it would be impossible for him to keep. Above all I should never have mentioned the word danger but I had done so and it was too late.

III

The walk through the tall grass has heated me. I wipe the sweat from my face. I can feel it running over my body beneath my clothes. My boots are covered in dust and grass seeds cling to my skirt. I take no notice of any of these things.

The air along the cliff is still. The noise of the surf comes clearly to me. I can feel the ground tremble beneath my feet as each roller rears against the rocks and wonder how it will be in this place when the winter storms arrive. I reach the head of the track. I do not hesitate but start straight down, feeling the heat coming up out of the ground, hands grasping at knots of coarse grass, feet slipping in the loose earth. The surface of the rock is smooth as glass. It gives no handhold. Emptiness yawns beneath my feet. I can hear the buzz of insects, feel the itch of pollen on my skin, smell the harsh dry smell of thrift and sun-hot grass. I slip and slither a yard or two, grabbing grass stems. I regain control and rest a moment, panting, eyes smarting with sweat.

As I have told no-one where I am going, there will be no-one to help me should I need help.

I come to a section even steeper than what has gone before. I lift my heavy skirt and tuck it into my waistband. My boots are not suitable for this sort of ground. There is a narrow crevice scratched between two flat rock faces. The rock is grooved vertically: no hand- or foot-holds there. I turn inwards to face the cliff, toes stretching for a roughness in the crevice that will provide some sort of hold. Through my straddled legs I see the sea surging against the gleaming rocks fifty feet below, hear the grate of shingle sucked to and fro by the tide. My boot rests on a roughness. Cautiously, I put pressure on it. It slips. It will never bear my weight. I turn my head with difficulty. On either side the rock stretches away.

How did Edward get down here? The question repeats itself again and again inside my head.

Perhaps he did not. It is the easy answer. Perhaps he slipped, as I almost slipped, and fell from this point straight into the sea. It would explain what happened. Except there were no broken bones, no lacerations as would be caused by a fall from this height. The only lesions on his skin had been caused after death, the body tumbling in the surf until it was wedged at last between the rocks.

No. He did not fall. Even if I had never seen his body, I would have known how my son died. I can see it as clearly as if I had been there: as in one sense, perhaps, I was. I know because the same thing almost happened to me in the bleak and frigid waters of the fjord that until I die will be home to me.

My foot stretches again, futilely, my fingertips, white with pressure, crooked around the top of the rock slab. I must not stay here too long. Do that and I shall lose my nerve to move at all, shall hang helpless until cramp prises my grip from the rock and gravity sucks me hurtling downwards. Even now I can feel the ache building in my bent fingers, my outstretched arms.

I twist my neck and stare downwards. Six feet below, perhaps eight, a bush grows out of a rock. If I let myself drop ... How securely is it rooted? If, as I suspect, Edward did the same it may prove strong enough, although Edward and I, of course, are not the same. I am not a heavy woman but heavier, I am sure, than a fourteen-year-old boy. Commit myself to the drop and there is no way back if the roots turn out to be insecure after all. Bush and human will fall helplessly together.

The sea surges, blue ringed with circles of white.

I doubt I have the strength to pull myself up. I open my fingers and let myself fall.

The rock face strips skin from my elbows, my knees. Branches score my legs with fire. I snatch, lose my grip, snatch again. The bush sways alarmingly. I cling, tight as a limpet. I can sense the strain my weight imparts to the roots: it is not a tree or even a very large bush. I doubt it will hold me for long. A foot away a shallow horizontal gash crosses the surface of the rock. I must not miss. I open my hands. As my body begins to fall I lunge at the gash. My fingers lock into the crevice. My body is a river of sweat but I do not care. I am safe.

Below the bush is a slope of earth. It is steep and treacherous, loose stones falling in a cascade as my feet touch them, but after the rock face it is nothing. I scramble down the last few yards and reach the lush carpet of grass at the foot of the cliff. I lie full length on my back on the moist cool grass. Far overhead the cliff top draws its stark line against the sky. My body is wracked with tremors. Slowly my breath eases.

After ten minutes I am strong enough to get to my feet. I walk to the edge of the grass and look down at the water. It surges below my feet, close enough to spatter me with the occasional gout of spray. It is not more than eight feet down to the strip of grey sand strewn with shells and pebbles that is rhythmically covered and uncovered by the falling tide.

The water must be only a few inches deep.

I look more closely. The sea has been working here. Over the centuries, the pounding waves have scoured the cliff into a deep curving wall. It is smooth, without cracks or crevices of any kind. There are no bushes, no vegetation. From the sand it will present a curving overhang, eight feet in height. As long as the tide is out anyone on that patch of beach will be safe. Once it turns, the only ways of escape will be up the cliff or out through the narrow entrance into the waters of the gulf. I watch the waves breaking heavily in the entrance. No-one could live in them, and the smooth rock overhang, eight feet above the sand, would be out of the reach of a fourteen-year-old boy.

I never warned him. I had been here before yet I never thought to say anything to him.

We fjord children were brought up by the water. It held few terrors for us but we learned early to treat it with the respect the sea demands. I must have been more or less the same age as Edward. With my father so often away, I grew up with greater freedom than most. I used to explore by myself. There was a cliff, dark, high and frowning, at its base the same curving inlet, the same circular overhang rubbed smooth by the sea. I had jumped down to the wet sand before I realised there was no way back. I would have drowned in the frigid water had a fishing boat not found me.

I have been here before.

I look at the surf thundering in the entrance, behind my back I feel the cliff looming high overhead, the sun-bright water is blurred by my tears.

I kneel, eyes screwed tight, clasped hands raised to the breaking waves. I hear their voice beyond the darkness of my closed eyelids, taste the mist of spray on my lips, feel the rock tremble beneath my knees at the relentless hammer-blows of the sea.

The sea has taken him, the child I loved. I am of the sea. I look to it for recompense.

BOOK ONE

PETREL

Petrels form an extensive family of seabirds common to the Southern Ocean. Individual birds are occasionally beached after storms along the South Australian coast.

ONE

Left hand clasping a tin pannikin brimming with hot rum, Jason Hallam came out from the shelter of the deck house and hurried aft, staggering and lurching against the wild movement of the hull. The gale sank its claws in him. Far above his head the three mast tops swung violently against the black clouds that drove in endlessly from the west. The few scraps of sail that remained unfurled strained full-bellied in the wind. Even from the deck Jason could hear the triumphant yell of the storm in the spider's web of rigging. The wind blew the tops off the waves and flung them over the rail in solid sheets of water, cold, salt and dangerous. They fell heavily on him. At once he was soaked, as he had been soaked so often since they had left Hobart Town five days before. Van Diemen's Land and his whole past life behind him, the unknown and his whole future ahead of him. If he had a future. If the *Kitty* survived.

Jason worked his way along the slippery deck, free hand snatching at handholds—stanchions, shrouds, the windward rail—all running with water.

It was lunacy to be on deck at all in this weather. No matter. Captain Hughes expected a prompt and unfailing response to all his orders and one of them had been to have the cabin boy deliver one pannikin of hot rum every half-hour to the captain's station beside the helmsman. The cabin boy: meaning Jason, aged fifteen. It was typical of Captain Hughes that he should call him by his function and not by his name, as it was typical to issue such an order at all, disregarding the near impossibility of getting the rum to him in such weather without losing most of it over the side. He demanded it and expected it. Failure would be the cabin boy's failure, to be punished when the opportunity for punishment occurred.

The weather had been unremittingly foul since the *Kitty* had put to sea and Jason had therefore had plenty of practice in delivering the precious container of rum. By now he had mastered the art to the point where he spilt hardly any of it and, if Captain Hughes did not praise him, at least he no longer gave him the crack around the head that had greeted his earlier and less successful efforts.

The great world was proving every bit as harsh a place as his brother Tom, slow-witted but five years older and vastly more experienced, had warned him it would be.

Not that Jason cared. He had been hungry for the chance to go with his brother, had warned him that if he did not take him on the *Kitty*'s next voyage he would stow away anyway.

Cheeky bastard, Tom had called him, but had gone to see the master, all the same. Hadn't had much choice, really, not with Jason alone in the world. He could have abandoned him, of course, plenty of brothers would have done that and thought nothing of it, but Tom had never been that sort: although Jason, big for his age and with a mind of his own, would no doubt have managed well enough.

It had happened so suddenly: their mother struck down with fever in Hobart Town and dead within a week; his father, liver destroyed by booze, disintegrating before Jason's eyes.

Tom had been a deck hand on the *Kitty* for three years. The last voyage had been a long one: up the coast to Sydney and then several times north to Moreton Bay with supplies for the settlers who had been pouring into the area since it had first been opened up three years earlier in 1842. It had been almost a year before the *Kitty* had re-entered the Derwent River. Tom had returned to find his mother dead, his father dying and Jason on the verge of being alone in the world.

'Be sure to mind your lip,' Tom warned him. 'You always was too smart for your own good, as I recall. Try anything on with the Cap'n, he'll put you over the side.'

Jason and discipline had never got along. 'Maybe I won't come at all, then.'

'Suit yourself.'

Wild horses wouldn't have kept him. Home was a tar paper shack in a confusion of other tar paper shacks. Both parents had been transported. Neither had had the energy, ambition or intelligence to rise above their miserable beginnings. All Jason had known had been a confusion of alleyways and mud-filled courts with sewage running in open channels down the middle, the stench of filth, poverty and despair.

It might have been enough for his parents but Jason wanted more from life. If this was home you could keep it.

'What's the captain like?' he asked curiously.

'He's all right.' Tom rubbed his chin. 'Won't stand no sass, mind. You jump when he says jump, you'll be right. Watch out for Lew Bone, though.'

'Who's he?'

'Bosun. Big bastard. Bit of a punch artist. Did some prize fighting in Sydney and never lets anyone forget it. Captain Hughes'll give you a clip round the head but it don't mean nothing. More for show, see? Lew Bone hits to hurt.'

'He don't scare me none,' Jason boasted.

Tom looked at him scornfully. 'You don' know you're pupped. Lew Bone will eat you for breakfast. You keep out of his way.'

Tom had spoken to Captain Hughes, a man with his own way of looking at things and God help you if you crossed him; at heart a fair enough man, nonetheless.

'God save us,' he had growled ferociously. 'Fifteen years, ye say? Next thing ye'll be wanting me to take babbies out of the cradle.' But the captain found Jason a berth, all the same. 'No cheek, mind. Understand me, lad? No cheek, no smart answers. One false step and ye're beached.' A bloodshot eye had scoured Jason's face suspiciously, looking for cheek. 'One false step, that's all it takes.'

'Yessir.'

His father had been a week in his grave when the *Kitty* put to sea. Jason stood at the stern and watched as the barque cleared the Derwent and headed westwards under a sky black with the threat of storm. The land fell back. Jason turned to face the dark sea, the heavy rollers shod with foam. The strengthening wind blew the black hair back from his face.

A gateway to the future, a door closing on the past.

20

As for Lew Bone ... Jason was the sort who had to learn everything the hard way. Half an hour after the *Kitty* entered the Southern Ocean the ex-fighter found him.

'Who the hell are you?'

Lew Bone stood in the forecastle entrance and stared at Jason out of eyes encircled with scar tissue. He was a big bastard, as Tom had said. His cheeks were hard with muscle and his back and shoulders were as broad as the deck but Jason had grown up as rough as any and wasn't the sort to be intimidated.

'New cabin boy. Who are you?'

Jason never saw the blow, just felt it explode in a scarlet burst of pain on his left ear. His feet left the ground. He crashed backwards into the bulkhead and slithered stunned to the deck.

Through hazed eyes, ear ringing like Hobart church tower, he saw Lew Bone glaring down at him. 'I'm the bloke what'll punch yore lights out, you give me any smart-arse talk,' he said, 'an' don' you forget it.'

'I *warned* you,' Tom told him later but made no attempt to interfere. In this world, as in the one he had left, Jason would have to fight his own battles.

I'll fix him, he promised himself but after five days the opportunity had still not arisen.

Staggering and slipping, half-running, Jason scooted down the deck, following the tilt of the hull, and almost collided with the captain as he stood with the mate at the helmsman's side.

'Steady, boy, dern you!' Hughes growled. Rum safe in his freckled paw, he took a half-hearted swipe at Jason's ear and missed; his mind was on other things. Water streaming from his collar, Hughes craned his head upwards. For the first time

Jason realised there were men clinging to the crazily swinging yards as they tried to see through the tumult of rain and spray that lay ahead of the plunging vessel.

'What d'you see?'

The captain's bellow was swept away by the wind: but not altogether, it seemed. A moment's silence, then from one of the tiny figures far above their heads came a faint answering hail.

'Nothing . . .'

Steam wreathed the captain's face as he took a deep swig of hot rum. 'I don't like it, mister,' he confided to the mate. 'By my reckoning we should be well into the gulf by now.'

'Maybe we are.'

Hughes shook his head impatiently. 'Talk sense, mister! How can we be in the gulf when the derned wind be still blawin' our heads off? A west wind, mister! We was in the gulf, we'd be sheltered by the peninsula, isn't that so?'

'Where are we, then?'

'That's what I don't know!' Without apparent regard for the movement of the hull beneath his feet, the captain stamped up the steeply inclined deck, seized the windward rail and stared out for a minute at the confusion of storm-lashed water before returning once again to the wheel.

'See that?' he asked the mate.

'See what?'

'The waves is running every which way. No pattern to them at all. The land's not far off, that's certain.' He shook his head, water streaming off his red face. 'But where, eh? That's the question. Where?' He glared angrily at the mate as though it were somehow his fault they were lost. 'Tell ya something, mister. I got a mortal hatred of standing into the land when I don't know where I am! Dangerous, see? Especially in thick weather.' His eyes lit on Jason. 'You, boy!'

'Yessir?'

'Ye should have sharp enough ears, your age. Get for'ard, see if ye can hear anything!'

'Hear what, sir?' Not knowing what he should be listening for.

'God save us! Breakers, boy! Breakers! Hear anything, give us a yell, right? And hang on tight. Go over the side, we shan't be coming back for ye.'

Forward the seas were coming green over the bows, the deck constantly under two feet of swirling water. The wind drove across the port rail with a vicious intensity that made it hard for Jason to open his eyes, never mind see anything. Teeth chattering with cold and fear, he clung to the heavy forestay and did what Captain Hughes had ordered. He listened.

The groaning, complaining hull. The banshee wailing of the over-stressed rigging. The rhythmic crash, crash, of some heavy object that had broken loose and was now rolling to and fro in the chain locker beneath his feet. The hiss and roar of the waves. Water bursting like hail about him. The fluctuating scream of the wind.

He listened.

In a world of sound, nothing.

He listened.

Overhead, one of the remaining sails blew out with a clap like thunder.

He listened. Nothing. Noth . . . Something.

A rhythm out of cadence with every other sound about him. A roar. Silence. Roar. Repeated.

Breakers.

He turned to scream his warning aft to the

captain. Even as he opened his mouth he knew that Hughes would never hear him above the keening of the gale but did the best he could, anyway.

'Breakers! Breakers ahead!'

He turned again to look forward. Through the maelstrom of driving wind and water he saw them: white teeth in the grey mouth of the sea lying dead ahead and stretching away half a mile at least on either bow. The vessel was driving straight down upon them, upon the rocks or shoals or whatever it was that was causing them.

Jason tried again to scream his warning to the captain then froze, terror seizing his tongue.

A huge wave, bigger by far than the rest, appeared from nowhere, rearing halfway up the masts. Its sloping face, green and wreathed in boiling spray, raced upon them. Its crest was crowned with foam and its voice was louder than thunder. Jason wrapped arms and legs around the forestay, clenched his eyes tight shut and hung on for his life. He felt the hull lift as it strove valiantly to ride the crest but it was impossible. The wave was too high, the angle of its face too steep. The hull faltered and skidded sideways in the water. Jason heard and felt the concussion of the sails as the wind took them aback. The monster wave fell upon them. It tore Jason effortlessly from the rigging and flung him into darkness.

Mura awoke to darkness and the sound of the wind.

In the language of the Narungga people *mura* meant hand. Had his mother followed tradition she would have called him Kartemmeru, meaning first-born; despite living in a world governed by tradition, his mother had always had an independent mind.

'I shall need him to help me,' she had said, 'to give me a hand.'

And so Mura it had been. Not that it had done her much good. Mura was fourteen now, his mother had been dead eight years and he had little recollection of her. The clan had been *kanggallanggalla*, or parents, to him.

It was utterly dark; no stars were visible and Mura knew that the sky was still covered by the dark mass of cloud brought by the wind that for days had been blowing furiously from the sea on the far side of the peninsula.

He lay without moving, dozing, waking, dozing again. Around him other members of the clan slept.

When he was awake, Mura listened to the wind. The coastline was only minutes from their camp but the wind blew from the opposite direction and the surf on that side of the peninsula was too far even for Mura's ears. On this side the wind carried away all sound of the sea but Mura knew it was there even if he could not hear it. He was still too young to have been taught any of the important secrets, but that much he had always known: the presence of the land, the encompassing arms of sea that bordered each side of the clan's territory.

The next time he woke a rent had appeared in the invisible clouds. A scattering of stars shone down. Mura watched them as the earth turned imperceptibly towards the sun. Around him others were awake now. Mura heard a thin cough, the murmur of voices. Silence returned. Beyond the shore, beyond the gulf, beyond the land that lay beyond the gulf came a faint softening of the darkness. A glimmer of light rimmed the distance, growing silently. The stars blinked and disappeared as cloud once again covered the sky. Behind the cloud the pearly greyness grew, turning slowly to pink.

There was a thread of sound now in the silence behind the wind, a voice chanting softly. It was the song of the land. It was so soft it did not disturb the tender dawning. Rather it greeted the returning light, celebrated it, was one with it.

Mura turned, eyes wide and reflecting the colours of the dawn. A few steps from him he could make out in the gathering light the seated figure of Mingulta, facing the dawn and intoning gently, so gently, the song of the land. As the light grew stronger, so did the song: light growing, life continuing, the circle of creation rounded as it had been from the beginning.

When it was fully light the party of men rose, took up the game they had killed the night before and set off together through the grass, the slender shapes of their hunting spears black against the storm-wracked sky.

The world was water: cold, violent, implacable. Helpless in its grasp, Jason could find neither light nor warmth nor breath. He was flung upside down, rightway up, tangled round and round in the sinuous force of waves, and buried deep. Bubbles burst frothing about him. Choking blackness consumed him. He flailed futilely, lungs on fire, not knowing which way to go to reach the air.

One breath. That was all it would take to end the terror, the unavailing struggle. One deep, choking breath, drawing the acrid water deep into lungs starved of oxygen. Peace. He would not. *Would not.*

Jason's head burst through the lethal skin of water. Immediately a wave slammed into him, burying him again, but in that second he had drawn a breath, one tortured breath, and it was enough. He surfaced again and this time stayed afloat long enough to see the *Kitty*'s topmasts as the barque sped away from him. It was two hundred yards distant, near as he could judge, and he remembered the captain's warning. *Go over the side, we shan't be coming back for ye.*

Better if he had stayed buried by that first giant wave. Better to have drowned than this.

Panic paralysed him. His face dipped below the water.

NO! Frantic now, Jason clawed his way back to the air. *I shall live!* I . . . shall . . . *LIVE!*

Jason heard a distant, grinding crash, a groan of timbers. He turned in the water in time to see the topmasts of the barque, only just visible beyond the rearing waves, topple wildly and come crashing down.

Jason did not know what to do. His instinct told him to swim towards the vessel but he doubted he could make it through the breakers. In any case, he was frightened of being swept on to the rocks on which it seemed the *Kitty* had run aground. On the other hand if he stayed where he was he would surely drown. Already he could feel the cold working on his legs and arms. He had only minutes before his limbs grew too numb to support him.

He had no choice: he *must* try to reach the ship. It represented his only chance of rescue in the wilderness of the sea. Fortunately he had been brought up on the banks of the Derwent and could swim like a porpoise.

Porpoise or not, the waves were too high and violent for easy swimming. Every time he reached the top of one wave, another one, even higher, was there to take its place. He tried to swim with his face towards the waves so that he could see them before they struck him but this didn't work. Perhaps because they were so close to the shoal where the *Kitty* had run aground, the waves had no pattern but came at him from all directions at once. Every time he opened his mouth to breathe a wave slapped water into it. It was infuriating. Worse, it threatened death. If he couldn't breathe properly his strength would soon be exhausted.

He was no longer sure where the grounded vessel lay. The waves cut off all visibility and he had been so buffeted by the water that he no longer knew in which direction he was heading.

Cold and sick with all the water he had swallowed, helpless and alone, he could see neither ship nor land. There seemed no prospect of rescue and, as he had feared, his strength was running out. The temptation to give up was almost overwhelming.

He tried to turn on his back, to float while he regained his breath, but the movement of the waves was too violent and erratic for that. A bullying wave submerged him.

This time it took him a lot longer to regain the surface. In his fatigue, the weight of his clothes dragged him down. He should kick off his boots but was afraid to do so: he had seen the wrecked feet of men who had been brought ashore on rocks. He didn't want the same thing to happen to him.

Jason thought he heard Captain Hughes speaking to him in words similar to those he had heard him use to the mate when he had brought him his last draught of hot rum.

Talk sense, mister. This rate ye'll be drowned long afore ye reaches shore. What difference do it make what state your feet be in?

Jason was too tired to argue but his boots stayed

on. He was much colder now. There was still no sign of ship or shore, no sign of anything. Hadn't the captain said they were near land? Where was it, then?

A wave broke over him, followed immediately by another. Once again, gasping, he fought his way up to the air.

I SHALL LIVE.

His strength was going fast now. His legs hung lower in the water. He could not feel them, neither warmth nor life nor movement. There was only weight, drawing him down.

I shall live.

He was no longer sure he believed it.

He began to feel warm, almost cosy in water that lapped his chin. Even the waves no longer seemed so violent.

I shall live . . .

Jason floated vertically in the water, eyes shut.

TWO

It was twenty feet long and four wide, each end armoured with jagged splinters a foot or more in length where it had been ripped out of the *Kitty*'s main deck. It was heavy, potentially lethal, potentially life-saving, and was flailing up and down in the waves like a stupendous hammer.

A blow from it would kill.

Nearly unconscious, Jason did not see the wreckage as it bore down upon him. It came so close that as it reared in the waves one of the long splinters ripped a ragged six-inch gash in Jason's shoulder.

It was what saved him. The sudden pain startled Jason into opening his eyes. He saw his danger and managed, despite cold and increasing torpor, to eel himself out of the way as the massive fragment crashed down in the very place where seconds earlier Jason's head had been.

It reared again. He tried to grab it, hands snatching and slipping over the planking, but it eluded him. He was like a small child trying to mount a giant brumby yet Jason knew that this fragment of decking represented a spark of hope in what until then had been a situation without hope. If he could clamber aboard the fragment he had a chance of life; without it he was as dead as he had so nearly been a moment earlier.

It was hard: impossibly, heart-breakingly hard. The decking must have weighed at least a ton and reared in the waves like a frightened stallion. Jason grabbed at it. It threw him off. Again. The same result. It slipped through his outstretched arms and within seconds had opened up a ten-foot gap between itself and him. He was going to lose it.

It would have been so easy to give up, to sink down in the water and watch the splintered wreckage carry his chance of survival away with it. By now the gap had doubled in size. So easy ... No more fighting, no more fear, no more pain.

Jason refused to give in. From somewhere he summoned the will to set his limbs in motion, to plough furiously after the wooden raft until once again it came within reach of his arms. The effort had drained him of his remaining strength; if he could not clamber on to the wreckage now he would never do it. The planking came slamming down in the water and he hurled himself at it again, managing somehow to get arms and one shoulder over the edge of the timber, fortunately at a point where there were relatively few splinters. The wreckage reared again, almost throwing him off. Somehow he hung on, fingers scrabbling, shoulders straining, mouth set in fear and determination. The wreckage came down again. He inched himself higher and then higher still. A protruding fragment like a ragged blade snagged in his jacket; he ripped himself free at the cost of another gash, this time on his chest.

Ripped clothes and flesh did not matter. What

mattered was getting himself on board this piece of wood and staying there. Little by little he managed it. At last, oblivious to how long it had been since he was first swept overboard, Jason dragged his legs clear of the sucking waves.

Utterly exhausted, chest heaving, he lay in a heap on the rearing piece of decking. It sped through the turbulent water with a force and speed that astonished him.

He had nothing to hang on to; at any moment a violent lurch might hurl him back into the sea. He would never climb aboard a second time. He lay flat, arms and legs spread, fingers scrabbling at the planking, trying to present the smallest possible target to the wind and waves.

For hours he lay there; hours that seemed like days. It grew dark and then, after what seemed an eternity, light again. He opened his eyes. It was indeed light of a sort: a full moon cast its mantle over a mad confusion of black and white waves, black and white spray, extending everywhere and forever. Jason stretched out his hand and looked at it. Black and white like everything else. He wondered with what remained of coherent thought whether he had died and this black and white world was eternity. Eternity was not something he had thought much about in his life. He lowered his arm, his head drooped, he slept.

When he awoke the moon had set and it was dark again. Now Jason was conscious of a raging, all-consuming thirst. He was cold, so cold, the wind penetrating the soaked clothing with such ease that he might have been wearing nothing at all, the gashes on his shoulder and chest stiffening and increasingly painful, but it was his thirst that dominated everything. He began to wonder whether he had succeeded in saving himself from the sea only to die on this piece of wreckage being swept at the mercy of the wind and tide. He closed his eyes and again, miraculously, slept.

It was light and the wind had eased. Jason opened his eyes cautiously. The lids were stiff and the eyes themselves burnt like fire. His throat burnt, his skinned fingertips, the two major gashes he had sustained: all burnt. He was scarified by salt. Pain filled him like a tide.

As he sat up, body groaning, what he saw put all thought of pain, of discomfort, even of the demon thirst itself, out of his mind.

Twenty yards away a group of small islands, some of them little more than rocks, raised their heads above the surface. Beyond the islands was an expanse of calm water. Beyond the water, and filling the horizon as far as he could see, was a yellow and grey sweep of cliff, one hundred feet and more in height.

After such relentless violence and turmoil, of screaming wind and near death, he had come, without noise or fuss, safe to land.

The raft of broken timber moved through the tranquil water. Revolving slowly, ponderously, it drifted past the islands and began to inscribe a lazy circle across the waters of the bay.

Jason studied the land. There was a headland at either end of the bay, pillars of rock jutting out into the water with a smear of green vegetation growing upon them. Between the headlands, the cliff drew a semi-circle against a sky which now was almost clear. Birds screamed and circled in noisy clouds above the cliffs and the breakers that fretted white along their base.

He could see no beach, no sign anywhere of a landing place, no route up the rocky face of the cliffs. It looked as though he were no better off now he had reached shore than he had been in the howling wastes of the sea.

The raft circled once more. Jason saw that it would pass close to the base of the cliffs that now loomed high overhead. If he stayed aboard it would eventually clear the further point and drift out to sea again. To go ashore might achieve nothing but to stay where he was meant death.

He stood, closing his mind to the thousand aches and pains that wracked him, and threw himself into the sea.

It was no distance at all: fifty yards, maybe less. He nearly didn't make it. There was a current setting off shore that had not been apparent from the raft. It was not particularly powerful but in his present weakened condition any current at all could easily have been too much.

He finally came ashore between two huge rocks where a jumble of boulders separated the base of the cliff from the sea. Somehow he managed to clamber over the smooth boulders, avoiding the slimy weed that clung to them, and hopping, jumping and slipping, came at last to the cliff wall.

He looked up. For the first twenty feet the rock, dark and moist as though covered by spray at each high tide, was sheer and utterly devoid of handholds. Jason's heart sank as he examined it. This first section ended in a rocky overhang. Beyond it the rest of the climb didn't look too bad but he doubted he would ever be able to scale that first section. Used to the water he might have been but climbing slippery rock faces was something entirely outside his experience.

However, that could wait. There was something he had to do before he could even think about climbing the cliff. Jason scrambled along the line of boulders, searching with increasing anxiety for a flat-topped or concave rock.

The sun's heat was increasing with every minute. He had to find water and a flat-topped rock above the tideline was the only place he could think of where some of the rain that had fallen in the storm might be trapped.

Within a hundred yards he stopped and looked about him in despair. Every boulder he had examined had been dry, smoothly rounded and beginning to warm ominously in the strengthening rays of the sun.

He found a crevice in the rock face, explored it desperately. It was dank and smelt of seaweed and the sea. After a few yards it ended at a wall of smooth rock. He retraced his footsteps and went on until he reached a second crevice, narrower than the first, running deeper into the cliff face. After a few yards it opened up into a cave wide enough for its sides to be invisible. There was the same dank smell and a bunch of weed lying on the cave floor in a scattering of wet sand showed that it was below high water mark. No sign of fresh water anywhere.

He turned to go back but paused as he heard a faint, intermittent pattering. He listened, holding his breath. It was too dark to see but he groped further, hands outstretched. A splashing trickle was falling from the roof of the cave. He shuffled in the darkness until he thought he had reached the spot. He could hear it clearly yet still could see nothing. He groped again. Still he could not find it and the sound of falling water, so tantalisingly close, made his thirst more intolerable than ever.

Something splashed on the back of his out-stretched hand. Quickly he ducked his head and sucked it.

Fresh.

He moved until the thread-thin trickle of water was falling on his upturned face. With agonising slowness he positioned himself until it fell directly into his mouth.

It had a harsh, metallic taste. He did not care. He developed a crick in his neck. He did not care about that, either. He felt giddy, swaying so that the water fell sometimes into his open mouth, sometimes on his face, sometimes in his eyes. He cared about none of it. He drank and drank.

He stood there for a long time while the water filled his mouth, his stomach, his whole *body* with liquid. Dimly he remembered being told that it was danger-ous to drink too much after a long time without water; he took no notice of the memory but stood there, swaying and ecstatic, until he was full. Saturated, delirious with relief, he returned to the light.

Now for the cliff.

He found a place where there was an angle in the cliff wall. There were no handholds but by pressing his back against the rock and his feet on the jumble of fallen boulders he might be able to lever himself up to a point above the tideline where he could grasp the overhang at the top of the first section of cliff. He tried, stretching as far above his head as he could. He failed, his fingertips a good two feet below the rim. He moved ten yards along the base of the cliff and tried again. The same result. He stood back from the cliff wall and looked as far as he could see towards the headland of rock. No change anywhere. The other direction was the same. There was no way up that first section of the cliff.

Jason turned, checking on the state of the tide behind him. It had gone out a long way since he had landed. An expanse of rock, pebbles and reddish-brown sand extended thirty yards off shore but the tide would turn, the sea would come back and when it did there would be nowhere for him to go. He was trapped at the foot of the cliffs as surely as he had been on the floating wreckage.

He had to be away from here before the tide returned.

He looked about him again and saw his chance. Just one: he must walk across the beach, while the state of the tide still permitted it. As to what lay beyond the headlands ... It could hardly be worse than his present position.

Moving as quickly as he could across the tide pools and bands of slippery rock, he made his way towards the nearer of the two headlands. As Jason came close he saw that it stuck so far out into the sea that there was still water swirling around its base. He reached the headland and plunged into the sea. He had been uncertain that he would be able to swim around the headland but the water was calm, making no more than a gentle swirl around the base of the cliff. Soon he had passed it and entered the bay that lay beyond.

There was a beach of yellow sand, bisected by a grey-brown line of what he thought was bleached seaweed. There was a cliff, broken in places as though at some time in the past sections of it had fallen into the sea. There was a fire. Beside the fire, the shapes of two men.

THREE

Jason's first reaction was to scream out to the strangers that he was *here*, he was alive, in a place where he had thought never to see another human being again; his second was to say nothing. Maybe they were survivors from the *Kitty*, maybe they weren't. The figures moving about the fire were too far away for him to be sure even if they were men or women, white or black. He should get a good look at them before letting them know he was here.

He swam cautiously ashore, landed behind a rampart of large boulders and clambered his way along the beach. He kept to the cover of the rocks until at last he reached a position where he could spy on the strangers without their seeing him.

They had their backs to him but were clearly white. That was something. All the same, he waited until one of them turned and he saw a face that he recognised. Lew Bone, the man of all men whom he would have wished not to see. While he hesitated, unsure whether to reveal his presence or not, the second man also turned and Jason's doubts fell away. It was Tom, his brother.

Jason rocketed out from behind his shelter and ran full tilt across the sand in the direction of the two men.

'I can't believe you're still alive,' Tom said for the hundredth time, a foolish grin plastered all over his face. 'I were sure we'd never see hair nor hide of you again.'

Lew said nothing: not with his mouth, anyway. His look said he would not have cared had Tom been right.

Little by little the two brothers unravelled what had happened to them. Tom had been one of the men up on the yards.

'Couldn't see nothing,' he confessed. 'Even thirty feet above the deck the spray were too thick for that. Saw that there wave, though, jest afore we struck. How you ever lived through 'er I'll never know.'

The *Kitty* had grounded on rocky shoals and in the heavy seas had broken up almost at once. There had been no time to launch a boat. Tom had found himself in the water, much as Jason had done, then a fallen spar had come past with Lew Bone clinging to it. Together, talking to each other to keep themselves awake, they had lasted through the night and the following morning had been washed ashore where they now were. Unlike Jason, they had found no water. They had lit the fire in the hope that its smoke would draw other survivors to them but so far they had seen no-one.

'Reckon we're all that got off,' Tom said.

'Where are we?' Jason asked but they couldn't tell him.

'Somewhere along the west coast of the gulf?' Lew Bone hazarded.

They were certainly on the western side of *something* but even if he were right they were no wiser. None of them had ever been ashore on this coast or knew anyone who had.

'Mebbe there ain't no white men in these parts,' Tom said disconsolately. 'Only them natives, mebbe.'

They looked at each other. How would the natives react to the presence of three shipwrecked white men? None of them had had much to do with the natives but the wild ones who lived beyond the limits of European settlement were supposed to be dangerous.

'Mebbe the fire weren't such a good idea,' Lew Bone said.

Their first priority was water. The two men had looked everywhere along this section of the coast but found nothing. Jason told them about the cave he had found.

'What we waitin' for?' Lew demanded. 'Let's get there afore the tide comes in.'

With Jason leading, they swam around the headland. When they reached the cave Lew Bone shouldered his way inside ahead of the others and stood under the fall, mouth lifted to catch the water.

'Tastes bloody awful,' he complained but drank his fill, all the same.

By the time they came out of the cave the tide was nearly full and they were faced with a long swim but they were all good swimmers and managed it without difficulty.

'What we need now is summat to eat,' Lew said when they were back at the beach.

They walked along the edge of the sea, looking not only for food but for a container to store the precious water. They found nothing.

'There's got to be fish,' Tom said.

'What we supposed to do?' Lew demanded. 'Catch 'em with our 'ands?'

It was easy to get up the cliffs above this beach and Jason clambered up to see what he could see. There was very little: an undulating plain of tawny grass and scrubby trees, empty as a desert, extending without interruption to the horizon. Neither to north or south was there any sign of human inhabitants—which might be a blessing—or of animals. Worst of all, there was no water.

He climbed back down to the beach and told the others.

'Jest have to stay put, then,' Lew said.

'Stay here we'll die,' Tom pointed out. 'Won't we?'

Lew scowled: he did not like his views questioned. 'Not while we got water.'

'We got to 'ave food, too.'

'Somen's bound to be washed up from the wreck.'

'Don't see why,' Jason said. 'Nothing's come ashore so far.'

Tom said, 'Even if it does we'll still 'ave to move eventually, won't we? I mean, it won't last forever, will it?'

Even Lew Bone could not argue with that, although from the expression on his face he would have liked to. 'Which way you want to go, then?'

'North,' Jason said. 'I heard Captain Hughes tellin' the mate there was settlers planning to move into the peninsula. Our best bet would be to try and reach them.'

'And if we don't?'

'Don't see how we can be worse off than we are here.'

They stayed where they were overnight. The next

41

morning they scoured the water's edge, hoping that something might have been washed ashore from the wreck, but again found nothing. They revisited the cave, drank as much as their stomachs would hold, climbed the cliff and set off northwards.

To begin with they made good time but it did not last. The sun grew hotter as the day advanced. Unlike Jason, the two men had kicked off their boots in the sea and the harsh ground was cruel to their feet. The few wind-blown trees offered little shade. They saw no signs either of animals or water. Before long Lew Bone was grumbling: a constant, furious complaint that grew worse as the day drew on.

'Save your breath,' Jason advised him wearily, 'you'll need it for walking.'

It made no difference.

By midday they were exhausted. They rested for an hour in such shade as they could find beneath trees that seemed to continue without variation forever. If it had not been for the coastline to their right they would have become lost hours before.

'Git down the cliff,' Lew instructed Jason, 'see if you can find any more caves.'

Jason needed no urging but when he had scrambled down he found nothing, neither water nor moisture nor even any damp grass to chew. Sunlight blazed painfully from white sand littered with fragments of quartz. The breeze whistled through tussocks of the wiry grass that was the only vegetation. Jason plucked a stem and chewed it but it was as dry as a dead twig. There was nothing.

'There *got* to be somen,' Lew complained furiously.

'Seaweed,' Jason said.

Lew stared, brow lowering. 'What's that supposed to mean?'

'There's banks of seaweed all along the beach.'

'We can't eat seaweed.'

'That's all there is.'

The idea frightened them all.

'We got to have water,' Lew said.

'Keep goin', maybe we'll find some.'

They plodded on through the hot afternoon. Overhead the sun seemed barely to move in a sky white with heat. Earlier, sweat had poured off them; now their bodies were too dehydrated to sweat.

The sun sank at last. The worst of the heat disappeared from a sky that darkened swiftly from white to pellucid blue. A gentle breeze from the sea cooled them, the steady rumble of surf at the base of the cliff drew them on. With water and food— even water alone—it would have been a pleasant place to be. Without either, it was a hell that could only get worse as the hours passed.

At this point the cliffs crumbled away to a line of low sand dunes. They stumbled across the dunes and tried to soothe tired and bleeding feet in the waters of the gulf. Each knew that the next day would be a trial far worse than anything they had experienced so far. If they did not find water, it would also be their last.

They looked longingly at the sky. If only it would rain . . . But there was no sign of that.

They decided to stay on the beach overnight. It was cooler and for Tom and Lew in particular the sea was a more natural element than the endless dry plains. They felt safer surrounded by the soothing noises of the surf.

Jason wandered along the high water mark, seeking whatever he could find, came back with a trophy: an empty bottle.

'Wouldn't you bloody believe it!' As always with Lew Bone, life was a conspiracy directed personally at him. 'What's the use of having it now?'

'Best hang on to it,' Tom said. 'We'll need it when we find water.'

When ... None of them dared think of anything else.

'As long as you don' mind carryin' it ...'

Slowly it grew dark. The stars came out. Beads of phosphorescence gleamed like jewels in the surf. Ahead of them the coast unwound: for how many miles none of them knew. It was not something they dared think about. The moon rose. They lay sprawled on the sand in exhausted sleep.

Jason could not have said what woke him; nevertheless, suddenly, he was awake. Warily he opened his eyes. The stretch of sand gleamed white in the moonlight. The sea was shot with silver ripples. The cliffs loomed, dark with shadow. Below the cliffs, dark shapes moved.

Jason held his breath.

The creatures moved, paused, moved again. He heard a soft crunching sound. They were animals, grazing on the harsh grass that bordered the beach. Every so often they sat up and looked about them before crouching down again.

Wallabies. He counted. Six of them. Meat. Blood. A dead wallaby would keep them alive through another day. If he could only get close enough ...

With agonising caution Jason turned on his side and began to crawl through the sand. One inch. Another inch. Another inch. His hand encountered the smooth shapes of pebbles. Without taking his eyes from the grazing animals, careful to make no sound, he selected a pebble and carried it with him as he edged forward again.

Now the wallabies were twenty yards away. Fifteen. Ten. How much closer could he get? Inch by inch the distance between them lessened. Nine yards. Eight. Five. He stopped. His limbs shook with tension. He fought to control them, to still his breathing. He saw the heads come up again. He dared approach no closer. He was kneeling, body absolutely still. He drew back his arm. The wallabies sat up, suddenly alert. The nearest was smaller than the others. Jason saw the liquid gleam of its eye in the moonlight. He flung the stone, heard the dull thud as it struck home. There was an explosion of movement and the wallabies were gone.

Except that the one he had struck was moving more slowly and erratically than the others, one hind leg splayed out at an angle. Jason was on his feet, chasing. In the moonlight he could not see what lay underfoot: could not take his eyes from the wounded wallaby for fear of losing it. His foot came down awkwardly on a rock and he felt his ankle turn sharply beneath him.

He could not permit it to stop him. Limping, he closed on the stricken animal. It disappeared into the shadow below the cliff and for a heart-stopping moment he thought he had lost it, then saw it again as it tried to scramble away from him across the coarse sand.

Two steps and he was on top of it. It kicked out at him. Tried to bite as he seized it. He drew his knife, cut its throat.

The rush of activity had set his thirst blazing once again. As the blood fountained from the slashed arteries he put his mouth to the wound and drank. After a minute he lifted his head and shouted to the others to join him.

*

They were replete.

'Blood!' Lew Bone snarled. 'Raw meat! Bloody cannibals, that's what we are.'

'Didn't notice you say no,' Tom pointed out.

Now that Lew was stronger his meanness had returned in full measure. 'Tell you somen else,' he said. 'You don' keep yore trap shut I'll shut it for you. I'm gettin' good and tired of people round 'ere telling me what to do.'

The next morning they dragged their painful way northwards.

'How far is it, anyway?' Lew wanted to know.

It was the first time anyone had talked about how far away safety was.

'Depends if there are any settlers on the peninsula,' Jason said and rubbed his swollen ankle painfully.

'What if there ain't?'

'Jest have to keep walking, won't we?'

From time to time Lew stopped and stared with angry eyes at the haze on the far side of the gulf where a blue line of land barely cleared the horizon. There would be people there, safety.

'If we had a boat ...' he repeated over and over again with thwarted fury: but they hadn't.

They found no water that day, either. By midday the heat was intense. The sand was so soft that it made walking almost impossible. They gave up trying to make their way along the beach and returned to the high ground. At least there the tangled trees shielded them from the worst of the sun but underfoot the ground was littered with fallen branches that snagged their feet and at times made the going almost as hard as it had been on the beach. Their path was crossed by innumerable gullies. Nevertheless they still managed to stagger along somehow, Jason and Tom in front, Lew bringing up the rear. They had no energy to speak or think or do anything but place one foot precariously before the other. From time to time, with increasing frequency, they fell.

If Jason felt anything through the tide of exhaustion that threatened to engulf him it was anger. His ankle was getting worse with every step. The gashes he had sustained in the open sea troubled him. Soon he would not be able to walk at all and he was angry that he had endured so much fear and pain and effort to come to this.

He might as well not have bothered to fight at all, he thought. If he had drowned he wouldn't be worrying now about how far it was to safety or where his next drink was coming from. Indeed, the prospect of death was looking more attractive with every step he took.

As for the others ... He could not imagine how they were still walking at all. Both men's feet were in ribbons, their blood staining the dust as they lurched agonisingly along. There was nothing to be done about it, about anything. They would walk until they could walk no more. As each man reached the end of his strength he would fall and that would be an end of him.

The world had contracted to each painful footstep. Each one was a victory; they must not let themselves think how many still remained before they had a hope of reaching safety.

The sun had begun its westerly descent when they came to a gully crossing their path. Its sides were steep, its bottom choked with vegetation. Earlier they had examined all gullies eagerly, hoping to find water running at the bottom. They had long given up hope of such a thing; this land seemed to have no surface water at all. On the other hand the gullies made an ideal hiding place for snakes; if they could catch one, they might at least fill their bellies.

This gully was less than a hundred feet deep. The undergrowth was dense but not impenetrable, yet in their exhausted state it was too much for them. They sat on the edge of the steep incline and stared at the vegetation below them. Suddenly the realisation of what they were trying to do overwhelmed them. They had at least a hundred miles to go, possibly double that, with neither food nor water nor, from what they had seen so far, any prospect of finding any. They had no idea what lay ahead of them. There could be rivers or deserts. For all they knew there could be *mountains*. Jason had heard there might be settlers but did not know for sure. They knew nothing.

They stared hopelessly at the vegetation crowding the gully beneath them, at the plain on the far side flowing endlessly northwards. So far . . .

'We're a bunch of goddamn fools,' Lew said, voice congested with anger.

'Why?' Jason asked.

The big man turned to Tom. 'How far we got to go?'

Tom had always been alarmed by direct questions; now he looked scared and opened his mouth once or twice before speaking. 'Dunno,' he said eventually.

'Hundred miles,' Jason said, 'maybe more.'

'And how far have we come?'

'Ten miles, maybe. Could be twenty, I suppose.'

'And he asks why we're fools. I'll tell you why,' Lew said angrily, 'because that's the way we was born, see?' Abruptly he stood up. 'I'm going to have a drink,' he said.

Tom looked at him, startled. 'Where you going to get it, Lew?'

Lew gestured through the branches of the trees at the beach below them. 'Plenty of water down there.'

'Salt water,' Tom said. 'You can't drink that.'

Lew's eyes were almost sealed in a face burned brick red by the sun. 'Who says so, eh?'

Tom said, 'You know what happens to blokes that drink seawater.'

They went mad and died, that was what happened; every seaman knew that.

Lew showed him his fist. 'I warned you before about telling me what to do.'

He limped over to the cliff edge and stared down through the tangled branches at the ocean. Jason watched him indifferently. If Lew Bone wanted to kill himself he could get on with it as far as Jason was concerned.

He told Tom, 'Let him drink if he wants to.'

Tom stared at him, frowning. 'It'll kill him.'

'Why not? If that's what he wants.'

Tom tried to puzzle it out. 'We got to stick together, Jason, don't we?'

'Stick with him, we're dead.'

Tom gave up. 'What's the difference? At this rate we'll all be dead, anyway.'

Jason turned to see what Lew was doing, half-hoping to see him forcing his way down the cliff, but Tom's warnings must have struck a chord, after all, because, as Jason watched, Lew turned from the cliff edge and came limping back towards them.

Rage twisted his features as he saw Jason staring at him. 'You know so bloody much, tell us 'ow we're goin' to get out of this.'

There was only one thing they could do. With agonising slowness they got to their feet and began to clamber down the steep side of the gully. They had gone perhaps ten yards when something made Jason look up. His sharp exclamation brought the others to a stop. They looked at him questioningly.

'Look!' Jason pointed.

They stared where he was looking. Above them the rim of the gully was lined with black figures, long, thin spears in their hands.

'My God!' Lew Bone's mouth hung open. He turned and began to thrust his way frantically through the bush, fighting to escape. 'We're dead,' he cried, voice shrill with panic. 'We're all dead.'

FOUR

Jason awoke suddenly. For a moment he thought
he was still dreaming. Nothing he could see made
any sense; then memories came flooding back; their
despairing struggle through the bush, the sudden
appearance of the black warriors.

He remembered the last words he had heard.

We're all dead.

Perhaps Lew Bone had been right. Perhaps they
were indeed dead, killed on the steep slope of the
gully where the spear-carrying black men had surprised them, and he had woken in the next world.

Cautiously, Jason flexed his arms, then his legs.
He didn't *feel* dead. His ankle was sore but even that
was better than it had been. Everything seemed in
working order. He had a ferocious headache and
was desperately thirsty but nothing else seemed
wrong with him. He looked around, trying to understand his surroundings. He was lying on his back
beneath a latticework of branches that formed a roof
a few inches above his head. His hand went to the
sheath at his waist but it was empty: his knife was
gone.

51

There was something between his body and the ground. His fingers explored. It felt soft: fur. He twisted his head to look beneath him. He was lying on a rug, made apparently from kangaroo skin.

As soon as he moved Jason was ambushed by weariness. He could barely stir. He turned his head again, looking about him. The hutch in which he was lying was very small, little more than a box of plaited branches six feet in length with one end open to the daylight. Light also came through the interlaced branches; if it was intended as a shelter, Jason thought, it wasn't much of one.

On the other hand, if he *had* fallen into the hands of the natives, and it seemed more and more certain that he had, they couldn't be planning to kill him or they would have done it already.

Thirst ravaged him. His eye lit on what looked like a gourd standing by the entrance of the shelter. His parched tongue flickered over dry lips. He was so frightened it might be empty that for a few seconds he didn't move; then he summoned up his courage, crawled across on his belly and looked inside. He let out his breath in a deep sigh. It was full of liquid. But what kind of liquid? It could be poison, for all he knew, but after a moment's reflection he realised that made no sense. Why should the blacks have brought him here just to kill him? They could have done that in the gully, if that was what they had wanted.

He sniffed warily, tested the contents with his tongue. Water. His eyes closed and his throat convulsed in ecstasy. Trembling, terrified of spilling even a drop, he raised the gourd to his lips and drank the contents down.

When the gourd was empty he let it fall to the ground and struggled back to collapse once again upon the sleeping rug. Now the torment of thirst was eased he was ready to faint with weariness. He wondered briefly what had happened to the others but before he could even begin to think about that or anything else his eyes closed and he fell asleep.

When he next awoke it was dark. For a while he lay still, trying again to work out where he was. The ruddy glow of a fire flickered just beyond the opening of his strange shelter and he heard voices and occasional laughter. He went to stand before he remembered that the shelter was too low to do that. He crawled to the opening and peered out.

Shadowed forms huddled about the leaping flames of a large fire. Firelight gleamed on black skin, the shine of eyes and teeth. He salivated as the smell of scorched meat came to him; it seemed a lifetime since he had eaten.

Jason did not know whether or not to go and join the people around the fire. They had not killed him although they could have done. They had not tied him up or imprisoned him. They had even given him shelter and some of their precious water. It didn't seem that they intended to harm him. He decided it would be safe to go out, or perhaps it was the smell of the cooking meat that drew him irresistibly into the firelight.

He walked forward two or three paces and stopped, casting his eyes about him, alert for trouble. No-one seemed to have noticed him. Another three paces; still nothing. The firelight reflected in the tangled branches of the trees. It shone on the faces and bodies of the natives. There were both men and women; children, too: a family group, then, not a war party. He smelt no hint of danger here.

The people about the fire became aware of his presence. The voices died. In the stillness Jason could hear only the crackle of flames, trees rustling in the wind.

He stood motionless, waiting to see how they would react. Eyes watched him. There was a low murmur. In response to the murmur, or so it seemed, there was a shift among the seated group and a figure came out to face him. It was a youth of about his own age, several inches shorter than Jason. In the dim light he looked as black as night. He stood motionless, his back to the fire and the people silently watching. He was absolutely naked. The two youths stared at each other across a gap that had little to do with physical distance and much to do with culture and comprehension, then the black boy's face broke in a smile. He reached out and took Jason's hand in his own, coaxing him forward into the group by the fire. His hand was warm, surprisingly soft. Disliking having his hand held by another male, Jason at first resisted but after a few seconds yielded and allowed himself to be drawn forward: he couldn't afford to offend these people.

The group made room for them. Following the black boy's lead, Jason sat on the bare earth a few paces from the fire. He glanced nervously about him. Grown men of all ages were sitting together, some with paint on their bodies, others without. Women were gathered about the fire attending to the cooking meat whose smell had enticed him out of the shelter. A handful of children was scattered through the group. Jason could see no-one of his own age apart from the boy who had drawn him forward.

There were about thirty people here. He could see no sign of his brother or Lew Bone but without one word of a common language there was no way he could ask about them.

For a while nothing happened. The watchful eyes, gleaming white in the firelight, targeted him. No-one spoke. Soon, however, the low murmur of conversation resumed. In a few minutes the adults seemed to have forgotten him and talked and laughed as though he were not there at all.

Some of the smaller children, fascinated by the white-skinned stranger, were slower to lose their curiosity. Jason found himself the centre of a group of wide-eyed faces staring wonderingly up at him. He tried to ignore them but it wasn't easy. One small girl plucked up courage to touch him, the black fingers exploring the white arm as though seeking an explanation for the strange colour. The first time it happened Jason jerked instinctively away. The sudden movement froze the children, but within no time, when he did nothing else, the wondering fingers were back again, the air around him bright with childish laughter.

Perhaps they had never seen a white person before.

There had been a few blacks in Van Diemen's Land. Jason had heard that when the whites first came to the country there had been many more of them but that had been long before he was born. The ones who remained wore cast-off European clothes and lived around the edges of the European settlement, scrounging what they could get. He, who thought of himself as having nothing, had been brought up to despise people who had even less, neither land nor wealth, no pride, no hope, no future.

These people he found himself among now were different. They were free and untamed yet seemed no wilder than many white people he had known. They were strange, though. Take the way they

55

spoke, the sound flowing like water. As for their appearance: it was not only their colour that set them apart from whites. The shapes of their faces, their noses, lips were different. Their arms and legs were longer and thinner than the limbs of white people. The way they walked about with nothing on startled and embarrassed him. He remembered the spear-carrying men coming after them in the bush. The confident way they had moved and handled their weapons, everything about them, had said that here was a people to be reckoned with yet now they had him in their power they ignored him.

He did not understand what was going on; was not even sure that anything *was* going on at all. If he got up and walked away into the darkness, would they let him go? Was he a prisoner or free to do what he wanted? For a moment he was tempted to find out but stopped himself. It was too soon for experiments.

The youth who had brought him into the group sat at his side, paying no more attention to him than the rest. Apart from the gaggle of children, their wide eyes, questing fingers, laughing mouths, he might have been invisible.

The small girl who had first touched him was now sitting in his lap exploring his shirt. The others stood close. Staring. None of the adults took any notice of them. Embarrassed by the girl's curiosity Jason would have pushed her away but did not, afraid of angering the rest. He sat still, fidgeting under her exploring fingers, pretending that nothing was happening.

A loud exclamation, laughter bright behind outstretched fingers, as she found the opening in his shirt and pushed her hand on to the skin beneath.

'Give over,' he muttered. He pushed her hand

away but she ignored the hint. She turned her head and spoke rapidly to the rest of her companions. Their eyes grew even rounder and they edged closer to him. She pulled his shirt aside while the rest of them peered, necks craning.

'Can't you tell 'em to stop it?' Jason appealed to the boy at his side whom in this gathering of strangers he already thought of as his friend. The boy smiled cheerfully but did nothing. The curiosity of children was obviously nothing to get excited about.

The child was pulling at his shirt now, exposing more of the skin beneath. She had probably never seen anyone wearing clothes, either. Perhaps she had only just realised that his shirt and breeches *were* clothes, something apart from his actual body. Quite likely she had thought that they were attached to him, like skin. Not that he was planning to let her take off his clothes to satisfy her curiosity.

For the moment there was food. The meat that had been cooking on the fire was now ready. The youth at his side eeled away and returned in a few minutes with two chunks of meat, one of which he offered to Jason.

'*Kambandi paru,*' he said.

Jason was famished, his stomach growling; even so, he regarded the hunk of meat with apprehension.

'What is it?'

'*Kambandi paru,*' the youth repeated helpfully. '*Wauwe.*'

'Don't know what you're on about, mate,' Jason said. Dubiously, he took the meat and inspected it. The fur had been burnt off and the skin seared but the meat itself seemed hardly cooked at all. Blood ran over his hands as he held it. The black boy sank large white teeth into his own piece of meat, nodding to Jason to do likewise. Hunger overcoming caution, Jason followed suit. The meat *was* almost raw, tough, too, but at least it was food. Soon he was tearing at it with his teeth, gulping it down into his empty stomach. All too soon it was gone.

He wiped his hands on his breeches and looked about him once more. Still no sign of Tom or Lew. He wondered if the blacks had killed them or if they had escaped. Even if they had got away he did not think they would get far. Neither possibility explained why the blacks were treating him as one of themselves, giving him food and water, permitting him to sit with them.

There was another thing. He must be as strange to them as they were to him yet they showed no sign of it. Apart from the inability to speak to each other they might have known him all their lives.

It was scary to realise how little he understood what was going on.

The food was finished. There was a stir and everyone stood. Jason looked around him. Now what?

The men with painted bodies separated from the rest. They picked up spears and shields and walked out into the clearing on the far side of the fire. Once again the black youth seized Jason's hand and tugged it, indicating that he should follow. They stood at the edge of the clearing, the rest of the people gathered about them.

The painted figures formed up in two lines and stood facing each other.

Jason turned to his companion. 'Is there going to be a fight?'

The youth stared back at him, face blank with incomprehension. He jabbered sibilantly for a moment and fell silent.

To one side of the painted men an older man,

tangled grey hair hanging almost to his waist, held what looked like a piece of wood at the end of a six foot line. As Jason watched he began to swing it with increasing force and speed round and round his head. The piece of wood whirling through the air emitted a low drone that increased steadily in pitch and volume until the clearing resonated with sound. Halfway between a groan and a screech, it assaulted the eardrums and raised the hairs along Jason's arms. At the far end of the lines of painted men another figure whirled a similar device. The two sounds mingled, the watchers shifted, murmuring, and the lines of painted men began to move.

The line nearer the fire swayed rhythmically to and fro for a few minutes before breaking into a sideways shuffling movement, quite fast, the other group following suit.

Comprehension dawned. 'They're *dancing*,' Jason said aloud.

His companion smiled quickly up at him but his eyes returned at once to the dancers.

After a few minutes the two lines changed direction and began to follow each other in single file round and round the clearing while the bellow of the whirling wooden instruments rose and fell about the bobbing, firelit figures. The sound was like a bird, flying, fluttering, soaring, enclosing dancers and spectators alike in wings of reverberating sound.

As one the men turned inwards and marched towards each other, stamping heavily on the ground at each step and clashing their spears and shields together with great force as they did so. Dust puffed about their naked feet and the air was full of the smell of sweat.

Jason had an idea. Other members of the audience were talking; perhaps it would be all right if he did, too. He put his hand on his companion's shoulder. The black youth looked up at him. Jason pointed at himself. 'Jason Hallam,' he said, enunciating the words slowly and carefully. He pointed a second time. 'Jason Hallam,' he repeated. He pointed at the black youth. 'What ... is ... your ... name?'

The dark eyes watched him expressionlessly.

Jason went through the procedure again. 'Ja ... son Hal ... lam,' he repeated. '*Jason Hallam*.' Again he reversed his finger. 'What is your name?'

Silence. We are getting nowhere, he thought. Then the black face cleared. The youth pointed at himself. 'Mura,' he said. He put his hand on Jason's chest and looked at him enquiringly.

Both names are too much, Jason thought. 'Ja ... son,' he said aloud. '*Ja ... son*.'

'Jayser?' Speaking slowly, the heavy lips writhing over the large white teeth as he tried to form the word. 'Jay-e-son?'

Near enough, Jason thought. 'Jason,' he said, laying his hand on his own breast. He pointed. 'Mura,' he said, hoping he had the pronunciation right.

'Jay-e-son,' the boy said happily. 'Mura.'

They smiled at each other, proud that they had made contact despite their shared incomprehension.

'Jay-e-son,' the black boy chanted, laughing. 'Mura.'

The dancers uttered grunting cries as they moved to and fro. As their excitement grew the audience started to echo the sound, the women keeping time by beating their naked thighs and buttocks rhythmically with the palms of their hands.

Jason was more interested in information than the dance. 'What have you done with my mates?'

Mura stared at him without comprehension.

'Look,' Jason said. He squatted in the dust and picked up a piece of stick. In the dust he drew a crowd of small stick figures, waving spears. Mura watched over his shoulder, breathing audibly through his nose, forehead wrinkled as he tried to understand what Jason was doing.

Jason pointed at one of the figures, then at Mura. 'Mura,' he said. He pointed at the rest of the figures, then at the people around them. 'And that's the rest of you.'

Mura's face cleared. 'Mura,' he repeated with emphasis, then pointed around him, uttering a word Jason could not grasp. It slipped away from him amid the sounds of the dance, the flickering firelight reflecting from the low-hanging branches of the trees.

'What did you say?'

Mura stared at him.

This will take forever, Jason thought.

He drew three figures, a little apart from the rest. Again he went through the procedure. He pointed at one figure, then at himself. 'Ja . . . son.' He pointed at the others. 'Where are they?'

Mura stared.

Jason went through the whole procedure again, pointing first at the drawing, then at Mura himself and the rest of the black group, then at himself and the drawing of himself, finally at the figures of his two missing companions. He looked about him, miming bewilderment. 'Where . . . are . . . they?'

Mura's eyes lit up and he spoke in a swift flow of sound, jabbing his extended finger repeatedly into the darkness. *There*, he seemed to be saying. *There*.

'Where? Take me to them. Please?'

It was no use. Tired of the game, Mura turned his attention back to the dance. Jason watched. As far as he could make out, the men were now miming a hunt, possibly of an emu or kangaroo, who could tell?

He was filled with determination. He *must* find out what had happened to Tom and Lew Bone.

Getting away would be the first step. Slowly, he moved a step or two backwards; paused. Mura felt the movement and turned to look at him. Jason smiled brightly at him. Mura's attention returned to the dance. Two of the dancers leapt high in the air, limbs cartwheeling as they sprang, firelight glinting on skins shining with sweat, on the spears and shields they waved vigorously about their heads. A low shout of approval rumbled through the audience.

Jason took another step backwards. Paused. Mura did not look at him again. No-one was paying him any attention. At the edge of the crowd three young women were dancing together, long limbs prancing, bodies swaying as they joined the palms of their hands above their heads, jerking out their legs repeatedly from the knee. They saw this strange white being watching the movement of their breasts against their ribs as they danced and laughed at him white-mouthed, not hesitating or losing a step.

Jason moved back again. The dancing women paid him no more attention, concentrating as they wove their own pattern of movement in the warm night air. A renewed rumble of voices flowered in the darkness, greeting another phase of the men's dance. Over the naked black shoulders, the attentive heads, he saw the movements, more frenzied now. A sigh from the crowd. A series of cries. The whirling wooden instruments droned. Jason turned and stepped beyond the circle of firelight, beyond the watchers, into darkness.

After the firelight and whirling movement, it was hard to work out where he was. He stood still, waiting for his eyes to get used to the dark. Shadowy trees hunched, their scrawl of branches obscuring the stars. Ahead of him the grass glowed with a pearly light, swaying softly in the breeze. At his back the noise of the dance accentuated the stillness that surrounded him. There were branch shelters similar to the one in which he had regained consciousness. Two or three dogs prowled the shadows, snouts questing suspiciously after him as he walked through the darkness.

He could see nowhere where two men might be imprisoned.

Could they be dead, after all? He could not understand why he remembered so little of what had happened. A fight would explain the deaths but neither his own survival nor his inability to remember.

He came to a patch of darkness more profound than anything that had gone before. Behind him the distant firelight varnished the underside of the leaves with orange. The whirling wooden instruments growled like bees, shrieked like banshees. The cries of dancers and audience came distantly to his ears. Ahead was silence. The ground opened at his feet. The sides of a gully plunged steeply into blackness.

Jason hesitated. He could escape, if that was what he wanted, and keep walking through the night. He doubted that the blacks would notice his absence or bother to follow him if they did. They had brought him in, fed and watered him, given him shelter, yet apart from Mura, the giggling children, the oblique, laughing glances of the dancing women, they had ignored him. Many things—imprisonment, death—

might have happened to him but had not. The blacks remained a mystery.

What if he did walk on and leave this place? He had seen enough to know that he would never survive to find his way to a settled area. His only hope would be to find more natives along the way but there was no reason to suppose they would be any better than the ones here. They might very well be worse. The blacks had no need for bars or walls. He was imprisoned as securely as one could be, a captive of the empty landscape, of distance, of a lack of water and of food.

Jason hesitated, on the edge of turning back, yet did not. He had come out here to find his brother. He would not give up yet.

He placed one foot on the steep slope of the gully, then another. Little by little he scrambled down it, slipping and sliding until he came into the trees. He looked about him, recognising the place even in the darkness. It was where they had first met the warriors.

He went on. The darkness swallowed him up.

FIVE

All Mura's life there had been rumours. White birds had been seen moving swiftly across the sea where nothing like them had been seen before. Word had come from other clans, which had in turn received the news from clans still further away, of white strangers in the land.

One day one of the strangers had come among them. Mura had been very small yet he remembered the occasion clearly. In the depths of winter had come a great storm that raged upon the sea for days and cast up quantities of wood and dead birds along the coast. Out of the storm, a man. They brought him into their midst and examined him with eyes at once curious and afraid. He was alone. It would be easy to kill him. There were those who said they should, remembering the stories they had heard of these strangers. There were others, more merciful or perhaps more cautious, who said they should not.

In the meantime, they studied him.

He was tall and powerfully made, covered in hair. He was frightened of them, cowering and smiling placatingly when anyone tried to speak to him. His only speech was a jumble of sound. No-one could make sense of it. Some questioned that he was a man at all but when they took away his clothes—how he had fought!—they found he was indeed made as other men.

The clan lost its fear of him. They permitted him to stay among them, a member of the clan yet not a member, uninitiated and therefore always less than a man, but in time even this distinction blurred. They called him Karinja, after the place where they had found him. Slowly he picked up the language. Always he spoke it badly, like a handful of broken stones in his mouth, but in time they grew used to that, too.

Now these new strangers had come, also. Nantariltarra, most important of the Council and leader of the group that had encountered the strangers in the gully near the cliffs, had ordered that the young one be kept separate from the others, allowed to wander freely among the members of the clan, eat their food, mix with them. And be watched, always. Nantariltarra said that if they understood the strangers they could perhaps in time come to overpower and kill them or, better, make them like themselves, another clan within the land, to find their own place as in the distant past others had found theirs.

Responsibility for observing him had been given to Mura.

'Because you are also young,' Nantariltarra said. 'Make him trust you. Be friends with him. We want him to become one of us so we can learn from him.'

It had proved easier than Mura had expected. The stranger had already begun to communicate with him, something that old one, the white man they called Karinja, had never done. This one called himself Jay-e-son, not afraid that by revealing his name he was also exposing the secret source of his power. Greatly daring, Mura had told the stranger his own name, too, although not of course his secret name, known and spoken only in the clan's greatest mysteries.

This was what Nantariltarra had hoped for. Mura had looked forward to telling him how well he had performed his duties; he knew how delighted Nantariltarra would be.

And now, as the Emu dance neared its conclusion—the dancers strutting, arms bent to imitate the bent necks of the birds, the hunters creeping up on them, spears pointing death—Mura realised that Jay-e-son had gone.

Mura would be blamed. He knew he must go after him at once and bring him back. In daylight this would have been easy enough but at night, away from the protective shield of firelight ... His heart sank. At night the world became the house of the spirits that wandered free. Yet Jay-e-son had gone out there. Perhaps he had some magic to protect him, the magic that Nantariltarra was so anxious to learn. Perhaps it would be powerful enough to protect Mura, too, if he followed him.

He went out apprehensively, eyes slanting at the darkness. The outline of a tree. Grass silvery in the starlight. Dust still warm beneath his feet. The voice of the breeze. Everywhere shadows. Everywhere the invisible eyes of the spirits watching him.

His own eyes grew used to the darkness. When he looked back he could still see the firelight, hear the sounds of the dancers, but Mura himself was one with the dark.

Fallen branches crackled beneath Jason's feet, loose earth slid. He was surrounded by an earthquake of noise. His headache was worse, he had given up hope of remembering what had happened, he had no idea where he was going or why.

... The crest of the gully had been spiked with spears, the lean figures of the blacks, bodies daubed with white, faces staring down at them ... Lew Bone, cursing beneath his breath, trying to run. The boy ...

Memory tugged, swirled, vanished. What boy? He could not remember.

I remember shouting out, he thought. Lew Bone said something, I think it was him. *We are dead*, something like that. Then the black men came running down the side of the gully. They ran as easily as on level ground, although the sides of the gully were so steep we could hardly walk at all without slipping. We had fallen a lot, I remember.

The black men were naked apart from a string about their waists with a tassel of fur or grass—one Jason remembered had a sea-shell—covering their private parts. They carried long thin spears. Some had boomerangs as well but all had the spears and long wooden shields covered in a pattern of lines. The spears did not taper to simple points but had carved teeth-like serrations along one side.

Lew Bone had tried clumsily to escape, slipping and falling down the steep walls of the gully. Panic in his voice as he yelled.

'Let's get out of here before we're all killed.'

Jason and his brother—recognising the futility of flight, realising that to show fear was the worst thing they could do—had stood where they were while the black warriors surrounded them, menacing faces, waving spears, gesticulating hands.

Jason recalled thinking, *So this is the end of it, then, the end of everything*, and then ...

Jason explored his aching head with cautious fingers. There was a lump above one ear. Must have knocked me out, I suppose. But remembered nothing.

The floor of the gully levelled out as he reached the bottom. It was darker here, the leaves of the trees quenching the starlight. He could barely see to put one foot in front of the other. He groped with extended leg, extended hand. Away to his right he could hear the distant susurration of the sea, the soft rumble of gravel stirred by the waves along the beach. He must be very close to the cliff here.

A wooden structure loomed out of the darkness: a scaffold fifteen feet high supporting a wooden platform. Jason could see no way up the scaffolding, had no way of knowing what—if anything—was on top, yet stared at it apprehensively. The mysterious structure made the hair crinkle on his arms. A scarf of mist wrapped itself about the wooden uprights, about him. He could taste the moisture, a hint in it of salt and decay. The area smelt dankly of earth and putrefaction. Giving the structure a wide berth, Jason almost walked into another one.

What are these things?

Panic was shredding his mind. He wanted to run, to plunge helter-skelter through the darkness, to escape from where he was, from the sudden dread that assailed him. He could not. It was too dark to run, too many obstacles to make flight possible. Who knew what he might run into next?

He had never been one for ghosts but had never before been in such a place, either. Sweat ran cold over his back as he stared about him. Nothing moved. The only sounds he could hear were the trees creaking in the breeze, the distant sibilance of the breaking waves: peaceful noises that helped to restore his calmness. He took a series of deep breaths. Nothing moved. Nothing happened. He walked cautiously on.

He passed three more of the strange structures, climbed a slope and came out at last on a stretch of ground devoid of trees. The cliff ran a few yards to his right. On the edge of the cliff was another structure—ten feet square, perhaps—of branches laced together by vines. It looked like a cage. Inside the cage . . .

'Who is it?'

The voice was stark with terror but Jason recognised it. Lew Bone. He had found the missing men.

Mura drew a wide circle through the bush, walking swiftly now, still frightened but forcing himself to ignore his fear. Not for anyone, neither Jay-e-son nor Nantariltarra nor the dreamtime spirits themselves, would he venture through the Place of the Dead, the smoked bodies placed on high wooden platforms to protect them from wild animals. The Council attended ceremonies here but only in daylight. Mura had never heard of anyone coming by darkness to the Place of the Dead.

'We thought you was dead . . .' Tom, eyes staring, hands gripping the bars of the cage.

'Never mind that,' Lew said, impatient as ever. 'Get us outa here, boy, we'll be off.'

A third figure swayed in the shadows behind the other two.

Jason eyed him uneasily. 'Who's that?'

'Don' take no notice of 'im,' Lew said. 'Ain't right in the 'ead, see?'

The stranger was tall, gaunt, wasted shoulders that had once been full of power, wondering eyes deep-set above a dark thicket of beard that covered most of his chest. He stank like a corpse and was completely naked. It was strange how he seemed so much more naked than the blacks whom Jason had just left.

'Why did they put you in here?' Jason asked Tom.

Lew interrupted before Tom could answer. 'Never mind any o' that. Git us *out*, that's the first thing.'

Jason hesitated. 'But what'll we do?'

'Do?' Derision in Lew's voice. 'Take off, o' course. What else?'

'That's right,' Tom fawned eagerly. 'Get us out and we'll be on our way. Like we was before, remember?'

Jason remembered only too well. The thirst, the despair, the certainty that without aid they would soon be dead. He would not go through that again for a thousand pounds.

'You'll never make it,' he said.

'You'll ... all ... die,' the naked stranger said, voice creaking like a worn hinge.

Jason stared open-mouthed, as astonished as though a tree had addressed them.

'Keep your damn mouth shut!' As always, Lew's immediate reaction was violent. 'Nobody asked your opinion.'

A high, keening sound. It took a moment to realise the man was laughing. 'All ... dead,' he said again.

Lew raised a sledge-hammer fist. 'Shut the hell up! He's barmy,' he said to the others, disgust in his voice.

''Ere forever, maties,' the man said, crooning to

himself, idiot smile on his lips. 'Jes like me. 'Ere forever.'

Jason looked at him. He was grinning and chortling to himself. Slobber ran down the heavy beard and gleamed in the starlight. As Lew had said, he didn't seem right in the head. Would that happen to him, too, if he stayed here? NO. He was strong. He would never allow such a thing to happen to him.

'Git on with it!' Lew snarled out of the darkness.

Jason hesitated: but why had he come, if not to release them? He inspected the cage. As he had thought, the bars were branches, secured by vines. He tested them, teeth clenched, arms straining, but could not shift them.

'Strong as rope,' he panted.

'Cut 'em, then!'

'Can't. They took my knife.'

The vines were lashed so tight he did not see how he could possibly undo them. One section formed a trap door, secured by a double thickness of vines fastened around two adjoining bars, the knots out of reach of the men inside the cage. Jason wrestled with them.

'For God's sake git on with it!' Lew's paw tried to cuff Jason through the bars.

Jason stepped out of range. 'You want me to get you out or not?'

'Leave 'im be, Lew,' Tom whined. ''E's doin' 'is best.'

'God help us if 'e ever does 'is worst, then.'

Jason's fingers discovered a knot drawn less tightly than the rest. He worked it to and fro until one end fell loose. Quickly he unravelled it and turned to the next one.

A burst of jumbled sound came from the old sailor. It sounded like words but was certainly not English. Jason looked up, frowning. The man was clinging to the bars, arm outstretched, finger pointed, eyes fixed on the darkness. Cold shivers prickling his spine, Jason turned and looked where the man was staring.

A dark figure stood watching them from the edge of the trees.

SIX

Jason's heart leapt painfully in his chest; then the figure moved and he saw that it was Mura.

Thank God, he thought, but his relief was short-lived. Mura stalked across the clearing towards him. He stopped two yards from Jason and pointed furiously at the cage.

'*Madlanna!*' he said. '*Madlanna! Wakkinna!*'

Jason did not understand the words but the meaning was plain. The next thing they'll be putting me in the cage, too, he thought. If they don't decide to kill me first.

'*Wakkinna!*' Mura repeated, scowling ferociously.

From the shadowy cage the old man said, ' 'E says you ain't got no right to try and get us out of 'ere.'

'These are my friends,' Jason said, eyes fixed on Mura's face. 'One of them is my brother.' Over his shoulder he said, 'Ask him why they put you in the cage.'

'They does what they likes.' The old man's voice was nervous. 'You don' ever ask 'em why. 'Alf the time I doubt they knows why themselves.'

'*Ask him.*'

The man said something. Even to Jason's ear, unfamiliar with the language, it sounded wrong, entirely different from the easy fluidity of Mura's speech.

He's been here for years and still can't speak the language properly, he thought. I'd have done better than that.

Mura spoke again.

'What does he say?'

'He says we got to stay 'ere until the others agree to let us out. That's what the Council decided.'

'You're bigger'n 'e is.' Lew Bone's voice hissed behind his shoulder. ''Ow's 'e goin' to stop you, eh? 'E gives any trouble, tap 'im on the jaw. That'll shut 'im up.'

Jason ignored the remark. No way was he going to hit the black youth; it would be asking for trouble. At the same time he didn't want Mura getting the idea that he would always do what he was told.

'He is my brother,' he repeated firmly. He mimed the cage door being open, the prisoners coming out. 'I want him out of there.' Even though Mura did not understand the words he hoped his tone and gestures would convey his meaning clearly enough.

Mura shook his head angrily.

He's scared, Jason thought. If I take no notice of him he knows he'll have to try and stop me.

'Tell him you promise not to escape if he agrees to let you out.'

'Not escape?' Lew Bone echoed indignantly. 'I ain't agreein' to nuthin like that!'

'Then you can stay in the cage,' Jason said but Mura would not agree, in any case.

'He got to speak to the others,' the old man explained. ''E can' do nuthin. It's the Council what decides.'

75

'Then tell him I'll go back with him and speak to the Council myself.'

The old man cackled derisively. ''Ow you goin' to do that when you don' speak the lingo, eh?'

'I'll find a way.' But had no idea how.

He waited until his words had been translated—this is impossible, he thought, if I'm going to be here for long I shall have to learn to speak to them—then smiled cheerfully at Mura's suspiciously frowning face.

'Let's go, shall we?'

'You *leavin'* us?' Lew Bone rattled the bars of the cage, his voice congested with rage.

You want me to strangle him? Jason felt like asking. That way you can be quite sure the rest of them will come after us and kill us all. But said nothing. You couldn't talk to men like Lew Bone.

Instead he began to walk purposefully in the direction of the blacks' camp. After a moment's hesitation, Mura joined him.

When they got back the dance was still going on. The air was heavy with dust. The smell of sweat was stronger than when they had left, sharp and acrid in the warm night.

Jason hoped that their absence had gone unnoticed but as soon as they emerged into the yellow circle of firelight a man, enormously tall and wearing a feathered headdress and leather apron, knobbed wooden staff in his hand, came striding across the clearing towards them. His feet raised little puffs of dust as he walked. He stared down at Jason. The heavy forehead shadowed his eyes like a cliff. Jason set his shoulders and stared back at him, trying to hide his apprehension.

The man shook the club and spoke threateningly: a heavy stream of sound. At Jason's side Mura said nothing and neither did he. The man spoke again, voice dark with anger.

Jason shrugged. 'No point getting mad at me, mate. I don't understand a word you're saying.'

The man must have recognised the tone if not the words. His eyes narrowed. The wooden club moved in a blur of speed. It struck Jason above the left ear. He saw a flash of coloured lights and the world turned black.

Pain was a pulsing agony, drowning all else. Slowly, breath ragged in his throat, Jason eased his eyes open to daylight that stabbed him like spears. The pain intensified at once and he shut them again but the flicker of his eyelids had been noticed.

' 'E's comin' round.'

A voice he recognised, he thought dazedly. A voice speaking English. The familiar language brought back his last memory, the voice of the huge black chieftain, if that was what he had been, shouting furiously, asking and re-asking the same incomprehensible questions, his cheeky answer, the change of expression in the angry eyes, the scything blow of the wooden club.

He opened his eyes again. His brother was staring down at him, a look of concern on his stupid face.

'How yer goin'?'

'Where am I?'

'In the cage.'

'The cage?' He seemed unable to focus on anything, mind as blurred as his eyes.

'They chucked you in 'ere along o' the rest of us.'

Tom's face vanished as he was pushed aside. Lew Bone, unshaven and belligerent, scowled down at him. 'You done wot I said, we'd be away from 'ere be now.'

Jason was not strong enough to argue: to talk at all, come to that. He closed his eyes, hoping they would leave him alone. Mercifully, they did.

When he woke again he felt a little better although pain still beat like a drum inside his skull. He worked his dry mouth and opened his eyes.

'Any water?' His voice was so weak it startled him.

Tom brought him a gourd, half full. Jason bent his head and drank, feeling the blessed relief of life slipping down his throat. He wanted to drain the container but forced himself to stop after two mouthfuls. 'Any more?'

'Drink all you want.'

'No . . .' He forced down the temptation, pushed the container away. 'Have I been here long?'

'Since first light.'

Tom told him how a group of blacks had appeared out of nowhere, running as lightly as though on open ground and unencumbered instead of carrying Jason's dangling body through the bush. At first they had thought Jason was dead and the blacks intended to kill them, too. They had decided to break out as soon as the door of the cage was opened.

'And?' Jason asked.

Tom shook his head. 'Never had a chance.'

Serrated-edged spears thrust through the bars of the cage had held them back while the men unlashed the trap door. They had thrown Jason's inert body inside, slammed and re-fastened the gate and gone away.

'They'll be back,' Jason said.

Lew growled. 'Could've left us 'ere to rot, all we know.'

Jason shook his head. 'Why leave us the water, in that case?'

But could not understand, any more than the others, why they were imprisoned at all.

'You'd think they'd *want* us to go,' Lew said. 'Then they wouldn't 'ave to bother with us.'

Jason turned to the old man sitting blank-eyed in a corner of the cage, mumbling quietly to himself. 'Seen any other white men since you been here?'

The man jerked, nervous at being addressed. His eyes wandered then focused on Jason's face. 'Eh?'

'What's your name?' Jason asked him.

The sailor sucked his lips over his teeth. 'Karinja,' he said eventually. He giggled, eyes squinting. 'That's what they calls me.'

'That's *their* name for you,' Jason said. 'What's your real name?'

The old man licked his lips. 'What you want that for?'

'So I know what to call you.'

'You don' tell folks your real name.' The old man winked craftily and lowered his voice. 'Gives 'em power, see?'

'What sort of power?'

'Power over you.' He lowered his voice. 'They kin put the devils on you, they knows your name. Them *quinkans*.'

'*Quinkans*?' Jason repeated. 'What's that?'

'Demons,' the man said. 'They lives in the rocks, comes out at night.'

'Ever 'ear such tripe?' Lew demanded, exasperated.

Jason thought, this is all too much for me. I am fifteen years old and I have to think for the lot of us. I have to find out what the blacks plan to do. I have to see if I can do anything to make sure we survive. The others are years older but they're no help at all. Self-pity stabbed him. It isn't *fair*, he thought.

Quickly he forced the sudden weakness down. His head ached, a thick crust of dried blood matted his hair, he was almost sick with fear, yet would not give up. I have to get us out of here, he thought. Then find some way to keep us alive. They're the only things that matter.

'Got to call you something,' he told the old man.

The sailor brooded for a while. 'You kin call me Fred,' he said eventually.

'All right, Fred,' Jason said, 'how long you lived with the natives?'

Fred shook his head. 'Long time, matey. Years.'

'How did you get here?'

'I were a sealer, see? We was shipwrecked an' I got washed ashore, years ago.'

'How many years?'

But years, time itself, had lost all meaning.

'Been here ever since?'

'Like I say, there ain't no way out. They're not so bad,' he added, 'when you gets to know 'em.'

'Oo cares whether they're bad or not?' Lew interrupted roughly. 'What I want to know is 'ow we get outa here.'

'You don't,' Fred told him. 'Ain't no water an' it's too far to walk wivout it.'

Lew said, 'Don' talk daft! Them savages *lives* 'ere. There's got to be water.'

'You'll never find it. Besides, all the springs are guarded. They don' let anyone near 'em. You try takin' any wivout their say-so, they'll kill you.'

Jason needed space to think. They were jammed too closely together in the cage for that but he did the best he could, sitting in a corner with his back to the others, trying to work out how they were going to escape. Earlier he had thought he would not leave at all, at least for the present, but being thrown into the cage had changed all that. The sooner he was away from here the better.

Water and food, he thought, that's all we need. As long as we've got them we'll manage, especially if we move at night. He grinned, remembering Fred's words. Maybe the *quinkans* will look after us. We should take one of the blacks with us, he thought. Someone like Mura. Make him show us where the springs are. God knows how we do it, though.

Lew Bone would be another problem. He and Tom might manage by themselves but he doubted they'd survive with Lew along. At the moment the bosun wasn't dangerous because he thought he needed them to help him escape. As soon as he decided they weren't necessary any more he would turn on them. They couldn't leave him behind, though.

Maybe I should kill him, Jason thought.

The trouble was there was no way he could take Lew in a straight fight. Catch him by surprise, he thought. That would be the only way.

In the hour before the dawn Nantariltarra sat cross-legged on the turf at the top of the cliff in the fore-front of the elders and looked out at the sea. Overhead the sky was a rash of stars. The breeze from the water blew cool on him, the sound of the surf was in his ears. He waited as behind him Mingulta sang the dawn.

The thread of sound rose. The voice, joined now by another voice, increased steadily in volume. Far away across the dark water the sky turned from black to grey to gold and at last to red. As the light increased the land on that side of the gulf showed as a dark blue line broken here and there by headlands. It was unknown land. From time to time men came from those distant places with goods—shaped flints for weapons, *pituri* plants, ochre, tanned kangaroo skins—to trade for fish, stone and shells but Nantariltarra had not been there, nor any of the people.

Some said it was the place where the white men came from. Karinja had come, long ago. Now there were three more. Soon, no doubt, there would be others.

Nantariltarra had thought that if they could take the young one and understand him they might learn what the white men were like. Of course the youth was too young to know all the secrets of his people. Only the elders would have that kind of knowledge, as only their own elders knew the secrets of the Narungga, but the chance of his meeting with one of their elders was small. Even if he did, the man would never reveal their secrets to him. No, the youth was their best, perhaps their only, chance.

I must find a way, he told himself. I must break him to our ways and use him for the safety of our people. He must learn, as we must.

Mura has done well. As soon as I decide what is to be done, I shall release the boy into Mura's care, as before. We shall keep him with us, teach him our ways, even, in time, bring him to initiation. There will be opposition to that, he thought. But it was the only way if they were to use him to the full. Make him one of us as well as one of them. Use his knowledge against those of his people who come after him. Otherwise they may end by destroying us all, he thought, reflecting on the rumours he had heard.

The song rose, fell, rose again. A golden blink showed above the distant land. The sea ran with liquid gold. Somewhere birds were calling. All life welcomed the day, the returning light.

Nantariltarra thought, I can talk about this with no-one. Mura was too young to share the weight of the decisions that must be made. He did not have the knowledge of the people, the spirits, the land, and without that he could not help.

Nantariltarra was alone. It was a heavy burden yet he would have it no other way. The spirits moved through him so that he and all who came after him would remain in the land that was mother and source of life to all of them.

The spirits have given the white boy into my hand. He is the sign I have been waiting for.

I shall not fail.

Jason turned to the others. 'Anyone got a knife?'

Lew Bone laughed. 'Wouldn't be givin' it to you if I had.'

He doesn't trust me either, Jason thought. Of course. But it had been a stupid question; naturally they didn't have knives.

He studied the earth on which the cage stood. The bare earth was hard and dry, but it *was* earth, not rock. And in the earth . . .

Stones.

He'd heard that people had used stones as tools for thousands of years. He knelt. The surface of the ground was as hard as any rock. He scraped at it with his nails but barely scratched the surface. He would have no nails or fingers if he tried to dig a hole like that. He took off one of his boots and tried to use the heel but that was no good, either. He would wear out the boot a lot quicker than the ground.

Frustrated, he looked about him. The others watched, Lew Bone grinning sardonically.

'Ain't no use, see,' Tom said. 'The ground's too hard.'

'There must be a way,' Jason said, more to himself than the others.

'There ain't.' Lew Bone was dismissive. 'Like Tom said, we already tried it.'

Wood, Jason thought, looking at the framework. Wood lashed together by vines. He rattled the uprights experimentally but they were too strong to break.

Jason set his jaw, thought: I will not sit here and wait for other people to decide what to do with me.

Fred was right. Even if they managed to break out the blacks could always track them down and bring them back but that was not the point. What was important was to keep trying: to refuse ever to give up.

He knelt down, checking how the uprights had been driven into the earth. At each corner of the cage unpeeled lengths of gumwood had been driven into the ground. They were rock-hard, rigid, several inches thick. There was no moving them. But the walls were made of lath-like timbers set a few inches apart. He tested one. It gave slightly. So did the next one. He thought about it, went to the middle point of one of the walls and shook it as hard as he could, eyes fixed on the point where the laths entered the ground.

They moved. Only slightly, but they moved.

He turned his head, spoke to Tom who was watching him with a placid lack of curiosity. 'See?' he said.

But Tom would go through life seeing nothing.

'These uprights aren't buried that deep in the ground. And the soil around them's not as hard as out here in the middle.' With his fingernails he scraped at the earth around the bottom of the laths. A few fragments crumbled loose. 'See?'

Lew Bone was as dismissive as ever. 'Coupla crumbs. Where does that get us?'

Jason stared at him. 'Got something better to do, have you?'

When he shook the walls the lath itself acted as a lever, helping to loosen the soil about its base. It was cruel work and there was no room for them all to work at once but they took it in turns, crumbling the earth around the base of the central lath, scraping it away, repeating the operation again and again.

Fred did nothing to help them. Lew tried to talk him into it but he would not.

'Bloody fine bloke you are,' Lew said, scowling savagely. 'It's for your benefit, too.'

Fred was not interested. 'I told you, there ain't nowhere to go. I coulda run away a thousand times over the years. Why should I? This is home, far as I'm concerned.'

Lew spat. 'Funny sort of home, you ask me.'

Not that anybody had: but he left the old sealer alone, after that. Even Lew Bone could see there was nothing to be gained by harassing him further.

The foot of the lath was buried six inches in the ground. It took them most of the day to get to the bottom but at last they managed it.

'Now what?' Tom asked, wiping sweat off his face.

'We shovel it all back.'

Lew scowled. 'You tryin' to be funny?'

Jason was sick of having to justify every word he

uttered but knew there was no other way. 'We leave it, the blacks will see what we've been doing when they bring us food, won't they?'

So back into the hole the powdered soil went. Sure enough, as it grew dark two women brought them food and water. One was fat and old but the other was young: pert breasts, bouncing buttocks.

Lew Bone's lips curled over yellow teeth as he watched the young one. 'Could do with a bit o' that,' he said. He put his hand between the laths. She laughed good-naturedly but avoided him, all the same.

'Got any sense you'll leave 'em alone,' Fred told him.

Lew turned on him savagely. 'Don' you tell me what to do!'

'I seen blokes killed before this.'

'Maybe I'll kill you too, afore I'm through.' But Lew spoke mechanically, reaching for the food.

'Don't take too much,' Jason warned them. 'We'll need it when we get out of here.'

Neither Tom nor Lew took any notice but Jason kept some of his own back, wrapping it in a square of grubby cloth that he found in his pocket and putting it away safely.

When they had eaten they dug the powdered earth out of the hole again. Little by little they enlarged the hole until they could move the bottom of the lath an inch or two in its socket.

'We must make the hole bigger,' Jason said and they did.

The moon rose slowly above the gum trees, shedding its pallid light over them as they worked.

Eventually the hole was big enough for Lew to curl his big fist around the bottom of the lath and lever it upwards. It came up only so far but no further. Lew gasped, sweating in the moonlight, muscles standing out along his quivering arm. The lath gave a fraction. Lew redoubled his efforts. There was a crack like a pistol shot and he tumbled backwards, the broken lath clasped firmly in his hand.

Using the splintered piece of wood as a tool, they made quicker progress. Within an hour they had exposed the bottom of the second lath. Confident now, Lew made swift work of it. The gap was still not wide enough for them to squeeze through but at least they were getting there.

'One more should do it,' Jason said.

The eastern sky was beginning to silver by the time they broke the third lath. Freedom beckoned but they hesitated, looking at the gap.

'Reckon we'll make it?' Tom wondered nervously.

'Not without food and water,' Jason said, 'but I've thought about that. We'll take one of the blacks to find water for us.'

Lew looked dubious. 'How you going to manage that?'

Jason did not know. 'Perhaps one of the young blokes?' he hazarded, thinking of Mura. He ought to have felt guilty—kidnapping him would be a poor return for friendship—but did not. Mura's friendship had not stopped the other blacks putting him in the cage.

Lew nudged him. 'Why don't we grab that young girl when she comes back? She'll be easier to handle than a man and she'll be able to show us where the water is, easy as a man could.' Teeth gleamed in the moonlight. 'Show us a lot of things, I reckon.'

Jason hesitated. He didn't like the idea—having a young girl with them was certain to cause problems—but Lew was right about one thing: to take a man they would have to raid the camp whereas they could ambush the women when they brought the food in the morning. Perhaps that was what they should do.

'It means waiting 'til daylight . . .'

'Got a better idea?'

That was the trouble: he had no other ideas at all.

Lew seized on his hesitation. 'We need to get out of here now,' he said. 'Wait somewhere where we can grab them when they come.'

'All right.' Jason turned to Fred. The old man had not moved, had made no sign he was even aware the others had broken out. 'You coming?'

Fred ignored the question; he had made his choice long ago. Jason said no more. Perhaps it was best to leave him to live out his life as he wanted.

He said, 'Let's get on with it, then.'

Without a word they took the gourd of water, squeezed through the gap in the wall and disappeared into the bush.

SEVEN

Once again the dawn-singing drew to a close, the ritual complete for another day as it had been each day since the beginning of time. The light returning, the earth returning, the return of the spirits that were the rocks and water and trees. The singer also a spirit as he sang.

Nantariltarra unwound his long legs and stood, the others following his example. He summoned Mura to him. 'Bring Jay-e-son here. Make him understand that he must not go off alone. Start to teach him the ways of the people.'

'How do I get him to understand?'

'Use Karinja. They speak the same language.'

'What about the others?'

'For the moment, leave them where they are.'

The others had no role in his dream of the future.

Soon Mura was back, alarm in his face, with the news that three of the prisoners had broken out of the cage and vanished.

'Karinja is still there,' Mura said, 'but there is no sign of the others.'

Nantariltarra was displeased but unworried.

There was no way the white men could escape. Bringing them back, however, was a job for men, not an uninitiated youth like Mura. Quickly, he issued orders to a six-man party armed with spears and boomerangs.

'What if they fight us?' asked Walpanuna, leader of the party.

Nantariltarra thought. The boy's co-operation was important. 'Don't kill any of them unless you have to. If you cannot avoid it, you may kill the other two. But the boy must not be harmed.'

Within minutes the group had vanished into the bush.

They had planned to wait, to ambush the women when they returned, but Mura's unexpected arrival had changed all that. His sharp eyes must have seen the broken cage as soon as he came in sight of it. They had caught a brief glimpse of him standing at the edge of the gully, hand shading his eyes as he stared towards the cage, then he had vanished again without coming close enough for them to have any chance of capturing him. His arrival forced them to change their plans.

'Best git movin',' Lew said nervously.

It was pointless to go without knowing where the water holes were but Jason, too, was not willing simply to sit down and wait to be recaptured. At least if they *tried* to escape they would be making a fight of it. Anything, rather than simply giving up.

To begin with they made good ground, anxious to get as far away as possible before their escape was discovered.

Doggedly they followed the coast northwards.

The cliffs were lower here, little more than mounds of broken sandstone. If they saw a boat and could somehow attract its attention they might be able to get away before the pursuit, if any, caught up with them. But the sea remained empty, the sun climbed steadily in the sky until once again they faced the familiar spectre of thirst.

At the beginning Tom had carried the water container but after he had stumbled a number of times Lew Bone took it from him.

'Can' afford to lose that,' he said.

Jason eyed him suspiciously. They could not afford to have one man drink it all, either, and Lew wasn't the sort to volunteer unless he got something out of it himself.

In the event it made no difference. They had been travelling for less than three hours when the pursuit caught up with them.

The first sign of trouble was a succession of flickering shadows moving swiftly through the bush ahead of them.

Tom stopped at once, pointing. 'What's that?'

'Maybe animals?' Jason said. He knew they were not animals.

Lew picked up a jagged rock.

Jason looked at him. 'What's that for?'

'If that was what I reckon it was,' Lew said, 'we're goin' to have to fight.'

'Stones against spears?' Jason was scornful.

'They ain' takin' me back to that stinkin' cage,' Lew said savagely. 'They ain't treatin' me like no animal.'

'They'll kill you.'

'Let 'em, if they can manage it. We show we're willin' to fight, maybe they'll leave us alone.'

Maybe they would. Maybe the party ahead was

91

there simply to escort them out of their tribal territory. If on the other hand the idea was to kill them, well, perhaps Lew was right. By all means let them make a fight of it.

They drew together. Jason found a stone for himself, saw Tom do the same.

Lew cackled, beads of moisture frothing his lips. 'Give 'em a run for their money, eh?' He turned, brandishing his rock in the direction of the bush where they had seen the shadowy movement. 'You wan' to fight us,' he yelled in his cracked voice, 'come on an' fight.'

The response was immediate. A thin shadow flew from the undergrowth and Lew was rolling on the ground, clawing and fighting at the haft of a spear protruding from his shoulder.

The others had no time to move. There were men all around them. Tom raised his stone and was at once submerged in a tide of warriors. Jason flung his own rock—somewhere, anywhere—and turned to flee, instinct overcoming logic, but before he had gone two paces was caught from behind. He turned, fighting with fists, feet, fingernails, but was flung down in his turn, face in the dust, a knee in his back.

Something cracked him on the head and darkness returned.

He opened his eyes to yet another blinding headache and had a second in which to think *not again* before he found himself looking into Mura's black face.

For a moment he did not understand, then his senses returned and he realised he was back where he had started, in the branch shelter where he had awoken after he had first been captured.

At least this time he did not feel as bad as he had

then; perhaps his head was getting used to blows. It should be: there had been enough of them recently.

Mura's eyes changed as he realised Jason was awake. He backed out of the shelter and ran away, presumably to pass the word that Jason had regained consciousness. Jason wondered what would happen next but his brain wasn't up to guessing games.

He dozed for a few minutes. When he next opened his eyes there were two faces staring at him from the entrance. The light was bright at their backs but he recognised them at once. One belonged to the tall, powerfully built man who had struck him when he had come back from his first visit to the cage. Presumably he was the man who had had him imprisoned. An enemy, then. The other face belonged to Fred.

'What's going on?' Jason asked.

Fred licked his lips but did not answer. The big black man spoke: the usual incomprehensible flow of sound without intervals or identifiable words.

'What's he say?' Jason asked.

''E says you gotta stay 'ere. When you're better they'll teach you to become a member of the tribe.'

Whatever he had expected it had not been that.

'What happens if I don't want to be a member of the tribe?'

Fred grinned, shaking his head. 'Don' 'ave no choice, matey.'

Headache or not, Jason still had enough spirit to object to that. 'I didn't ask what you thought. It's him I'm talking to. I want to know what he's got to say about it.'

Fred's face closed resentfully. He said something to the black man. A moment's pause; again the flow of sound as the black man answered.

Fred said, 'You got to stay 'ere, same as me. 'E wants you to learn how folks live in this part of the world.'

Jason did not like the idea of anyone telling him what to do. 'If I try to go will he stop me?'

Jabber jabber.

''E says they won' stop you but without food or water you'll die, anyway. Like before.'

There was sense in that, at least. One important point remained unanswered. 'Where's my brother?'

Fred looked blank.

'The two men who were with me,' said Jason impatiently. 'One of them's my brother. What happened to them?'

Fred looked awkward. 'I dunno, matey—'

'Him,' Jason interrupted, pointing. 'Ask *him*!'

A pause, some limping questions, a curt and vigorous response.

Jason studied the black man's features as he spoke but they gave no hint of his thoughts.

Fred said, ''E says they're dead.'

Jason stared at him foolishly, his mind refusing to comprehend.

Dead . . .

He had seen Lew Bone writhing on the ground, fighting and cursing the spear in him, but Tom . . .

Dead?

He could not get a hold on the idea.

They had never been close: too many years between them for that, too many years apart.

Dead.

They'd had virtually nothing in common. Tom had been slow-witted, placid, willing to follow his younger brother's lead, an uncomplaining man. He had been tough, loyal. His brother. His dead brother.

Faced with the enormity of the news Jason could

not speak. He'd had no time for Lew Bone, the bully, the braggart, had even thought of killing him himself. But Tom . . .

He managed to ask, 'How?'

What was the good of questions, of answers?

'They was goin' to bring 'em back, matey, but they wouldn't come. One of 'em had a spear in 'im—'

'That was the other man.'

Fred jerked his head at the black man standing beside him. ''E says they wouldn't stop fighting. In the end they 'ad to kill 'em both to stop 'em killing them.'

Grief was replaced by anger: a red tide mounting in his brain. 'There was a whole mob of them, only two of them. They didn't need to kill them!'

'That's what 'e says, matey.'

Jason would have fought the black man but was too weak even to crawl.

'Tell him he had my brother murdered.' Fury made his voice ugly even in his own ears. 'Tell him there'll be a reckoning. Tell him—'

'I ain't tellin' 'im nuthin like that,' Fred said firmly. 'What you tryin' to do, get yourself killed, too?'

The blinding rage overflowed. 'I . . . want . . . you . . . to . . . tell . . . him!'

''Ave to tell 'im yourself, then.'

'You know I can't do that.'

''Ave to learn the lingo, then, won't you, matey?'

'Don't think I won't!'

'Tha's all right, then. It's what 'e wants you to do, anyway.'

Jason and Mura sat cross-legged in the dust at the edge of the trees. Through the leaves sunlight shed patterns of light and shade across the ground. Ten yards away a group of women sat gossiping, a scattering of tiny children—boys and girls, one of them the squirming girl who had climbed into his lap on his first evening with the clan—shrieked and tumbled together, playing like puppies. A dog, little more than a puppy itself, bounded forward barking from time to time or stood watching them with a pleased expression on its face.

Mura held up the spear, its notched blade of polished wood wicked in the sunlight. He said something that Jason could not catch.

'What?'

'*Winda*.'

'*Winn-derr*.' Jason tried to get his tongue around the sound.

'*Winda*.'

'*Winda*.' That was better. He could hear it himself. '*Winda*.'

Mura put the spear to one side. He pointed at himself. '*Nunga*.'

That was easier. '*Nunga*,' Jason repeated. 'Man,' he guessed. He pointed at himself. '*Nunga*?'

Mura shook his head vigorously, laughing, and pointed again at himself. '*Nunga*.' Pointed at Jason. '*Kuinyo*.' Pointed at Fred, off to one side, brought along to help when things got too difficult. '*Kuinyo*.'

Jason shook his head. Too hard. He appealed to Fred. 'What's he saying?'

'*Nunga*'s what they call themselves. *Kuinyo*'s their name for us.'

'Black and white?' Jason guessed.

Fred shook his head. 'Not colour. It's just that they think of themselves as different, I s'pose.'

'The same as we do,' Jason said. He turned back to Mura. '*Kuinyo*,' he said, placing his hand on his bare chest. He had decided to follow his hosts' example as far as his shirt was concerned but could not yet bring himself to go as far as Fred who sat now, naked as he was born, scratching unconcernedly between his legs. Jason pointed at Mura. *'Nunga.'*

Mura's grin widened. He clapped his hands softly together.

Jason wanted to confirm what Fred had said. On the other side of the clearing the small girl ran helter-skelter between the trees, pursued by another slightly older. Jason pointed at her. *'Nunga,'* he hazarded.

Mura nodded, beaming. *'Nunga.'*

Progress. As for understanding what the blacks said among themselves ... He still had no idea. At least he was beginning to break the flow of sound into identifiable words but it would be a long time before he could attempt a conversation.

Days, weeks passed. Words became phrases, phrases sentences, sentences conversation. Slow, halting and often incorrect, but conversation nonetheless.

Jason had learned that the tall man's name was Nantariltarra, a proper jaw-breaker. He practised saying the name silently to himself, listening to the sound inside his head.

Nantariltarra. *Nantariltarra.*

From time to time Nantariltarra came to listen to the lessons. He gave no sign of being pleased by Jason's improving skills but since it had been his idea to teach him the *nunga* language Jason thought he must be.

Jason made no attempt to address him or even acknowledge his presence. He would always think of him as the man who had killed his brother. The waste and futility of Tom's life and death were always with him. Tom had been a threat neither to the clan nor to any person on earth, not even to himself. There could be no excuse, no forgiveness, for what had happened. Jason watched Nantariltarra out of the corner of his eye. There would be a reckoning.

One day Nantariltarra said something to Mura, speaking brusquely and far too fast for Jason to understand, and Mura looked thoughtfully at Jason, no smile for once, and Jason knew that something important, possibly even momentous, had been decided.

Yet for days little changed. One variation was that now Fred was seldom there: Jason's understanding had reached the point where an interpreter was rarely necessary. Once or twice an older man joined them. He had grey hair and an infirm way of walking, his chest and back marked with even lines of scar tissue. He sat and observed, saying nothing, but once when Nantariltarra was there they walked away together, Nantariltarra towering over the older man, and Jason heard their voices raised in what sounded like heated argument.

'*Worrarra*,' Mura explained in an undertone after the old man had gone.

'His name?' Jason guessed.

Mura shook his head. 'Magic man,' he explained, using words that Jason understood.

Magic man ...

'Magician,' Jason said. 'Sorcerer.'

He took care to treat the old man with extra respect after that. No future in getting on the wrong side of a sorcerer.

Days later Mura said, 'We are to meet the old ones.'

Jason looked at him enquiringly. 'Old ones?'

'Those who will make us men,' Mura explained.

'I am already a man,' Jason boasted, believing it was true. He was as strong as most men and alone in the world. He still missed his brother but not as he had.

Mura explained there were rites to be undergone before anyone could become a man in the eyes of the clan. The visit to the old ones, the elders, would be the first step in the instruction that would lead in time to Jason's initiation.

'What about you?' Jason asked. 'You going to be initiated too?'

Mura nodded. 'That was why Nantariltarra wanted us to be together from the beginning. So we could become men at the same time.'

The proceedings were drawn out over many weeks and shrouded in ritual and mystery. There was instruction in the meaning of things, in the ancestral beings, in the laws that governed the people.

In addition to instruction there was pain. The first steps towards initiation began with a physical test of worthiness.

A glowing fragment of red coal, clamped firmly between the upper and lower arms at the elbow.

'What's this all about?' Alarm rang in Jason's voice despite efforts to conceal it.

'A man shows no fear of pain,' Mura told him.

It was excruciating. The sweat burst in torrents from him but Jason willed his face to show nothing. The agony, the sickening stench of burnt flesh, almost made him faint. He sat expressionless under the watchful gaze of the old men, his skin a river of sweat, the pain eating his flesh.

Then there was the knife, by comparison much easier to bear, the ritual cutting of parallel incisions in the skin of chest and back.

'*Manka*,' Mura called it.

Blood ran thick. Ash was rubbed in the wounds. The scars would always be borne proud of the flesh, Mura said, as a reminder of how a man should bear all suffering.

Dizzy with pain and loss of blood, confused by so many strange things, Jason heard the voices of the instructors chanting, explaining, expounding, telling him the truths that a man must know, that a woman must never learn.

'There is women's business, too,' Mura said. 'Things they learn that we don't.'

'What things?'

'I don't know.'

Of course: but Jason wanted to learn everything. He felt resentment that there should be knowledge forbidden him.

'Why?' he asked.

'It is the way things have always been.'

Whenever he raised an awkward question that was always the answer. There were things he must know, things he was permitted to know, things he was forbidden to know. Why? Because that was the way it had always been, the way it would always be.

'Does nothing change?'

It seemed not.

'Then how . . .?' But said no more.

How do we learn new things? he had meant to say but did not. Such a question was meaningless, might even be dangerous. To Mura and the rest there were no new things nor could ever be. Yet there were new things in the world, Jason knew. He was one of them. No white man had ever been taken into the clan, had any of its secrets revealed to him.

Fred told him, 'Taken a proper shine to you, they have. An honour, that's what it is.' He showed no resentment that such honour had never been paid to him.

'Some honour,' Jason said, the pain of the burning still with him. Yet was proud of the pain, the way he had proved to the elders his ability to withstand it. Already he felt apart from Fred, superior to him.

It *was* an honour, he knew. The clan was on the way to accepting him. With the initiation he would become one of them. He was pleased without knowing why. He no longer thought of running away, as once he had, although he also never thought of spending the rest of his life here, either, initiated member of the Narungga people or not.

For the moment he was prepared to live from day to day. As to the future ... Something would happen. He had no doubt of that.

EIGHT

Asta Matlock kneaded the damper and put it into the cinders at the edge of the glowing coals to cook. While she waited she busied herself with the meat that she had left soaking in fresh water to rid it of the salt in which it had been preserved. She made a face as she took the strip of meat out of the water and laid it on the wooden table top. The salt was supposed to stop the meat from going putrid but seldom did the job properly. It was usually half-rotten by the time they ate it and, judging by the smell, this piece was no exception. It was ironic that they should have to rely on salt meat when they had so many sheep but Gavin had been adamant: no sheep to be killed unless absolutely essential. The demands of the flock took precedence over their own.

'We need a new pickling barrel,' Asta said out loud. She had been telling herself the same thing for weeks but had done nothing about it.

'Perhaps tomorrow,' she told herself with little conviction.

Since Edward's death she had taken each day as

it came, drifting mechanically through her life. She carried out her duties, kept the house as clean as was possible in a place like this, prepared the meals and cooked them, did the laundry, looked after the cows, made butter and cream, tried—and failed—to grow vegetables in a soil that was alien even to her fingertips. She permitted her husband the use of her body although the first time it happened after Edward died it had been all she could do not to cry out in protest, to beat her clenched fists against his hard flesh in outrage that he could even *think* of such a thing. She had not done so. She had lain there, enduring, until it was over. Not only enduring, in truth. Although she had told herself then and on every occasion since that the act did not touch her, that she was no more than a receptacle for her husband's lust, it was not true. Always her flesh betrayed her, kindling the response of the flesh with a power greater than anything her will could muster against it. She despised her body and herself for it, despised Gavin, too, but accepted it might be different for a man.

Now Asta cut and slashed, turning the meat, cutting again, discarding the worst pieces, hands moving automatically, mind busy with her thoughts. She put the meat into a pot with a few precious onions and potatoes—they had brought with them large supplies of both but they were running low now—and placed it on a trivet at the edge of the coals. Slow cooking would soften the tough meat a little.

Face hot and flushed from the fire, Asta went out of the kitchen into the sunlight, crossed to the main house and went inside. She removed her apron, put on shawl and bonnet, changed her boots. She went out into the harsh glare of the day and walked down the sloping paddock towards the distant line of cliffs, as she did every day at about this time.

Gavin had spoken to her several times about it. 'I don't like you going out alone,' he said. 'Ian saw a group of natives near his place only a week ago.'

'Did they do anything?' she asked.

'They watched him from the trees. When he walked towards them they ran away.'

'To me they do not sound very dangerous,' she said, accent lilting and foreign-sounding in air that would always be foreign to her.

'They've killed plenty of people in other places. You know that as well as I do.'

'It is their land, after all.'

Gavin shook his head. 'Not any more.'

'Perhaps nobody has told them that,' she said.

He was right, of course. It *was* dangerous to go out alone but she was unable to prevent herself. Every day she had to go to the sea, every day she had to wait. What she was waiting for she could not have said but that did not matter. It was the waiting that was important.

The sea stretched like a piece of crinkled silk to the horizon. Where sky and sea met she could just make out the triangular outline of headlands marking the other side of the gulf. They thrust through the haze: blue sea, blue land, blue sky. They were the limits of her world: remote, alluring, unattainable, the gateway and symbol of everything she had lost.

At the foot of the cliff the sea tumbled ponderously, the sound of the breakers compressed, it seemed, by heat. The air was swimming with insects. In front of her the dusty path unwound down the cliff. The tide was in and she could not see the sickle of sand-girt stones, so insignificant from here, where her son's body had been found.

Perhaps I shall conceive again, she thought, knowing she did not want that.

The sea has taken him, she told herself, eyes fixed on the blue expanse. In its own time the sea will return what it has taken. It was crazy, she knew. She heard her thoughts, there were times when they frightened her, yet she believed.

There was always Alison, her brother-in-law's twelve-year-old child, but Alison was a girl. There was Blake Gallagher: but the farm supervisor was a harsh, brutal man and, at sixteen, his son showed every sign of growing up to be the same.

Someone else's child was not the answer, either.

There was alarm in the clan, anxious discussions, slanted glances aimed Jason's way. The Council had been talking for hours, seated in a circle on the ground in their usual place well away from everyone else, but the sound of their voices carried to the rest of the camp and the voices were often angry.

'What is going on?' Jason asked Mura.

His friend would not answer.

'What is it? Why won't you tell me?'

He went to look for Fred but he was no wiser than Jason was.

'They're allus gittin' worked up about summat. Their nature, see? Maybe it's to do with one of them there initiation ceremonies they're always on about.'

Jason knew it couldn't be that. The next phase of his initiation was due very soon and as far as he knew everything to do with that had been running smoothly. He was reasonably sure that the present excitement had nothing to do with the clan's normal routine but was something new and possibly threatening, not only to the clan but to himself.

The sun was well down in the western sky when a Council messenger, tall and stern-looking, a long spear in his right hand, came stalking across the clearing and stopped in front of Jason.

'The Council will question you.'

Jason knew he had been with the clan several months but could not be sure how many; he had lost count of the days in a world where days did not seem to matter. It had been winter when the *Kitty* sank and now, after the long heat of summer, the days had shortened, the nights were cold once more. In all those months this was the first time Jason had been summoned in such a way. The brusque order bothered him: how was he supposed to communicate with them? He had learnt enough of the language to carry on a simple conversation but to be questioned by the Council would be an entirely different matter.

Nerves jumping, he scrambled to his feet and followed the messenger to where the elders were seated on the sun-warmed dust.

Jason had long ago given up wearing clothes. At first he had felt awkward, afraid that every male and—much worse—every female in the clan had been watching him, possibly even laughing at him, but he had soon got used to it. Now he wished he had something to cover himself. Clothes were more than a covering, they were something to hide behind. Naked, he felt that his thoughts were as exposed as his body. In the present circumstances that might not be a good idea.

A few yards from the circle of seated elders the messenger stopped and raised his hand. 'You will wait here until you are called.'

Jason waited self-consciously, trying not to fidget. To begin with, the elders gave no sign that they knew he was there. They continued their discussion, often several of them speaking at once, but eventually the talk petered out into an expectant silence. Several heads turned in Jason's direction.

The messenger pushed him forward. 'They are ready for you now.'

Nantariltarra watched as Jay-e-son came forward. The other Council members seemed to believe that this *kuinyo*, washed ashore in a storm, must know everything there was to know about others of his own people.

What nonsense, thought Nantariltarra. Do we know everything that happens among the Kaurna? Or the Nugunu? Of course not. Yet they are *nunga*, as we are. Jay-e-son knows nothing about this latest news, I am sure of it. I have to allow the Council their chance to question him because if I do not they will say that I am hiding something, but their questions will uncover nothing.

Jay-e-son stood to one side of the circle.

'Stand here, in the centre,' Nantariltarra instructed him, 'where everyone can see you.'

Nantariltarra watched the members of the Council studying the white man: almost man. He doubted they saw what he saw. He saw Jay-e-son as an ally, the only hope they had of surviving the threat that was coming down on them, whereas he suspected they saw someone strange, an enemy because of his strangeness and because of what they had heard of others of his kind.

'The Council wishes to ask you what you know about the *kuinyo*.'

Jay-e-son nodded but did not speak.

He no longer even looks like a *kuinyo*, Nantariltarra thought. *Kuinyo* meant dead person. Before a corpse was placed on the funeral platform to enable wind and rain to do their work the top layer of dark skin was removed, leaving a pinkish under layer. The colour of the first newcomers had reminded those who saw them so forcibly of the pink colour of death that they had given them the name of a corpse.

'You are *kuinyo*,' Nantariltarra said, speaking slowly so that Jay-e-son would understand him. 'Tell us how you came here.'

'I was on a ship that sank in a storm,' Jason said. 'I was washed ashore.'

'Where do you come from?'

'From a land far from here. We call it Van Diemen's Land. I don't know what it is called in your language.'

'When you came ashore were you alone?'

'No. There were two other Europeans with me.' He used the English word European but saw at once that they did not understand. '*Kuinyo*,' he explained.

'What happened to them?'

Nantariltarra saw anger flash in Jay-e-son's eyes. 'You killed them.'

'Do you know why we did not kill you?' Nantariltarra said.

'No, I do not know why.' Jay-e-son's eyes met his and Nantariltarra was pleased to see no fear in them, nothing but anger and pride.

No, he thought, nor will you know until we have learnt everything you can tell us about the *kuinyo* and their ways.

He could sense the Council watching him.

'Where do the *kuinyo* come from?' he asked.

'From over the sea,' Jay-e-son said.

'From where over the sea?'

'Far. Travelling as long as I have been living here with the clan.'

Disbelief rumbled around the circle of seated men. What this youth was saying was impossible. No-one could live so long on the salt waters. What would they eat? What would they drink? Was this boy claiming that the *kuinyo* had powers beyond ordinary men? Even, perhaps, beyond the spirits?

Nantariltarra saw that Jay-e-son's answer had angered them: not because they knew it was false but because, in a hidden part of their minds, they were afraid that it was true. It was inconceivable that the *kuinyo* could have such powers yet Nantariltarra too was inclined to believe. The newcomers were so different yet no-one had ever heard of them until recently. It made sense that they should come from far away.

'Why have they come here?'

It was the only question that mattered. If he knew why the *kuinyo* had come he might be able to anticipate what they planned to do now they were here.

Jay-e-son hesitated. 'I don't know.'

Again the hiss of disbelief. This *kuinyo* was lying: Nantariltarra could read the thought clearly in the down-turned mouths, the lowering brows of the Council. They believed Jay-e-son did know, that he denied knowledge not from ignorance but from guile. It confirmed what they had always suspected: that he was an enemy, part of whatever it was the *kuinyo* planned to do.

Nantariltarra knew he must be careful. Against the wishes of the majority he had forced through the decision to initiate Jay-e-son, to admit him to at least some of the clan's secrets. If it was now agreed that Jay-e-son was an enemy then Nantariltarra himself would be guilty of betraying the clan by having revealed to him what should not have been spoken.

109

'You are a *kuinyo*,' he said coldly. 'How can you say you do not know why you came here? You will be telling us next that you do not know what the *kuinyo* are planning to do now they *are* here.'

Anger and frustration rose in Jason like a hot tide. These men knew nothing of the outside world, did not even admit that it existed.

How could he explain to them what the European arrival meant, that they had travelled all the way from Europe to take this land, that they had no intention of leaving, that they thought of it as their own? Even in English it would have been impossible to explain. In a language that he spoke only haltingly, understood even less, it was doubly impossible. The worlds of the European and black man were too far apart for understanding. He looked around at the eyes watching him and saw only suspicion.

Be careful, he warned himself. If you tell them that the whites are here to stay these men may kill you. On the other hand if you say the opposite, that the *kuinyo* will *not* stay, they may kill you later when they find out you lied to them.

Jason said, 'All the *kuinyo* think of the place across the sea as home. They think of going back there.' It was the best he could do.

There was a gabble of controversy as all the members of the Council began to speak at once. The talk was too fast for Jason to understand so he waited, trying to hide his increasing apprehension.

'Why have they come here if they intend to go back again? If their home is as far away as you say it is?'

Jason did not know why the Europeans had come to Australia. Some, like his parents, had been convicts brought here to be punished, but why here and not somewhere else he had no idea. He had been

110

born here, it was his home. He had never given any thought to *why*.

Think, he told himself furiously. He remembered something Mura had told him about how the clans traded with each other, how some of their weapons were tipped with special stone that had been quarried from an island far away to the north, in a place where no-one whom Mura knew had ever been.

Perhaps the Council would understand *that*.

'It depends on the type of people they are,' he said.

Nantariltarra frowned. '*Kuinyo* are *kuinyo*,' he said. 'They are all the same. What do you mean, the type of people?'

'They are *not* all the same. There are sailors, farmers, traders . . .' He chose the categories least likely to offend them. 'Perhaps they have come to trade,' he said.

'Trade in what?' Nantariltarra asked.

Jason did not know what trade the Europeans would be willing to make with the blacks. 'Wool, sealskins, maybe weapons,' he guessed. 'I don't know. You'll have to ask them.'

Nantariltarra watched Jay-e-son closely as he spoke. He did not think the *kuinyo* had come to trade. The reports he had heard had said nothing about that.

'Perhaps you should ask them yourself,' Nantariltarra said.

'How can I do that?'

'There are some only two days march from here.'

Thunderstruck, Jason stared at him. 'Two days . . .?'

He had always believed that white people would come eventually but for them to be here already . . . And so close . . .

111

Just to *see* them, Jason thought. That would be something. 'I could try,' he said, not wishing to sound too eager.

Nantariltarra turned and spoke briefly to the other Council members. Some dubious head-shaking but nobody spoke. He looked back at Jason. 'Go, now. I shall tell you later what you must do.'

Ian Matlock, tall and yellow-bearded, riding long and easy in the saddle, rode up to his cousin's house one morning in June, three months after they had first arrived on the peninsula. His daughter Alison, twelve years old and as dark as her father was blond, rode behind him, arms clasped around his waist.

The cousins saw each other most weeks but this was a special occasion.

'Mary will be along later,' Ian said, beating dust from his clothes, clumping into the house. The small room felt smaller with the two men crowded into it. 'She's still got some baking to finish.'

Alison had gone looking for Asta; now they both came into the room, making it smaller than ever.

Ian was on his feet, kissing, hugging, eyes probing, bright with laughter that did not soften the knife slash of his mouth.

'And how is the birthday girl?'

With a strained mouth in a face grown bony since her bereavement, Asta said, 'Feeling her age. But I thank you for the good wishes.' Trying to bring warmth into her face, her words. Failing.

'That's good.' The eyes appraising her, possessive as ever.

'Thirty-two is not old,' Gavin protested, good-natured but bereft, too, the loss of his son a constant ache. Concerned as well for his wife, who showed no sign of recovering from what had happened.

'Not young, either.'

Ian fidgeted. Life was too short for sorrow over what could not be rectified. He said, 'Good rains we've had, the last few days.'

It had rained heavily day and night for nearly a week. It was the season for rain but welcome nonetheless.

'We have indeed,' Gavin said. He fetched a bottle, poured two glasses.

'Still some left, then,' Ian asked, nodding at the bottle.

'We only touch it when there's something to celebrate,' Gavin said.

Asta laughed without humour. 'Thirty-two years old. What is there to celebrate in that?'

Life was passing her by in this little hut in a land without hope or pity. Bitterness would make her old, she knew, but could do nothing about it.

'Come,' she said to Alison at her side, 'let us go to the kitchen and get ourselves each a glass of fruit cordial.'

'Bring them back in here,' Gavin said.

'Oh no.' Asta wanted to be away, preferring the girl's company and her own to that of the men. 'There are things we must do in the kitchen.' Any excuse would do.

Gavin insisted. 'Of course you must come back. It's your birthday, after all.'

She saw there was no way out of it. She led Alison to the kitchen, they poured themselves a tiny glass of cordial each. Like the alcohol, when it was gone there would be no more. They returned to the men.

'A happy birthday,' Ian said, glass raised. 'Many of them.'

They drank.

'Thank you,' Asta said to no-one in particular. 'Thank you.'

Happiness, she thought. What is that?

But she was also determined to make the best of things, hating self-pity to which she feared she was prone.

'How are your sheep?' she asked for something to say.

'Good,' Ian acknowledged. 'The rain will be good for the grazing.' He looked at his cousin. 'You expecting the Gallaghers?'

'Hector said he would drop in. He'll probably bring Blake.'

Hector Gallagher, a widower, divided his time between both runs as part supervisor, part shepherd, and full-time bully to his son and anyone else he could find to dominate, which excluded, most emphatically, the Matlock men. Was not above trying it on the women either, although with little success as far as Asta was concerned. Sixteen-year-old Blake, blond hair almost white in the sunlight but heart as black as night, looked set to follow his father's example. Hearing he might arrive, Alison made a face, hating him but knowing better than to say so.

'We are a small group,' her mother had warned when Alison told her how she despised Blake's braggart ways. 'We must learn to live harmoniously with each other.'

Harmony was Mary Matlock's grail. Small wonder, with a husband who ruled the roost as Ian did.

Blake is my cross, Alison thought. She was going through a religious phase but with little help or encouragement from her parents: a father who loudly professed disbelief in anything he could not see, a mother dedicated to the avoidance of conflict.

'Someone for you to play with,' Asta said but without conviction, knowing more than she would admit.

That boy needs a strap, she thought. But knew that neither she nor anyone would give it to him. At sixteen Blake was already beyond her reach, beyond the reach of them all.

'Hector was telling me he's seen natives again,' Gavin said.

'They'll stay away from my place if they know what's good for them,' Ian said, but with little heat, equal to the challenge of the natives.

Asta felt uncomfortable, as always with such talk of the natives, who had been here first. But said nothing.

'They've been known to steal sheep,' Gavin warned.

'I'll shoot a few, they try that.'

Ian finished his glass, stood and refilled it uninvited. 'I brought a bottle of my own in the saddle-bag,' he said, in case Gavin might object.

'Help yourself,' Gavin said, now that Ian already had. 'Pour one for me, while you're about it.'

It was a birthday, after all. Another drink wouldn't hurt.

Hector and Blake Gallagher arrived at the same time as Mary Matlock, the Gallaghers on foot, Mary riding the spirited grey filly that was her pride, knowing how to dominate horses in a way she had never learned with humans.

The three men sat in the room and talked sheep, the two women went to the kitchen. Alison would have preferred to join them but something perverse in her nature prevented her. They thought she should entertain Blake. Very well, entertain him she would, or try to.

'There are kittens,' she offered, but Blake was too old, too masculine, for kittens. It would have made no difference what she suggested. Blake was contemptuous of Alison and saw no reason to hide it. She was too young; she was female; there was nothing to be done with her. He should have been with the men, a man among men, and the fact that he had been left with this child mortified him. Kittens . . . Next thing might be dolls. He wanted to be away by himself, looking for mischief. His father would thrash him if he knew but Blake was used to that. Another year, maybe two, he would be beyond his father's reach, too.

On the other hand kittens might be just the thing he needed. He smiled at Alison. 'Let's see them, then, shall we?'

His sudden change of manner made her suspicious. 'Are you interested? Truly?'

'I said so, didn't I?'

Alison's screams brought Asta and Mary running.

Blake with a kitten clasped in a beefy hand too big and powerful for a boy his age. Face white, voice whispering hoarsely, 'Quit your screeching!'

Asta stopped in the doorway to the hay barn. Her attenuated shadow lay across the dirt floor. 'What is going on in this place?'

Blake crouched in a far corner, in shadow. His eyes hunted to and fro, caught in the midst of whatever he had been doing. His lip curled back in defiance as he turned to face the light. 'Nuthin!'

Mary stood at Asta's shoulder: shorter, rounder, her face concerned. 'Alison?'

116

'He's killed one already! He said he was going to kill them all!' Distraught, voice choked with sobs, with shock.

'I never!' Blake opened his hand. The kitten fell, spread claws like needles raked his bare leg. 'Ow!' His foot lashed out but in an eye's bat the tiny creature had landed, turned and was gone. He inspected two or three drops of blood glistening on his leg. 'Look what it did!'

Alison was already in her mother's arms, tears wetting the silky grey skirt. 'He killed one already! He stamped on it! He said he was going to kill them all!'

Mary looked around her helplessly, action not her forte, but Asta marched purposely forward, seized Blake by the arm and shook him.

Big boy or not, he is not spreading his terror in my house. She was surprised how much she disliked the firm white flesh beneath her fingers. 'So? Explain yourself, Blake.'

He wrenched his arm free, glaring defiantly at her. 'I didn't do nuthin!'

Muffled sobs. 'He did ...'

Blake yelled with sudden violence, 'I didn't! It was her! She did it!'

Shaking, Alison pointed into the far corner. Asta looked. A spill of blood. A dead kitten, its head crushed. She turned in outrage. Blake backed off but she went after him, eyes a pale fire.

He raised his fist. 'Don' you touch me!'

She ignored that. Her rage overwhelmed his defiance. She snatched his arm again, held him firm. 'How dare you come to my house and murder my animals!'

'I didn't! I didn't!' Screeching, shaking, face red with blood and terror. 'She did it!'

Any lie would do, anything.

'Be silent!' Shake, shake. Willpower generated the strength to drag Blake forcibly across the barn to the dead beast. 'Pick it up!'

Horrified eyes glared at her. 'What?'

'Pick it up,' she repeated. 'You kill my animals, you will bury them.'

Blake stood still, frozen between fear and defiance.

'Now!'

Her icy will overpowered him. He bent, took up the tiny body. Its fur, matted with blood, smeared his fingers.

Next, the row of tools hanging from hooks along the wall. The timber smell mingled with rage, fear, death, the sun's heat, the dust's placid swirl in the still barn.

'Take down a spade.'

They went outside. Asta pointed. 'Dig a hole. There. Bury what you have done.'

The kitten's body out of sight, the dirt raked across, Blake wiped his fingers on his breeches, defiance returning. 'I never done *nuthin*!'

'You are a liar,' Asta told him. 'A liar and a bully.' She pointed imperiously towards the house. 'Go. I want nothing more to do with you.'

Blake ran.

Asta shouted after him. 'Put the spade back first.'

He turned, halfway to the house, free from the influence of her will. He threw the spade on the ground. 'You wait,' he shouted at them all, at a world that dared tell him what to do, 'you just wait.'

By the time the women reached the house, Alison dragging her smeared face and woeful expression behind them, Blake's father was standing in the doorway.

'You been speaking to my boy, missus?' Voice congested, face dark.

Asta faced him, chin up. 'I have, Mr Gallagher. And shall do so again, if the need arises. Which I hope it will not.'

'You got something to say, say it to me, not him.'

His tone threatened her but Asta disregarded it. 'This is my house, Mr Gallagher. In my house I speak to whom I please. You wish me to speak to you? Very well. This boy of yours is becoming a menace to us all. Teach him to behave, Mr Gallagher, or we shall all live to regret it. You, too.'

Gallagher set his surly shoulders. 'What's he supposed to have done?'

'Supposed nothing, Mr Gallagher. What he has done, actually done, is to kill a cat.'

Intervals of stained teeth showed through Gallagher's thick-lipped grin. 'Kill a *cat*? Lord love us, missus, he was doin' you a favour, then. Got to control 'em, see, or they runs out of control.'

'With his *boots*, Mr Gallagher?' She swept past him into the house. 'Teach him to behave, he is welcome in my house. Until then, I am sorry.'

'We came to wish you for your birthday, missus.' Gallagher's voice was derisive behind her.

'Good,' she said without turning her head. 'Teach Blake to behave like a civilised being, it will be a gift I shall cherish.'

Later, after all the visitors had gone, Gavin said, 'Gallagher's a useful man. I don't want to fall out with him.'

'Gallagher is an animal.' Asta was unrepentant. 'And Blake is worse.' She turned to him, appealing. 'Someone has to control him, surely?'

'Are you sure it is our place to do it? Blake is not our child.'

Asta's face was white. 'Our child is dead. We are in this wilderness alone. We have to behave well, all of us.'

Gavin shrugged. He walked across the room to the cupboard, poured them both a drink, came back to her, handed her the glass. 'It *is* a wilderness. You can't expect people to act civilised in a wilderness.'

Vigorously she shook her head. 'It is because it is a wilderness we must behave well. Otherwise how are we to bring civilisation to this place?'

'Is that what we're supposed to be doing?' He found it hard to take what had happened as seriously as she did. It was only a cat, after all. 'And there I was thinking we were trying to raise sheep.'

Asta ignored that. 'Of course we are bringing civilisation. Otherwise what is the justification for our being here at all?'

He strolled across to his chair and dropped into it. He stretched out his legs, crossed his boots and grinned lazily up at her. 'What justification do we need?'

'This is not our country,' she said. 'There were people here before us. If we bring civilisation, if we make things better here than they were before, good. *That* is our justification. But if we do not we have no business to be here at all.'

He shook his head. 'Blake kills a cat and you think we should all move out?'

'Of course not.' She came and sat on the arm of his chair, looked down at him with troubled eyes. 'You know what I mean.'

He shook his head. 'No, I do not know what you mean. I am here, so are you, so are we all, and we are staying. That is something I know. Nobody is going to stop me. Not Blake, not the blacks. Nothing.'

'Not me, either?' she asked softly.

He avoided the challenge. 'We are going to do big things here: for you as much as for me.'

Her wounded eyes regarded him. 'You and me, yes. And after us, it will all have been for nothing?'

'God willing, no,' he said. 'It is not what I want.'

'*You* want?' she repeated, crying. 'You think *I* want it?'

'All I am saying,' he said carefully, 'is that we are here and we shall stay here.'

'By force?'

He took a deep breath. 'If needs be. If the blacks try to drive us out, yes.'

'You mean as we are driving *them* out?'

He did not know what she wanted from him. A tiny incident, trivial it seemed to him, and now all this. 'Yes!'

'So force becomes our justification. Is that it?'

Gently he drew her to him. For a moment she resisted, then yielded. He cradled her, her hair fragrant against his mouth. 'The strong overcome the weak,' he said. 'It is the way of the world.'

She shook her head resolutely without looking up. 'It is a bad way.'

'It is the natural way,' he corrected her. 'The strong must prevail.'

His hand moved over her body, caressing, seeking. She stared at him, eyes swollen with the tears she had shed, yet did not push his hand away. Something was happening; a door, closed since Edward's death, was slowly opening. All the same, his argument troubled her.

'You are saying that strength is all that matters? That right and wrong have no place? Blake is strong,' she said. 'Bad, I think, bad through and through, but strong, certainly. You are saying that Blake and people like him must prevail?'

He supposed that *was* what he meant but had the sense not to say so. 'All I am saying is that this is our place and I'm not going to leave it.' Gently, he kissed her forehead. His hand resumed its exploration. 'As for Blake ... I think we can safely leave Hector Gallagher to deal with him.'

'That is something we cannot do,' she said. 'Hector Gallagher is as bad as Blake. Worse, if anything. He has made Blake what he is.'

But Gavin was thinking of other things than Blake Gallagher. He stood and took her hand. 'Come,' he said.

She went with him gladly. For the first time since Edward's death she was as eager for him as he, thank God, was for her.

Afterwards, Gavin sleeping at her side, Asta thought what a strange thing life was. A man and a woman, separate in every way, came together and from their physical union came new life. A personality, a soul, that did not exist before became a being entire in itself, totally separate from the parents who had created it. It was a mystery as great as death.

What lies before life? she wondered. If there is nothing, why should we assume that death is not the end of everything, too? Out of nothing, into nothing? In which case Edward, her son, was nowhere; gone into the dark. From dark to dark in fourteen years. A creature of flesh and bone, laughter and sorrow, wants, hopes, love. All gone. What is the point of life, Asta asked the sky in anguish, if at the end there is nothing? If we cease utterly to be? Surely there must be more than the memory of ourselves that we leave behind? Because, she thought, if there is not there is no point to anything.

Yet perhaps things were not as bad as that. Whether there was something after death or not, life still had to be lived. All, in time, would go into the dark but not yet, not yet. Asta's fingertips traced the line of her lower ribs, the soft fall of her belly. Now, with the return of her feelings for her husband, she felt for the first time since her child's death that she was indeed coming back to life. Now, perhaps, it might be possible to face the future with something like hope.

Riding homeward Ian thought, I doubt seriously whether Gavin and Asta will survive.

He said as much to Mary, trotting at his side.

She glanced across at him. 'Why?'

'Because it's a hard country. We have to be hard ourselves if we're going to make a go of it. There's no room for softness.'

'I've never thought of Gavin as soft,' Mary objected.

'He was hard once,' Ian allowed. 'As hard as any man I know. Asta's made him soft.'

'Asta wasn't exactly soft today,' Mary protested tentatively.

He dismissed it. 'All that fuss about nothing . . .'

She said, 'Blake's a horrible boy.'

'He's tough. It's what this country needs.'

She thought of Blake's wanton cruelty and shook her head. 'No-one needs a person like Blake.'

'They would probably have drowned the damned cat anyway,' he said. 'Anyone would think it was a *child* he killed.'

'I wouldn't put it past him,' Mary said.

They rode in silence, listening to the rhythmic thud of hooves on the grass, and started up the hill beyond which, sheltered from the hot north wind, they had built their house.

If Asta is so upset by the death of a kitten, Ian thought, how will she take it if it ever comes to a fight with the blacks?

It probably would: it had everywhere else. The sooner the better, as far as Ian was concerned. Back in Adelaide, shortly before they had left to come here, people had been using a new name for the blacks: aborigines, abos for short. He liked that. Abos: it had the right sound to it, easy to say, with a ring of contempt. He had nothing against them as long as they left him and his flocks alone but they were savages, after all, barely human. They had to give way to the Europeans, that was inevitable. He couldn't see it mattered. There was plenty of land in the interior. Let them go there.

Alison's small arms were wrapped tightly about his waist.

'You all right, baby?' he asked over his shoulder. 'We'll soon be home.'

'I'm all right.'

Ian couldn't find it in his heart to make much of what had happened to the kitten but he did feel it was a pity that Alison's day had been spoiled by it. Heaven knew she had few enough treats in her life.

Seeking to make amends to her he said, 'How would you like me to ask Auntie Asta for one of her kittens?'

'That would be very nice,' Alison said politely, disappointing him with her lack of enthusiasm, 'if you think that would be all right.'

Ian, Mary and Alison dismounted outside the house. After their hour or two of holiday the duties of the

124

farm surrounded them again. There were cows to milk, chooks to feed, sheep to pen against the coming dark. The three shepherds—Luke Hennessy, Cato Brown and the black man with the unpronounceable name whom Ian called Sinbad—looked after the stock in the outlying areas while Gavin and Ian handled those nearer home.

Ian thought that next day he would ride out and see how the shepherds were going. Check, check, check: it was his way. He took nothing for granted, never had, never would. No doubt the men cursed him at times but he cared nothing about that. All his life he had taken what he wanted from life and held it. To hell with what men thought.

At least they didn't have to worry about fences around the perimeter of the run but he supposed that time would come, when other settlers arrived in the district. Work, he thought, there is no end to it. The thought pleased him.

Appetite—for work, for the future he sensed ahead of them all—gave a spring to his step as he went to fetch the hurdles he would use to pen the sheep against the forthcoming night.

Inside the house Alison went into the curtained-off section that was her bedroom. She sat on the bed, feeling the house draw close and comforting about her. The wooden walls, the thatched roof, creaked softly in the heat. The house had the mixture of smells that in only a few months had come to mean home to her: sun-warmed wood, cooking, the tanned kangaroo skin rugs on the floor, others used as bed coverings at night, the fresh smell of the material that Mother had brought with her from Adelaide and used to make curtains and cushion covers.

It was a nice house, Alison thought, much nicer than the one they'd had before coming here. She wondered if they were going to stay now or if they would just get settled and then decide to move on again. She had heard there were some families that never settled at all. She hoped they weren't going to be like that. She liked it here despite what had happened to Edward. She had thought the sun rose and set on her cousin. Everything about Edward—the way he looked, the things he did—had been wonderful. He had even let her go with him when he had inspected the stock—not all of the time, of course, that would have been too much to hope— but at least sometimes. On the long journey north he had kept her company, told her stories . . . It was hard to think that he was dead.

Oh God keep him safe, she prayed, *wherever he is*.

When she had first heard the news she had refused to believe it—someone as alive as Edward couldn't just *die*—yet part of her must have believed or she would not have cried so much.

Crying had done no good. It hadn't brought Edward back. And now she was discovering how difficult it was to keep the memory of someone— however dear—whole and clear in her mind when they weren't around any more. He had been her true friend; it should have been easy to remember him, and it puzzled and upset her to find that it was not.

Now I have no friend, she thought, suddenly filled with self-pity. Then a flash of anger: one thing was sure, she certainly did not want to be friends with Blake Gallagher.

The house creaked quietly around her as she thought about Blake. She hated him. He had always been a bully but today had been the worst experience of all. She had known how mean he was but

126

would never have imagined him or anyone stamping on the kitten's head the way he had.

Once, not supposed to be listening but doing so anyway, she had overheard Mother and Papa talking about Blake, saying he was horrible because of the way his father treated him. Papa had said that things had got so bad he'd spoken to Mr Gallagher about it, that Mr Gallagher used to beat Blake until he was almost unconscious. It was difficult to imagine anyone beating Blake, almost a man himself, but Alison supposed it was possible. If Alison herself had been beaten like that perhaps she too would want to take it out on something that couldn't hit back. Yet she thought Blake had done what he had done more to hurt her than the kitten: although why that should be she had no idea. She had never done anything to make Blake Gallagher angry with her. She hardly *saw* him, even.

Shivering away the thought, she hoped she would never find out what it felt like to be beaten as Blake had been.

NINE

When Nantariltarra went to meet the *kuinyo* he took with him Jason and several members of the Council. Mura and about half the clan, men, women and children, went along, too.

They headed north along the coast in the direction of the newcomers' camp. The rumble and suck of waves along the shore, the grate of pebbles, was never far away. Except at the cliff edge there was little cover. Grassland, tawny now at the beginning of winter, extended inland as far as Jason could see.

A few miles northwards the cliffs petered out in shallow dunes of coarse yellow sand. The beach smoked with spray from the tumbling waves; above high water mark lay piles of sea grass, grey and dry.

The children ran laughing and shrieking along the edge of the surf, water drops bright on their dark skins.

Jason said, 'It looks more like a party.'

'Why not?' Mura walked at his side, long-legged and confident, as much at home here in the tawny grass as in the gum scrub they had just left. 'They want to see what the *kuinyo* look like when we're all together. Besides, the *kuinyo* are still far from here.'

'I thought the idea was to see them without them seeing us. With this racket they won't need to see us. They'll hear us ten miles off.' Jason was surly, uneasy about what lay ahead, remembering only too well what white attitudes to the blacks had been in Van Diemen's Land.

Mura did not share his misgivings. 'They'll be quiet enough when we get closer.'

Jason thought it would make little difference. Nantariltarra was fooling himself if he thought that seeing the white strangers would give him a better idea how to handle them. The Europeans were here to take the land; spying on them would achieve nothing.

At midday on the second day they came to the valley, little more than a shallow fold of ground, where the *kuinyo* had set themselves up. The valley ran east and west across the peninsula and was choked with trees and bushes. On the far slope and sheltered from the north by a low hill there were a number of buildings: a house of timber slabs with four smaller buildings around it, some paddocks marked off by paling fences.

The house was shaded by a cluster of trees. A feather of smoke came from the stone chimney, some hens scratched in the dust around the door, there were a number of lambs in one paddock, three cows in another.

Nantariltarra and Jason advanced cautiously across the valley bottom and up the far slope until they reached the edge of the undergrowth. The house was no more than twenty yards away. They parted the branches and stared out at the innocent curl of smoke, the hens quietly pecking. It looked peaceful enough but Jason did not trust it. Somewhere there would be men with guns. They would be quick to use them if they felt threatened; even if they didn't, perhaps.

'*Kuinyo*,' Nantariltarra said, a breath of sound.

Jason nodded. 'Farmers.' He did not know the phrase for sheep run but that was what it was. Behind the buildings large numbers of grazing sheep spread out across the slope of the hill.

'They have not come to trade?' Nantariltarra asked.

Jason shook his head.

'Where are they?'

'I don't know.'

A figure came out of the house: a girl dressed in a long green dress with a white apron. Dark hair reached to her shoulders from beneath the white cap that covered her head. She called to the hens, or possibly to someone inside the house: a clear, high cry, too faint to make out individual words. She disappeared around the corner of the building and a minute later re-emerged, running away from them up the hill.

Instinctively Jason drew back into the undergrowth. Two days earlier, standing in front of the Council, he had been acutely aware of his lack of clothes. Now, as he watched the running figure of the girl, dark hair flying, he felt something of the same: a hot sense of shame.

If she sees me like this she'll think I'm a savage.

He was not a savage. He was white, civilised. He was not a Narungga and never would be. He was a *kuinyo*, a dead man living. It was good that it should be a term of abuse. It made him proud to be what he was, made clear what the clan's real feelings towards him were. I almost lost myself these past months, he told himself. No longer. I am a European. My place is there, with those people, not here in the bushes.

When we get back to the camp I shall have to look for my breeches, he thought.

The child was coming back towards the house. With her was a man, tall, with high boots, breeches, a long-sleeved shirt. A cabbage palm hat was pulled low over his eyes. Sunlight glinted on the long-barrelled rifle that he carried over one shoulder. The child skipped along at his side and again Jason caught the ripple of her voice. They went into the house together.

'Come . . .'

Nantariltarra moved away and Jason followed, the pair of them slipping silently through the trees. Before they rejoined the rest of the clan Nantariltarra stopped and looked at him. 'Well? Do they intend to stay or not?'

The answer was obvious yet Jason found himself protective of the unknown settlers: the European man, the child skipping so gaily at his side.

'Who knows what they plan to do?'

'They plan to stay,' Nantariltarra said.

Jason bit his lip. Anyone with half an eye could see that these people with their flocks of sheep, their hens, their buildings and fenced paddocks, were going nowhere. He said nothing.

'What must I do?'

Jason stared, startled that Nantariltarra, a member of the Council, should ask such a question of someone who was uninitiated, a *kuinyo* like those whom they had just seen, a threat to the stability and possibly even the survival of the clan. He was tempted to lie, to say *leave them alone, they won't trouble you*. He could not do it. Nantariltarra deserved the truth, however unwelcome.

'I think you must learn to live with them,' he said.

'We could kill them,' Nantariltarra suggested.

'You could,' Jason agreed, 'and then more *kuinyo* will come with guns and hunt the Narungga out of this land—those they don't kill first.'

The truth burdened the air between them. Jason was exasperated that the black man should still be clinging to hope when it was obvious that there was no hope, no future at all now that the white men had come. But it was not something he could say.

'Go to them,' he suggested. 'Get to know them, like you've done with me. There's room enough here for all of us.' Knowing that there was no room for the black man now, that the whites would take all and grant no space to anyone else.

Nantariltarra considered. 'Very well,' he said. 'You will talk to them. And I shall come with you.'

'I shall need clothes,' Jason said.

'Why?' Nantariltarra's eyes were dark with suspicion.

'They won't respect me, otherwise.' Jason remembered his first sight of Fred, how he had seemed so much more naked than the blacks around him. Not for anything on earth would he walk out naked in front of that girl.

Jason's breeches were no longer big enough to fit him. Instead they found him a kangaroo skin kilt that had been traded long ago from a group of the Ngarrindjeri from the other side of the gulf. It was a kind of apron and had been made for a woman. There were smirks and nudges from some of the men when he put it on but at least it fitted around his waist, more or less, and hung to his knees. His chest, arms and legs remained bare but that was all to the good: cover any more and the people they were planning to visit might shoot him before they realised he was white. As it was, his skin was so tanned by the summer sun that from a distance he looked almost black.

'I should go alone,' Jason said. 'They see you with a bunch of spears in your hand, they'll be likely to shoot the pair of us.'

Nantariltarra would not hear of it. 'I also wish to meet with these *kuinyo*, to see how they live.'

Unspoken between them was the thought that if he went alone Jason might not come back.

A woman brought a bunch of leafy twigs.

Jason stared. 'What's that?'

'A sign of peace,' Nantariltarra told him. 'When they see the leaves they will know they have nothing to fear.'

'It is not their custom,' Jason said. 'How will they know what the leaves mean?'

Nantariltarra glared. 'It is *our* custom. They wish to stay here, let them learn our ways.'

With Nantariltarra beside him, Jason crouched in the bushes at the very edge of the cleared ground and waited for someone to come out of the house. His chest felt tight, his breathing constricted.

I am an ambassador for the Narungga to the *kuinyo*, he told himself, and strutted a little.

You are a sixteen-year-old boy, he reminded himself. There will be guns over there and you will be walking straight into them. It'll serve you right if they shoot you.

He felt Nantariltarra's hand feather-light upon his arm and, glancing at him, saw him point with his chin. Jason squinted through the screen of leaves at the cluster of buildings, dark with patches of shadow or varnished to bronze by the afternoon sun. The white girl had come out of the doorway and was busy twisting round and round, hands held high above her head, skirt swirling, in a game he did not understand.

Jason stood, a gaping hollow in his stomach beneath the awkwardly slung kilt. Over Jason's strong objections, Nantariltarra had insisted on bringing a shield and spears; he heard them rattle as they got to their feet. Jason took a deep breath and stepped forward into the sunlight.

Alison had dreamt of an angel, a being white and shining and wondrous, clad in a diaphanous garment of silver and gold, with wings like an eagle. She had never dreamt of an angel before and the memory of it had entranced her all day. Now she stood on tiptoe, turning and turning until the whole world spun, too. Round and round, eyes shut, then open, watching the swirling blur of the bush, the grass, the pristine blue vault of the sky. The angel danced with her, a glory of gold and silver, smiling, smiling. Grave, courteous, kind.

She would not say to herself it was Edward; would not say it was not him, either. Edward had drowned but was not dead. Edward was in heaven. Who was to say he could not come back to her in the form of an angel, if he wanted to?

The bush rippled and swayed, blurring before her spinning eyes. Something out there moved. She stopped. Looked. Heart pounding, she ran to the open door of the house.

'Papa! Papa!'

'What is it?' Ian Matlock running, wiping his mouth.

Alison pointed.

'My God . . .' Diving back into the house, grabbing for his rifle.

'What is it?' Mary's knuckles clenched white before her breast.

'Abos . . .'

He ran back outside. He had cleared the ground a week earlier, afraid of fire, and so saw immediately two men, spears bristling, marching towards them, halfway between the scrub border and the house.

A second glance showed him that only one of the men was carrying spears. It could be a diversion. Ian's eyes scanned the scrub on either side of the house for signs of others, saw nothing. Rifle ready in his hands he stared at the advancing men. A tall man, a giant, skin as black as night, with shield and spears. His companion was carrying what looked like leaves and wearing an apron of some sort about his waist. His limbs were stockier than the other, his chest and arms brown, not black. His hair . . .

Ian stared, unable to believe his eyes. A *white man*? Barefoot, dressed like a savage, accompanied by a savage?

White man or not, he would not let them come too close. He cocked the rifle, threw it up to his shoulder, took a bead on them.

'Far enough, mister. Stop right there.'

Ten yards. Already it was too close for comfort.

'We're not looking for trouble.' The stranger *was* a European, then.

'What do you want?'

'To talk.'

Ian hesitated. 'Tell the abo to put his spears on the ground, then.'

135

The white youth—Ian could see now that he was little more than a boy—turned and spoke. The black man protested angrily but the youth persisted. Eventually, with obvious reluctance, the native laid his spears carefully on the ground and stood erect.

'Come closer.' Ian gestured with the muzzle of the rifle. 'Slowly, now . . .'

They came forward. Ten yards, five yards, three . . .

'Stop there.' Ian was conscious of Alison behind him, eyes bigger than her face. From the corner of his mouth, not taking his eyes from the strangers, he said, 'Get into the house.'

Mary was in the doorway, fingers as tight as claws on the frame. The three of them stared at the newcomers, at the black face and the brown.

Ian addressed the youth. 'What are you doing with this bloke?'

'I was shipwrecked, months ago. Been here long, have you?'

'Three months. Give or take.'

Jason's eyes checked the buildings, the fenced paddocks, the flocks on the slopes of the higher ground. 'Got yourself well settled in,' he said.

'A lot still to do, though.'

The words marched awkwardly between them. A white man living with natives like he was part of the tribe . . . Ian found that hard to take.

'The clan won't like it.'

Ian bristled at once. 'Planning to do something about it, are they?'

Jason shook his head. 'They don't want trouble.'

'Try messing with me, it's what they'll get.'

'If you stay, where's the clan supposed to go?'

'Anywhere they like. So long as they stay well

away from me and my sheep. Tell your mate this,' he said, beginning to bully, 'they start stealing my sheep or bothering my shepherds, anything like that, I'll come after 'em.'

Mary murmured behind his shoulder. 'Ask him if he'd like some buttermilk.'

'Why should I do that?' The idea affronted him.

'He's white, isn't he?'

'So?'

'So perhaps you can get him to tell you what they plan to do about things.'

'There's nothing they can do.' But it made sense, he supposed.

He sensed Mary go back into the house. Alison was still there. He didn't like her seeing the naked black body although the native hardly counted as a man, he supposed. 'Go with your mother,' he instructed her.

'You heard her,' he said to the white youth. 'What are you going to do now?'

'It's not up to me what they do.'

The three men stared at each other in spiky silence until Mary came back with a jug, some mugs.

'Sit down.' Ian gestured at the ground between them.

'What is it?' the white youth asked curiously.

'Buttermilk. You must know it, surely?'

'I never had it.'

But sat, all the same. After a moment's hesitation the black man followed his lead.

They looked at the jug, the mugs. Suspicion curdled the air.

'Come on,' Ian said. 'Help yourselves.'

Geniality fitted Ian as uneasily as the apron around the waist of the young stranger. He leant forward, poured milk into a mug, drank it down with ostentatious pleasure. Perhaps now they would accept that it wasn't poisoned.

'Can always try it, I suppose.' The white youth poured and drank.

His eyes widened. He wiped his mouth. 'Good,' he said.

He turned to his companion and talked, gesturing. The black man drank, too, with difficulty—not used to drinking mugs, Ian saw—and smiled like a child. He looked curiously at the buildings, the chickens chuckling about the door, the sheep on the hill's shoulder.

'You say it's not up to you. Tell me what your mate wants, then.'

Jason, sitting cross-legged on the ground, watched the man. He was tall with a bold, assertive face, eyes that missed little. He was certainly here to stay, Jason saw, would expand when he could and fight to keep what he had taken. For the moment he seemed friendly enough but his hand never strayed far from his rifle.

'These are their lands,' Jason said. 'As far as the clan is concerned, you've got no rights here.'

Ian Matlock lifted the rifle a few inches. 'This is the only right I need. Don't think I won't use it if I have to.'

Jason could see that he would indeed use it without hesitation, possibly even with enjoyment.

'Face it,' Ian said. 'These friends of yours . . . Their day's gone.'

'Perhaps they don't think so.'

'Who cares what they think? This one's the chief, is he?'

'They don't have chiefs.'

'Tell him, anyway. This land is mine. I'm not looking for trouble, either, but if I get any I shall repay it ten times over. It's not just me, remember. There's others coming will make me seem a right softie, by comparison.'

'You're saying there's no place for them in their own land.'

Ian glared: shut face, shut mind. 'I'll tell you one last time, I am the master here now. They get in my way, I'll kill them.'

'You talk as though the clan is helpless.' Jason stood. Recognising the anger in his voice, Nantariltarra stood too, his face glowering. 'This is their *home*. If I tell this man what you just said they'll likely kill you first, before the rest of your people get here.'

Ian said, 'The ones who come after me will wipe them out, they try that.'

'Won't help you, though, will it?'

'Get out!' Ian's face was brick red with anger. He thumbed back the hammer of the rifle. 'Before I use this.'

Jason was determined to have the last word. 'You're not the only one, remember. You've got women here, too.'

Jason turned. With Nantariltarra following, he stalked away across the open ground towards the shelter of the bush.

TEN

Gavin Matlock and Hector Gallagher were inspecting a ram with suspected foot rot when Ian burst out of the undergrowth and rode furiously up the slope towards them.

They ran towards him as he brought his mount skidding to a halt.

'What's up?' Gavin demanded.

'Blacks are what's up.' Breath coming in great gusts after his furious ride, Ian dismounted and told them about the visit he had received an hour earlier.

'Where are Alison and Mary?'

'Back at the run.' Ian saw Gavin frown. 'We decided they'd better stay. Mary's got the rifle. If the blacks saw us all leaving together they might burn the buildings.'

'They still might,' Gavin said grimly. He turned to Hector Gallagher. 'Fetch the shepherds and get over to Ian's house, quick as you can. Take Blake with you. I'm leaving now. I'll meet you there.'

At least he needn't ask if Gallagher was armed. The overseer was the sort to take his rifle with him to the outhouse; he wouldn't be without it now. Not one to waste time talking, either. Gallagher ran to his horse, swung himself into the saddle and within seconds was galloping across the grassy plain, the reins rising and falling as he lashed the horse's neck.

Gavin ran towards the house. Asta came out to meet him.

'What is the trouble?'

'Blacks over at Ian's place.'

He pushed past her into the house, scooped up his rifle and began to fill the big cartridge belts with bullets.

'Blacks?' Asta repeated. 'What have they done? Are Mary and Alison all right?'

'As far as I know they've done nothing yet.' He pushed the last cartridge into its retaining loop and slipped the straps across his shoulders, buckling the belt about his waist.

'Ian left Mary and Alison behind?' Asta was indignant.

'It was either that or risk losing the farm.' He cinched the gun belt tight and headed for the door. 'Mary's got the rifle. She'll be all right.'

'I certainly hope so. Are you going over there?'

'Where else?'

'I'll come with you.'

Gavin barely hesitated. 'Hurry, then. I'm not waiting around.'

His big body darkened the doorway as he went out into the sunlight. Asta snatched her own gun from its place beside the door and ran after him, pulling the door shut behind her, knowing that if it came to a fight she might never see her home again.

Gavin was already mounted, the big bay wheeling.

A pang of doubt as she put her foot into the

stirrup. 'What if they come here while we're away?'

'We'll have to chance it.'

She nodded, swung herself into the saddle and gathered the reins in her hands.

'Let us go, then,' she said.

The three of them rode fast, Ian and Gavin in front, Asta right behind them. They reached the house to find everything as Ian had left it.

'Thank God,' Asta said.

'There could be an army hiding out there and we wouldn't see them.' Gavin watched the under-growth but all was quiet. Hopefully it had been a false alarm, after all.

White-faced, Mary came out of the house to meet them, rifle in her hand.

'Everything all right?' Ian demanded.

'Fine.' But swayed as she said it.

Asta went to her at once. 'Let me take this . . .'

She eased the rifle out of Mary's stiff fingers. Alison's scared face stared from the shadows inside the house. Asta turned to her. 'Your mother would like some hot tea to drink,' she told her. 'Make it for her, please.'

'This isn't a tea party, you know.' Ian's voice was rough behind her.

She ignored him. 'Quickly now,' she told Alison's back as the girl disappeared into the house. 'Put in plenty of sugar if you have it.'

'I'm going to have a look round,' Gavin said.

'Be careful,' Asta admonished. 'They probably have spears.'

'That white kid may have a gun, for all we know,' Ian said.

Asta frowned. 'White kid?'

Ian explained what there had been no time to explain before.

Asta stared at Ian. 'You let him go back with them? A European boy?'

'He threatened to kill my wife and child. You think I was going to take him in after that?'

'And you didn't threaten him, I suppose?' Tartly, her dislike gleaming momentarily in her words.

'I didn't do anything. He asked what we were doing here and I told him, that was all.'

'You threatened them, all right.' Asta knew Ian too well.

'All that's beside the point,' Gavin said. 'Now we've got to make sure they don't kill the lot of us.'

At her side Asta felt Mary's body grow taut, tremors running like ague through her limbs. She went to the open door, calling inside to Alison. 'Is that tea ready yet?'

'Coming . . .'

Asta put her arm around Mary's shoulders. 'Come,' she said. 'We shall go inside.'

The contents of the mug were steaming, almost stiff with sugar. 'That is very good, Alison,' Asta congratulated her. 'Thank you.' She turned to Mary, coaxing her. 'Drink it now. Quick as you can.'

Mary tried, made a face. 'It's too hot.'

'Never mind. Drink it so. It is good for you. Good for the nerves.'

Mary tried a smile. 'What nerves?' Her teeth rattled on the rim of the mug.

Outside the house Gavin prowled, Ian at his side. Fingers taut around their rifle triggers, their eyes watched the undergrowth but there was no movement, no sign of the blacks at all.

Ian said, 'I didn't imagine it, if that's what you're thinking.'

Gavin shook his head. 'I'm thankful we got here in time.'

'What do we do now?'

'Wait until Hector arrives with the rest of the men.'

'And then?' Ian was insistent. He had been frightened, for all his bravado, and now was thirsty for action.

Gavin would not be drawn. He suspected the blacks had come peacefully and Ian had sent them away with a flea in their ear: that would be his style. It was a pity they hadn't come to him first but it was too late to think about that.

'It'll be dark soon,' he said. 'We'll be safe enough then.' It was well known that the aborigines did not like to fight after dark.

Ian was unconvinced. 'With that white renegade leading them I wouldn't bet on that.'

'Renegade? I thought you said he was a kid?'

'He was leading them, all right. Threatening Mary and Alison like that . . .' Ian burst out angrily. 'I should have shot him there and then.'

'Thank God you didn't,' Gavin said. 'There'd have been hell to pay if you'd done that.'

A drumming of hooves as Hector Gallagher and his men rode up.

There were five of them: Hector, Blake and the three shepherds, Luke, Cato and Sinbad. Hector was a good man in a crisis; Blake would be the same, Gavin thought, even though he was so young. The shepherds should be fine, too, even though one of them was black. Men who worked in outlying places knew the risks.

'What you want us to do?' Hector asked.

Gavin said, 'We've two runs to defend and a couple of thousand sheep. We can't be everywhere at once whereas they can hit us anywhere.'

'We should get in first,' Blake said. 'Shoot some of 'em, the rest'll do a bunk and we won' 'ave no more trouble.' He grinned cockily at the faces around him, enjoying their attention.

'When we want your opinion we'll ask for it,' Hector told him. To Gavin he said, 'The boy's got a point, though. Why wait for 'em to attack us? Makes sense for us to move first, don't it?'

'They've done nothing to us so far.'

Ian was having none of that. 'You call threatening to murder us nothing?' He turned to the shepherds. 'You're the ones they'll kill first if there's trouble. What do you think about it?'

'Reckon Blake's right,' Cato Brown said. 'Knock off a few of 'em, the rest'll take the hint and move on.'

'You'd better be sure he's right,' Gavin said. 'You're a softer target out there than we are.'

'I'll tell you what's a softer target still,' Hector said. 'The blamed sheep, that's what.'

Silence as they thought about that. The flocks were scattered across miles of countryside; if the blacks wanted to attack them they could do a tremendous amount of damage with little or no risk to themselves. Wiping out the flocks would be a blow almost as damaging as killing the humans who guarded them.

'All the more reason to sort 'em out first,' Blake said.

Gavin considered. It made a lot of sense. And the men were thirsty for action. Very well. He would give them action.

He said, 'We'll move against them tonight.'

*

'How will you know where to find them?' Asta stood in the little shed that would be their bedroom for the night. 'And what is to stop them attacking us here while you are gone?'

'They don't move at night. They are frightened of the dark.'

'And this white boy? Is he also frightened of the dark?'

'How am I supposed to know?' Asta's questions exasperated Gavin, as always. 'I've never seen him, even.'

'Ian spoke to you about him, though.' Asta was fascinated by the idea of the white boy. 'Tell me what he said . . .'

'He said he was young, dressed in some kind of kilt. Spoke good English. Said he'd been with them for months—'

'He must have come from the sea,' Asta said. 'There is no other way for him to be here.'

'Ian said something about a shipwreck.'

There was a long silence between them.

'And now you intend to kill him.'

'I'll tell you something, girl. If he'd threatened you the way he did Mary and Alison I'd have shot him myself.'

Asta shook her head. 'You must not kill him.'

'I may have no choice.'

'No!'

'Why not?'

She ignored the question. 'How old is he?'

'Ian didn't say. Does it matter?'

Again Asta did not answer. She walked to the open door and stared out towards the invisible sea.

Gavin watched her, troubled. She had such strange ideas. Perhaps it was coming from Norway that did it. Mostly he never thought about her background but whenever there was trouble he saw at once that her brain worked quite differently from his own. This sense of difference had been one of the things that had attracted him to her in the first place but nowadays there were times when it made him uneasy.

'There'll be bullets flying about,' he pointed out. 'There's always a chance he might get in the way of one.'

'Tell the others they must not shoot him.'

'I say that, like as not Blake will do it deliberately.'

'Blake is a mad dog,' she said.

'Happen he is. That's why I can't promise.'

'You will promise me one thing.'

'What's that?'

'You will never abandon me, the way Ian did Mary.'

'I would hardly call it that—' Awkwardly.

'Oh? What would you call it?'

'He had to think about the farm—'

'Which of course is much more important than his wife and daughter. It certainly makes it plain where we women stand.'

He was irritated, having to defend the indefensible. 'It was a situation that called for an immediate decision. And as it happened they were perfectly all right.'

'As it happened.'

'No-one came near them. I am not prepared to judge him—'

'No? Well, I am. I have.'

'I see you have.'

'I am glad you see.' Her anger flared. 'Do not let me delay you. I am sure that butchering aborigines is far more important than wasting time with your wife. Who is, after all, expendable.'

Gavin stared at her, angry but knowing better than to argue when Asta was in this mood. He turned and went out into the gathering dusk.

Asta stood in the dark hut. Slowly her anger ebbed. In truth she did not believe Gavin would abandon her, whatever Ian might have done. Thank God, the two men were totally different. As for the white youth living with the blacks . . . She stood with clasped hands, eyes staring at mystery. Conviction was a cool flood through her body.

The strange white boy. That was what Ian had called him: a boy, not a man, yet old enough to talk like a man. The boy who had come to them out of the sea.

She followed her husband outside. The sun had set beyond the rising ground and the western sky was awash with the deepest rose. Someone had lit a fire. Its flames cast shifting orange and black shadows over the faces of the men gathered about it and glinted on the dull steel of the firearms they carried. Mary and Alison were there, their white aprons patches of brightness against the sombre clothes, the firelight, the gathering darkness. She walked over to them.

'Sinbad will guide us,' Gavin was saying as she arrived at the group. 'When we find them we shall form up and fire one volley into the camp before we go in. Only one, mind, or we may end up shooting ourselves. Cato, you stay here to guard the women.'

'Aw, come on . . .' Cato was indignant.

But Gavin's mind was made up. 'I'm not arguing about it. You stay.'

'We expectin' trouble?' Luke Hennessy asked.

'Not if we're careful. Catch them by surprise, they'll be too busy trying to get away from us.'

'What about the white bloke they've got with 'em? What we goin' to do 'bout 'im?'

'Reckon 'e'll die jest as easy as a blackfeller.' Blake's voice was like a rasp.

Asta stared at Gavin's back, willing what he must say. He said, 'I want him alive. We won't get rid of more than a handful of them. He'll be able to tell us where to find the rest.'

'Sinbad'll find 'em for us,' Blake said, teeth grinning white in the firelight.

Asta watched, hating him. A mad dog she had called him and a mad dog he was. She hoped that there would be resistance, that a spear would find Blake Gallagher. A mad dog needed to be put down before it could infect the rest.

The men lined up, the black shepherd Sinbad in the lead, then Blake with Gavin next to him, the others behind. Only the clink of weapons, the occasional murmur, disturbed the silence.

'I wish I was coming with you,' Asta said.

'Well, you're not.' Gavin was impatient to be gone and indignant, still, over what had been said. 'You'll be safe enough with Cato here to look after you.'

It is not because I am afraid that I want to come. She wanted to scream the words at him, her nerves wound tight by his obtuseness, the tensions of the night, the thought that out there, somewhere, the white boy lay unknowing while these men made ready to kill him and his friends. She said nothing, as she had said nothing so often before in her life. Ultimately, she thought, we are all alone.

She stood back. The outflowing of her will faltered and ceased. Her spirit drew back within herself. What was destined would be.

After the men had gone the three women looked at each other, the firelight staining their faces with flickering orange light.

'Best get in the 'ouse,' Cato Brown was sour at being left behind. 'Anythin' happens to any of you, the captain'll have my skin.'

The captain: it was what the shepherds called Gavin, although he had no right to the title.

'The blacks do not move around at night,' Asta said. She wanted to stay outside. In the open she felt closer to what was happening out there in the bush.

'Who knows what them savages might get up to?' Cato grumbled.

It made sense, of course it did. And it seemed that the boy *had* threatened something, at least.

'Very well,' she conceded. 'We shall wait indoors, as you say.'

But indoors the tension was worse, as Asta had known it would be. Perhaps they were safer but she did not *feel* safe. She felt suffocated by the stagnant air, the walls of the tiny room cutting her off from life.

'What do you think about what they're doing?' Mary asked.

Asta hated the idea but would not say so. 'It is a way to protect us from being attacked.'

'Will it not be dangerous?'

Except for hoping that harm might come to Blake she had not thought about it. 'I suppose it might be.'

'If anything happened to Ian I would die.' Mary's voice full of terror and self-pity. She took no notice of the child at her shoulder, what her words might be doing to her.

'Why should anything happen to him? Our men have guns. The blacks don't.'

'They have spears.'

'Gavin would not have gone if he had thought there would be danger.'

They both knew it was a lie but the pretence gave a form of protection more easing to the spirit than Cato Brown and his gun.

How strange it was, Asta thought. Here was Mary terrified for Ian's survival whereas her own fear was not for Gavin at all. Gavin was strong, the rock upon which she had based her life. Without his granite strength she would never have come to this far country. It was unthinkable that anything might happen to him. In a trivial night skirmish with a group of tribesmen armed with spears? Never! No, her concern was less for her husband than for the unknown boy whom she had never seen.

There is a resonance in my soul, she told herself. I felt it when Gavin first told me about him. The child taken by the sea; the youth emerging unexplained from the sea. From infancy I was brought up to believe that the sea settles its debts. When I see this unknown youth I shall feel the same pang of recognition I would have experienced had he in truth been Edward returning from the waves. Fate will not permit anything to happen to him; the idea is unthinkable.

But feared for the boy, nevertheless, and for herself.

Let him be safe, she prayed, but was uncertain to whom the prayer was addressed. It should be to Odin and Thor, she thought. Odin with Gungnir, his magic spear, and Thor of the double axe. They had embarked on war tonight and it was the war gods of the north they needed now, not the muling Mediterranean Christ. The gods of Valhalla had always understood the need for death, the ritual of cleansing inherent in the spilling of blood. But how powerful could these gods be, so far from their own land? And felt abandoned by them, as by so much else.

She would be better off praying to herself, she thought, but could not, acknowledging her helplessness.

She knew better than to say any of this to Mary and Alison. Instead said, 'It is not right that we should sit here frightening ourselves over what may never happen. We should start preparing some food so that when the men come back we shall have something for them to eat.'

Doing something would occupy their minds as well as their hands, help to keep the shadows away.

As soon as they had returned to camp Nantariltarra went off by himself. He sat cross-legged on the bare earth, eyes staring across the land that for countless generations had been theirs. The breeze rattled the leaves of the trees but he did not hear them. Parrots flew in the undergrowth and he did not see them. Magpies, emboldened by his monumental stillness, hopped closer, preening their black and white plumage, cocking their heads to one side and watching him with beady eyes. He did not see them, either, or hear their bubbling calls. People eyed him cautiously and walked in a wide circle around him, knowing that he spoke with the spirits. Finally, shortly before dark, he summoned the Council and told them what he had seen, what the white man had said to them.

'We should kill them while we can,' Minalta said, and several others agreed.

'They are few. It would be easy. And once they are gone their flocks will give us enough to eat for a long time.'

'If we kill them, others will be frightened to come

here after them. Things will continue as they have always been.'

Nantariltarra let them rave on, giving no lead to their words. Eventually, as he had known they would, they fell silent, watching him expectantly, waiting for him to make the decision for them.

'We shall seek to be friends with the *kuinyo*,' he said. 'We shall not kill them or attack them. We shall help them in every way we can. Jay-e-son will act as our spokesman.'

'How do we know we can trust him?' Yarnalta demanded.

'We know,' Nantariltarra said. '*I* know.'

'How do we know we can trust *them*?' A more telling question than the first.

'Because I have seen them. They want peace, as we do. We are many more than they. Their animals are scattered. They cannot hope to defend them all against us. They would not be able to defend even themselves. I shall talk to them again, in the morning.'

He was stiff and tired by his long vigil. He rose without another word, went to his wurley and slept.

'We must get away from here as quick as we can.' Jason was exasperated by the inaction. 'Wait any longer, it'll be too late.'

'The Council says that the *kuinyo* means no harm.' Mura, trained in the ways of obedience, was alarmed by Jason's independence.

'The Council is wrong. I was *there*. I saw how he was.'

'He will live in peace with us.' Mura was not prepared to accept that the Council might be mistaken.

'There'll be peace, all right,' Jason scoffed. 'After

they've killed the lot of us. I'm not staying in camp tonight. You won't, either, you got any sense.'

Apprehensively, Mura eyed the darkness. 'Where will you go?'

'Out in the bush somewhere.'

Mura hesitated.

'The darkness won't hurt you, for heaven's sake.'

The darkness itself, no. The spirits that walked in the darkness were another matter.

'I'm going, anyway,' Jason told him. 'Stay behind if you want. But don't say I didn't warn you.'

Mura did not want to go but if he stayed he would be unable to keep his eye on Jay-e-son, as Nantariltarra had directed. What would the Council say if Jay-e-son went off alone and in the morning they found that he had joined the other *kuinyo*? Mura shuddered, the thought of the Council's anger too awful to contemplate. If the two of them stayed close together, perhaps Jay-e-son's magic would keep him safe from the *quinkan*.

'I shall come with you,' he said.

The camp was settling to sleep. The fires had burned low. The leaves of the hunched trees reflected hardly any light. Jason leading, Mura taking care to stay close at his heels, they walked out of the firelight into the darkness of the bush. Two hundred yards from the fires Jason paused and looked about him. Eyes used to the darkness, he could see that they were in a shallow hollow ringed by trees.

'This'll do,' said Jason.

They lay side by side. The stealthy noises of the bush enclosed them: the rustle of leaves, the creaking of branches, the chirruping fidget of possums and other small animals in the undergrowth.

They slept: Jason deeply, despite his concerns,

Mura with one eye partly open, as always. When he heard something he was instantly awake. Quietly, he shook Jay-e-son's arm.

'What is it?'

'Listen . . .'

A faint crunching, too regular to be the random movement of the tree branches. A clink of metal. A murmur, shushed at once into silence. The slightest breath of air as dark shadows stole through the undergrowth.

ELEVEN

Kudnarto was five years old and the youngest of her mother's three daughters. When she had first seen the *kuinyo* she had been frightened. Such a strange creature, like a man yet not a man, skin pink and brown, legs a different colour from the body, body from the face, harsh and rough all over, with lumps and flaps where real people had nothing like that. His face was wrong, too, not like the face of a real person.

Kudnarto had watched him from the corner of her eye when Mura had first brought him to sit among them by the fire. He had been clumsy, not able to walk as a real man would. She had watched him, wondering what he would do.

To begin with she thought he might be dangerous but he did nothing. At last she summoned up her courage and got close enough to look at him, to touch him, though always ready to run for her life if he became angry. He did not seem to mind her so she climbed into his lap and found that what she had thought was skin was a covering, like the aprons and cloaks that old people sometimes wore in winter. His real skin was underneath. How stupid she had been to think the brown covering was his skin!

Jay-e-son: his name was as strange as his looks. She would never have believed it had she not heard people call him that. Jay-e-son; she practised the sound when no-one was listening.

She asked Mura where Jay-e-son had come from but he would not tell her. She thought perhaps Mura did not know either, although it might be because he was too big to be bothered with girls as little as she was. Yet not all the time. There were times when he teased her, pretending to chase her, so that she laughed and ran away as fast as she could, her whole body hot with tingly fear and laughing, always laughing.

After a time she grew used to seeing Jay-e-son among them, used even to his looks so that he no longer seemed strange to her, just Jay-e-son. She still did not understand what he was or where he had come from, but that did not matter any longer.

When he saw her he smiled at her, sometimes he ruffled her hair as he passed by; she liked him.

Then came a day when things were different. The men of the Council sat for a long time, talking, talking, no-one smiling, then they called Jay-e-son to them and talked some more. Some of the men were angry, you could hear it in their voices, feel it in the air. When the talking was finished the clan moved north. They travelled for two days along the edge of the sea. Kudnarto played in the surf with the other children. It was fun. When they reached where they were going they made camp. Jay-e-son went away for a while. When he came back Kudnarto could not believe her eyes. Jay-e-son had long ago given up the strange clothes he had worn when she first saw him but now he was wearing an apron. It was not an apron like the old men wore in winter but a woman's cloak they had got from the people who lived by the mouth of the great river.

Kudnarto laughed, fingers over her face, wondering if Jay-e-son knew he was wearing a woman's cloak, but no-one laughed with her and she wondered what had happened that everyone should be so serious.

Jay-e-son went off with Nantariltarra. They were away a long time and when they came back their faces were more serious than ever.

All the children watched, all the women watched, no-one said anything. Whatever had happened must be very bad. For the first time Kudnarto felt fear in the air about her. It frightened her: it was not the nice fear she felt when Mura pretended to chase her but something quite different, cold and horrible. By the looks on their faces the grown-ups felt it, too.

Nantariltarra came, talking harshly to the men around him. His face was angry; everyone was angry. Some of the men shook their spears, the fighting spears with the notched edges and sharpened flints on the tips. Others carried shields and boomerangs. They talked together for a long time.

It grew dark. The fires were lit. The sunset was sung. Everything was normal yet nothing was normal at all. Grown-ups murmured to each other, nervous sounds in the gathering dark. The children crept about, eyes wide, mouths shut, keeping out of the way. Even the dogs slunk with tails between their legs, bellies cringing close to the earth.

Kudnarto was frightened, too. She found her mother, clung close, smelling fear on her also, the tremble of terror beneath the skin.

'Mama?' Voice high, close to panic.

'Hush now, child.'

'What is it? Why are people frightened?'

'It is nothing, nothing.'

Kudnarto was stabbed by the terror she felt in the air and was not comforted. She clung close, arms around her mother's neck. Nothing happened and eventually weariness at the day's end weighed more than fear. Kudnarto fell asleep.

Blake Gallagher was a youth filled with hate. He hated the people he knew, believing they despised him. He hated the countryside. He hated those born above him in the world. Above all he hated the black people of the country with a passionate intensity that had nothing to do with wrongs, real or imagined. He hated them for existing, would have killed the lot of them if he could.

The present expedition was right up his street.

He was a good shot and knew it; was not easily frightened by darkness or danger and knew that, too. Except for Sinbad, the black tracker, he was better in the bush than the other men. Excitement made his heart beat fast as they moved silently through the undergrowth on the way to the aborigines' camp. He was eager to kill, could hardly wait to get on with the job.

The blacks were vermin. He would shoot them as cheerfully as he would a pack of rats. It was his duty to do it.

They had been walking for twenty minutes when, two paces in front of him, Sinbad paused. Blake's ears had caught the same sound: the faintest creak and rustle, little different from the hundred other sounds with which the bush was filled yet out of harmony with them. Whatever had caused it was as much an intruder in the bush as they were themselves.

Behind him the rest of the party stumbled to a stop.

Blake could have screamed at them for their clumsiness. His head turned slowly, eyes probing the darkness. He saw nothing and the sound was not repeated. After five minutes Sinbad began to move forward again. Blake followed him. Perhaps it had been an animal, he thought, not believing it.

Another five minutes and Sinbad paused, holding up a cautionary hand. Blake looked over the black man's shoulder as he pointed silently through the tangle of branches. They had arrived at their destination.

There was a fire at either end of the camp; the dying coals glowed red in the darkness. In the faint light Blake could just make out the humped shapes of the shelters in which the blacks slept. Nothing moved. Blake's eyes ranged carefully, systematically, over the camp. There seemed to be no guards; his lip curled contemptuously. They knew the whites were in the area and still had done nothing to protect themselves. They deserved everything that was coming to them.

The other members of the party were lining up on either side of him. When they were in position they raised their loaded guns. Breath hot and eager in his throat, Blake watched Gavin with avid eyes as he waited for the command to open fire.

Gavin looked along the line of waiting men, turned to stare once again at the sleeping camp. He hesitated. He had expected to come across an armed camp making ready for war. What he had found was entirely different: people sleeping, at peace with the world. There was no threat here, no danger, yet having brought the men to this place he could not simply tell them to turn around and go home again. It was too late for that. He took a deep breath, committing himself to the action he no longer wanted.

'Fire!'

The silence was shattered by the bellow of the guns.

The two youths froze, watching the men go by.

Mura's hand tightened on Jay-e-son's arm. Mouth close to his companion's ear he said, 'We must warn the camp.'

Jason's face showed grey in the darkness as he turned. 'How?'

'We must go there. Get ahead of them.'

'It's too late for that.'

'We've got to do something.' Passion made Mura's voice too loud. He drew a deep breath. 'Stay behind if you want,' he said more quietly, using the exact words that Jason had spoken earlier. 'I'm going back.'

He scrambled to his feet and began to run through the trees, his night-adjusted eyes, instincts, warning him of branches with which he might collide, of hollows in the ground into which he might fall. He had covered twenty yards before Jay-e-son joined him, running silently at his side.

It was an impossible task. They had been only two hundred yards from the camp. There was no way they could bypass the attackers and still arrive in time to warn the sleeping clan of the danger descending upon them. They were still running when they heard the first volley of the sounds that Jason recognised as shots.

'Too late.' He grabbed Mura's arm.

161

Mura tried to shake him off but Jason tightened his grip, dragging him to a halt. *'Listen,'* he said urgently. 'There is nothing we can do now.'

They stood side by side in the undergrowth, chests heaving, eyes and ears probing the darkness.

A chorus of screams and cries came to them, punctuated by yells and the repeated volleys of the guns.

'What are they *doing*?' Mura's eyes were wild.

Killing them, Jason thought but could not bring himself to say so. He said, 'They're attacking the camp.'

Mura was not fooled. White eyes flashed in the black face. Fiercely he said, 'I am going to help.'

Jason still clung to his arm. 'Do that, they'll kill you, too.'

Mura was beyond reason. The sounds of gunfire dinning in his ears, he wrenched his arm free and took off pell-mell towards the camp. Jason hesitated but could not stay here in safety by himself. Mura had called them his people. Well, to some extent they had become his people, too. He sighed once in resignation and went after him.

Kudnarto awoke to uproar. Screams slashed the darkness. A violent noise, louder and sharper than thunder. Smoke swirled in acrid clouds. People were racing here, there, turning, fleeing, turning again. That was the most frightening thing of all: the panicked charging to and fro while the thunder roared, the smoke rolled through the camp and people fell, crawling, crying, or lay still.

Her mother snatched her up, ran with her into the darkness. Kudnarto could feel her mother's breathing, gasping in horror. Her mother's sister ran after them. She was younger than Kudnarto's mother and unburdened by a child. She ran more easily. She drew level with them. Kudnarto saw her falter, stop. There was a surprised look on her face. She opened her mouth. Her teeth were red. The blood flowed out of her mouth and down her chin. She fell. Terror wrenched at Kudnarto's pounding heart. Eyes screwed tight, she clung to her mother as they plunged through the darkness.

There was a fresh salt air blowing, the sound of waves. Kudnarto opened her eyes. Sand dunes humped, mysterious in the darkness. The line of surf gleamed silver.

Her mother lowered her to the ground, whispering, 'You must walk now. I cannot carry you any longer.'

Kudnarto did not want to walk. She clung tighter, arms wound about her mother's neck.

'Let go of me, child.'

She trembled, eyeing the dark, remembering the stories of ghosts, the *quinkan* that would steal her away.

'We are safe here,' her mother said.

There was a hollow in one of the dunes. They crouched within it, hearing the sound of the waves, smelling the harsh dampness of sand around them. The sea sucked over the rocks along the water's edge and ran in sparkling tongues up the shelving beach. Kudnarto burrowed into her mother's warm flank.

Through the swirl of powder smoke Blake saw the aboriginal camp erupt into frenzied movement. It was like watching an ant's nest turned over by a stick. There were figures everywhere, running, turning, none with any idea where to go or what to do. He would have laughed but had no time to laugh. The killing frenzy was on him. Rifle butt smooth against his cheek, the recoil bruised his shoulder each time he fired. He moved like an automaton: home on a target, aim, fire, watch the target go down, reload, seek another target, re-aim, fire, watch it go down, reload ...

The bitter smoke swirled, his ears rang with the crash of gunfire, there were bodies everywhere.

Blake's body was shaking uncontrollably. A frenzy of excitement fed his heart, his blood. He did not want the killing to stop. He needed more targets, always more, he searched for them eagerly but soon there were no more to be had.

The gunfire petered out. Silence returned to ears still ringing with the noise of violence.

'That's it, boys.' Gavin's voice.

Blake wanted to shout aloud in protest. No! That's not it!

There were still lots of them left, the ones who'd got away into the darkness. They couldn't afford to let them go. None of them would be safe if they did that. They had to get rid of the lot of them.

Blake caught his father's eye, knew they were thinking the same thoughts.

Guns at the ready, the men moved forward cautiously into the clearing. Blake strolled to the seaward side of the camp. He could hear the surf breaking beyond the sand dunes. His father joined him.

'Reckon a few went this way,' Hector Gallagher said softly.

Blake nodded. 'Let's see if we can find 'em.'

Silent as shadows, they drifted down to the beach. The humped shapes of the dunes rose at their backs. As far as they could see along the dim grey outline of the beach, nothing stirred. The two men moved, paused, moved again.

'I'm sure some of 'em came this way,' Blake whispered.

His father turned and looked back along the beach. Nothing moved. He turned again. His rifle clinked on a stone.

Blake said, 'If it wasn't so dark maybe we could see somen.'

He walked forward a couple of steps, paused again. His body craved action, something more physical than shooting people at a distance.

I want something I can get my hands on, he thought. He grinned in the darkness. If I could wring someone's neck I reckon I'd feel better.

A faint, low sound came out of the darkness. Most men would have missed it but not Blake.

'What's that?'

His father paused. They both listened but the sound was not repeated. My God, Blake thought in frustration, these damn noises are haunting me tonight.

'Didn' 'ear nuthin,' Hector said.

'Shut up!' he told his father fiercely. '*Listen*!'

He listened: with his ears, the tingling nerves of his skin. There *was* something . . .

His breath caught in his throat. Inch by inch he stretched out his hand, groping in the darkness in front of him.

Kudnarto felt the sudden tension in her mother's body before she heard the sound of footsteps, heavy upon the beach. They clung close, trembling. Their terrified eyes stared.

A voice spoke, so close.

'Imsuresomeofemcamethisway . . .' A sound without meaning, heightening their terror.

They held their breath. A dark shadow moved between them and the sea. Another followed. The shadows stopped and there was a clinking sound.

'Ifitwasntsodarkmaybewecouldseesomen.'

The men moved closer, so close that Kudnarto could see the starlight gleaming on their eyes, smell the rancid stench of their bodies.

She felt the tremors running through her mother's body, heard the moan of terror gathering in her throat.

'Whatsthat?'

Silence.

'Didnearnuthin.'

'Shutup*listen.*'

So close. She could have touched them. Her mother's arms were clasped tight about her. She could sense the wave of panic welling unstoppably in her mother's trembling body.

A hand groped, stopped.

'Whattheell?'

The wave broke.

Movement erupted under Blake's hand. Two figures exploding into movement, hurtling away from him along the beach. One was large, the other small, dragged stumbling along.

Blake grinned. Too easy. He gave himself a second to enjoy the sense of power that filled him, then loped after the fleeing forms.

Moaning, her mother ran, Kudnarto's hand tight in her own. Kudnarto ran, too, stumbling, slipping, running, fear driving her feet. Something behind them, a sound quick and purposeful. A terrifying shadow swooped across the darkness.

Blake caught up with them easily, raised the butt of his gun and brought it crashing down on the head of the taller figure: a woman, he saw now. She threw up her arms, collapsed like a felled tree.

When her mother opened her arms and fell forward Kudnarto did not stop, ran with screams bubbling in her throat. Something seized her, a hand wrenched at her hair, forcing her head back. She was lifted, released. She fell heavily.

Blake's grin widened. He reached out, fingers closing in tangled hair. He lifted the child, kicking, screeching, struggling, and flung it down on the sand in front of him. It fell with its face in a rock pool. Without thinking, instinct moving faster than thought, he put his foot on the back of its neck and pressed down.

Salt water covered her face. A heavy weight on the back of her neck pressed her down. Her body convulsed, seeking air after her panicked flight. There was no air. The weight on her neck grew heavier. She opened her eyes. Splintered starlight danced in the water of the rock pool. The roughness of the rock ground against her cheek. She had clenched her teeth shut but the need for air was too great. Her mouth opened, sucking water deep into her starving lungs.

Squirming vibrations ran in waves up his leg but Blake did not move. They stopped soon enough.

'Enjoyin' yourself?'

Blake heard contempt in his father's voice, reacted to it with his normal anger.

'I thought we come 'ere to kill 'em. Maybe you'd be 'appier if we kissed 'em?'

He never saw the blow that hit him above the ear and stretched him flat on his back on the sand.

His father looked down at him. 'Don' start bein' smart with me.' Contemptuously, he rested his boot on his son's chest, pinning him to the damp sand. 'I was you, I'd stick to little black kids that can't hit back. That's about your mark.'

Blake thought, One of these days I shall kill you.

Something of the thought must have communicated itself to his father. Hector's cruel grin widened. 'I wouldn't try nuthin. You ain't man enough to take me yet and I doubt you ever will be.'

He turned on his heel, walked across to the fallen figure of the woman and checked it briefly.

'Stone dead,' he said. 'Some would say that was a waste. Though mebbe you're the sort that fancies dead blackies?'

Laughing, he turned and began to climb the steep face of the dune towards the camp. Blake got to his feet and followed, the soft sand dragging at his boots, rifle heavy in his hand. Ahead of him his father's head bobbed as he climbed.

It would be so easy, Blake thought. One shot, that's all it would take.

Hector turned. 'Thinking of shooting your old dad in the back, by any chance?' His voice was rich with contempt. 'About your mark, I reckon.' He waited until Blake came up to him. 'Seein' I don't want my only son to hang, maybe you'd better walk ahead of me, eh?'

Face congested, eyes hot with fury, Blake shoved past his father's mocking laugh. Shoulders squared, he marched on towards the devastated camp. Hating. Hating.

They were too late, as Jason had always known they would be. In mute horror he and Mura stared through the latticework of branches at the line of barely visible men, the muzzle flashes of the guns, the swirling smoke, the crumpled, crawling, fleeing people.

Mura gathered his resolve to hurl himself forward in a futile charge against the guns.

'No!'

Jason's hand clamped tight on his arm, restraining him by sheer force from throwing his life away. For a minute Mura fought him in passionate silence, face closed, eyes blank with shock and fury, but Jason hung on until suddenly he slumped, breath noisy in his throat, watching in sullen silence the continuing massacre of his people.

Jason put his mouth to Mura's ear. 'Nothing we can do here ...'

He turned, arm protectively around Mura's shoulders, and on trembling legs guided him away from the sounds of slaughter into the darkness of the bush. A hundred yards was all they could manage before shock stripped the remaining strength from their limbs. They slumped to the ground. Around them the peaceful voices of the bush contrasted bitterly with the mayhem they had just witnessed.

'Why?' Mura stared unseeing at the darkness. 'Why did they do it?'

Jason's head was filled with the vision of hell they had just seen, the darkness riven by gunflashes, the contorted, motionless bodies, the dragging movement of the injured. He said nothing.

'Nantariltarra said there would be peace,' Mura said.

'Yes.'

Neither of them would admit what they both knew, that Nantariltarra had fatally underestimated the savagery and ruthlessness of the newcomers.

Mura stared at Jason with hostile eyes. 'Your people—' he said.

Jason interrupted him at once. 'No.'

'They are *kuinyo*.'

'I never saw them until yesterday.' But knew it was useless. Mura was right: they *were* his people. He had to share whatever guilt existed because of this night's work but there were more important things to think about now than who was to blame. They were in mortal danger. Judging by tonight's performance the *kuinyo* would kill them, too, if they found them. They had to get away but where and to do what he did not know. The night's events had fractured the framework of their lives.

The initial fury had faded from Mura's face. He looked at Jason appealingly. 'Do you think they killed all of them?'

'No.' It was hard to believe that anyone could have survived the carnage yet reason told Jason they must have done. 'We'll stay here tonight,' he decided. 'In the morning we'll find the others.'

For the survivors—somehow—life would start again.

'Where's the rest of 'em?'

Hector Gallagher looked about him in baffled

outrage. Six bodies plus the two more they knew about on the beach: that was all. He would have been prepared to swear they had knocked over twenty or thirty at least, yet there it was. Six. Somehow the rest had managed to sneak off into the bush.

He went looking for Gavin and found him standing with Ian in the middle of the camp.

'Looks like we missed most of 'em.'

Gavin looked around at the woven shelters, the handful of bodies, the silent bush at their backs. 'Looks like it.'

'We'll 'ave to go after 'em,' Hector declared.

Gavin shook his head. 'No.'

Hector was horrified. 'We can' let 'em get away, not after tonight. Won' 'ave no peace, we do that.'

'We wanted to give them a warning,' Gavin said. 'We've done that. We're not trying to wipe out the whole tribe.'

Hector disagreed. 'That were why we come 'ere. Six dead?' he scoffed. 'Ain't nothing, only six. We don't follow 'em up while we got the chance, you mark my words, we'll be havin' a war on our hands. Won't be a sheep or shepherd safe in the whole district.'

Ian said, 'He has a point, Gavin.'

'We can't go chasing them in the dark.'

'I don't see why not. We got here all right, didn't we?'

'We knew where we were coming. And they weren't ready for us. They'll turn the tables on us soon enough if we start chasing them through the bush.'

'That's crazy,' Hector said belligerently.

'You'll have to live with it.' Gavin did not take kindly to argument from his employees.

'Aye,' Hector said unrepentantly. 'Or die with it.' And stamped away, set shoulders shouting outrage.

'I think he's right,' Ian said.

'Well, I don't.'

Gavin was troubled, nonetheless. He had convinced himself that they were in danger of imminent attack. The peacefully sleeping camp had given lie to that but he had gone ahead anyway. Now their situation was far more dangerous than before. In his heart he knew that Hector was right—they had turned the blacks into enemies without weakening them sufficiently to make them harmless—yet could not bring himself to go after the survivors. The whole expedition had been a catastrophic mistake.

At least the white youth was not among the dead. Asta would be pleased about that although why she should care he did not know. His father had warned that was what you got by marrying a foreigner but he had taken it for granted that she would adapt to his ways, the ways of their new country. There were times when he wondered whether she had done so as successfully as he would have wished.

He put the thought from him; there was work to be done.

'We'd best bury this lot and burn the camp,' he said. 'Then we can get back.'

And carry on our lives as normal? He would have liked to believe it but did not. After tonight there would be small chance of that.

Blake was not prepared to go along with it. They had come out here to deal with the goddamned abos, hadn't they? They'd hardly started and now Gavin bloody Matlock was saying they should tidy up and go back home. Lily-livered, that was his trouble. If the man had any guts he would let them finish the job but no, he'd seen a handful of dead blacks and got in a panic over it. Blake bared his teeth and prowled deeper into the bush, rifle ready in his hand. He hadn't come out here to make things nice and tidy; he had come to give the natives such a lesson they would never again raise their heads to a white man. If it had been up to him he would have gone after them this minute. Shoot the lot before they had the chance to sort themselves out, that was the way to do it. Treat them with kid gloves, there would be nothing but trouble later.

He drifted silently through the trees, enjoying his own skill. Since he was a kid he'd been at home in the bush, could travel through it as quietly as any black man. Quieter than most. He wasn't scared of the dark, either, which gave him a powerful advantage now. Scared of the shooting, the abos would be even more frightened of the dark. They would not have gone far.

He intended to find them.

Above him, the spreading branches obscured the stars. Behind him the gun party was making a lot of noise in the camp. That was fine: it would help to distract attention from himself. He snarled silently, teeth bare. Maybe he'd be able to give them another surprise before the night was over.

Diminishing sounds behind, the silence punctuated by night noises, he drifted stealthily through the trees.

Where are you? Silently he asked the question. He took a step, another, froze again. *Where are you*? His head turned slowly, eyes seeking. They were here somewhere. He could feel them: smell them, almost.

He went on.

*

The night was full of unseen eyes. Jason could feel them about him. They were still too close to the camp. If the whites came looking for them they would almost certainly find them.

As he had said to Mura, there must be others who had managed to escape but he had no time to think about them now. It was all he could do to look after Mura and himself.

Come to that, the survivors could be as dangerous to him now as the whites. One glimpse of his white skin and they might have put a spear through him before they realised who he was. It was a risk he had to take. Anything was better than staying where they were.

He put his mouth close to Mura's ear. 'We can't stay here. We do that, they'll find us for sure.' He drew Mura to his feet. 'Let's get moving.'

The faintest flicker of sound.

Blake froze. Slowly, his head turned, instincts screaming. There was something moving out there. Not far away, either.

Muscles tense, cocked rifle ready in his hands, Blake took a step, paused, another step, paused. His eyes searched the darkness. He moved again, paused again.

The sound he had heard was repeated. He paused, feet spread, body finely balanced. Every sense alert, he tried to identify what he had heard.

There. His eyes probed further. The faintest . . .

. . . Murmur.

That was what it was. Someone whispering, trying to keep quiet. Fugitives.

Even for Blake's eyes it was too dark. He moved forward again. His senses reeled in sensations:

leaves shifting infinitesimally upon the faintest breath of wind, the spongy texture of soil beneath his feet, the scent of dry vegetation, of dust, of fallen leaves. The scratch of twig on leaf, a tree sighing to itself, timber creaking as it swayed in the breeze.

Blake was listening for something out of harmony with the noises of the bush.

The murmur came again. Again he turned his head, seeking its source.

Mura's body was inert, reluctant to move.

'Come on!' Jason said again, frustration tight in his throat. He seized the black arm, trying to drag Mura by force. It was like trying to shift a tree. 'You want them to find us? They'll kill us if they do. You know that? Is that what you want?'

Blake moved towards the sound. A voice, speaking in agitated squirts of sound, too softly for words to be audible. Had to be an abo: unless it was the white fellow who was with them. Blake hoped it was. Hanging was too good for people like that. It would be a pleasure to put a bullet through any man who had chosen to turn his back on his own people.

He moved forward another inch. His eyes jumped as something stirred. Body motionless, muscles spring-taut, he tried to identify what he thought he had seen: a shadow of movement, black against black.

There.

A movement, definite this time. Two figures. They were moving ever so slowly. Blake inched his rifle up into his shoulder. He must be sure before he fired. Miss and he would lose them. Engraved against the stillness, Blake waited, finger rigid on the trigger, breath controlled in his throat, waiting for the moment when he could see them clearly enough to fire.

Behind him, a sudden blossom of orange light rose into the sky and shed a pattern of shimmering brilliance through the trees.

'Where's that son of yours?' The tone of Gavin's voice said it all. Angry over how the night had gone, he was looking for someone to blame.

Hector said, 'Maybe he's gone to look for more of the natives.'

'Asking for trouble,' Gavin said.

'Not Blake.' Hector had no need to say more; both men knew Blake was the best bushman they had.

'We'll fire the camp,' Gavin said, 'then head back. If Blake isn't here by then he'll have to find his own way home.'

The fires were ready. The men stood waiting for Gavin to give the word.

'Let's do it.'

The fire crackled, raced in blue and yellow streams through the grass and took hold. The men shielded their eyes as the flames, orange now, tipped with smoke, reached quivering amid a crackle of sparks into the night sky.

In the bush, the sudden glare of the conflagration caught in its brilliant light the shapes of trees, of bushes, of grass and of two figures frozen in the moment of moving deeper into the safety of the bush. Pinned by the flames against the undergrowth, they turned and stared in the direction of the revealing fire. Their faces, one black, one white, were clearly visible.

Blake drew a deep breath, steadied the muzzle of his rifle against the trunk of a convenient tree and tightened his finger around the trigger.

The hungry flames leapt roaring into the sky.

'Tell them to keep an eye on it,' Gavin shouted to Hector Gallagher, 'we don't want to set the bush alight.' With all the rain they'd had recently there should be no danger of that but it paid to be careful.

Hector's teeth gleamed in the flame. 'Might be the best way of dealing with them. Burnin' 'em out should be better even than shooting.' He cackled. 'Cost less than bullets, an' all.'

'Might find we'd trapped ourselves,' Gavin pointed out.

'You're right.'

But regretted it, Gavin could see. No doubt the idea of an ocean of flame bearing down upon the trapped aborigines appealed to Hector's imagination.

Hector went to give the men their instructions, paused and looked around as a shot echoed dully through the undergrowth.

'What was that?'

Gavin said, 'It must be Blake. We'd best go after him in case he's in any trouble.'

Hector shouted instructions to the men watching the fire then, rifles ready in their hands, he and Gavin plunged into the undergrowth.

The firelight made the going easy but knowing exactly where the sound of the shot had come from was not easy at all. After a hundred yards they stopped, looking about them at the confusion of branches, leaves, shadow all shimmering in a confusing dazzle of firelight.

Hector shouted: 'Blake . . .?'

A distant voice answered. 'Over 'ere . . .'

They ran towards the sound.

Blake was on one knee, peering around the trunk of a tree. They crouched beside him. Gavin scanned the bush in front of them, could see nothing. 'What is it?'

'Two of 'em over there.' Blake pointed. 'One of 'em were that white fellow the blacks 'ave got with 'em.'

Gavin remembered Asta's words, how anxious she was that no harm should come to the mysterious white youth. 'White? You're sure?'

Blake nodded. 'He turned to look at the flames. I saw his face, clear as clear.'

'Did you get either of them?'

'Dunno,' Blake said. 'The flames startled them and they dropped just as I fired. Reckon I may have winged one of 'em, though.'

'Were they armed?' Hector asked.

'Not that I saw.'

'Let's go and see if we can find them, then,' Gavin said and stood.

'Just because Blake didn't see no spears don't mean they ain't got none,' Hector cautioned.

'If we wait we'll lose them,' Gavin said.

He supposed that in a sense it didn't matter but remembered his wife's words, her strange obsession with the mysterious white youth. He would save him, if he could.

Stepping cautiously, guns at the ready, they moved forward into the bush.

*

'We must keep moving,' Jason urged but knew that Mura had no strength left. The bullet had creased the flesh of Mura's left shoulder: a nasty wound, although not a dangerous one. He was losing blood with every step. The front of his body glistened red in the firelight and he staggered as he walked, breath whistling painfully through his sagging mouth.

'If we stop here they'll catch us in no time,' Jason said but Mura was done.

His legs folded beneath him as he collapsed. 'You get out,' he said. 'No need for them to find you too.'

Jason shook his head. 'I'll stay.' They would certainly kill Mura if they came on him alone. If there was a white person with him they might—just might—spare both of them.

Crouched in the undergrowth, they waited. They heard the pursuit before they saw it: the sound of leaves and branches crackling beneath the *kuinyos'* boots as they advanced slowly but steadily towards them.

If Mura hadn't been wounded they would never have found us, Jason thought, contemptuous of the pursuers' woodcraft, but it was too late to think about that. Mura was shaking, his face grey with terror and the loss of blood.

The undergrowth parted. Jason looked up, saw the questing muzzles of the guns, the hard and searching eyes behind them.

'Beauty!' A young voice, brutal and merciless. A rifle muzzle swung, focusing hungrily on him. I am dead, Jason thought. He stared back, unblinking, forcing himself not to close his eyes. He heard the click of the mechanism.

The food was ready by the time the men returned. They went outside to greet them, Mary and Alison running, Asta following more slowly.

The men were excited, talking, laughing, smelling of wood smoke and burnt powder and something less easily identified: the hot, animal stench of death. Asta wrinkled her nose in distaste.

From the corner of her eye Asta saw Mary run up to Ian, throw her arms about him. Gavin strode towards her, smiling, but she evaded him.

He was safe: good. It did not mean she wanted to be held by him while the reek of death was still on him. It was something that men did, she thought, no doubt necessary on occasions—although not this time—but that did not mean she would welcome her husband hot from the slaughter, whatever other women might do. Besides, she had other concerns. She looked about at their faces, seeking . . .

. . . The face swung into focus between two others. He must have felt the weight of her gaze upon him; he looked up, hostile eyes smudged with fatigue, mouth set in a bitter line, and saw her staring. His expression did not change but his eyes held her gaze.

It will take time for him to understand, she told herself, but I shall bring him round in the end.

My child.

Ecstasy ran in a warm tide beneath her skin. Someone to solace me for the loss of my son, she told herself exultantly. My gift, returned from the sea.

Without looking at anyone else, her eyes fixed on those of the strange white youth, she walked towards him through the cluster of men.

BOOK TWO

STORM HAWK

*The black falcon is an uncommon to rare nomad
on tree-scattered plains and watercourses
throughout the arid areas of Australia. Because
its arrival often signalled turbulent weather
conditions, it was known to certain of the*
nunga *people as* karrkawara *or storm hawk.*

TWELVE

Outrage; shock; hatred.

Choked by waves of conflicting emotion, Jason stared about him. Gunfire still rang in his ears, the powder-stench was still acrid in his nostrils. He had seen the rifle muzzle seek him out, the killing lust in the eyes of the man who held it. He had tasted death yet, inexplicably, was alive. He felt his life flood through him, not understanding why he was not dead.

A couple of the men around him carried flares; the flames pulsed in the breeze, reflecting in a hundred silver glints from the spear-shaped leaves of the trees that surrounded them. At his side Mura swayed with weakness; in the flickering light his black chest shone red with the blood that still seeped from the wound in his shoulder. The night air, the dry mustiness of the gum trees, smelt indescribably sweet.

I am alive, Jason thought. The breath of the wind is real. The oily crackle of the flares is real. I can feel the roughness of the ground beneath my feet, the stretch of my muscles as I move. I am alive.

It was a wonder to him, indescribable, but with the wonder came anger. Alive or not, they were prisoners. Not for long, perhaps, but for the moment they were guarded too closely to have any hope of escape. In any case Mura was not strong enough to get away; he doubted he was strong enough himself.

The men were laughing and boisterous, excited by what they had done. Their teeth gleamed in the light. What they intended to do with Mura and himself, why they had brought them here instead of killing them like the rest, he had no idea. Not that it mattered. He thought, they could have killed us but didn't. More fools them. The first chance we get we shall escape. Then, perhaps, we shall be killing some of them instead.

He needed vengeance as a man in the desert needs water. If these men wanted war, war they would have.

There was movement beyond the circle of light. From the buildings a woman—tall, grey-eyed, face the colour of ivory in the guttering yellow light—walked purposefully across the cleared ground towards him. Her eyes seemed to focus only on him. She came right up to him.

His first thought as he stared back at her: Thank God I am still wearing my kilt.

She took his hands in hers—cool, slim hands—and stared intently into his face.

'Yes,' she said, eyes devouring him. 'Yes.'

He was dumbstruck. He did not understand what she wanted from him but before he could gather his wits to ask she had dropped his hands and turned her back.

More confused than ever, he watched her walk away. Someone barked an order and he and Mura were hustled into a slab-walled hut, small, earth-smelling, dark. The door slammed shut behind them. They heard the thud as a bar dropped into place.

'What will they do to us?' Mura's voice was edged with fear.

They could barely see each other in the darkness. 'Nothing.'

Jason hoped he sounded more confident than he felt.

No water, no food, no certainty. He sat on his heels on the earth floor, trying not to think what the morning might bring. Slowly he slipped into a fitful doze. Hours later, a line of light now visible around the door, he awoke to dread.

Why had the massacre happened?

Why had they been brought here?

What was going to happen to them?

Why . . .?

Why . . .?

Questions without number. No answers.

Mura was burning with fever, teeth chattering, skin hot. They sat side by side, shoulders touching, and watched the growing brightness around the door, the chinks of light in the rough walls. They said nothing, waiting . . .

For what?

Later—no way to know how much later—the door creaked as the bar that had been placed across it was removed. They had time to glance at each other, eyes apprehensive in the gloom, before it swung open. Light flooded in. Eyes squinting, Jason made out the shape of the woman who had spoken to him before, etched in sunlight.

'I have brought you food.'

She spoke calmly, as though there was nothing

extraordinary about their situation. She bent over them, eyes fixed on Mura's shoulder, sore and swollen where the bullet had seared it, the blood dried now to a crust.

'Let me see that.'

Nervous as a colt beneath the foreign-seeming hands, Mura strained away from her.

'Let her look,' Jason said.

Obediently Mura sat rock-rigid, enduring the gently probing fingers.

'I'll get something to put on that,' the woman said. She stood. 'Wait here.'

She went out without another word, leaving the plate of food on the floor of the shed, the door ajar.

They looked at it, at each other.

'Can you walk?'

Mura nodded.

She had been kind but Jason did not trust her. Who could trust people who had behaved as these had?

'Let's get out of here.'

'What about the food?'

'Who knows what they might have put in it.'

They got as far as the edge of the scrub, walked into a yellow-haired giant with huge shoulders and cold grey eyes. With him was the youth, a rifle slung from his shoulder, who had found them in the bush the previous night. Then he had not concealed his desire to kill them; he did not conceal it now. He snatched the rifle off his shoulder and levelled it, would possibly have fired had not the older man put out his arm to stop him.

'Leave them!'

Jason stood rigid, hearing the scratch of breath over the back-drawn lips. He thought, he may shoot us anyway.

The yellow-haired man must have thought so, too. His huge hand seized the muzzle of the rifle, forced it upwards.

'I told you, no.'

For a moment the young man struggled, then surrendered. He glared furiously at them, eyes hot. 'We should get rid of 'em,' he said to the yellow-haired man. 'They'll be nuthin but trouble, else.'

'I said leave them.' To Jason he said, 'You get back in the hut until I decide what to do with you.'

They were led back to the hut. Once again they were locked in.

Jason remembered the cage at the edge of the cliff. He thought, all I ever do in this country is try to break out of gaol.

Once again he sat down, back resting against the wall's rough slabs. Breaking out would come later. Now there was nothing to do but wait.

Asta sat in the house, hands clasped in front of her, ears hearing yet not hearing the words that Gavin directed in a furious monotone at her bowed back.

'Why do you want them? Tell me that, at least.'

'Not them. You can do what you like with the black one.'

'Blake would have shot them both if I'd let him. You saying you wouldn't have cared if it had been just the black one?'

Asta hunched her head into her shoulders, not deigning to acknowledge such a question.

'What will you do with him if I agree to keep him?'

'Raise him as my own.'

'To take Edward's place.' He had told himself not

187

to say it but felt better with the words out in the open.

'No-one will take Edward's place,' she said. It was true, yet Edward was dead, after all.

'Then I don't understand you.'

She did not care whether he understood or not. What mattered was that she should no longer be alone in this arid land.

'They may not want to stay,' Gavin said.

'I will speak to him.' I shall make him stay, she thought. How, she did not know.

'They're a pair of savages. Give them half a chance and they'll cut your throat.'

'They will not hurt me.'

She believed it absolutely without knowing why.

'I'll come with you,' he offered.

Asta shook her head. 'He will not speak if you are there.'

It was strange how certain of the boy she was, knowing nothing of him. But I *do* know him, she thought. I have always known him.

Asta went back to the hut, its secured door concealing who knew what future. She lifted the bar and went inside. The two youths crouched with their backs against the far wall. Light gleamed in their eyes as they watched her from the shadows.

She said, 'Perhaps you should start by telling me your names.'

The faces as unmoving as the wall behind them.

'Very well,' she agreed pragmatically, 'names later. Tell me, please,' she said to the white boy, 'how you came to be with the native people.'

He ignored the question. He said, 'We want to go back.'

'You think they would have you back? After what happened?'

'That had nothing to do with me.'

'Perhaps not. But you are white.'

He glared his defiance. 'They are my people.'

She shook her head. 'If you go back they will kill you.'

Hatred spilled. 'As you killed them, you mean?'

'I do not deny it,' she said. 'As we killed them.'

The eyes of the black youth moved between them as he tried to guess what they were saying.

'Here you will be with your own kind, at least,' Asta said.

'My own kind?' he repeated contemptuously. 'That bloke with the gun was going to kill us.'

'I shall deal with Blake,' she promised.

He watched her, his face hard, a hint of contempt on his lips. 'Maybe I should kill him first,' he said.

'I wish no killing here,' she said.

'You going to keep us locked up?'

'Your friend may go if he wishes.'

The white face turned to the black, they spoke softly together.

'If I stay he'll stay,' he said.

'And do you wish to stay?'

'I'll think about it.'

'What is your name?'

A pause. At length: 'Jason.'

'Jason . . .' She tested it on her tongue. 'And your friend?'

He shook his head. 'They don't like people knowing their names.'

'I must call him something.'

Jason thought about it. 'Call him Michael.'

She went to the door, turned to look back at them. 'If I leave the door open, will you run away again?'

'One way to find out,' Jason said, not in the business of making promises.

'Very well.'

She went out. Once again she left the door open. She walked across to the house without looking back.

It was not much but it was, perhaps, a start.

Alone on a hillock overlooking the sea, Nantariltarra wrestled with the spirits. He sat for the whole of one day and night and far into the next day, mind blank, eyes closed and unseeing. He had thought to summon visions that would tell him what he must do but had seen nothing. We are nothing, he thought, we know nothing.

More and more he was convinced that the *nunga* were no more than the dust. For centuries they had lain undisturbed but now a wind had arisen that would blow them all away. A white wind, he thought. A deadly wind.

Deadly it certainly was. There were eight dead out of a clan that numbered less than one hundred. He had known each of them; all the clan had known them. Five men, two women, one child, all henceforth nameless in accordance with custom. Their spirits accused not only the white men who had killed them but himself and the rest of the clan for having failed to prevent it.

Eight dead. Plus the white boy upon whom he had pinned so many hopes. He too was gone, as dead as the rest. His name, too, could not be spoken.

If we attack the *kuinyo* they will kill us, he thought, but what of it? By their raid on the camp they have already begun to kill us. If we are to die, whatever we do at least let us fight. It was easily said but in his heart he was afraid of the white man's power. What did the spirits want?

He waited, eyes closed. Silence, darkness encircled him.

Wait, he instructed himself. Listen. Guidance will come.

Through the silence came a cry, faint and shrill.

He focused, senses drinking the sound.

It came again.

Nantariltarra opened his eyes.

A blaze of light flooded him. After so long in darkness his eyes should have been dazzled but were not. Clearly, calmly, they surveyed the sky over the sea. A tiny hatchwork of cloud against the blue. Against the cloud . . .

A far dot, circling.

Doubt trembled, wounding his certainty. Karrkawara, the storm hawk, was the totem of the Warree clan who lived on the far side of the peninsula, facing the setting sun. Why should it appear to a man of the Winderah?

The circling dot swooped, a sudden lunge across the wind. It swung above him as he sat, legs folded beneath him, facing the wrinkled sea. He heard the rush of air in its wings. Its reed-thin cry filled his head.

Sharp wings swept back, fierce eyes watching the ground, the hawk swung across the fish-scale glitter of the sea. A silent shape hurtled up to meet it. From a crevice in the cliff face, Winda the owl rose to challenge the hawk that had invaded its space.

Long ago Winda was formed like a man. He lived in a cave overlooking the beach. One day when he was hunting he found the children of Tuketja, the curlew, who in those days was also shaped like a man. Being hungry he ate them. When Tuketja returned and saw what had happened he was angry. He laid his complaint before Nantha, the red kangaroo who was the totem of the Winderah people. Nantha pitied Tuketja and laid a curse upon Winda so that henceforth he would be able to leave his cave only at night. Men are frightened of the night and the quinkan who hunt at night, so Winda turned himself into a bird, the owl, that also hunts only at night.

Now here Winda was, hunting in broad daylight.

Winda the bird of Narungga tradition.

Karrkawara the storm hawk from the west, the direction from which the white youth had said his people came.

Winda challenged Karrkawara and chased him away.

Slowly Nantariltarra uncoiled his legs and stood. He had been sitting for a very long time yet stood without touching the ground with any part of himself but his feet. Nantha, Winda, Karrkawara, his dreaming filled him.

The sign he had sought had been given him. They would watch the *kuinyo*, learn the pattern of their movements. When they were ready they would find Mura and bring him back. They would kill the white youth without name. They would kill the *pindranki*— the white women—and the men who guarded the sheep. Finally, they would kill the yellow-haired men who led the white clan. The wisdom of the dead *kuinyo* would enter them. They would learn everything there was to know about them, their ways and dreaming.

They would drive them away, as Winda had driven away Karrkawara. The death of the *kuinyo* would restore life and hope to the clan.

THIRTEEN

Shearing time.

At Whitby Downs, named by Gavin after his Yorkshire birthplace, a group of riders and dogs was driving a mob of sheep across the plain towards the shearing sheds constructed from the bent branches of felled trees. The midday sun lay like a brand upon the grass, the cluster of buildings, the slowly moving flocks. Everywhere was noise: sheep bleating, dogs yapping, stock whips cracking, men yelling. The air was filled with dust from a thousand hooves rising in a golden haze into a sky bleached white by heat.

Ian Matlock had ridden over to help. When the shearing was finished at Whitby Downs the team would move south to Bungaree.

'Bungaree?' Gavin had been amazed that Ian had chosen an aboriginal name. 'How come you picked a name like that?'

'Sinbad told me it means "him my country",' Ian said. 'I liked that. Him *my* country now and the sooner the blacks accept it the better for all of us.'

Although by the way they had been behaving—

constant pin-prick raids, sheep speared, an unsuccessful attack on one of the shepherds—it seemed unlikely that would be soon.

Ian turned in his saddle to look at his cousin. 'Those two you picked up on the raid. I reckon you're crazy to keep them.'

Gavin would not admit it was Asta's idea: no woman told him what to do, at least not officially. He said, 'Got them digging a well. They've been no trouble.'

'Nor will they be till the day they cut your throat. Then it'll be too late.' Ian brushed flies from his face. 'They won't trust us either, after what happened. In my book that makes them dangerous.'

They rode for a while in silence, watching the ambling flocks, the darting, pink-tongued dogs, the boiling clouds of dust.

'Do they ride?' Ian asked.

'Had a job getting either of them into the saddle,' Gavin confessed. 'Jason—the white one—kept falling off to start with but he's getting the hang of it now. The blackfeller looks like he's a natural.'

Ian grunted sceptically. 'Make sure they don't steal the horses, that's my advice to you.'

Ian was right; Jason trusted none of them, least of all Blake Gallagher. His hackles rose each time he saw the cocky strut, the glowering face, the ever-present gun.

I'll deal with that bastard one of these days, he promised himself.

As for the woman . . .

Jason did not know what to make of her. She was friendly but made him uneasy, too willing to invade his space. He could not see why she should be so interested in him. What was he to her?

Uneasy or not, he had given up the idea of running away. As the woman had said, he had nowhere to run. To the men here, Mura was black before he was a person. The clan would think of Jason in the same way.

If he went back to them now, after what had happened during the raid, they might decide to kill him because he was white.

Blake and his father stood over the box press, loading fleeces into bags for shipment to Adelaide.

It was hard work and sweat streamed off them. Blake secured the mouth of the bag with twine. Together they lifted it out of the press and carried it to join the growing stack inside the shed.

'Should fetch a right fair price in Adelaide,' Hector said.

Blake grunted. 'If it ever gets there.'

They walked back to the press.

'What's that supposed to mean?'

'Jason and the blackfeller . . . Gavin should have let me get rid of the pair of 'em when we shot up the rest.' Blake stretched the new bag within the press. 'We'll 'ave to do it sometime.'

Hector rammed a folded fleece into the bag. 'Maybe, maybe not.'

'If it had been them as raided us, you reckon we'd just accept it?'

'We ain't black.'

'Neither's that Jason.' A second fleece joined the first. 'We could lose the whole clip.'

'They'd never do it,' Hector said.

'You'd better be right, Da.'

Hector thought about it. Blake might be right, at

that. He said, 'I bin wonderin' why they was still 'angin' around . . .'

Blake straightened. 'Now you know.'

'It makes no sense,' Gavin said but was troubled, Hector saw.

'We killed their mates, didn't we?'

'What are you saying?'

'Get rid of 'em while we got the chance, that's what I'm sayin'.'

Gavin turned away, exasperated by the situation. Get rid of them, indeed . . .

Whatever that was supposed to mean.

Asta's fingertip touched the line of scars on Jason's chest.

'Tell me about these.'

Embarrassed, Jason drew back from her touch.

'It's the way they do things.'

'Why?'

He did not know how to explain the acceptance of pain, the test of courage. He said nothing.

'Do you know why you were brought here?'

How he resented the way she tried to strip him with her never-ending questions.

'No.'

'Because I wanted it.' She laughed. 'Although that is not the real reason. You were shipwrecked, I think?'

'Yes.'

'Always, when I was a child in Europe, I was taught that the sea repays its debts.'

He stared at her, no idea what she was talking about.

'I had a son, you see. He was drowned. It was the greatest pain I have known.' She smiled at him brilliantly, stretched out her hand to touch his. 'That is the reason you are here. To do the things he would have done, had he lived.'

Her words alarmed him, seeming to lay claim to him. 'I don't want to do anything. The men brought me here, that's all.'

He saw she was not listening. Maybe he would have to run away, after all. Anything, rather than this.

Two weeks of driving rain brought a break in the shearing when it was only half-finished. Ground that had been as hard as granite turned to liquid. Work was impossible.

'What a country . . .'

Gavin stared fuming at the lashing downpour.

'It will be the death of us, I dare say,' Asta agreed. Yet privately she did not believe it. The death of others, perhaps, but herself . . . It would take more than this land to kill her. She stood at her husband's side and stared out through the open doorway, seeing the sheen of standing water reflecting clouds that sagged grey bellies almost to the ground, the landscape half-drowned in mist.

You hate me, she told it. But I shall beat you. Never doubt that.

If needs be she would fight it, as with new-found determination she knew she would fight the circumstances of her life, and she would win.

The men sat around grousing, watching the rain. Devil's weather, Asta thought. Everyone idle and out of temper, everyone with plenty of time to dream up trouble. She watched Blake in particular but nothing happened and eventually the rain stopped. The sun came out. She might have been imagining things but knew she was not. Trouble, now or later; she could smell it.

The wet land steamed, new grass shone like emerald fire. Ian Matlock, who had gone home when it started to rain, returned, Mary and Alison with him.

He clumped into the house, careless of the rich mud clinging to his boots.

'There's water in all the gullies and the tanks are full,' he said. 'Pity it didn't wait until we finished shearing, though.'

'At least the fleeces will be clean,' Gavin pointed out. 'Just like at home.'

In north Yorkshire they had washed the fleeces on the sheep's backs, standing with them in the ice-cold streams of the northern moors. For this year at least they would be able to do the same here.

'Doesn't mean we should stop drilling wells, though,' Ian said. He sipped the glass of spirits that Gavin had put into his hand. 'How are those two boys coming on?'

'Fine.'

'Under supervision?'

Gavin shook his head. 'They're not going any-where.'

'More's the pity.' Ian up-ended his glass.

'Two pairs of hands,' Gavin pointed out. 'Not costing me a penny, either.'

'You'll live to regret it.'

'We can't turn our back on the white lad,' Gavin protested. 'He's one of us, after all.'

'You're wrong. Have you seen the scars he's got?'

'The scars don't signify—'

'They're *ritual* scars,' Ian corrected him. 'He may

have been one of us once but not any longer. As for the other one . . .'

'What about him?' Gavin was displeased, not about to accept criticism in his own house.

'He's a savage, Gavin. They're all savages. Keeping him here is asking for trouble. I'll tell you something else: our boys don't like it. If you don't get rid of him they may decide to do something about it themselves. I for one wouldn't blame them if they did.'

Gavin glared, master here and intending to stay that way. 'Any man lays a finger on either of them, he'll answer to me for it.'

In the kitchen Asta, Mary and Alison were surrounded by the warm steam of cooking.

'Ian says you have a black man here,' Mary said.

'Two of them,' Asta corrected her.

Mary looked more flustered than ever. 'Two? But I thought—'

'Sinbad the shepherd,' Asta said. 'And Michael. He's quite young. More of a boy, really.'

'Oh Sinbad . . .' Mary dismissed him as too familiar to pose any threat. 'Ian says the wild ones are dangerous.'

'Can be, I am sure,' Asta agreed, 'as we are.'

A typical Asta remark, Mary thought, the sort Mary hated, never knowing whether she was supposed to take it seriously or not. She decided not to hear it.

'Why did the men bring Michael back with them?'

Asta inspected the contents of an iron pot through a gushing cloud of steam. 'By accident. I wanted them to rescue the white boy but the black one was with him so they brought them both.'

She replaced the lid; the rush of steam was cut off.

Alison had been listening round-eyed. She asked, 'What is the white one's name?'

'Jason.'

'Jason what?'

'I don't know.' Asta laughed. 'It was hard enough to get that much out of him.'

'Why?'

'The black people like to keep their names secret.'

'You said he was white,' Alison objected.

'I think perhaps he picked up some of their ideas.'

'Does that make him a savage, too?'

A good question, Asta thought. 'Not very savage. The two of them are digging a well down in the gully. If you go down there you will see them.'

Alison hesitated. 'He's not like Blake, is he?'

'Not at all like Blake,' Asta told her. 'He may be savage but I do not think he is cruel.'

'Don't go far.' Mary was uneasy at the idea of her daughter leaving the house when there were such men about, savage or not.

'She will be safe enough,' Asta assured her. To Alison she said, 'Your mother is right. You need be afraid of neither of the boys we have here but there are others in the bush, as you well know.'

Not only in the bush, she thought, thinking of Blake.

'I hate the idea of the blacks,' Mary confessed after Alison had run outside, banging the door behind her. 'I know that one of these nights they will break in and kill all of us.'

'I understand they do not move at night.'

'Day or night,' Mary said, 'what difference does it make?'

*

Blake Gallagher was chopping firewood. He stood at the woodpile, shirt off, axe blade shining in the sun, revelling in the air on his bare skin, the pull of his muscles, the solid thunk, thunk, as the axe head buried itself repeatedly in the sawn blocks of wood that he was reducing systematically to kindling.

The door of the house opened and Alison came out. Blake watched as she crossed the corner of the paddock towards the gully fifty yards away.

Going to the new well, then.

He scowled. He had always despised her for being soft, for being a girl, but these days was beginning to think differently about such things. If she wanted to talk to someone, what was wrong with him? At least he wasn't a savage. He watched her figure flitting lightly through the trees. She was pretty, he thought. Too pretty to waste on the likes of Jason and his black mate. His scowl darkened. Have to do something about them two, he thought. Reckon they've over-stayed their welcome. As for Alison . . . She needed someone to show her the difference between a savage and a proper man. His scowl dissolved into a slow smile. Heated by images of white flesh, he wiped his mouth with the back of his hand. Keep her in line, like. He reckoned he'd enjoy that.

He turned back to the stack of freshly cut timber gleaming the colour of cream in the sunlight. He hefted the axe, brought the head crashing down.

At the fringe of the trees, Alison paused and stared at the new well in the centre of the clearing. There wasn't much to see; a wooden tripod six feet high with a rope disappearing into the ground beneath it, a pile of yellow earth off to one side. No sound, no movement. Cautiously she stepped closer. Somewhere in the bush a bird gave a long, bubbling call. The rope from the tripod tightened and began to shake.

The silent movement scared her but she stood her ground. They are only boys, she reminded herself. What harm can they do me?

Heart pattering for all her brave thoughts, she waited until a head appeared above the rim of the hole and a young man climbed out into the light.

He was filthy, dressed only in breeches, his body streaked and clotted with yellow mud. Beneath the mud his skin was white. He turned and for the first time saw her watching him. Momentarily he froze, then dropped the rope and walked slowly towards her.

I will not run, she told herself.

'Who are you?' Jason's tone was unfriendly.

Alison's chin went up. 'I am Alison Matlock. My uncle owns this run.'

Jason's sardonic eyes studied her. 'Is that so? What are you doing here, then?'

'I wanted to see what you were doing.'

Jason studied her silently, seeing the slight quiver of her lip, the way she tried to conceal her fear of him. It was the girl he had seen from the bushes the day he had come with Nantariltarra to talk to the white people. It was sight of her that had reminded him that he was not a black man or ever would be, that these were his people, after all.

But were they? How could they be, after what they had done?

She was staring at the scars on his chest. 'Did you have an accident?'

He shook his head. 'They were deliberate.'

'They *tortured* you?' she asked, awed.

He laughed. 'No. They do it so you can show how brave you are.'

'Are you brave?' she asked him seriously.

'Very brave.'

She looked around her. 'Where is your friend?'

'Down the hole.'

Jason stepped over to the well head and shouted down the shaft in a language Alison did not understand.

'What did you say?'

'I told him to come up.'

Jason liked her for controlling her fear of him. Scars and all, she made him feel normal for the first time since he had come here and he liked her for that, too. He watched her as Mura emerged from the hole, his black skin shining with water and daubed with clay. She did not flinch as a lot of white women would have done.

'This is Michael,' he told her. 'He is my friend.'

Mura recognised the word *friend*. His white teeth gleamed as he smiled. 'Fren',' he repeated, touching his chest with the tips of his fingers.

The black boy, the white girl, stood examining each other with interest.

'She is the child of the other one,' Mura said to Jason. 'The one from the place where we first met them. Has he come here, too?'

'Probably.' To Alison, Jason said, 'I saw you the first day. Do you remember? When I talked to your father.'

She nodded. 'When you told him the black people would kill us all if we didn't go away.'

Jason stared at her. 'I never said that.'

*

203

Ian Matlock smiled humourlessly and lifted the rifle a few inches. 'This is the only right I need.'

'You're saying there's no place for them in their own land.'

Ian glared. 'They get in my way, I'll kill them.'

'You're not the only one, remember. You've got women here, too.'

Angrily Jason said, 'Instead you came that night and killed them. For nothing.'

Alison nodded, face serious. 'They were frightened you might do it. They thought they should get in first.'

His liking for her vanished at the thought that he might have had something to do with what had happened.

'They did it because they wanted the land! That was the only reason!'

Alison seemed no more afraid of his anger than she had been of Mura, emerging from the well like a demon from the pit. 'Papa told me he paid the government for the land. It belongs to him. The reason he went with Uncle Gavin and the others that night was because you told him they would come and kill us.'

Jason stared at her. 'I never said we would kill anyone.'

But had meant it.

Ian thumbed back the hammer of the rifle. 'Get out! Before I use this.'

And his reply: *'You've got women here, too.'*

*

204

What else was that supposed to have meant? What else could Ian Matlock have understood by it?

All of a sudden he hated her. 'You don't know what you're talking about.' Before he could stop himself he was shaking her. 'I could drop you down the shaft for making out it was my fault!'

He let her go. She edged away but her voice when she spoke was unafraid. 'It *was* your fault! If you hadn't said what you did they wouldn't have done it!'

And, turning, ran away from them through the trees.

Jason watched her go. She came to be friends, he thought, and I drove her away.

His mind seethed with memories. Of Ian Matlock raising his rifle and his own instinctive reaction. Of the nightmare scene of death and terror, of screams and swirling clouds of biting smoke.

His fault?

The running figure of the girl had disappeared.

He thought, The last time I threatened them they brought their guns. What will they do when she tells them I threatened to drop her down the well shaft?

'We're off,' he said to Mura.

'Where do we go?'

'Find the clan, of course. What else?'

Mura shook his head. 'No.'

'Why not?' Jason stared at him, knowing the answer before he heard it.

'They will not accept you now.'

'What happened wasn't my fault!'

Wasn't it?

Mura said nothing.

Anguish turned to anger. 'Why stay, then? If you blame me?'

'You saved my life,' Mura said simply.

It was not the only reason. He had discovered that the white men knew many secrets unknown in the ages-old world of the clan. He wanted to learn those secrets, not turn his back on them.

Jason said, 'When that girl tells them what I said there'll be hell to pay.'

There was nothing he could do about it. If the clan truly had turned its back on him he would have to stay where he was, whatever the consequences.

'Let's get on with the damn well, then,' he said furiously, and swung himself over the lip of the hole.

Their future—even their survival, perhaps—depended on what the girl said when she got home.

'Thank God!' Mary said as Alison came into the house. Relief made her cross. 'What took you so long?'

Asta studied Alison's eyes, unnaturally bright in her flushed face. 'Did you find them?'

'Yes.'

'Were they savage?' Teasing.

'Not savage at all. I liked them.'

Especially Jason, she thought but did not say. As far back as she could remember, Edward had been her idol. Jason had made her feel the same way. He was not a savage but as soon as he spoke to her she knew that he was someone who would not let anyone tell him what to do. Edward had been like that. One day she wanted to be like that herself. Jason had been angry and had scared her but now she was annoyed with herself for running away. She knew that tomorrow she would go back and see him again.

'Jason was nice,' she said.

*

After it was dark Blake came out from the shed where he had been pretending to sleep and made his way cautiously around the corner of the building. The surrounding swell and fall of land lay floating in the cold light of a full moon. Shadows of buildings and trees lay black upon the brilliant surface of the ground and overhead, dimmed by the blaze of moonlight, stars glittered in a clear sky.

Without haste, Blake made his way to the small barn crammed with hay where he knew Jason and the blackfeller would be sleeping. At the back of the house a dog barked once, sleepily, and Blake froze, another shadow in the moonlight. Silence returned and he passed on. The night air stung his lungs and he shivered. Winter had set in.

The barn door stood an inch or two ajar. He paused, testing the texture of the darkness within. All was still. Cautiously, without turning his head, he let his eyes move around the buildings, the railed paddock where the clustered sheep grazed audibly in the moonlight, the hills beyond. The sounds of grazing accentuated the stillness. Nothing moved.

Let's do it, then.

He teased a handful of straw into a loose ball, dug his tinder box from his pocket.

Set this lot ablaze, the barn would go up in seconds.

Blake steadied the tinder box in his hands.

Hector Gallagher did not believe in taking chances. He had never believed the yarn that the blacks never moved at night. If you had an enemy and wanted to attack him, what better time could there be?

He was not a man who needed much sleep and had got into the habit of spending half the night sitting up in a gully he had found halfway up the hill. The massive trunk of a gum tree was at his back so that nothing could come at him from the rear and he was free to concentrate on the buildings of the run spread out two hundred yards below him and clearly visible in the moonlight.

He saw the shadowy figure come out of the darkness and cross stealthily towards the hay barn.

Quick as thought, Hector was on his feet. He had his rifle but in the moonlight it was too long a shot to risk. He would have to get closer. Besides, shooting might not be the best answer.

Never came at night, did they?

His lips parted in a savage grin, instantly extinguished. Catch him and question him first, that was the way. The killing could come later.

Carefully his eyes searched the ground separating him from the buildings but nothing stirred. The intruder was alone.

Hector moved stealthily down the hill, a deadly shadow in the moonlight. He reached the nearest building, flicked an eye around the angle of the wall.

Nothing.

He moved a yard or two, conscious of sweat starting along his hairline. He paused. Looked again.

Again nothing.

The dazzling mix of moonlight and shadow made it difficult to see anything. He moved another foot, looked again, hand sweaty on the stock of his gun.

A figure crouched at the door of the barn. Hector could not see what he was doing. He hesitated. He had meant to grab him; now was unsure. The man was up to some mischief, that was certain. He was bound to be armed. Where was the point of getting into a scrap with him? It made more sense to knock him over from here. That way there would be no danger: at ten yards he could hardly miss.

He clicked back the hammer of his rifle and raised the butt to his shoulder. The sound must have carried; the figure straightened, turning swiftly towards him. Hector's trigger finger tightened.

Gavin sat up.

'What was that?'

Even as he spoke he was out of bed, dragging on breeches, thrusting bare feet into boots. He pushed his arms into his shirt, snatched up the rifle that he always kept primed and ready against the wall beside the bed and ran to the door.

'What is it?' Asta stared at him from the bed.

'Sounded like a shot.'

'Be careful . . .'

Asta's warning died disregarded on the night air behind him. Rifle in hand, he raced out into the moonlight.

For a moment he could see nothing beyond a confusion of shadow and brilliant light, then made out two figures standing by the door of the hay barn. He ran towards them. They turned to face him: the Gallaghers.

'What's going on?'

Hector answered. 'Saw a blackfeller. Thought he was trying to set the barn on fire. I took a shot at him but I reckon I must've missed.' His voice quavered; he sounded like an old man.

Gavin squinted at him in the darkness. 'You all right?'

'Why not?' Belligerently.

Now was not the time to argue the point. Gavin peered into the moon-dazzled darkness. 'Where did he go?'

Hector waved his hand towards the bush. 'That way.'

'Was he alone?'

Before Hector could answer the barn door creaked open. Jason stood there, eyes half-sealed with sleep. 'What's going on?'

'Someone tried to burn the barn,' Gavin answered abruptly. 'Your mate there, is he?'

Jason was wary. 'They don't go out in the dark.'

Gavin exploded in exasperation. 'This fellow tried to make bacon out of you! Get Michael out here, see if he can find any tracks. If we get on with it we may still have a chance to catch him.'

'Too late,' Blake said. 'He'll be long gone.'

Jason turned back into the darkness of the barn. The men by the door heard the murmur of voices. Eventually Mura sidled into the moonlight. His eyes, wide and apprehensive, watched the darkness.

'Get on with it, man,' Gavin said impatiently. Now was not the time to be too tender about the black's fear of darkness. Someone had tried to burn down one of Gavin's buildings and he wasn't going to let him get away with it if he could help it.

Mura shuffled forward, Jason beside him, the men bringing up the rear. Mura's shoulders were hunched, his eyes quartering the ground. For a time he stood motionless, eyes seeking, then raised his head and spoke to Jason.

'He says no-one's been this way.'

Blake said derisively, 'How can he see in the dark, anyway?'

Gavin looked at Hector. 'Where did you say the man went?'

Again the vague gesture. 'Over there . . .'

'And you saw him by the barn door?'

Hector nodded.

'Then he must have come this way. Tell him to look again.'

'It's too dark,' Blake said.

'Be quiet.' Gavin was in no mood for Blake.

Again Mura looked, eyes scanning the ground. He walked forward a few steps, crouched down, examined the ground, then repeated the process until he had covered the whole area. He stood. Without looking at Jason he threw a few words into the air.

'Well?' Gavin demanded.

'Nothing.'

Hector said, 'I *saw* him, I tell you. Bloody black don't know what 'e's doin'.'

Perhaps recognising the contempt in Hector's voice, Mura took a few steps to one side, pointed forcibly at the ground—*there* and *there*—spoke again.

Jason told Hector, 'He says the only person who's been this way tonight has been you. You came down this way from the hill and went behind the other buildings.'

Gavin stared at his supervisor. 'Is that what you did?'

'There was someone here, I tell you. Where's he supposed to have gone?'

'Perhaps he hasn't gone anywhere,' Jason said.

'What's that supposed to mean?'

Jason stared deliberately at Blake. 'If there really was someone, it means he's still here.'

'What the hell's that supposed to mean?'

'This is getting us nowhere,' Gavin decided. 'I'm going back to bed.' He turned away.

'Ain't we goin' after 'im?' Blake demanded.

Gavin shook his head. 'Too late now. If there was ever anyone here at all he'll be long gone by now. As you said earlier.'

He went back into the house and slammed the door.

Blake sidled a step, threateningly, towards Jason. 'You don' learn to shut your mouth, one o' these days I'll be shuttin' it for you.'

Jason looked him up and down. Blake was bigger than he was but he was not frightened of him. 'Sure you haven't tried it once tonight already?'

'Why you . . .!'

Blake gathered himself to spring. At once Hector backhanded him viciously and he fell sideways. He shook his head, twisted as quick as a cat and was about to spring up again, then paused as Hector raised a ham-sized fist.

'You done enough all ready tonight!' He was shaken how close he had come to killing his own son; would have done so, had Blake's reflexes not been so good. He turned to Jason. 'An' you get back in yer box, too, if you don' want a taste of the same.'

And stood there, as big and solid as one of the buildings, until the tension went out of the air and they obeyed him.

FOURTEEN

A month later, in the relative peace that followed the departure of the drays loaded with fleeces, Asta sat in the open doorway of her house and stared unseeing across the stump-pocked ground that flowed away towards the distant sea. Her mind was peopled with images.

A white face as she had first seen it: grimed with dirt, heavy with suspicion, eyes shuttered against her. Jason, she thought, my consolation and my cross.

Jason's companion, stick-limbed, heavy-featured, eyes and teeth a white glare against the dark skin.

The two figures, white and black, were set against a kaleidoscope of other images: grass bending before the wind as storm clouds surged across the vast and empty plain; rain marching in grey columns across the land and rebounding a foot high from earth dry after months of sunshine; lambing, shearing, crutching, fencing, the repetitious shift and stir of life on a sheep run. Too much rain followed too little; whirlwinds stamped their trails of destruction through the crops and scattered the panicked flocks in empty-headed confusion; the natives, invisible but ever-present, waged spasmodic war against them.

Sheep speared. A shepherd's hut burnt. A second unsuccessful attempt to kill Cato Brown. Frontier country.

Blake Gallagher was constantly nagging Gavin to mount another expedition against them.

'Sort out the bastards once and for all . . .'

Blake grew taller and harder with every day. He dominated all but Gavin himself and his dark eyes were filled with hatred for the black people whose land they had taken.

Not only for the black people, perhaps.

He has always been trouble, Asta thought. He always will be. I said he was a mad dog and so he is, too strong for the bars of convention and discipline that presently contain him. God help us all when he breaks through them.

God help Jason, in particular. He and Blake had hated each other from the first. Gavin had told her little of what had happened during the raid on the camp—which told her a good deal—but she had heard how Blake had almost killed both boys when he had come across them in the bush after the raid.

Asta eventually heard other things, too, that several of the natives had been killed, women and at least one child among them.

'Why?' she had screamed at her husband, her anger and despair beating like the wings of birds against the walls of the wooden house. 'What had they done to us?'

The dead child in particular haunted her, bringing back the sharp-edged agony of Edward's loss.

'My gift from the sea,' she said now, mimicking savagely the fulfilment and delight she had felt when first she had seen Jason's face among those of the returned men. A gift polluted by blood.

'A house built in blood will be destroyed in blood.'

She uttered the words to the sloping land, the penned sheep, the rumbling and invisible sea. They had stained the land with blood and, some day, blood would be demanded of them in return. She knew it as she knew that tomorrow the sun would rise in the east; it was inevitable.

Asta's thoughts moved to the place on the cliffs, a hollow in the crumbling rock where a seep of water nourished a profusion of moist growth: ferns and creepers, lichen staining the rocks in patterns of brown and green. She had chanced on it on one of her rambles, a cool grotto shielded from the sun by a rocky overhang.

She had told no-one of its existence. It was private, the one place that brought her a measure of peace. After rain, the seep trickling audibly over the broken stone, she liked to sit there alone, eyes shut, ears and senses opening like the petals of flowers to the coolness, the trickling sounds of moisture, the damp exhalations of the green plants, and imagine herself back in Norway, the cliffs black and welcoming above her head, the white-painted houses reflected in the dark waters of the fjord.

She had found a large, flat stone. She placed it on other stones, an altar crowned with greenery that she replaced on every visit. The water flowed across the stones like a libation.

I am the high priestess, she thought, the guardian of honour, love, decency. If I try hard enough, perhaps the light will still conquer the dark. Was not forgiveness a feature of civilisation, too?

Sitting now in the open doorway of the house, Asta's thoughts returned to Jason. So far forgiveness had not been a characteristic of Jason's attitude to her, to any of them. He had been sullen, resentful, and Gavin, predictably, had grown sick of it.

'What do you want him for?' he had demanded for the hundredth time.

Gavin had put away from him the remorse he had felt after the raid on the native camp; indeed, after the niggling rash of attacks, the deaths of precious sheep, he would not have undone the events of that night even if he could.

'I've half a mind to let him go,' he told her. 'And he can take that black mate of his with him. The others don't want them around, I'll tell you that.'

'I suppose they would feel happier if you killed them, too,' Asta said, stiff back, stiff words, bleak and snapping eyes.

Gavin grew angry, feeling under attack. 'Maybe in Europe people can take time to argue about right and wrong. We can't. This is survival country.'

'Kill or be killed,' Asta said. 'Very civilised, I am sure.'

'It's the way life is. If we keep them we'll live to regret it.'

Echoing Ian's words.

Gavin was a harsh man but until now the harshness had always been tempered by an underlying gentleness. Now his eyes were like grey ice, his face set in planes of uncompromising determination, and Asta saw that the gentleness was gone, stolen by this land of fire and stone in which, it seemed, there was no place for kindness or compassion or humanity. Even the youth she had thought would in time come to replace her own son remained as unrelentingly hostile as the land in which they had found him.

Since his arrival she had tried without success to make friends with him. Now Gavin wanted to be rid

216

of him. From his point of view she could understand that but would never agree. She had set her heart on the boy. There were dangers for her in doing so; if she could not win him she would be alone as never before. Yet without him she faced a future filled only by heat and isolation. In the truest sense there would *be* no future.

She would not accept it. Her lips set in an implacable line.

No.

No.

She shouted her defiance into the brazen shimmer of the sky.

'NO!'

If it were her destiny to live out her days in this harsh and unforgiving land it would not be because she was the sacrifice for other people's ambitions. That would be intolerable. She would decide her own destiny.

Jason would stay.

She stood, brushing dust from her black dress. There was food to prepare. While she was doing it she would consider what must be done about Jason, the future.

Resolutely she turned her back on the sunlight and went into the house.

The empty drays returned from Adelaide, bringing with them the news that the wool clip had fetched a price more than three times Gavin and Ian's most optimistic predictions.

'Fair snatched it off the waggons,' Luke Hennessy said. 'There was clippers lined up all along them new wharves they've built down at the port. Counted ten of 'em alongside or anchored out in the bay. Never seen nuthin like it.' And sucked his teeth, remembering the scurry and bustle, so strange after the emptiness of the bush.

Gavin sent word to Ian and the next day the Bungaree contingent rode in. They were all hungry for news and were not disappointed. There were tales of settlers moving into the empty land to the north of them, of farms and even towns spreading like a rash across the Adelaide Plains on the far side of the gulf, of inns and staging posts lining the route to the city where before there had been nothing.

'That mine done it,' Luke said. 'The one they call the Monster. They say it's the biggest copper mine in the world. There was drays full o' copper all the way to Adelaide.'

'A long haul,' Gavin said, remembering the drays they had passed on their way north.

'Not for long. They're opening up a trail to Port Henry at the head of the gulf. Save 'em weeks, they reckon.'

Gavin frowned. 'Port Henry? When we came up that way, I didn't see anywhere that would serve as a port.'

Luke cackled. 'It ain't much. No more'n a creek a few yards wide. They bring the barges as close inshore as they can at high water and wait till the tide goes out. Then the drays go alongside and they put the copper on board before the tide comes back in again.'

The two cousins went into the house, opened one of the remaining bottles of wine to celebrate their good fortune, looked awkwardly at each other.

'Quite a moment,' Gavin said.

A month ago they'd had the two runs, the sheep and the clothes they stood up in; now money was running out of their ears. It was hard to get used to the idea. A few more seasons like this and they would be rich, not that either of them was about to tempt providence by saying so.

Both of them felt that one or other of them should say something to mark the occasion but what was there to say, after all? You did the best you could. Sometimes the hard work paid off and sometimes it didn't. This time, it seemed, it had. Nothing to make speeches about.

Ian raised his drink. 'Here's to next year.'

He tipped the contents of the glass down his throat.

'Cheers . . .' Gavin followed suit.

They stood side by side in the doorway and stared out at their property, seeing not only the paddocks running away from them up the hill, the creeks swollen with water from the rains that continued to fall, but the invisible rise and fall of their land stretching from the coast to far beyond the skyline and southwards towards the tip of the peninsula.

'Maybe we should think about getting more land,' Ian suggested.

'Doubt there's any available,' Gavin said. 'Be a steep price if there is.'

'We can afford it.'

'I was thinking of something different.' Gavin topped up his glass and gazed at it reflectively. 'Luke talking about the Monster Mine reminded me. There's a German fellow, Walter Lang, owns a copper mine down Kapunda way. Neu Preussen, he calls it. He wrote to me when we were still living outside Adelaide. Said he was looking for an investor to help him develop the mine. We didn't have any money so I did nothing about it. Maybe I should get in touch with him again, see if he's still interested.'

'What do we know about mining?'

'We know there's money in it. Dutton and Bagot were making a killing out of the Kapunda Main before we left Adelaide and by the sound of it this Monster Mine is doing even better.'

'Mining's a risky business,' Ian said.

'Show me something that isn't. We could all be dead tomorrow if the blacks turn nasty. Besides, it spreads the risk. Where are we if the price of wool collapses?'

That night, as the light was beginning to go, Mura made his way from the well head to the cluster of farm buildings. He and Jason had nearly finished the new well—hard work with all the rain they'd been having—and he was tired, his body aching from the effort of swinging a spade in the confined space at the bottom of the shaft.

Thirty yards ahead of him Jason had already reached the first building. At Mura's back the bush crouched, dark and dripping with moisture. Something on the path caught his eye.

Three feathers, black and white, in a group.

Mura crouched, studying them. He did not touch them. They were oyster catcher's feathers. What were they doing so far from the sea?

Mura stood, watching Jason's back, but his friend did not turn. He looked cautiously about him at the darkly shadowed bush. A glint of white caught his eye. Another feather, seemingly caught in the lower branches of a tree. He stepped into the dripping undergrowth. The shadows devoured him.

The next morning dawned overcast but by midday

the clouds were thinning. The Bungaree visitors had stayed overnight and Asta suggested the three women should all go for a picnic on the cliffs.

'A picnic?' Alison repeated, delighted.

'We have worked hard,' Asta told her, 'now it is time to celebrate.'

They had indeed worked hard, baking bread, cooking meat and vegetables, preparing great fruit tarts as large as waggon wheels for what would be the first party ever to be held at Whitby Downs. With the news the drays had brought from Adelaide they had something to celebrate, after all.

Celebration or not, Mary declined the invitation, saying she must stay behind to look after her mare that had started coughing.

'An hour,' Asta said, 'maybe two. Surely you can spare that?'

Apparently not.

Asta was not prepared to argue. If Mary did not want to accompany them, so be it.

'It will be the two of us, then,' she told Alison.

'Where are we going?' Alison asked.

'To the cliffs.'

They packed a basket—a small cake she had baked especially, a tart, cold meat, cordial—covered it with a cloth and put on their bonnets and cloaks. As they opened the door of the house the sun broke through the clouds and shed a yellow beam of light upon the grassy slope leading downhill towards the invisible sea.

'The sun,' Asta said, laughing, lifting her arms towards it. 'It has come out to greet us.'

What better omen could they have than that?

They walked side by side down the hill. The grass-clad slope flowed ahead of them without cover of any kind while to their right the bush along the creek lay dense and impenetrable, a dark cloud against which the sun was powerless. The creek had been brought to life by the recent rain. They could hear it splashing through a series of low cascades on its way to the cliff top and its long, final fall into the sea.

Asta smiled at Alison as they reached the secret grotto. 'I have never brought anyone here before.'

Was not sure why she had done so now but was pleased that Alison was delighted with the place.

'So pretty . . .'

Asta picked ferns for the altar to replace those that had died. The rain had increased the flow of water so they could hear the spring above the rumble of the sea one hundred feet below them. Asta watched Alison as the girl listened, entranced, to the restless scream of gulls, the trickle of water, the reverberating crash, crash of the distant waves.

'This is a secret place,' she said. 'I didn't know it was here.'

'Nobody knows it's here,' Asta told her.

'Apart from us.' Alison was delighted with its romantic secrecy. 'Thank you for showing it to me.'

They spread the folded cloth on the emerald turf, began to take the food out of the basket and arrange it on the cloth.

Alison was puzzled. 'Has Uncle Gavin never come here?'

'He is too busy for picnics,' Asta explained.

It had not always been so. Inland the plain stretched for miles to the far coast and the other gulf that lay beyond it. Asta sat on the edge of the cliff, listening to the breaking waves, remembering . . .

Shortly after their arrival on the peninsula she and Gavin had gone inland together, riding hard across the wind-rippled grass, the horses' manes tossed by the wind, Gavin's hand never far from the rifle holstered by his saddle. It had been a wild, exultant ride. The wind had filled their hair, their lungs, their being. When they reached journey's end they had made love passionately in the grass on the cliff top. Asta would never forget the feel of the sweet-smelling grass crushed beneath her naked body, flowers stitching the grass with bright threads of red and yellow and blue. She had drawn Gavin down so that lying together on the sun-warmed ground the heads of the grass were above their heads and they lay immersed in a green and rustling sea.

In those days she had still wanted to make love with her husband, had been eager for the weight of his body on hers, the hard male thrust of his body inside hers, the sharing and mingling of breath and body, the cries upon the wind as they clung entwined together.

Then and now, she thought.

There was a loose pebble by her feet. She leant forward, picked it up and weighed it contemplatively in her hand before tossing it into the void. She watched it fall.

She remembered when she had last had such a feeling. It had been the evening of her thirty-second birthday, before she had known that Jason existed. The day when Blake had killed the cat.

Another world. Another lifetime.

It was not only Jason; this place itself had changed them. It would change them more if she permitted it. That was the key: *if she permitted it*. Things did change, even the earth had its seasons, but they were not the earth. They had a choice.

Streams *could* flow in the desert. If Gavin will not come to me, she thought, I must go to him. I will not permit things to die between us. Easily said, no doubt, but Asta was determined and what she determined she would do.

She smiled gaily at Alison, filled with joy and, at that moment, faith in a shared future.

'Come,' she said. 'Let us enjoy the food we have brought.'

'Two of their women are alone on the cliffs,' the messenger said.

It was the opportunity for which they had been waiting yet still Nantariltarra hesitated. To kill the women would mean war. He did not see how they could hope to win yet knew he had no choice.

The warriors were clad in their fighting paint, white lines forming traditional patterns across the black bodies, spears and woomeras in their hands. They looked expectantly at Nantariltarra.

He had no wish to kill anyone but there was no way back. With heavy heart he gave the order. 'Let us go, then.'

He led the way through the dense covering of bush that fringed the creek.

Something was troubling Mura, and Jason did not know what it was. Asking him about it did no good: he put on his sullen face and pretended he didn't know what Jason was talking about.

They had finished the well and that morning Gavin had set them to building a dam to contain the water that flowed down the creek during the wet season. It was miserable work. Jason was cold, wet and covered in mud and did not appreciate mysteries. It was the first time since coming here that Mura had shut him out. There had to be a reason for it: an important reason, perhaps.

He had known from the beginning there was bound to be trouble with the clan: not the pin-prick raiding they'd had so far but something more serious. He thought Mura's furtive behaviour might have something to do with that. It was important to know; if he failed to ask the right question it might mean a spear in the guts.

He rested his shovel on the ground and looked at Mura working beside him.

'On our way back last night . . .'

Mura neither looked at him nor stopped working. The skin over his shoulder muscles gleamed as he drove the shovel into the earth and levered out another dollop of heavy clay to add to the wall that was beginning to take shape.

'What happened to you?' Jason asked.

'Nothing happened to me.'

'I was a yard or two ahead of you when we left but you didn't get back until at least ten, fifteen minutes after I did.' He watched Mura from the corner of his eye but the black face revealed nothing. 'Thought maybe someone spoke to you on the way back.'

Mura chucked another lump of clay to join the other lumps, said nothing.

Jason said, 'If anything's happened that affects me or the people here I reckon I should know about it. *Atjika.*'

That stopped Mura, as he had intended.

'What?'

'I said *atjika,*' Jason said. 'Mate. You're my mate. You know that.'

Mura wiped his face with his hand but would not look at Jason. 'I know it,' he said.

'If something's going on I reckon I've the right to know.'

The chop, chop of the shovel in the heavy ground. Mura paused, wiped his face again.

'You hear me?' Jason said.

'I hear you.'

'So talk.'

Mura had to choose. Last night, at the meeting to which the feathers had summoned him, he had already chosen by refusing to return to the clan, by deciding to stay here in the camp of the white men. Now, it seemed, he had to choose again and he hated it.

He looked at Jason. 'How do you know there's anything going on?'

'I know.'

Mura looked intently at the yellow mud before him, the blade of the shovel shining with water.

'The women . . .'

'What about them?'

'Maybe they shouldn't go off by themselves.'

'Why? What's going to happen to them?'

Mura shrugged.

Jason seized his arm. '*Tell me!*'

For a moment he thought he would get no answer, then, reluctantly, Mura said, 'That Mrs Matlock, she's always wandering about. You tell her, she keeps doing that she might meet trouble.'

'What sort of trouble?'

Beneath the heavy brows the dark eyes showed nothing. 'Plenty of snakes along the cliffs,' Mura said.

'Snakes? More like a war party, eh?'

'People are dead,' Mura said simply. 'The spirits tell them to kill. You tell Mrs Matlock, better she stay home.'

'And you? Am I going to have to kill you, too?'

'*Atjika*,' Mura told him. 'Like you said: I'm your mate.'

Jason risked one more question. 'When?'

'Tell them today. Otherwise it may be too late.'

'Jesus!' He turned away, paused. 'Mura . . .'

'What?'

'Thanks, eh.'

Jason climbed up the muddy bank and began to sprint across the paddock towards the house.

'Where you think you're going?'

He turned. Hector Gallagher came stumping towards him from one of the lambing pens.

'Looking for Mrs Matlock.'

The overseer scowled. 'You're here to work, my beauty, not lounge around chattin' to the ladies.'

Jason glared, not attempting to conceal his dislike. 'Two minutes, that's all.'

Hector set big fists on his hips and thrust out his chest at Jason. 'Not two minutes. Not two *seconds*. You get back to the work Mr Matlock give you.'

'I don't have time to argue with you,' Jason said and went to push past him. Hector grabbed him, Jason raised his arm to break Hector's grip and the burly overseer hit him once, savagely, in the face.

Jason fell full length on the wet grass, staggered to his feet, nose swelling already, saying thickly through a mouth hot and coppery with blood, 'Now just a minute . . .'

And Hector hit him again in the same place, as savagely as before. Jason felt his nose break in a blinding flash of pain and once again measured his length on the ground.

He was up even before he knew it. He saw Hector's expression change from contempt to alarm, then saw nothing, all sensation swept away by a wave of scalding rage. Hector stepped away, trying to evade him, but Jason was all over him, punching, butting and gouging. Hector tripped, they both fell, arms wrapped around each other, rolling to and fro across the ground, until Jason ended on top, knees on either side of Hector Gallagher's chest, clenched hands driven up to the knuckles in the overseer's thick neck. Gallagher flung his body from side to side in a frantic attempt to dislodge him but Jason clung on, knees tight, clenched hands tightening inexorably while Hector's face turned red then purple and the furious eyes stood out of his head.

A metallic click somewhere behind his head. A voice said something. Caught up in rage, Jason barely heard it.

Beneath him Hector's body heaved once again but his strength was going and Jason hung on without difficulty. There was a deafening explosion and scorching blast of air beside Jason's ear.

A voice said, 'If you don't let go of him the next one will be through your head.' Gavin's voice.

'How old are you now?' Asta asked.

'Almost fourteen.'

'You will soon be grown.' Holding up for their shared wonder the mystical experience of being a woman. 'Growing up in a wilderness. We must make sure you have some education, at least.'

By education Alison knew that Asta meant book learning. She was not in the least interested. Such information would not help her at all in her life. She sought to change the subject.

'Tell me what things were like when you were a child,' she asked, not altogether deviously. She liked hearing about Asta's childhood in Norway, the shivery stories of the old Norse gods.

'You have heard all those old stories before,' Asta said, pleased nonetheless. 'What do you want me to tell you?'

Gavin was spitting with rage. 'Any more of this behaviour and you can get out, the pair of you.'

Massaging his neck Hector said, ''E's been a troublemaker since the day 'e come 'ere.'

He, too, was furious: at Jason for attacking him, at himself for letting it happen, most of all at Gavin for not taking his side as he had expected.

'When I want your opinion I'll ask for it,' Gavin said.

'But—' Jason tried to interrupt.

'And you,' Gavin said, cutting him off. 'I told you to dig out the dam. Why are you wandering around over here?'

'I was on my way to warn you,' Jason said.

Gavin's eyes sharpened. 'What about?'

'I think there may be trouble from the blacks.' Jason repeated what Mura had said.

'Is it true?'

'It may be.'

Gavin nodded. 'We'll take no chances. You,' he said to Hector, 'find Blake. The pair of you get out there and warn the shepherds, quick as you can. My cousin, too. He's out there somewhere. Bring them all back here to help defend the place. When you've done that—'

'I don't think they'll try a full attack,' Jason said.

'Why not?'

'It's not their way. They're more likely to try and pick us off one by one. The women in particular.

Especially if they're alone and unprotected.'

'Where's Mrs Matlock?' Gavin interrupted. 'Where's my wife?'

'That's why I was going to the house,' Jason said. 'To find out.'

'We'll check. You come with me.' He turned to Gallagher. 'What are you waiting for? I told you what to do. Get on with it. And *hurry*, man!'

He ran to the house, Jason on his heels, shoved open the door.

'Asta . . .'

Silence greeted them, a thin swirl of dust in the empty room.

'Damn!' He came out into the daylight and saw Mary with her horse in the nearest paddock. 'Have you seen Asta?'

'She's taken Alison for a picnic on the cliffs.' She came to the paddock rail. Her face was anxious. 'Why? What's wrong?'

'Blacks on the war path.'

Her face went white. 'Oh God . . .'

But Gavin had no time to spare for Mary. He turned to Jason. 'Go and look for them. I'll stay and keep an eye on things here.' He thrust his rifle into Jason's hands. 'Know how to use this, do you?'

Jason looked at it, its weight easy in his hands. He had never handled a rifle in his life but felt immediately at home with it. 'I'll manage,' he said.

'Take my horse and get down to the cliffs as quick as you can. Find Mrs Matlock and Alison and bring them back here.'

Jason was already running for the horse that was tied by a halter to the corner of the barn.

Gavin ran also: into the house, picking up the gun that he had told Asta always to take with her but that she always forgot. He went back outside and looked about him. Across the paddock Jason, hair flying, head stretched forward over the horse's neck, was just disappearing over the crest of ground that lay between the farm buildings and the sea. All seemed still, unchanged. Sheep grazed peacefully upon the slope behind the house. Along the creek bed, the undergrowth held its breath.

From up the hill came the thwuck, thwuck of a spade. With all the excitement Gavin had forgotten about the black boy. He hefted his rifle and walked up the hill towards the sound.

Jason rode over the brow of the slope and straight into them.

There were about a dozen of them, loping swiftly across the open ground towards the cliff top. They heard the horse's hooves on the turf and spun to face him, spears ready. The white paint on the black bodies gleamed like bones. Jason was on them before either he or they could do anything about it. The faces, the painted limbs, were all about him. He had a fleeting impression of spears thin as reeds but deadly, oh yes, he had seen what those spears could do. His mount reared, feeling itself surrounded. He had a second in which to think, *So Mura was telling the truth*, black bodies scattering, dust blowing in clouds, and he had a glimpse of Nantariltarra's face, clearly recognisable beneath the paint, as he broke through them. He twisted his neck to look behind him as he rode; he tried to tighten his legs around the horse's sweating barrel but knew how insecure he was, riding not one of his skills. A couple of spears flew after him and fell harmlessly in the dust. They would certainly have recognised him but he could not tell whether it was this or the fact that he had taken them by surprise that had caused their low-key response.

Asta and Alison must be somewhere nearby. It was too late to collect them and take them back to the house as Gavin had wanted. Yet if he dismounted and confronted the blacks . . .

Body reacted before thought could reason. He hauled in on the reins, bringing the horse sliding and snorting to a halt. He leapt to the ground, rifle in one hand. That should be a help—they knew only too well the power of rifles—or would it? The possession of a gun marked him as an enemy. They had enough spears to take care of a single enemy, rifle or no rifle.

The war party was thirty yards away. Moving deliberately, Jason raised the rifle above his head, lowered it ceremoniously to the ground before him, straightened, stepped across it to leave it lying behind him on the grass and again raised his hands, empty now, above his head.

He thought, flesh cringing, if they are going to kill me they will never have a better chance.

Among the party of blacks, no-one stirred. The massed bodies were a shadow against the light.

Heart beating suffocatingly in his chest, Jason walked slowly towards them.

Jason returned with Asta seated on Gavin's horse, Alison walking at his side. By the time the little party reached the run it was like an armed camp. Gavin came out to meet them, the slab buildings at his back bristling with the muzzles of guns.

'You took your time! If anything had happened—'

Anxiety had stoked his rage.

'Something did happen. I met a whole war party of them on the cliffs.'

Gavin stared, unsure whether to believe him or not. 'Then why . . .?'

Aren't you dead?

The unspoken words hung between them.

'They knew me.'

Gavin hated things he could not understand.

'You'd best tell me about it.'

Jason told him of his meeting with the armed men. 'I made a deal with them.'

Gavin eyed him suspiciously, trusting only arrangements he had made himself. 'What kind of deal?'

'We'll let them stay, use their traditional hunting grounds, let them take a sheep from time to time. In return they'll leave us alone.'

'Take my sheep!' Gavin exploded indignantly. 'Never, by God!'

Jason was walking two feet above the ground; it was the second time since his return to the world of white men that he had thought he was dead yet had somehow survived. Not just himself; he had managed to pull this man's wife and niece from the jaws of death, too. Now Gavin Matlock was complaining about the odd sheep.

'Seems a cheap price to pay for your wife.'

Gavin's eyes sharpened at his tone. 'I do my own deals. When I want you to act for me I'll tell you.'

Jason had thought he would be a hero but heroism, it seemed, was not so easily acquired.

'Would you have preferred us to be killed?'

'I'd have preferred you to use the rifle! That's why I gave it to you!'

'One rifle against twelve spears? What would be the good of that?'

Gavin hated being told. 'Now you listen—'

Asta said, 'I cannot believe what I am hearing! Jason saved our lives and now you talk to him as though he is a criminal.'

Gavin did not look at her. 'I'll thank you to stay out of my business, Asta.' His cold eyes remained fixed on Jason. 'As for you ... Any more arrangements, I'll make them myself. Understand?'

'One thing I wish to make clear,' Asta said. 'I am not your servant nor do I expect to be spoken to like one, least of all in front of the men.'

Gavin wondered at her cold dignity but was not about to have his wife tell him what he should and should not do. 'And I do not expect you to interfere when I am talking to them!' Yet the last thing he wanted was a fight; he decided to appeal to her emotions. 'I was frightened for you. Can't you understand that? I had visions of you speared to death! How do you expect me to react?'

Asta was not so easily placated. 'The point is we were not dead. We did not know even that there was anything wrong until Jason came down the cliff and told us. He saved our lives, Gavin! And because he promised them a few stupid sheep you treat him like a thief!'

'Those few stupid sheep, as you call them, are our living!'

'And your wife and niece are unimportant?'

Gavin was in the wrong and knew it. 'For God's sake, woman, stop nagging me!'

Asta had something further to say but knew better than do so at the moment. That evening, however, sitting in front of the fire, after the Bungaree party had departed and they were alone again, she brought up what was in her mind. Deliberately, however, she came at it from the side.

'You do not like me talking about business,' she said. 'Why is that?'

Gavin's feet were stretched peaceably to the flames but all his senses came abruptly awake at her words.

'It's not a woman's place to worry about such things.'

'Why is that?'

Despite himself Gavin felt exasperation mounting. 'A man concerns himself with business, a woman with the home. That's the way it's always been! I want no changes in my house.'

'You think the success or failure of the business does not affect me, too?'

'Of course it does—'

'Then it is right you should discuss it with me, is it not?' Her smile as warm as a northern glacier. 'It is your decision, that I understand. But to talk first, is it so unreasonable? Who knows, I might even contribute some useful ideas.'

Gavin thought that was unlikely. 'And what words of wisdom do you have for me tonight?'

He heard the sarcasm in his voice. It outraged him to discuss with Asta something that by rights should have been none of her concern. It was a reflection on himself, a sign of weakness that he did not have proper control over his wife.

If she noticed his tone she gave no sign. 'The money from the shearing. What had you thought to do with it?'

He watched her cautiously, trying to read her thoughts. 'Ian was talking about buying more land.'

'And you? What do you feel?'

'I was thinking of trying something different.'

'Not to leave here?'

He laughed. 'Certainly not. But spread our risks a little.'

'Into what?'

'There's money in mining. That German in Kapunda wanted me to invest with him.'

'Walter Lang. I remember the name. You said he was not an easy man.'

'Not easy at all but I reckon he knew what he was doing.'

'Does he still want capital?'

'One way to find out.' He looked at his wife, the flames flickering golden across her face. He took a deep breath. 'What do you think?'

It was the first time he had asked Asta's opinion about anything to do with business. He was surprised how easy it was.

'I think it is a good idea. Write to him, why not? Go to see him, if he sounds interested.'

The next day the cousins met again.

Ian said, 'This business of the blacks will have served one good purpose, anyway.'

'What's that?'

'It'll have made up your mind about the black boy. You won't be keeping him now.'

It was bad enough hearing this sort of thing from his wife; he was not about to take it from his cousin.

'Why shouldn't I keep him?' Letting his exasperation show a little.

Ian laughed. 'Not if you want to sleep at nights.'

'I went and talked to him, while Jason was looking for Asta and Alison. He was still working, good as gold. I see no reason to get rid of him just because of what his mates in the bush have been doing.'

'You're off your head.'

'When I want your opinion I'll ask for it.'

Ian stared, anger rising. 'Now wait a minute—'

'No, you wait a minute.' The frustration of having to put up with Asta's interference had bitten deep and he was not about to take it from anyone else. 'This is my run. I'll do what I want on it.'

Ian breathed deep. 'Not if it endangers the rest of us! My daughter could have been killed.'

'But wasn't. And the man who saved her was obeying my instructions.'

'By chance.'

'Not by chance! By my specific orders. I don't recall you doing much.'

They glared at each other, anger spilling over after the trauma of the previous day.

'You've said enough,' Ian said.

'No more than I should have said long ago. You don't run this place nor are you likely to. I reckon you'd best stay away until you remember that.'

FIFTEEN

Three months later, after the exchange of several letters, Gavin set out to meet Walter Lang in Kapunda.

He took Asta and Jason with him. The journey on horseback took them north around the top of the gulf to Port Henry, already renamed Port Wakefield, then south down the drovers' road, even more rutted and dusty than when Gavin and Asta had seen it last.

A week after leaving Whitby Downs the travellers reached the summit of the last range of hills and rode down into the smoke and commotion that was Kapunda. In the midst of a group of buildings a tall stone-built chimney belched clouds of acrid smoke. Supervised by a pale-faced boy in rags, an undernourished horse drove a creaking whim round and round amid piles of grey stone. Everywhere was steam and the clatter of machinery.

'Doesn't look much of a place,' Gavin said.

Jason stared with interest at the scurrying figures of men. 'Got a bit of life about it, though.'

Gavin had brought Jason to provide extra firepower, should they need it on their journey. Blake or one of the shepherds would have served as well, possibly better, but Jason was more easily spared from the run. He had also wanted very much to come and that, too, was important: Gavin was uncomfortably aware how much he owed him for saving Asta's life.

Asta, too, had pushed him to bring Jason along—pushed to the point where he had almost said no—but it had made sense and at last he had agreed in spite of her.

Gavin beckoned to a man blinking suspiciously from the open door of one of the shacks.

'How do I get to Mr Walter Lang's house?'

The man scratched his head. 'Up along,' he said, pointing beyond the belching chimney. 'Tesn't likely he'll be thur now, mind.'

Gavin struggled to understand the man's speech. 'Where can I find him?'

'This time o' day he be underground, I blaw.'

'Underground? But he is expecting me.'

'Don' know nuthin 'bout that,' the man said. He turned an indifferent back and went into the shack. The flimsy door clapped shut behind him.

Gavin's tight mouth expressed exasperation. He turned to Asta. 'I'll drop you off at the hotel and go on to the house myself. There's bound to be someone there who can tell me where he is.'

The house, stone-built and substantial, was surrounded by open land set with strictly disciplined bushes and young trees, a patch of what looked like vegetables standing to attention in one corner.

Gavin rode up the driveway, dismounted and knocked on the door.

'Mr Matlock for Mr Lang,' he told the maid.

She stared suspiciously at his travel-stained clothes.

'*Moment*.' She disappeared into the house, closing the door firmly behind her.

A minute later and she was back.

'Please to come in,' she said in a heavily accented voice. '*Herr* Lang will see you.'

She showed him into a room crammed with furniture as heavy and solemn as a troop of dragoons. The walls were papered in maroon silk and hung with a myriad of small portraits—oval frames, square frames, rectangular frames—and knick-knacks of various kinds. In one corner a palm in a large copper container thrust leaves like sabres halfway to the ceiling. The windows were small and shaded by the overhanging roof of the outside veranda. Even the air held its breath.

'Please to wait,' the maid instructed him. 'The master will come.' And went out. The door closed behind her.

The silent room, ponderous with the manifestations of wealth and power, conveyed to Gavin the message that was no doubt intended, that Walter Lang, late of East Prussia, was a man of consequence, a personage of weight and influence.

Gavin was not a man easily intimidated. He strolled to a window and stared out. The house overlooked the mine. What view it had was of earth scarred by workings, a wilderness of broken stone beneath a pall of steam and grey smoke.

He couldn't imagine anything worse than living in such a place, however smart the furniture.

He turned away from the window as the door opened. Walter Lang was physically as imposing as the heavily furnished room: stout and tall, with big shoulders and a strong neck, eyes hard and commanding in a square face framed by mutton chop whiskers. He came forward, feet soundless on the thick carpet, powerful hand outthrust.

'Mr Matlock, how good it is to meet you at last.'

His grasp was firm, too firm perhaps, but Gavin was no weakling and gave as good as he got. Honours even, they smiled at each other, recognising in each other a potential opponent as well as—possibly—an ally.

'You had a good journey, I hope?'

Gavin shrugged. 'Long.'

'Then you will have some refreshment.' He rang the bell. 'Come . . . Sit, sit.'

The same maid came, Lang barked instructions in what Gavin assumed was German, she withdrew to return a minute later with a silver tray: two small glasses and a bottle containing a colourless liquid.

'Schnapps.' Lang filled each glass to the brim. He raised his, waiting until Gavin had followed his lead. '*Prosit*!'

He tossed the contents of the glass down his throat. Gavin did likewise. It was the first time he had tasted anything like it and its harsh heat caught his throat. Somehow he managed to avoid coughing.

'Strong,' he said, smiling into the hard eyes assessing him above the empty glass.

'A man's drink. Another?'

Gavin nodded, not trusting his voice, and held out his glass. Lang refilled it and settled back in his chair. 'So,' he said, 'you also are a victim of coppermania, is that so?'

'I wouldn't say so,' Gavin said, 'but I'm not averse to making a mining investment if the returns are there.'

'The returns are very good,' Lang told him, 'but only with a successful mine. It is a speculative business, you understand.'

'You seem to have done all right out of it,' Gavin offered.

241

'Neu Preussen is a good mine. New Prussia, you understand? You speak German, perhaps?'

'No.'

'Ah. Well, it is unimportant.'

Gavin thought it was perhaps more important than Lang was prepared to admit.

'When we corresponded before I left for the peninsula you told me you were interested in outside capital to develop the mine. From our recent letters I understand that is still the position.'

'The position has changed,' Lang said. 'When we wrote originally I was by myself but since that time I have gone into partnership with Mr Joshua Penrose, a mining engineer from Cornwall. His knowledge is very useful to me.' Lang's smile glittered like sunlight on ice. 'That and his capital, *ja*? But now we are thinking of expanding further, so additional capital will be needed. We had thought to raise it from our own resources but if a suitable outsider wished to make us an offer . . .' He shrugged: take it or leave it.

Gavin saw he was in for a long, hard bargaining session.

'What inducements do you have to offer an outside investor?' he asked.

'Inducements?' Lang laughed: ho, ho. 'Risk we offer our investors,' he said. 'Danger. The possible loss of capital. Mining is a risky business. More people lose than gain. Especially those lacking the technical knowledge,' he added, ice-floe smile glinting.

No-one hearing Lang would have guessed that Gavin had come to Kapunda in response to his specific invitation. Perhaps it was time to remind him of that. Gavin drew Lang's letter from his pocket and opened it slowly and deliberately.

'Let us talk some more about the contents of your letter,' he said.

Alone in her hotel room Asta stripped off her travel-stained clothes and stood naked, looking about her. The mattress on the brass bed was lumpy, the water cloudy in the washing jug, but Asta had long grown used to worse inconveniences. She poured water into the china basin and sponged herself all over, scrubbing her skin until it glowed. She dressed herself in clean clothes, putting on some of the garments, fashionable once, that she had brought with her. Her dark green satin dress had a tight-fitting, boned corsage adorned with a fan-shaped piece of blue silk and full-length sleeves puffed moderately at the elbows. Kapunda might not be much of a town but was the only one Asta had seen for years and she was determined to make the most of it.

Finally she brushed her fair hair until it gleamed, put gloves on her hands, a hat with a small peak and decorative feather on her head and was ready to face the town and whatever it had to offer.

She went out of the room and knocked sharply on Jason's door.

'Come,' she said without opening it, 'let us go and see this town.'

He opened the door. He had not washed, was wearing the same dusty, creased clothes in which he had arrived.

'*After* you have smartened yourself up,' she said.

Jason scowled but she took no notice of that, had indeed expected it. Clothes for him had been a problem from the first. When he had arrived he had been wearing nothing but a kilt made out of skins.

It had been patched, filthy, fit only for the fire. Asta had taken the kilt, nostrils fastidious, and destroyed it. She had not asked his permission, had been determined that from the first he would be clean, at least. Gavin was twice Jason's size but she had taken some of her husband's old shirts, a pair of breeches, and fashioned them to fit the new arrival. She had presented them to him, he embarrassed and hostile. She had wondered if he would refuse them, would perhaps confront her without clothes at all, but he had not. Fortunately his savagery seemed no more than skin-deep.

'You have another set of clothes,' she instructed him now. 'We should make ourselves smart before we go out to see this new town.'

'Town?' Jason was derisive. 'Rat hole, more like.'

But went back into the room, having learned respect for this strange woman and her whims. She was quite capable of dressing him herself and he was not prepared to risk that.

'And wash your face,' she hectored him through the closed door.

Outside the hotel they paused, deciding which way to go. It didn't seem to matter. In either direction the view was the same: piles of grey stone, rutted tracks, sparse vegetation scorched black by fumes, the groan and clatter of machinery.

'How people live in such a place I do not know,' Asta said.

'I've lived in worse than this,' Jason said, remembering the stews of Hobart Town.

It was the first time he had volunteered anything about his past and she willed him to go on but he did not.

'People like you don't know what it's like to be poor,' was all he said.

Passers-by, some ragged, some sturdy, clumped along heavy-booted. Women in sacking aprons stood at the doors of the hovels that lined the rutted lane. All of them stared as Asta and Jason passed but none of them answered when Asta, feathered hat and quality gown, greeted them.

'Are they deaf?' she wondered.

'They dislike us. You in particular.'

Asta stared at him, astonished. 'Why should they dislike me?'

'They think you're some rich woman slumming it.'

'I am not rich.' She laughed at such an absurd notion.

'You don't have any money but in your head you're rich and it shows.'

'How do you know such things?' she asked him.

'I was born in a place a lot worse than this. In Hobart Town I had nothing at all.'

'Did your parents not look after you?'

He laughed bitterly: the only answer she needed.

Pensively she resumed her walk. 'It seems you know more about these things than I do,' she told him.

'Why exactly have we come here?' he asked.

'Mr Matlock is thinking of going into partnership with the mine owner.'

'What does he know about mining?'

Asta did not reply and Jason wondered why he had bothered to ask. Whatever the Matlocks did would not affect him one way or the other. However friendly Mrs Matlock was, the gulf between them was unbridgeable. At heart, without even knowing it, she was rich, with the attitudes and assumptions of the rich, whereas he was poor and would always be poor, never mind how much money he might accumulate in his life. The way of life of the people they saw about them in this raw mining town was utterly foreign to her whereas to him it was like coming home.

'These are my people,' he said with satisfaction.

She thought, I do not care what your background is. *We* are your people now, not these slum dwellers. But had the wisdom to say nothing.

I shall win him over, she told herself, as confident of this as she was of all things concerning him. It is just that he does not know it yet.

'We shall go back now,' she said.

At Lang's house the two men had finished their initial discussions. There would be many more talks before a deal could be struck but they were both satisfied with how things had gone so far.

'Perhaps you and your wife will honour me by coming here to dinner tonight?' Lang suggested.

Gavin hesitated, testing the invitation for possible dangers, but could find none. 'That would be very civil.'

'And perhaps the young man you have with you.' Lang smiled genially.

It had been too much to expect that Lang would not have been aware of everything about them from the moment they had entered the town; he owned a goodly proportion of it, after all, along with Dutton and Bagot who had been the first to discover the rich lode of copper on which the various mines were now based.

Gavin kept his face expressionless. 'I am not sure he is ready to eat in civilised company.'

Lang raised shaggy eyebrows. 'How so?'

Gavin explained how Jason had come to them. Lang smiled, saying nothing. He made it his business to know what was going on in the world about him and was already familiar with the story. He thought it would be interesting to see the boy for himself.

'Bring him anyway,' he said. 'It will be interesting to ask him about his experiences.'

'If you can get him to talk about them you will have done better than we have,' Gavin said.

But it was not himself the miner had in mind to ask the questions of Jason. 'It will also give him an opportunity to meet someone of his own age,' Lang said. 'My son Stefan.'

He smiled genially and stroked his whiskers. Let the two boys make friends with each other and I shall soon know all there is to know about him. About Matlock, too, perhaps.

'Perhaps you would like to take a look around the mine before you return to your hotel?' he suggested.

The two men rode down the hill side by side, Walter Lang on a grey the size of a war horse, Gavin astride the bay gelding that had brought him from Whitby Downs.

The miners' cottages were clustered around a spring about half a mile from the main workings but had already begun to extend up the hill towards the site of the mine itself. The tiny buildings were mostly of wattle and daub construction, whitewashed and thatched with straw. Bags covered the open window spaces and blew gently in the wind.

'They have no glass,' Lang explained as they rode past. 'Glass is expensive, not so?' His barking laugh was as hard as his eyes. 'At least the bags help to keep out the flies.'

'Must be hot as Hades, this time of year,' Gavin commented.

'As ovens,' Lang agreed. 'Some of the men have built their houses partly underground to try and get away from the heat. One or two wanted to dig burrows along the creek bank as they have done at the Burra Burra mine further north but I would not allow it. Too much danger of disease, you understand.'

As they approached the mine workings they passed long tables strewn with mounds of broken rock. Gangs of barefoot boys clustered around the tables, picking over the lumps with a speed and dexterity that Gavin found extraordinary.

'Mine pickers,' Lang explained in his lordly way. 'We pay them six shillings a week to separate the ore from the dross.'

Lang reined in by a half-built chimney spiked with scaffolding around which a gang of men laboured furiously. From a large brick building fifty yards away came the thunder of machinery, the constant hiss of steam that hid its roof in a swirling grey cloud. 'Smelt house.' Lang had to shout to be heard above the din of the machinery. 'We refine our own copper here.'

'What is the chimney for?'

'The mine output has been falling,' Lang explained. 'There is too much water. We have bought a pump and condenser from England to pump the mine out. It should be operating in June. Then we can follow the lode deeper.'

'So we cannot see the new workings now?' Gavin asked.

'They do not exist.'

'And the present ones?'

'You can see them, certainly. But it will be dark and dirty and in some parts dangerous.'

'Dangerous?'

'There are holes, flooded sections ... Mining is dangerous, Mr Matlock. Physically and financially. As many speculators have learned to their cost.'

'So I can see nothing?'

'Would you know what you were looking at if you could?'

'Perhaps not.' He could see the frenzied activity that surged about him; perhaps that was all he needed to see.

'This town is going ahead,' Lang told him. 'Since we have been in correspondence for so long I would like to make you the first offer to join Penrose and myself in our new extension. But you understand it is not our most important concern. Mr Penrose owns another mine—Wheal Sennen—and I also have other interests. Besides, if you feel you would rather not join us I am sure there will be many other takers.'

Gavin suspected Lang was right but was uneasy at investing so much money in a venture which he understood so little and which, at this stage at least, he could not even see. Lang was looking for five thousand pounds. It was a fortune. There was another problem, too. Lang's bluntness grated. Gavin was used to being in charge of his own affairs; how would he feel investing money in an operation where this man would be calling the shots?

'I should like to meet Mr Penrose,' he said.

'You shall. At dinner.'

Joshua Penrose turned out to be a garrulous, red-faced Cornishman of perhaps fifty, not tall, with broad shoulders and a winning smile.

'Welcome to Kapunda, Mr Matlock,' he said. 'And Mrs Matlock, of course.' Bowing.

'You will pardon Mrs Lang's absence,' Lang told Asta. 'I own another house at Langmeil, in the Barossa Valley, and she seldom comes to Kapunda.'

Penrose winked at her. 'I'm afraid, Mrs Matlock, that you will also have to put up with me by myself since there is no Mrs Penrose at all.'

'You are a widower?'

'Bachelor, ma'am. Could never find a woman to take me.'

They went in to dinner: Lang at the head of the large mahogany table, Gavin and Asta on either side of him, Penrose next to Asta and the boys Jason Hallam and Stefan Lang at the foot.

'I hope you are enjoying the Miners Arms?' Penrose smiled ironically.

'We are used to plain living,' Asta told him.

'You'll get that at the Miners Arms, sure enough.' He stared at her frankly, moist lip and lively eye. A bachelor he might be but one who evidently enjoyed the company of women. More than their company, perhaps. 'There is talk of a new hotel,' he told them, 'but that won't be for a while yet. Always assuming they can get a licence for it.'

'They will get it,' Lang said. 'Mr Whittaker is behind the venture and he is no fool.' He turned to Gavin. 'Mr Whittaker runs the store and post office. He is one of our leading businessmen.'

'I thought you were that,' Gavin said.

'I have certain interests,' Lang conceded. 'It is necessary to diversify to survive, is that not so?'

'Survive?' Penrose laughed, face redder than ever. He raised the glass he held and tipped its contents down his throat. 'Mr Lang owns half the Barossa Valley.'

'You, of course, are the true adventurers.' Lang addressed Gavin as he had all evening; Asta was a guest at his table but not, it seemed, to be included in his conversation. 'Living on the very frontiers of civilisation.'

'It can be basic living, at times,' Gavin acknowledged.

'There is a Lutheran pastor wishes to minister to the natives in your area,' Lang said.

Gavin had little time for ministers, Lutheran or otherwise. 'I would not advise it.'

'Is it true you lived with the natives?' Stefan asked Jason.

In this grand house, seated at the elaborately laid table, Jason felt as out of place as a pig in a tree. He looked closely at the youth facing him, unsure whether to respond to this initial overture or not.

'Yes,' he said cautiously.

'What was it like?'

There was no way of explaining what he had learnt and experienced during his time with the *nunga*. He compromised. 'It was different.'

'Different in what way?' Stefan was slightly built, perhaps a year younger than Jason, with brown eyes and a deeply cleft chin.

'Nothing like this,' Jason said, gesturing at the room. 'They don't have houses at all.'

Stefan's eyes grew round. 'Where do they sleep, then?'

'On the ground. It's not too bad, when you get used to it.'

'And where you are now . . . Do you sleep on the ground there, too?'

'Of course not.'

'What's it like?'

'Oh,' Jason said airily, thinking of the hay barn in which he slept. 'Like this. Only larger,' he added.

'Do you have mines there?'

251

Jason was not prepared to admit to the complete absence of mines in the area of Whitby Downs. 'Not yet,' he said.

'Have you ever been down a mine?'

'No.'

Stefan glanced cautiously up the table but the other diners were listening to one of Joshua Penrose's anecdotes and were paying them no attention. He leant across the table. 'Would you like to?'

'Can you arrange that?'

'Of course. I go down all the time. My father doesn't know. He'd stop me if he did.'

'Why would he do that?'

'He says it's too dangerous.'

Just the challenge Jason needed.

'All right,' he said. 'Let's go down the mine.'

The banshee howl of the mine whistle fractured the early morning air as Jason slipped out of the hotel and made his way along the lane towards the clutter of mine buildings.

They had agreed to meet at the site of the new chimney. A team of men was already at work. Jason expected that any moment someone would ask him what he was doing but no-one took any notice of him.

He looked about him. Spindly wooden gantries, connected to each other by a spider's web of ropes and pulleys, leant this way and that like a party of drunks. Around the workings piles of dirt several times higher than the buildings rose into the early morning sunlight. Over everything was an air of ferocious and focused energy the like of which Jason had never witnessed before. Everyone was working as fast as they could and, watching the scurrying, purposeful figures, he felt something of their excitement stir in him.

'I wondered if you'd come.'

He turned: Stefan stood grinning at him. He was holding two resin hardened hats, each with a tallow candle secured to the brim.

'What do we want the hats for?'

'In case we hit our heads.'

The shaft was a square of darkness descending into the earth.

'How deep is it?' Jason did not often feel apprehensive but did so now.

'Fifteen fathoms.'

Ninety feet . . . He had climbed a lot higher on the *Kitty*'s rigging but there he had been able to see what he was doing. Here it was the darkness rather than the depth that troubled him.

'They wanted to go deeper but they hit water. They've brought out an engine from England. When it's working they'll be able to pump out the water, then they can go further down.'

'Why should they do that?'

'Because that's where the best ore is.'

'How do you know?'

'My father says so.'

How does *he* know? Jason wanted to ask but did not.

'Let's go down,' Stefan said.

'How?' Sounding nervous despite his efforts.

'Down the ladder, of course.' Stefan looked at him. 'You scared?'

'No.' But was.

Stefan swung himself over the lip of the shaft and climbed out of sight. Jason hastened to follow him. The blackness of the shaft was a horror to him but it would be a hundred times worse if he had to grope his way down alone. Of course there was nothing to make him go at all but not for the world would he back off now.

He lowered himself backwards over the edge of the shaft, feeling the depths sucking at him. His arms and stomach were trembling, his feet groping for the first rungs of the ladder fastened to the timber framework of the shaft.

He tested the first rung nervously. It felt secure enough. He lowered himself, feet groping, hands groping, until he found the next rung. His breath was loud in the narrow shaft. Below him was a rustle of diminishing sound as Stefan clambered swiftly down the ladder.

Jason gritted his teeth and followed, foot by foot, yard by yard.

It grew dark, utterly dark. He could see nothing at all. The weight of the blackness pressed upon him. He craned his head to look upwards, trying to gauge how far he had come. Above him the rectangle of light shone with a painful brilliance. It was difficult to judge how far away it was; certainly not as far as he had hoped.

No help for it. He went on down. Slowly his arms and legs got more into the rhythm of things, panic ebbing as he went.

The air was warmer here, stagnant, as though it had been lying at these depths for a very long time. It was wetter, too, the ladder's rungs slippery with moisture. Jason looked down and saw a faint flicker of light far away in the depths of the earth. He hoped it marked the bottom of the shaft. He went on, the flickering light drew nearer, and as he came to it realised that it was not the bottom at all but the entrance to a horizontal tunnel opening up from the main shaft.

Stefan was there, candle burning on the brim of the hat that he was wearing. Jason stepped into the tunnel beside him. Beneath their feet the shaft continued its silent plunge into darkness.

'Let me light your candle . . .'

They moved down the tunnel, Stefan leading. The roof was low and they had to crouch almost double to get along. Before they had covered fifty yards Jason's back muscles had begun to protest at the unnatural way of walking.

Imprisoned in his fluttering cone of light, Jason heard sounds of activity emerge from the tunnel ahead of them. The sounds grew louder until the tunnel opened into a chamber hewn from the rock and Jason saw about him the smoky flame of candles and hunched, scurrying shapes of miners working. Picks rang on rock, boots clattered, loads of broken stone were shovelled into wheeled skips. The din was as absolute as the silence that had preceded it. There was dust as well as noise; it swirled about them, irritating eyes and throats, casting a grey pall across the candlelight.

It was like arriving in hell.

Once again Jason was mesmerised by the frenetic movements of the miners: everyone active, everyone knowing what he was doing. Hell it might be but it excited him, the idea of extracting riches from the rock.

'How do they know what they're doing?' He had to shout to be heard above the din.

'They know.'

Which was no answer.

'How did anyone know the copper was here?'

'They found the lode on the surface and followed it down.'

A dark oval in the rock wall on the far side of the

chamber showed where the tunnel continued. Stefan gestured towards it.

'We'll go through there in a minute.'

Jason was anxious to explore further. 'Why not now?'

'Because they'll be blasting soon to bring down more rock.'

A whistle blew, the sound penetrating in the confined space. A number of figures emerged from the far tunnel. The men took cover. Activity ceased. They waited for what seemed a long time.

'What—' Jason began and the earth shook.

The flames of the candles gusted sideways. A cloud of dust and smoke jetted out of the tunnel opening, the dull thud of the detonation followed by a clatter of falling stone. Acrid fumes billowed through the chamber and set them coughing.

'Come on,' Stefan urged, 'before they start working in there.'

Without waiting for an answer he got to his feet, ran across the chamber and disappeared into the opening, Jason hard on his heels.

The fumes were far worse inside the tunnel but they groped their way along until they reached the place where the explosives had brought down the rock. The charges had been placed in a side gallery that was now half-filled with fallen stone. Light from the candles played over the rock's gleaming surface.

'How do we get through there?' Jason wondered.

'We don't,' Stefan told him. 'We go straight on down the tunnel.'

'Where does it take us?'

'To some old workings. I often go there. Come on!'

On the other side of the chamber the tunnel went on, dipping and ducking, splitting and re-splitting into side workings so confused and extensive that it seemed a marvel to Jason that the rock roof above them had not collapsed long ago.

They came to another shaft and, looking up, saw daylight far above their heads.

'One of the first shafts,' Stefan said. 'No-one's worked it for years.'

Jason knew he would have been lost here within minutes but Stefan made his way through the maze with the confidence of one who had been here many times before.

The Neu Preussen mine had been open only five years yet already these early workings, abandoned after the ore had been stripped from them, had begun to revert to the rock. The air tasted dead on their tongues, piles of fallen stone lay at intervals along the deserted tunnels, the timber shoring that held up the roof had begun to buckle under the unrelenting pressure of the hundred feet of rock and earth above them.

The process was still continuing; occasionally, above the sound of his own breathing, Jason heard a creak, a groan, from the roof to show that up there the earth was still working.

'Is it safe?'

Stefan's laugh rang off the rock walls. 'Of course it's not safe. That's what's exciting about it.'

It *was* exciting; frightening, too. Stefan was right: the sense of fear caused some of the excitement yet there was more to it than that, a sense of adventure that had nothing to do with danger. Riches that had lain undisturbed for millions of years ... Jason was excited by the idea that you could find them and by discipline, knowledge and determination bring them into the light. The thought had ignited a slow fuse within him.

'Look at this,' Stefan said.

On the far side of the chamber there was an opening in the ground. Jason went cautiously to the edge and looked down. A shaft, sides lined with timber, plunged vertically downwards. Twenty feet beneath them reflected candlelight danced on the sullen surface of water.

'This is as low as we can get until the engine's running,' Stefan whispered, the sound magnified by the closeness of the rock walls about them. 'Below this level everything's flooded.' He leaned right out over the edge of the shaft, staring down at the mirror of the water below them. 'Imagine what it would be like to fall in there. You wouldn't get out in a hurry.'

Jason could imagine it only too well: the darkness, the choking water, the futile screams echoing within the rocky chamber, the terrifying certainty that rescue would never come.

Fear destroyed his pride. 'Let's get out of here,' he said.

Stefan laughed. 'You're scared.'

It was true but even now Jason was not prepared to admit it. 'You said yourself we can't go any lower.'

Stefan's eyes reflected the candlelight, their expression unreadable. 'I spend hours down here, sometimes.'

'Doesn't your father mind?'

'He doesn't know. He's too busy.'

'Don't any of the miners tell him you come down here?' Jason asked.

Stefan laughed scornfully. 'He doesn't talk to them. Besides, they hate him as much as I do.'

'Why do you hate him?'

'He cheats. Me, everybody. He'll cheat you, too, you give him half a chance.'

He turned and led the way back through the

workings until they reached the area where the miners were clearing the stone that had been brought down by the blasting. What had first seemed hell now welcomed them like home. Surrounded by the scurrying figures, the shadows that leapt and pranced across the candlelit walls, Jason's fear evaporated. Stefan did not stop and Jason followed until they reached the main shaft down which they had entered the mine.

They looked up. Far above, daylight blinked.

'This is where they have the most accidents,' Stefan said. 'After a twelve-hour shift the men are tired. Sometimes someone falls.'

'What happens then?'

Stefan laughed. 'It depends how far they fall.'

He swung himself out over the drop and began to swarm up the ladder. A heartbeat and Jason followed him. As he climbed higher fear returned but above his head the rectangle of light grew steadily until at last, scarcely out of breath, he reached the surface.

The sunlight struck him like a blow, the breeze smelt indescribably sweet, the sounds and movement of the living world were all around him. He had come back out of the dead earth.

'Thank God,' he said aloud, not caring if Stefan heard him. He flopped on his back on the warm grass at the side of the shaft.

Yet something other than relief remained: the memory of the excitement he had felt at the idea that men with knowledge and imagination could claw riches out of the earth. It was a feeling he knew he would never forget.

He had found what he wanted to do with his life.

SIXTEEN

'My province,' Lang said. 'No discussion!'

The three men had met as always in the drawing room of Lang's house.

'We can guarantee nothing,' Penrose said.

Gavin stared them down. 'Consider it from my point of view. You say there's rich ground below the fifteen-fathom level but you can't show it to me because of the water. I don't know if you're telling me the truth or not.'

'Neither do we,' Penrose said. 'That's the point.'

'You have seen the reports,' Lang pointed out stiffly. 'You know as much about the mine as we do.'

Gavin hesitated. Did he trust these men enough to let them have five thousand of his hard-earned pounds to play with? Did he trust their experience, their instinct, above all their integrity? Did he trust himself to trust them?

Ultimately nothing else mattered.

'Perhaps I can say this,' Penrose said. 'We aren't in the cheating business. Mr Lang's other interests are all in this part of the colony. I've got Wheal Sennen, a piece down the road. Neither of us is going anywhere. We can't afford to cheat you, that's the size of it. Lose your reputation in this game, you lose everything.'

It was the truth. Gavin recognised it yet still hesitated.

Lang stroked his mutton chop whiskers. 'The first time we met I warned you that mining is a risky business. Risk to the miners' lives; risk to the financiers' capital. The rewards are high but the risks are high also. I am sorry if that is too strong for your stomach but there is nothing either of us can do to help you.'

Lang's words had the ring of truth, too, yet it was typical of the man that in his mouth even sound advice sounded like an insult.

There was nothing more that any of them could say.

Gavin stood. 'I shall let you know my decision by morning.'

For the twentieth time Gavin turned restlessly in the broken-backed bed.

Five thousand pounds. Enough to add five thousand sheep to his flocks. Enough to buy four thousand extra acres *plus* grazing rights to eleven thousand more and still leave him with a thousand pounds for additional stock. Five thousand pounds.

He turned again, arms and body fighting the thin blanket.

The same five thousand pounds would buy a quarter share in Neu Preussen mine, with all the risks of a mining venture thrown in, all the frustrations of having to deal with the stiff-necked Walter Lang. Lang would continue to own fifty percent of the mine, Penrose the other quarter.

He would be days' travel away. It would be impossible to keep an eye on his investment, even if he had understood what he was looking at. It was idiocy even to think about it. Yet if things worked out it would provide him in the space of only a few years with a return far above anything he could hope to receive from his land holdings. It would spread the risk so that if anything went wrong at Whitby Downs he would still have a measure of financial security.

Twist and twist again, brain seething.

At his side Asta said, 'I think you should invest the money.'

His immediate reaction was irritation. 'I am grateful for your advice. Perhaps you can also tell me how I keep an eye on things when I am so far away?'

She turned in the bed to look at him. A gleam of light from the starry sky outside the window shone in her eyes. 'Jason will represent you.'

He stared at her, thunderstruck. 'I daresay he knows even less about mining than I do.'

'Lang could train him. That would be part of your agreement. At least he has been down the mine. Lang's son took him.'

'He told you so?'

'Yes.'

'A mine is a place of work, not somewhere to go exploring. I shall speak to him in the morning.'

Asta placed her hand on his in the darkness. 'Please don't.'

'Why not?' Gavin was exasperated by her growing habit of telling him what to do.

'Because he told me in confidence.'

'A confidence you broke.'

'My dear, I have a loyalty to you, too.' She

paused. 'It seems that Jason was fascinated by what he saw.'

Gavin grunted. 'Extraordinary what some people like.'

'But don't you see? If he likes mining . . .'

He thought about Asta's suggestion. A youth, little more than a child, whom he barely knew and had no reason to trust, raised first in the slums of Hobart, then by a tribe of aborigines . . .

'Lang would run rings round him.'

'I don't think even Walter Lang would find it easy to run rings around Jason.'

From outside the window came the sound of drays passing. The creaking wheels, the volleys of yelled oaths and crackle of stock whips rose slowly to a crescendo and as slowly diminished.

'But what does he know?'

'If he is interested he will soon learn.'

Without conscious movement, they had drawn closer together in the bed. Gavin could smell Asta's hair, feel the warmth of her body beneath the bedclothes.

The closeness, the hint of intimacy, made him uncomfortable. Recently they had drawn apart, no question about it. She had changed and that had affected their relationship. Perhaps he had changed too. Determination, will, *did* change people, not always for the better, but without them he would have no hope of achieving what he had set himself to achieve.

He couldn't bear lying there a moment longer. He got out of the bed and thrust his legs into his breeches.

'I need to walk,' he said. 'I need to think. Alone.'

She neither spoke nor moved; he guessed she felt the same need as he to put space between them. He finished dressing and went out.

Outside a misty rain was falling. Up on the hillside an engine clanked hoarsely. Gavin walked through the darkness. The rain beaded his face and beard, ran moist fingers inside the collar of his coat. Another dray passed, the drover hunched deep into his coat and ignoring Gavin's greeting. He walked until the last buildings were behind him and he came out in open country. He climbed towards the summit of a grass-covered hill. It was a long way to the top yet as he walked he was conscious not so much of distance or time as of a sense of loneliness that increased with every step he took. Near the crest of the hill he stumbled over an outcrop of rock and remembered what Lang had told him, that eight years earlier Dutton had discovered the Kapunda reef by coming across such an outcrop bearing traces of green copper ore. From such findings millions were made . . .

Cloud covered the sky, an unseasonably chilly breeze brought tears to his eyes. He looked out at the blackness of the surrounding countryside; no lights, no hint of people, nothing. He wondered where he was going in his life and why.

From the first he had been concerned about Asta's unhealthy obsession with Jason. She had called him her gift from the sea, a hundred times Gavin had wished he had never come into their lives, yet without a future, a generation to inherit Whitby Downs, he supposed their lives would have no meaning.

Jason *was* the future: the only future they were likely to have. Perhaps, if he really did have an interest in mining, Kapunda might offer a useful niche for him: useful both for him and themselves. And perhaps, after Jason's help in saving Asta's and Alison's lives, might he not owe him as much, if he wanted it as Asta seemed to think?

As for Asta ... If he loved her (*surely he did*?) why hadn't he put his arms around her? Were they destined to drift ever further apart because neither of them was willing to make an effort to prevent it? It was a pretty damning indictment, if so.

From the valley beneath him came the thin, mournful shriek of the mine whistle. Today he would have to give Lang and Penrose his answer. Without someone on the spot to represent him he would never dare invest so much money in a project he did not altogether understand. Asta, Jason, Whitby Downs, now the Neu Preussen mine ... A dynasty in the making. But it would ultimately mean nothing, without the next generation to inherit it. We build not only for ourselves but the future, he thought. Without that, there is no point.

Jason meant far more to Asta than he ever would to himself. Why then had she suggested Jason should come here to work, so far from Whitby Downs?

He knew the answer even as his mind formulated the question; by persuading him to bring Jason into their affairs she was creating a family unit that in time would establish their line.

Yet for the future to be significant the present had to mean something, too. All their plans would be pointless without that.

He moved restlessly, thrusting his hands deep into his pockets against the cold. He identified what it was he had felt as he came up here, what he felt now. It was need. Need for a unity in his life. Need for Asta. Need for love. He thought perhaps, with luck, she needed it, too. He—they—needed to be made whole again.

'Pray God,' he said aloud to the misty darkness, the dagger-bladed wind. 'Pray God.'

After Gavin had gone out Asta lay for a long time, eyes staring sightlessly at darkness.

He had been right; they both needed to think what they were doing. By getting up and going out he had demonstrated what she had lacked: the courage to admit to herself that when it came to the important decisions in their lives they were better apart.

By his actions, she thought, he has done what I could never have done for myself. He has acknowledged that, whatever we may have been to each other in the past, we are no longer one.

She was grateful—or at least hoped that in time she would be grateful—for being forced to face that fact.

When we get back to the run, she thought, there are many things I shall be able to do to make my life worthwhile. Even if Gavin will not let Jason take a hand in his affairs—and he won't, I see that clearly now—I will still be able to do something for him, to help build the future, if he will let me. Otherwise why are we alive at all? Simply to be: she could not bear to think such a thing. To be and then to cease . . . She would never see that as a worthwhile objective.

The first thing she would do would be to arrange for Jason to be educated. She would make him belong. God knew how, but she would manage it somehow. *I shall be content*.

Lying there she told herself it would be easy, knew it was not. Nothing lessened the ache she felt, the sense that by getting up and going out in the middle of the night Gavin had drawn a line under everything that had happened in their shared lives until now.

'And I let him go . . .'

Distressed, she uttered the words aloud to the dark-blanketed room, yet did not know why the idea troubled her so much. If it was the right thing for him to have done, why should she feel such emptiness at what his action implied?

It would be light soon. Gavin would make his decision. He would invest in the mine or not. They would return to Whitby Downs. Life, one day following another day following another day, would continue.

Dear God, she thought, I cannot bear it.

She heard the building creak, creak again. The door opened.

'Who is it?' Voice nervous despite herself.

'I'm back.'

He came to the bed, groped, took her warm hands in his cold ones. The room was too dark to see anything but in her mind's eye she could see him: face grave, yellow hair swept back.

'I have come back,' he repeated.

She knew he meant more than that he had just returned from a walk. 'Have you?' she asked. 'Have you?'

She felt a wave of emotion so intense she thought it might carry her away. To save herself she held out her arms to him, groping blindly; he, somehow seeing or sensing her movement in the darkness, put his arms around her, cold strong arms about her soft warmth, and she felt herself dissolve, melting into him. Tears ran down her face, moisture down the inside of her thighs, everything breathless and yielding. Her mouth sought his, her arms enfolded him, hands clutching ribbed muscle as hard as stone, he was naked in the bed with her, fire and stone united, he was looking down at her as he penetrated her,

267

she biting her lip to prevent herself crying out, hips, thighs, body writhing sinuously beneath him.

She said, breath tangled with the words, 'I cannot believe you're back.'

He paused. 'I cannot believe I went.'

The searching, the probing, the mingled breath and cries, the future charted by the shared movements of their bodies.

'Now and forever,' she cried into his mouth as her first climax erupted.

'Now and forever . . .'

She came again, a third time, her voice a breathless echo, a sigh of fulfilment, the rounding of their refound unity.

'We do not have time for such things!' Lang slapped his hand impatiently on the surface of the mahogany table. 'Time is money, as you know very well!'

'That is my condition for investing in your mine,' Gavin told him.

'That you will nominate a representative to look after your interests in this town?' Angrily Lang repeated Gavin's proposition. 'We can represent your interests as well as anyone, I suppose. Better, I should say.'

'I want someone independent.'

'This is a slap in the face to us. It tells the world you do not trust us.'

'It is a matter of business.' Gavin had had enough of Lang and his bullying bluster. 'Take it or leave it,' he said.

'Perhaps we should leave it.'

'Please yourself.'

'And who would this . . . independent representative be?'

'I shall tell you within a month.'

'A month is too long.'

But the flame of Lang's anger had died to sullenness and Gavin knew he had won. He thought the time had come to raise the other matter he had in his mind. He had little time for the church but thought that Asta, though not religious herself, might welcome its presence in their area as a sign that civilisation was on the increase.

'The other evening you mentioned a Lutheran pastor who wants to minister to the natives in our area.'

'Reverend Laubsch? What about him?'

'If he likes he can come with us when we go back.'

'Why do you suggest it?' The lode of suspicion never ran far beneath Walter Lang's surface.

'It makes more sense for him to accompany us than travel alone.'

Lang pondered, looking for hidden motives but finding none.

Grudgingly he said, 'We could perhaps suggest it to him.'

'It is pretty country,' Asta said.

Riding alongside the waggon Jason turned in his saddle to look at the view. She was right. In front of them the ground fell away in a series of gentle waves until it reached the floor of a broad valley three or four miles across. On the far side of the valley the setting sun cast ribbons of golden light down the eastern face of another line of hills that barred the western horizon. Ripple by ripple the hills rose in a series of purple steps against the sky. Shortly before the hills an undulating band of green showed where a river wound peacefully along the valley floor. Here and there stands of gum trees gleamed white as bones in the last rays of the sunlight.

They had left Kapunda eight miles behind them and were planning to camp for the night on the banks of the river where there was a crossing and an inn. They had stayed there on the way south and Jason was looking forward to what was likely to be their last night in civilisation before they headed north on their long journey back to Whitby Downs.

'Pretty enough,' Jason agreed.

Asta smiled coquettishly at him from beneath the brim of the bonnet she wore against the sun and dust.

'Pretty enough,' she mimicked. 'Is that the best you can say?'

He didn't know what she wanted him to say but there was nothing unusual about that. For the last two days Asta Matlock had been acting in a way that Jason found quite extraordinary: laughing to herself—once out loud in the street, in full view of half a dozen astonished passers-by—making jokes, generally behaving like a girl of fifteen instead of an old woman in—what?—her mid-thirties.

Perhaps she was pleased that her husband had made up his mind to put money into Lang's mine. That could be it. Jason could relate to that—he had thought it a good idea himself, when she told him—but suspected there was more to it than that. For those two days she had seemed unable to leave her husband alone, touching and pawing him in a way utterly different from how he had ever seen her behave before. If Jason hadn't known them he'd have said they were in love but they had been married for years so that was clearly out of the question.

By the time they reached the river it was dark.

The lights of the inn cut the gathering darkness and cast long yellow gutters across the rippled surface of the ford, making the countryside on the northern bank seem even blacker and more desolate than it would otherwise have been.

They splashed their way through the shallow water and dismounted before the inn door. The main road north crossed the river at this point and a number of drays and waggons were drawn up in the shadows at the back of the wood-slab building. By the trail a sign had letters roughly scrawled upon it. Rifle Inn.

A gale of laughter and voices came through the door to greet them as Gavin shouldered his way inside, Jason at his elbow. The Reverend Laubsch stayed in the waggon. Gavin had expected nothing else. Julius Laubsch was built like a tower but was the meekest man he had ever met. He seemed interested in nothing but bringing the heathen, as he called the blacks, to the one true God. It was a vocation for which his training at the Hermansburg Lutheran seminary in East Prussia had ideally equipped him but unfortunately it had not made him a conversationalist. All the way from Kapunda he had sat with his nose stuck in a book and had made no more noise than a mouse.

There were half a dozen men inside the inn. There was a break in the conversation as they turned to look at the newcomers but seeing nothing remarkable about them began talking again almost at once. The man behind the bar shrugged his way towards them.

'What'll it be, mates?'

'Brandy,' Gavin said, 'and we'll want something to eat. There's a couple more of us out in the waggon.'

'Don't be shy,' the barman said. 'Tell 'em to come in.'

'One of them's a woman and the other's a preacher.'

A cocky-looking little man, cheeks flushed by drink, laughed. 'Bring the woman in here. The preacher can stay in the waggon.

'The woman's my wife.'

The man looked up at him, a half-full glass slopping in his hand. 'We all got our problems. Bring her in, who knows, maybe someone here will make you an offer for her.'

Gavin put down his glass.

'Excuse me,' he said to the bar keeper. He turned back to the man who had spoken to him. 'I said she's my wife. You trying to make something of that?'

The cockerel shrugged, grinning. 'Every wife I heard of got the same gear as other women. What's so special about a wife?'

Gavin hit him once, hard. The man's heels left the ground. He flew backwards into the wooden wall behind him and slithered down to the floor where he lay stunned.

Gavin massaged the fingers of his right hand.

'Pardon me,' he said to the bar keeper. 'I can't get used to the idea of a man speaking that way about my wife.'

'Be my guest,' the barman said. 'He's been nothing but trouble since he got here a few hours back.' He came from behind the bar and hauled the stunned man to his feet. 'On your way,' he said. 'We've had enough of you for one night.'

The man massaged his jaw, gave Gavin a baleful glare. 'I'll be looking for you.'

He staggered out of the doorway, turned to yell incoherently, vanished into the darkness.

Gavin shrugged, turned back to the bar. 'What's to eat?'

The man had no chance to reply before an outcry came from outside the inn: voices upraised and furious, one of them a woman's.

Asta's last two days had passed in a rosy haze of contentment. Overnight the months of growing estrangement had vanished. One evening had re-awoken in her all the emotions she had ever felt for her husband, emotions that she had believed had vanished without hope of recovery.

It was a good feeling. She had forgotten what it felt like to have a man in her arms who was not only loving in his behaviour but whom she realised she had never ceased to love. It gave her a feeling of hope as well as contentment. It gave her faith that they could do anything they wanted. Life had a new symmetry. Gavin would run Whitby Downs, Jason look after their interests in Kapunda. And she? She would hold the family together, combining all the qualities they needed of love and faith, the looked-for victory of light over darkness.

She smiled, at peace.

Tonight they would eat, talk around the red heart of the fire. Later she and Gavin would lie together in their blankets beneath the waggon, listen to the water flowing over the ford and watch the stars revolve in slow majesty across the night sky.

A din of raised voices came from the inn. A runtish man came stumbling through the doorway, arms gesticulating furiously. He yelled something over his shoulder then staggered towards the waggon.

'Hey . . .!' His gaze scoured her face.

Asta froze, very much on her dignity. 'I beg your pardon?'

'That your bloke jest gone in there?'

'What about him?'

'You 'n' me's goin' to have a chat, *that*'s what's about him.'

His words were so garbled that Asta could scarcely understand him. While she was still trying to work out what he was saying the man reached the waggon and began to scramble on to the wheel. Suddenly she realised that he was planning to get into the waggon with her.

'What do you think you are doing?' She tried unavailingly to push him away.

The man laughed. A gale of stale alcohol blew across her. 'Comin' to 'ave a chat, that's what I'm doin'.'

'Get off,' she cried and the Reverend Laubsch, motionless until now, joined her in trying to push the man off the wheel of the waggon.

'Get off!' he cried. 'Get down!'

Gavin was through the door in an instant, Jason and the bar keeper on his heels. The first thing he saw was Asta and Laubsch in the waggon, batting at the head and shoulders of the same man with whom he'd had the trouble inside the bar and who now seemed to be trying to climb into the waggon with them.

In three strides Gavin reached the man, seized him by the shoulder and dragged him off the waggon.

'I believe we've had enough of you.' He shook him until his teeth rattled. 'On your way before I do you some real damage.'

Standing five yards away Jason saw the man bare his teeth and clutch Gavin as though to steady himself. He saw his hand go to his waist, the gleam of metal. The man's arm went back, came forward again. The blade disappeared into Gavin's body with a meaty thunk. It was a slight yet portentous sound and Jason heard it above the voices from inside the inn, the ripple of water from the ford, the breath of air stirring the grasses along the river bank. A slight sound that filled and altered their lives.

Thunk.

Looking down at the two men Asta heard the thud of the blow, the grunt of effort that accompanied it, and saw the dark flood of blood that discoloured Gavin's plaid shirt. She had no time even to scream before Gavin sat down on the ground, a foolish, surprised look on his face. He coughed. Blood ran down his chin.

She had no time to think, no time for anything. Afterwards she could not remember moving yet one moment she was sitting in the waggon, the next she was on the ground, arms cradling Gavin's head, his dead weight dragging at her.

'There,' she said, 'there now.'

Even as she tried to soothe him she knew it was no good. There was a collapsed feel about Gavin's big body as though the muscles, the very structure of bones and flesh, had given up on him.

Through a froth of blood he said, 'He was rude about you.'

'Rude about me?' She did not understand. 'But I never knew him.'

What the man had said or done she never discovered. All her attention was focused on her husband's face, all her will directed towards making him mend.

Other men had come from the inn and stood in a silent half-circle around them. They were as helpless as she and she paid them no attention.

You will not die you will not die you will not die . . .

. . . The thought, determination, instruction running over and over in her head even as she knew that he was indeed dying, that all her hopes and plans were crumbling into dust at her feet, that what had been offered so miraculously was being snatched away again.

Because of a chance meeting, a fight it seemed about nothing, her husband, a man perhaps a hundred times better than the man who had killed him, was spilling his life blood in the dust and the future of all of them was placed in jeopardy.

Gavin's face convulsed, his eyes sought hers.

'Hush now,' she told him, 'hush.'

The world was a silent, anguished cry. She cradled him closer; his blood soaked her dress. Its sticky wetness was against her skin, she could smell it combined with the odours of dust, alcohol and flowing water.

She was close to tears, would not let herself cry. She was close to anger, used it to drive away the pain and fear that threatened to overwhelm her at the prospect of being left alone, of being forced from now on to make those decisions that Gavin had always been so reluctant to share with her but that from now on she would be unable to share with him.

Her world was torn by fear and grief.

Gavin coughed; a fresh spurt of blood ran over his lips. The harsh whistle of his breath pained her. She could do nothing beyond what she was already doing, cradling him, soothing him as best she could, sensing the life seeping away from him, from them both. She knew it was not enough.

I love him and hate him at the same time, she thought, hate him all the more for loving him so much. She felt betrayal at being so bereft. God damn him, how can he go and die on me now?

The tears came at last, despite her efforts.

Perhaps he felt the tears on his face; she never knew.

He grinned up at her: a twisted, cock-eyed grin. 'Don't worry about it,' he told her, voice broken, everything broken. 'Everything's going to be all—'

Never managed to finish the sentence.

Asta laid his head gently in the dust. She stood. The stranger who had caused the trouble was standing a little to one side, guarded by the bar keeper and two of the inn's patrons.

She walked over to him. He flinched from the expression in her eyes but said nothing.

'They will hang you, I suppose.' Words like ice from lips like ice. 'May God curse you. I would hang you myself if I could.'

Jason was swaying helplessly, face chalk-white.

'Put him in the waggon,' she told him. Her voice was cold, aged. 'We will bury him in the morning on the north bank of the river. I would take him home to Whitby Downs but it is too far.' She turned to the bar keeper. 'We shall need food. Death or no death, the rest of us have to eat.'

He looked at her. 'Right,' he said.

They fetched food from the bar and sat down beside the waggon. Jason found it hard to accept the idea of eating with Gavin's tarpaulin-wrapped body in the waggon beside them but she was right, the living needed food. Certainly Reverend Laubsch had no difficulty with the idea: he worked his way through the contents of his plate with a grunting enthusiasm that, had Jason not been so hungry, might have spoiled his supper more effectively than the presence of the corpse in the back of the waggon.

When they had finished Asta put her plate on one side.

'Mr Matlock and I have no living heirs,' she said. 'Everything that belonged to him therefore comes to me. That is the law. Whitby Downs was my husband's; it is now mine. His interest in Neu Preussen: that is mine, too. I shall continue to run things as he would have done had he lived.'

Whatever Jason had expected her to say it was not that. He had never heard of a woman running anything: neither ship nor mine nor sheep run. It was not the way of nature.

'Do you think you'll be able to do it?'

'Tell me one reason why I cannot.'

He thought, the Gallaghers, there are two reasons, but said nothing. If Asta Matlock did not know it now she would learn soon enough without his sticking his nose in.

'I shall need you to help me in Kapunda,' Asta said. 'Mr Matlock wished it. So do I. I must have someone I can trust to keep an eye on things for me. Someone who knows about mining or is willing to learn.'

'I don't know much,' Jason said.

'All the more reason to apply yourself to your lessons.'

Jason's face showed alarm. 'Lessons?'

'Of course lessons. Mr Laubsch will teach you to read and write and reckon figures. That is all that will be necessary.'

'What will Mr Lang say about that?'

'He will say nothing. It is none of his business.'

Jason looked dubious. He doubted he would be able to handle a man like Walter Lang at all, whatever Asta Matlock might think.

'You will learn to deal with Mr Lang,' Asta told him. 'I have watched you. I know you can do it.'

They arrived at Whitby Downs on a calm day of bright sunshine. She had sent Jason on ahead with the news and Ian Matlock was waiting for her. Only then did Asta's nerve fail her. The face that had been so calm and resolute shattered into a hundred lines of grief and doubt. She walked into the house, Ian stepping behind her as though he owned it.

He said, 'A terrible tragedy, my dear. I rode over as soon as I heard. Don't worry. You'll be all right. I'll take care of everything.'

'Thank God,' she said. Relief flooded her like the tides. 'I intended . . . so much. But now I look around me and see what has to be done—'

'Don't fret about it, lass,' he said kindly. 'We'll go through his things, you and I. I'll help you throw out what you don't want. Some of his clothes could go to that aboriginal lad, maybe. Tog him out decently, they would.' He nodded at Gavin's rifle propped by the door. 'I'll find a good home for that, never fear. Treat it like my own, I will.'

Her uncertainty was reflected in her face. She ran her hand through her hair. 'Thank you, Ian.'

'I'll get Mary to come and give you a hand. We'll join the runs into one unit. Makes better sense that way. I'll get a count of the flocks, work out what I owe you.' He laughed, let his hand linger momentarily on her shoulder. 'You needn't worry, I shan't cheat you.'

'Of course not.'

He smiled kindly at her evident confusion, went back out into the sunlight.

Funny how things worked out. She was lost, completely out of her depth. Well, it was to be expected. Alone in the world with problems she had not the first idea how to resolve ... He would take care of them, as he had promised. No cheating, either, that wouldn't be right. Probably the best thing once she was over the worst of her shock would be for her to go back to Adelaide, to Europe, even. Yes, happen that would be best. He would take care of everything.

He stood, hands on hips, looking about him. Well, Gavin, he thought, we fell out, you and me, and now here I am and you're six feet under. I'd not have thrown it in your face when you were alive and I'll not do it now but that's the way of things. This whole area is mine now. In time it'll pass to Alison's husband, then to her children. A regular dynasty we're building here, by God.

He saw Jason loitering by the side of the house.

That was one thing he'd sort out straightaway. If the lad was prepared to work, know his place, he could stay but no more of this long-lost-son nonsense.

He hailed him sharply. 'You. Come here.'

On top of the waggon, Hector Gallagher hefted the last bundle of stores that the returning party had brought from Kapunda. He passed it down to Blake, noting the ease with which his son accepted the heavy load.

Aye, he thought, you're getting stronger by the day. The next generation, by God. Won't be long before you're ready to take over. You think you're ready now but it takes more than muscle to run this operation. It takes brains: and that's where I come in.

He said, 'This is your opportunity, lad.'

Blake placed the crate on the pile of other crates. 'What opportunity's that, Da?'

'Now Gavin Matlock's dead, Ian will take over.'

'We don't know that.'

'Who's to stop him? Asta Matlock will never run it by herself, will she? There's no-one else.'

'What difference if Gavin or Ian Matlock run things?'

God save us, Hector thought.

'Alison's the difference. The man who marries her stands to inherit the lot, in time.' He laughed, slapped his son on the shoulder. 'Needn't look like that! I've seen you watching her! You wouldn't mind getting aboard her, I can tell.'

'Alison Matlock hates my guts.'

'So do something to make her change her mind! There's only one person you need watch out for.'

'Who's that?'

'That Jason.'

'I just want to know, that's all. If I'm to take orders from Ian Matlock or not.'

Asta felt herself drowning in confusion. I am *helpless*, she told herself.

'Perhaps it would be best,' she said uncertainly. 'For the time being—'

'If you've a mind to run things you must do it now. Otherwise Ian Matlock will take over and you won't be able to do anything about it. Of course, maybe that's what you want—'

'No,' she said, 'it is not what I want but I know

nothing about sheep or mining or money. Tell me, what would you do?'

'If it was mine? I'd fight him for it.'

She took his hands in hers, looked searchingly into his eyes. 'And will you help me if I fight him?'

'I can't. No-one can. What you don't know doesn't matter, you can always learn that. But standing up to Ian Matlock . . . No-one can help you there. You have to do that alone.'

A spark, a stream of sparks, ran between them. 'You are right,' she said slowly. 'Of course you are. How do you know these things at your age?'

He laughed awkwardly and withdrew his hands from hers. 'I don't know a lot,' he said, 'but I know that much.'

'I will do it,' she said. 'And I shall never forget it was you who helped me to see what must be done.'

'Ian Matlock told me to go out to the north of the run, give Sinbad a hand with the flocks. You want me to do that?'

'You stay here. Go and find Mr Laubsch, tell him I want a memorial service conducted outside the door here in, let me see, twenty minutes' time. Make sure everyone is here for it.'

'You want me to *tell* Ian Matlock or ask him? He's likely to throw a fit, I start giving him orders—'

She smiled grimly. 'Tell him,' she said.

Standing in the yard with the rest of the group, the sun beating down on her head, Asta listened with impatient half-attention to the missionary's heavily accented voice braying of memory and memorials. Trepidation, excitement, resolve sent the blood coursing through her body. She thought, the only memorial that Gavin needs is this run and he won't have that if I don't take a firm grip of it *now* and run it the way it must be run. Jason was right. It is *now* that matters. No-one, least of all Ian, must have time to draw breath, to think about what is happening.

She stepped forward, hand raised. Laubsch hesitated, broke off what he was saying.

'Thank you, Mr Laubsch.'

She faced the rest of them. 'Mr Laubsch has spoken well. I thank him on behalf of all of us. More than anyone, my husband carved this run out of the wilderness. There is a lot still to be done. The best way we can honour his memory is to build on his work. Let us get on with it.' She turned away. 'Mr Gallagher!'

Hector hurried to her side. 'Yes?'

'Let the men get to work. The sledge we used for the timber when we were erecting the buildings, I want it harnessed and brought around to the front of the house.'

She loaded it, first with wood from the log pile, then with Gavin's possessions: clothes, boots, saddle, papers. She did it herself, allowing no-one else to touch anything. The only items she retained were the government deeds to Whitby Downs, a handful of sovereigns in a leather wallet, Gavin's correspondence with Walter Lang and his rifle. She hefted this last, left it in its habitual place against the wall beside Gavin's side of the bed. It was a fine piece, the stock inlaid with ivory, the hammerlock mechanism chased with silver. Too heavy for her but she would not get rid of it. It was not its intrinsic value that mattered; more important even than the legal documents, her husband's rifle was like a sceptre, representing her title to the land.

'What you going to do with that lot?' Hector asked.

She gave him her coldest look. 'Why?'

Hector Gallagher was not easily cowed. 'There's an English saddle there. Good leather. If you're thinking of getting rid of it I'll take it myself. A good saddle always comes in handy.'

'No-one is taking anything, Mr Gallagher.'

Even then he wouldn't give up.

'A waste, that's what—'

Asta was climbing up behind the sledge. She paused, looked down at the importunate supervisor.

'Do you have no work to do?'

'Yes, but—'

'Then do it. If you would be so kind. As to what is waste and what is not, I shall decide that. Is that clear?'

Gallagher flushed angrily, rubbed his jaw with his hand, said nothing.

She drove the sledge down to the cliffs, the pile of Gavin's possessions swaying as she crossed the rough grass. She reined in and unloaded the sledge, piling everything on the edge of the drop. Beyond the cliffs and extending to an horizon shot with black and scarlet cloud, the sea spread wings as peaceful as a blessing.

When everything was ready Asta faced the sea. This was her place, now. To assist her to consolidate her grasp upon it she summoned to her aid the gods that she also thought of as her own. She said, 'Lords of Fire and Air, take my husband. Let me never forget him or what he tried to do. Let me build a memorial to him in this place.'

She lit a brand and thrust it into the heart of the pile. The flames flickered, spread. She stood unmoving until the gods had taken everything. She stamped out the embers and went home.

*

When Asta got back Ian was waiting for her with a storm-dark face.

He said, 'I think it's time we had a word.'

'What about?'

'The run. Who is going to operate it?'

'I am going to operate it.'

He gestured impatiently: don't let's waste each other's time. 'Impossible.'

'Oh? And why is that, please?'

'No woman alive can operate a sheep run.'

'No other woman, perhaps.'

They stared at each other: no love lost.

'We don't want to fall out over this,' he said.

She inclined her head, acknowledging his words. 'I am glad of that. Living in this country, on the frontiers of civilisation,' she waved her hand at the rolling landscape, 'we have to rely on each other. But I'll do a deal with you. I won't tell you how to run your property if you don't tell me how to run mine.'

He flushed brick-red beneath the yellow hair, tipped back the drink she had given him. 'I don't know how you think you're going to manage—'

'I shall manage, don't worry about that.'

She stood at the door and watched him ride away, shoulders stiff with outrage, his family following obediently behind him.

Pray to the gods, she thought.

'I ain't goin' to do it!' Blake stared furiously at his father. 'Go to *school*? What kind of game is that?'

Hector Gallagher thrust his face threateningly into Blake's. 'You want to end up owning this place or don't you?' Hector's voice dropped. 'Gavin's dead and there ain't no son, right?'

'Right.' Uncertainly.

'Ian's got just the one daughter. *Right*?'

'Right.'

'Ever hear of a woman running a place like this?'

'Asta Matlock sounded like she was planning to run it ...'

'Never!' Hector shook his head. 'Marry the daughter and this will all be yours. But you got to be educated, see? You'll never manage the way you are now.'

Blake turned and looked about him at the fold of hillside, the creek with its line of trees, the rolling acres of pasture that his mind's eye could see beyond the hill's crest, the dust-brown mobs of sheep feeding on the land.

The land. *His* land?

It had never occurred to him but now Hector had planted the idea it began to take root. *My land*, he thought.

Hector said, 'Won't be easy, mind. That Jason: I don't trust him.'

'What can he do?' Sneering.

Hector cautioned him, 'Don't muck up your chances by taking anything for granted.'

Blake was puzzled. 'What do you want me to do?'

'I want you to be *mates*.'

'*Mates*?' Blake stared. 'With Jason?'

'Know your enemy, see? Get him to trust you, he won't care when you take charge. He'll *help* you! Why not? What does he know about sheep?'

SEVENTEEN

Jason stood on the cliff top with Alison beside him.

Ever since Gavin's death, almost three years ago now, they had grown steadily closer to each other. In that time there had been changes, both in their world and in themselves.

Asta had taken a firm grip on Whitby Downs and ruled it with an iron hand. The wool price had stayed high and she was now a wealthy woman. In the changed circumstances Jason had never been able to return to Kapunda after all but Asta received regular reports from Walter Lang and it seemed the mine was prospering as well. Blake and Jason had become what passed for friends. In particular, Alison—sixteen now to Jason's nineteen—was a very different person from the child she had once been.

Now she tossed a pebble over the cliff edge and watched it fall.

'I hate him,' she said. 'He frightens me.'

Jason mooched at her side, hands in his pockets. He was embarrassed having to defend Blake to Alison now that Blake had become his friend. 'He's not so bad. Besides, what can he do to you?'

'He watches me.'

Jason smiled. 'I watch you myself.'

'That's different.'

She did not know how to say that she welcomed Jason's attentions while Blake's made her blood run cold.

'Not so different.'

She glanced up at him, smiling. The light breeze of late summer flattened the front of her dress, reminding Jason—if he had needed reminding—that Alison was a child no longer.

'When are you going to Kapunda?'

'In two months time. Mr Laubsch thinks I should be good enough at reading and writing by then.'

Discontentedly Alison kicked at a pebble. 'I wish I could go to Mr Laubsch's classes.' There had been a time when she had wanted nothing like that but those days, like so much else, were past.

'Asta did ask your father.'

'My father doesn't think a woman needs an education.'

'Well,' Jason said, 'why does she?'

'Because I feel so stupid, knowing nothing!'

He teased her. 'If you came to the classes you'd see even more of Blake than you do at the moment.'

'That's the only reason I'm glad I don't go!'

'He's not so bad,' he told her again.

'Never turn your back on him,' she said.

Mura had said much the same. 'He's putting on an act. He'll turn on you soon enough when it suits him.'

At the beginning Jason, too, had been suspicious of Blake's motives but in a world without friends he had been willing to take friendship where he found it and ever since Gavin's death Blake had been friendly enough.

288

'It's up to us now, eh?'

He had said it the day after Jason and Asta got back from Kapunda. Laubsch had preached his sermon, Asta had burnt Gavin's things down at the cliff, Blake had seemed as truculent and unfriendly as ever. The following day he had changed.

'Time for the next generation to take over, I reckon.'

'I doubt Ian Matlock will agree to that!'

'Ain't nuthin to do wi' him! He does what he likes at Bungaree but here at Whitby Downs . . .' His voice sank to a whisper. 'You reckon yon woman will be able to run things?'

'I don't know.'

'Well, I do! No woman's goin' to run me: nor you, neither, if I be any judge, and without us how can she operate, eh?'

Initially Jason had been on his guard, expecting this new friendship to go as swiftly as it had come, but it had not. Little by little, without being aware of it, he had come to accept Blake's attitude as genuine. Over the years since he had come to accept it unquestioningly.

Time had proved Blake wrong about Asta, certainly, but only in one area did they remain opposed: what needed to be done about the blacks who lived in the bush around them. Asta had continued to honour the arrangements that Jason had made with the clan, permitted the taking of the occasional sheep. Blake was bitterly opposed to it.

'Makes no sense. Here we be workin' our guts out to grow a decent crop o' wool and we let these bastards butcher 'em as they likes!'

And of Mura: 'I knows 'e's your mate, Jason lad, but I can't abide to see a black man treated like a Christian. No offence, like, but I reckons he should be off wi' the rest o' his kind, like in the old days. We all knows where we be, that way.'

Translated: *they're our enemies, let them behave like enemies, give us the excuse we need.*

Blake added: 'They won't never be civilised an' there ain't no sense pretendin' they will.'

So long as Blake *did* nothing Jason was content to let things be. Talk hurt neither Mura nor the rest of the clan.

As for Alison . . .

She had grown up out of nowhere, one day a child, the next entirely different. The transformation had astounded Jason. He knew nothing about women. The shapes both of their temperaments and their bodies were strangers to him. At the time he had not been sure he *wanted* to know them, forming as they did part of the unfamiliar adult world which he, too, had been beginning to enter. All the same, he had begun to watch her, despising himself for doing so but unable to help himself, drawn by the differences he sensed in her: different from what she had been in the past, different from what he himself was becoming.

Now, at nineteen, he saw things very differently. When he could get away he tramped along the cliffs, sometimes with Mura, sometimes alone, carrying with him not only the reality of the wind in his hair, the noise of the sea on the rocks below him but an image that was becoming increasingly important to him: of a young woman, presumably Alison, walking ahead of him along the cliff, dress as white as the slender body it contained, his own body filled by conflicting tensions of tenderness and a fierce and implacable desire.

As to what she felt for him, if she felt anything . . . He had no instinct for that at all.

Two years earlier Mura had disappeared without a word. He had been gone for three weeks. When he came back he had changed. He would not talk about it but Jason knew that he had returned to the clan to undergo the final ceremonies for which they had trained together, ceremonies from which Jason was now permanently shut out.

Hector had wanted to get rid of him for going off in such a way.

''Ow can I plan the work if I never know from one day to the next whether 'e's goin' to be 'ere or not?'

'It is their way,' Asta told him.

'Damn stupid way, you ask me.'

'I did not ask you.'

She disliked her supervisor. More stiff-necked than ever, she saw no reason to conceal it but needed his expertise. She felt no conflict between disliking him and respecting his competence.

'I see us using increasing numbers of the aborigines,' she said, 'as we all become used to each other. It will be good for them and for us. This is as much their country as ours, after all.'

It was a sentiment with which Hector Gallagher would never agree.

'*Their* country?' he said to Blake and Jason. 'That'll be the day!'

Cato Brown shared Hector's views.

'God-rottin' savages lay a finger on my flocks I'll sort 'em out double damn quick, you see if I don't.'

A week later he came on a raiding party with a sheep they had butchered. True to his word he fired on them, killing one. The next day two things happened: Mura disappeared and Jason and Alison broke through into the adult world.

*

Jason had ridden over to Bungaree with some supplies. When he had off-loaded them he strolled down to the cliffs. He met Alison, it could have been by chance, and they walked together.

'Your dad had better not catch us like this,' Jason said.

Alison regarded him gravely. 'What is wrong with it?'

'I'm sure he would find plenty wrong with it.'

'He is on the far side of the run.'

Which Jason already knew.

They walked further; at one point in their conversation Alison placed her hand on his bare arm. The shock of her touch jarred him. He turned, placed his hands on her shoulders. She made no attempt to avoid him or draw away but looked gravely up at him. Waiting. He leant forward. She did not move. He kissed her.

She kissed him back, clinging to him while his hands moved over her in a kind of ecstatic wonderment: *yes* and *yes* and *so this is what it is like*.

At length she rested her forehead against his chest. She was breathing deeply. She pulled her head back and looked up at him and he saw a halo of light around the darkness of her eyes. Gently he caressed her.

She said, 'You mustn't do that.'

Instinct made him say, 'You don't want me to?'

'I want you to very much. That's why you mustn't do it.'

'Why mustn't I?'

'Because we have no future, you and I.'

'You don't know that.'

She smiled ruefully at him. 'I doubt there's many places will hold you. This one never will. Kiss me like that, touch me, I shall lose my heart to you. If that happens I won't be able to bear it when you leave.'

'I'm not going anywhere.'

'You're going to Kapunda.'

'Only for a time. She'll want me back at Whitby Downs later. You'll see,' he boasted, 'I'll be running things there before I'm through.'

Alison shook her head. 'Asta will never let you do that. All the things that matter to her are at Whitby Downs. What she wants out of life, her memories—Edward, Gavin—they're all there. She'll never share them. Not with you, not with anyone. They're too important for that.'

'I don't understand what you're saying.'

'The run is everything to her. It's her justification for living. She cares for you but her dream is more important to her than you are.'

A dark flicker fell between them; a breath of air touched their cheeks. They turned, staring. A thin spear quivered in the dust at their feet.

Jason spun round, grabbing Alison's hand. Thirty yards away three warriors stood, spears bristling, white paint stark against the glossy black skins. As Jason watched the arms of the men went back in unison.

'Run!'

They took off without looking back, plunging down the slope towards the cliff edge.

'Wrong way,' he gasped. 'We're getting further away from the house.'

Alison kept going. 'We can't go the other way. They'll cut us off if we try it.'

It was true: but this way there was no shelter either, no place to hide. Jason risked a backwards glance. They had gained on their pursuers. The men were now at least fifty yards behind them but loping easily along and showing no signs of giving up. Already he could hear the sound of Alison's breathing. Neither of them was any match for their pursuers. They had to find a place to hide. If they didn't the men would soon run them down.

They ran on. A minute later he stumbled over a chunk of stone lying hidden in the grass at the cliff edge. He staggered and almost fell before recovering. He increased his speed at once but had lost a few precious seconds. Worse, he had twisted his knee. Pain sliced like a knife blade into the joint as he ran.

A track slanted off down the cliff. Without thought they followed it. It angled sharply down and around a rocky overhang and at once they were out of sight of the cliff edge above them.

'Quick!'

The path forked, one branch descending precipitously towards the sea, the other disappearing into a gully past an area of lichen-yellow rock. The seawards path was very steep and obviously led nowhere. They ignored it and ran on. Jason was hobbling now, his breath coming in painful gusts.

They found a cave: a black crevice like a knife wound in the rock. Jason hesitated. Ahead of them the path snaked upwards towards the rim of the cliff. No cover, no hope of evading their pursuers. On the other hand the cave might be a dead end. He remembered climbing down the mine shaft at Kapunda. Would Alison be able to find her way in the dark? Would he?

It was a risk they would have to take.

'In here! Quick as you can!'

He led the way into the fissure, Alison not hesitating but coming in right behind him.

Darkness pressed upon them.

*

Mura had known from the first whom they were pursuing.

The rule was rock-hard. A black man had died; a white must die in retribution. As soon as he had heard what had happened he had gone back into the bush, knowing that by doing so he was almost certainly shutting behind him the door to any hope of a life with the whites.

More and more he had come to doubt whether there was any real hope of such a life, whatever he did. He knew so little, would not have minded if their attitude had been based on his own ignorance; ignorance could always be overcome. Ignorance had nothing to do with how they treated him.

Mulatji, the man whom the whites called Sinbad, had said it. 'They will never treat you as a man.'

Apart from Jason, they never had. He knew that men like Blake Gallagher and his father never would. Mura had hoped the raid would flush Blake out. He would have got a lot of pleasure from killing Blake. But Jason and Alison . . .?

He knew where the two fugitives were going. How could he not? He had lived in this area all his life. There would be time enough to decide what must be done when he came up with them: not that there was much choice. The rule was rock-hard. He ran on, unhurried in the sunlight.

Hand groping before his face, Jason inched himself through the darkness of the cave. Rocks bruised his shins; the air smelt stale and dirty as though the cave were home to a multitude of bats. Jason went on inch by inch, yard by yard, his foot searching the ground ahead of him. He was afraid of holes that for all he knew might open up in the rocky floor in front of them. It was utterly dark. The cave must have changed direction as it burrowed deeper into the cliff; looking over his shoulder he could now see no sign of the entrance behind him.

'Can you see anything?'

Alison's voice hissed in the darkness.

'No.'

At least if they could see nothing the blacks would be unable to see them, either.

'I'd like to get a bit further yet.'

Stumbling, groping, almost as frightened of what lay ahead as what lay behind, they went on.

The cave opened up. The rock had pressed upon them; now it withdrew. Arms outstretched, they could feel nothing. Space surrounded them. A step. Another step.

If we lose our direction here we'll never find our way out.

The empty darkness surrounded them like a scream.

Jason stumbled over something on the cave floor. He cursed, heart pounding. He crouched, exploring with cautious hands. A pile of stone. He felt further. Not stone. Bones.

'God!'

'What is it?' Fright in her voice.

'I'm not sure. I think, somebody's skeleton.'

'Someone who got lost in here in the past?'

'Perhaps.'

His hands explored further. A roundness, a dryness. A skull. It felt old beyond imagining.

'How do we get out of here?'

A good question; he had no idea of the answer.

He listened. Silence. No; something less than silence. Somewhere in the blackness, something was tapping.

'This way . . .'

Alison's hand in his, he groped his way through the darkness towards the sound.

Water, dropping from a great height.

He craned his neck, staring up into . . .

Nothing.

There was a real danger of getting lost in the vastness of the cave.

'We should stay here.'

The whisper kindled an echo like a murmur of distant thunder.

'For how long?' Her voice was sharp with the beginnings of panic.

His shrug went unseen in the darkness.

The water pattered down a yard or two ahead of them yet he felt no spray. He paused as a sudden thought occurred to him, explored the ground ahead of him with a cautious foot.

A foot away it ended. Beyond it . . . Space.

A shudder quaked through his body.

'Don't move!'

'What is it?' The panic manifest, now.

'I'm not sure . . .'

Cautiously he knelt, his hand moving ahead of him across dust . . . rock . . . empty air. The water pattered into the void: no splashes, no rocky base to create splashes. Emptiness.

'There is a hole right in front of us.'

'I'm going back.'

'You're staying right where you are. We get separated here we'll never find each other again.'

He drew her unresisting towards him; she came into his arms. He felt her trembling warmth, heard the infinitesimal chattering of her teeth.

'Be quiet,' he instructed her, 'if you don't want them to hear us. '

Time passed. Jason counted slowly. One and two and three. Five thousand, six thousand, seven. When he reached ten thousand without sound or movement he said, 'I don't think they're here.'

'How do we find our way out?'

The same question. The same answer: he had no idea.

He had no idea in which direction the entrance lay, no idea at all. The only focal point in the whole cave system was the fall splattering in front of them. The entrance tunnel might be anywhere.

He took a deep breath. At all costs he must avoid panic.

'There's got to be an end to the cave,' he said. 'It can't go on forever.'

His idea was that they could feel their way around the wall of the cave until they reached the outlet: but what if there was more than one tunnel? Pick the wrong one and they might go deeper and deeper into the cave system until they were irretrievably lost. Without light, without any idea where they were, their bones would in all probability be doomed to join those they had happened upon earlier.

There seemed no alternative.

The first thing was to get away from the chasm. Probably the hole had been opened up over the centuries by the falling water; the fact that it was there at all, however, had destroyed his confidence in the security of the cave floor. The only way to go was to crawl, exploring the ground in front of them as they did so.

He explained to Alison what he wanted her to do; on hands and knees they crawled back until, quite gently, he butted his head into the encircling wall of the cave.

Now to find the outlet.

They had to be inside, Mura knew. If they had carried on along the path he would have seen them. Very well. He told his companions to go ahead while he waited here, listening to the silence of the cave within the cleft, the faint and repetitive susurration of the sea at the foot of the cliff.

He had never been inside the cave and almost certainly never would. It was a site that had been used long ago to bury the medicine men, those who had been the guardians of the spirits. The cave was taboo and no member of the clan had entered it for a very long time.

He waited, spears clutched in his hand, white paint reflecting the sunlight.

It took a long time but eventually Jason found an aperture, six feet or so wide, leading off the main chamber.

'Are you sure it's the right way?' Alison's voice was spiky with incipient terror.

'I think it probably is.'

Even so, he hesitated before committing himself to it. *Probably* would hardly be enough, if it came to it.

He felt something and paused, eyes closed, concen- trating . . .

Felt it again.

He spat in his hand, smeared the spittle, held the palm up. The lightest of breezes blew cool upon his skin.

He said excitedly, 'I can feel air moving . . .'

Inch by inch they made their way down the stone corridor towards the as-yet invisible light.

*

The sun had gone round to the west. Mura now stood in shadow. Once he had heard the distant rattle of gunfire. His two colleagues had not returned but he was unworried. What had happened to them was not his immediate concern. Jason was in the cave, he was sure of it. That was what mattered.

He waited until he heard the faintest of sounds from inside the cleft. He glanced along the path in both directions, saw no-one. He settled more closely into the shelter of the rocks. The grip on his spears tightened.

They saw the reflection of the light before the light itself: a puddle of greyness upon the walls and floor of the stone passage. To begin with it was so faint as to be barely visible. Cautiously they drew nearer. The light was still faint, yet bright enough after the cave's darkness to make them squint. They reached a corner. The corridor twisted, twisted again. Light grew stronger, flooded in.

Jason paused, watching the entrance. They had escaped from the cave but he had not forgotten why they had taken refuge there in the first place. Foot by foot, he stole closer. Beyond the opening the sky was a peerless blue. He could hear the rumble of the sea, smell the grass and hot sand of the cliffs. Life beckoned him.

He could see no sign of anyone waiting. The blacks must have given up and gone away. He walked out into the sunlight. A figure, dark skin daubed with paint, emerged from the rocks at his side.

*

It had been a half-hearted raid at best. A few shots, a scatter of spears, and it was all over. No injuries on either side. All the same, Ian was uneasy; if he had not arrived at the house in the nick of time Mary would have been there by herself. She had a gun; she ought to be capable of looking after herself but he knew, no-one better, how she hated this frontier living. He had wondered more than once whether it would not be kinder to send her back to the city but saw no reason why he should deprive himself of the physical comforts of his wife. Of course, now that Asta was a widow ... It was true she disliked him but that, he thought, could be changed. His mind roamed over possibilities, then he put them to one side. For the moment Alison was of far greater concern.

When he had got back to Bungaree there had been no sign of her and he had no idea where she was. Now the attack was over he knew he must go out and look for her.

'Will you be all right by yourself?'

'Of course,' Mary said. Her expression gave lie to her words but they both knew there was no choice.

A clatter of hooves. Ian ran to the door. Blake and Sinbad reined in their horses before the house.

'Alison's missing. You seen any sign of her?'

They had not.

Blake said, 'I said when that Michael went, it was time we sorted these blacks out once and for all. I've said it all along.'

'Let's not waste time talking about it,' Ian said impatiently. 'Let's get out there and look for her.'

Rifles in hand, pistols thrust into their belts and a great and rising anger in their hearts, the men rode out. Sinbad scouted ahead of them and within yards had picked up a trail that appeared to head down to the cliffs.

'What the hell's she up to?' Ian demanded of the trees. Which did not answer.

They rode furiously, reined in at the head of the track that snaked down the face of the rock towards the sea. They looked around them but could see nothing.

'Down there?' Blake suggested.

Who knew? There was certainly no sign of her anywhere else. They left the horses. Guns in hand, they began to scramble down the cliff.

'You get out of here, quick as you can.'

It was Mura; the instinctive shock that had drawn Jason's knife into his hand now ebbed. He shoved the blade back into the sheath. Gradually his breath stabilised.

'Where are your mates?'

'They've gone on ahead. I saw it was you so I waited to warn you.'

Jason's hand was on Mura's arm. He squeezed it briefly. 'Thanks, eh.'

From the top of the cliff came the sound of a misplaced stone skipping free over the broken ground.

'You go,' Mura said urgently. 'They are coming back.'

A figure appeared at the top of the cliff followed by another one. White, not black.

'That's Blake,' Alison said, 'and my father's with him.'

Jason turned swiftly to his friend. 'It's you they'll be after when they see you. You'd best get out of here.'

An expression of resignation crossed Mura's face. 'They have guns. You tell me how I get away from a man with a gun.'

In a fever of impatience Jason pushed him into the cave opening. 'Get in there.'

Horror. 'I cannot—'

'It's either that or be killed.'

It was useless. Terror transcended mere physical danger. Trying to shove Mura out of sight was like trying to shift a stake set in the ground: the more Jason tried, the more he resisted.

'Then run!'

But both knew to do that would be to invite a bullet or several. Then it was too late.

'Look at this.' The rifle muzzle came up, was thrust into Mura's neck. 'Paint and spears ... Planning on attacking someone, were we?'

The hammer of the gun clicked back. The muzzle carved a circle of flesh beneath Mura's chin. Blake's forefinger whitened on the trigger.

'No!'

Alison's protest was as faint as a bird cry in the sea-washed air.

Blake's eyes moved but the gun did not. 'This bloke was goin' to kill you!'

'He saved us,' Jason said.

'Lookin' like that?' Blake's grin tightened the muscles in his cheeks. 'You been mates a long time, Jason lad. You wasn't thinkin' of covering for him, by any chance?'

Jason stared; so much for friendship.

Impatiently Ian said, 'Let's get back to the run. I'll decide what to do about him later.'

'What's the point of taking him back?' Blake demanded. 'Why don't I shoot him and be done with it?'

'I told you no!'

Ian's dilemma was simple: his instinct, also, was to shoot the prisoner and be rid of him, but Michael was under Asta Matlock's protection and he did not want to endanger their relations further.

'We'll take him back.'

They climbed back up the path. At the top the horses were as they had left them. Alison and Jason had been through so much. Now it was hard to believe that anything had happened. The nightmare of the pursuit and the cave had become unreal, something that existed only in their imaginations. The terror had gone. What remained—the rolling landscape, the puffball clouds in the blue sky, the sounds of wind and sea—was the only reality.

Ian said, 'We'll lock him up in the barn. Then I'll decide what to do with him.'

Alison said, 'I'd better move before my father realises I'm here.'

The straw in the stable sighed as, restlessly, Jason turned. Beyond the plank partition one of the horses whickered and blew softly. The warm smell of horseflesh was all around them.

'I'm afraid they're planning to kill him,' he said.

'They would never dare.' Eyes round in her sunburnt face.

'Blake would. I must get Mura away before it's too late.'

What about us? If you take Mura and run away? She wanted to say it but did not. Instead she asked, 'How are you going to do that? Blake's sitting on guard outside the shed door at this minute.'

'I've got no choice,' he said. 'Surely you can see that?'

She did see it. Love, she thought. It means sacrifice, then. 'I'll get him away. Be ready to get Michael out as soon as Blake moves.'

'What are you going to do?'

Alison smiled, put her hand on his arm. 'Trust me.'

They looked gravely at each other. Today had seen a change in their relationship. It was what was meant by growing up. Now truly they had escaped from the after-mists of childhood. For practical purposes Jason had been an adult all his life but for Alison, with her more sheltered background, it was a new world. From now on she would have to find her way through it unaided.

She shivered, said, 'I don't want to go.'

Meaning, *when I leave I shall be putting all this behind me.*

Meaning, *when I go through that door into the darkness, I shall be turning my back on everything that has happened in my life until now.*

Meaning, *I do not know when I shall see you again or that, when I do, I shall see you as I see you now.*

Meaning, *You are my love.*

But knew she would go, nonetheless. Because she had said she would, because the moment demanded it, because Jason needed her to do it.

Softly he said, 'Come here.'

She came into his arms at once. No hesitation, no shyness, simply the need to share with him the moment that had come upon them both.

She asked, 'Where will you go? If you get away?'

'I haven't thought.'

Had, in fact, but was reluctant to talk about it, even to her. What she did not know she could not reveal, however inadvertently.

Her warmth invaded him. He felt her breath on

his neck and moved his head to kiss her, their mouths coming together as naturally as though they had been doing nothing else all their lives. His tongue probed between her teeth, he felt her quiver and strain closer to him, the warmth of her breasts against him, her slender arms around his neck. He explored her, tenderly, pausing before each instinctive moment, giving her the chance to make the rebuff that never came.

She gasped, sighing, doing some exploring of her own. She said, 'I can't bear it,' but could and would, having no choice.

Trembling, breathing fast and shallow through her open mouth, Alison said, 'Wait. Wait.'

He paused, feeling her warmth, her movements as she disposed of clothes, did whatever it was she had to do in the scented darkness.

She said, 'There, then,' and he came together with her, a tension indescribable, a rendering, a fulfilment beyond expectation or dreaming.

Jason saw everything and nothing: the grain and odour of her skin, the rounded firmness of her breasts, the hair at the nape of her head and on her body: all of this. He saw nothing and everything. He had lost sight of the detail in attaining the universal. She had superseded the sum of her parts.

Gently, he lowered his head down her belly.

Alison, moved by awakening passion, the moment frozen, ephemeral yet eternal. Even at the moment of union she understood instinctively that the instant, the emotion, could not be captured; knew, too, that ever after the memory of that instant would call her back. It was the distillation of life, a pulse quivering in her sundered loins.

The beginning called to the future.

Later, she cradled him.

'What did you say? Just now?'

'Nothing.'

What will happen to us?

He had thought the words but had not realised he had actually spoken them. He stared at the shadowed recesses of the wooden stable. The future was a shadow far darker than anything he could see here. It lay between them like a curse.

Through a crack in the planks Jason watched in angry trepidation as Alison went out into the cool darkness and made her way across to the shed outside which Blake was sitting, his back against the door.

It didn't matter that he had agreed to her doing it; it didn't matter that he knew she was acting only as a decoy so that he could get Mura away before they did anything to him; what mattered was that she was his woman and he was jealous.

He visualised Alison's smile as she talked to Blake (*smiling at Blake Gallagher!*) and it was all he could do to stay where he was. Her smile ... He could have killed for it.

'What you doin' out here?' Blake made a special effort to be friendly.

'Came to give Jason his supper.'

''Ow come 'e gets special treatment?'

'Because when he came here first you wouldn't let him eat with you.'

'That were years ago. Any case, it weren't 'im. Were yon black bastard. And now you've fed him,' he asked, 'what you doin', eh?'

'I thought I'd go for a stroll before I went back inside, get some air, but now I'm not so sure.' An exaggerated shudder. 'It's dark out there.'

'You don't want to go wanderin' off,' he told her. 'You never knows what you might meet up with.'

'It's hot in the house,' she said.

And no-one of her own age to talk to. She was—how old?—fifteen? Thereabouts. No wonder she wanted to come out of the house in the evening. Blake thought, maybe the old man knew what he was talking about, after all.

With visions of spreading acres before his eyes he said, 'Wan' me to come with you?'

'Would you?' Eyes round.

'Reckon the blackie's safe enough locked in there. He ain't goin' nowhere.'

He stood. He was taller than Jason and more powerful. His skin was stained dark by the sun, his brown eyes looked at her admiringly. She felt nothing for him at all.

'We'll stroll a little,' Blake told her, arm around her shoulders as he smiled down at her.

It was all she could do not to draw away from him, agonisingly conscious of Jason watching them from the shadows.

She smiled back at him. 'My father may be watching.'

He grunted with displeasure but withdrew his arm, all the same, and she breathed a little easier.

'Let's stroll, then,' she said.

As soon as they were out of sight Jason moved out of the stable and across the patch of bare ground. He stopped by the shed door, mouth close to the wood.

'Mura . . .?'

'What is it?' Barely audible through the wood.

'I'm opening the door. We're taking off.'

He lifted the bar; the hinges creaked as the door swung open and Jason flinched, looking over his shoulder to see whether Blake Gallagher might be bearing down on him.

Mura's dark eyes gleamed out of the darkness.

'Where are we going?'

'Away from here.'

'Now?'

'Of course now. You want to wait until they can see us?'

But even after all these years Mura's fears of the night were not so easily dispelled. He hesitated and Jason was suddenly blazingly angry. Here he was, putting his own neck in danger, only to come up with this sort of nonsense.

'We stay around here they'll hang you.'

He did not think that Asta Matlock would allow such a thing but never mind.

'They know I helped you, they may hang me, too!'

Mura's heavy lips worked uncertainly, his eyes examined the night for demons.

'I'm coming . . .'

Alison and Blake had gone off towards the creek; Jason and Mura headed the other way, up the hill and along the crest of the range. Gradually the valley fell away behind them. The stars-bright sky looked down on a sleeping world.

Jason paused and glanced back. Nothing showed of the settlement they had just left: neither roofs nor buildings nor lights. They might have been the only people in the world.

He thought of Alison down there with Blake; forced himself to put such thoughts out of his mind. It would be a long time before he saw her again; in the meantime, he had more pressing matters to think about.

He turned to Mura. 'Let's get moving. We've got a long way to go.'

EIGHTEEN

The mangrove swamp stretched for miles along the coastal flats that separated the plains of the interior from the coast. To the north the low ground ended in a line of hills but here the shore seemed to breathe with the movement of the tides, water and mud mingling and often indistinguishable in salt-scoured channels where crabs, tiny fish and wading birds were the only inhabitants. A couple of miles from the head of the gulf a narrow creek ran inland, drying at low water to a series of muddy pools no more than a few yards across. Everywhere was the smell of silt, salt and decay under a sky so vast that it, like the swamp itself, seemed endless.

At the mouth of the creek a few shabby buildings had been erected, little more than shacks, at the end of a mud-churned track rutted with wheel marks and thick with bullock dung. The buildings were Port Wakefield and the track ran inland to Burra Burra, the huge copper mine several days into the interior. The creek, unpromising though it was, was the point at which the copper ore was loaded for trans-shipment to Adelaide a hundred miles down the coast.

Jason and Mura had come to Port Wakefield through the desolation of mangrove flats that fringed Wild Horse Plains. The journey from Bungaree had taken them several days, a large portion of which they had spent hiding: from settlers likely to shoot them on sight, from bands of aborigines whose territory this had been before the arrival of white men.

At last, half-starved and close to exhaustion, they had arrived. They stood at the edge of the grey water and looked through the last fringe of mangrove at the solitary barge that lay propped upright on the mud half a mile to the south. Around the barge a number of drays was assembled while hoists hauled heavy sacks over the side.

'What are they doing?' Mura wondered.

'Loading the ore to take it south to Adelaide.'

'What will they do with it when they get it there?'

'Turn it into copper.'

The idea that it was possible to take sand out of the earth and turn it into a metal hard enough to cut was something that Mura could not imagine. It was incomprehensible, like all the other incomprehensible things he had seen since he had been brought into the world of the white man.

'Why have we come here?' he asked.

Mura had followed Jason here unquestioningly, knowing that Blake would have killed him had he stayed behind. Why not? After helping Jason to escape from the clan, he no longer had a home, not even a way of life. He was like the tidal fringe on which he now stood: neither water nor land. He no longer knew where his home was.

'To get a job on that barge, if I can arrange it.'

'Where will it take us?'

'To Adelaide.'

'And then?'

'To Kapunda. I shall get work in Kapunda.'

Another meaningless concept: the idea of work as the *kuinyo* understood it.

'You stay here,' Jason instructed him. 'I'll go and see the master of the barge.'

He walked out of the shelter of the mangroves and crossed the mud to the circle of drays that surrounded the beached vessel. Scrollwork about her stern announced her name to be *Tulip*, of Port Adelaide.

He ignored the curious looks he received from the waiting drovers. There was a blue-jerseyed man standing at the rail of the vessel, supervising a lift bulging with sacks as it came swinging and creaking over the side and disappeared into what was presumably the hold. He was the man Jason wanted.

It was obviously a bad time to talk to him but Jason doubted there would ever be a good one.

'Mister . . .'

The man ignored him.

'Mister . . .'

'Piss off. Can't you see I'm busy?'

'Need a deck hand?'

The man's eyes remained fixed on the sacks as they swung in-board. 'Half my crew gone off to the mine and he asks if I need a deck hand. What I need is an experienced man, not some copper bunny that don't know port from starboard.'

'I was deck hand on the *Kitty*,' Jason said, lying.

The man looked at him then. 'The *Kitty* was lost years ago. Where you been since?'

'Working on one of the sheep runs.'

'What you doing here, then?'

'Time to move on.'

'Why not up to the Burra Burra? That's where everyone else's headed. There's money there: more'n you'll ever find here.'

Jason shrugged, not wanting to leave a trail by mentioning Kapunda.

'If I find out you killed someone,' the man warned, 'I'll hang you meself.'

So he had the job, then. But.

'There's one more thing,' Jason said.

'What's that?'

'There's two of us.'

It proved a trouble-free journey. The master of the *Tulip* was an easy-going man for all his ferocious talk and had raised no objection even when he found that the second man was a black. The gulf was calm and it took only three days to complete the journey.

'Now for Kapunda,' Jason said.

It took another week to get to the mining town. Nothing much had changed. The new chimney was now complete but apart from that things remained as they had been. The same ragged urchins picked at the ore tables, the same miners crunched hard-soled along the dirt streets, the same smoke and fumes poured into the air.

Jason went to Lang's house and knocked on the door. The same forbidding servant opened to him.

'Ja?'

'Stefan Lang.'

Before the woman could say another word she was pushed to one side as Stefan hurled himself at his friend.

*

'My father won't let you stay in Kapunda.'

'It was arranged I should come here to learn mining and watch out for the Matlocks' interests in the mine.'

'That was before you ran away. He'll never agree when he finds out about that.'

'That was the agreement. What difference does it make how I got here?'

'Because he never wanted to keep to the agreement in the first place. Now he's got an excuse not to.'

'Then I'll get a job at Kapunda Main.'

'You don't know my father. You're lucky he's away. You'll be safe for a few days but you won't be able to stay anywhere in Kapunda once he's back. He'll have you sent back straightaway, you try that.'

'But they would have killed Michael if we'd stayed.'

Stefan shook his head. 'My father won't care about that. He thinks the blacks *should* be killed. Why don't you go to Burra Burra? There'll be work up there for both of you. You said you can read and write? We'll fix you up with a job in the office. That way you'll learn all about how a mine operates.'

'Can you really do that?'

'Why not? My father's a very influential man.'

'But why should he do it for me?'

Stefan winked, grinning. 'It's amazing how things can be arranged.'

'And Michael?'

'He'll be able to get a job, too: above ground or below, it doesn't matter. There's plenty available. I'll write a letter to Challoner.'

'Who's Challoner?'

'The mine accountant. The real boss is a man called Henry Ayers but he's based in Adelaide and I don't know him.'

If Kapunda had seemed busy the Burra Burra mine was ten times more so. The workings sprawled all over the hillside and down in the valley the miners had built their homes along the banks of the creek. The sheoaks that had previously covered the lower slopes of the hills had been cleared to provide fuel for the furnaces, and the whole district, it seemed, rang with the sound of hammers, the rumble of engines and metal-wheeled trolleys, the yelling of men, the shrill wail of whistles. Over everything hung a pall of acrid smoke.

Challoner said, 'Have you ever worked for a mining company before?' His lips were drawn together disapprovingly, as wrinkled as prunes.

'Never.'

'I can't think what Mr Lang was thinking of.'

Once again the mine accountant picked up the letter that Jason had brought and stared mournfully at it.

Dear Mr Challoner

In his absence I am writing on my father's behalf to request that you find a position at the Burra Burra mine for Mr Jason Hallam. Mr Hallam is well known to me as a conscientious and loyal person. In my opinion he will be an asset to the workings of your office.

I have the honour to be, sir, yr most obt servant

'Can't imagine what he was thinking of,' he said again.

Jason did not look at the letter. There was no need; he knew it by heart. He and Stefan had spent the best part of an afternoon concocting it, copying it painstakingly from a number of other letters that Stefan had found in his father's study.

Challoner rubbed the tip of his nose with his quill pen. 'I suppose it's all right,' he conceded reluctantly. His voice scraped like a quill drawn across paper.

It had been dark for over an hour yet behind the accountant's table jacketed figures still bent attentively across high, sloping desks. Pens scratched. Everywhere piles of papers—orders, invoices, sales dockets—lay in apparent confusion, illuminated by a wan and guttering lantern that provided the only light. The air was stale, redolent of dust, ink, paper, an infinity of boredom and routine.

Jason thought, *I stay here I'll go mad*.

But it was a start, at least, and as Stefan had said, a man who kept his eyes open would be able to learn more about mining in six months than he could hope to pick up in a lifetime of manual work.

Dubiously Challoner eyed his sturdy shoulders, his work-toughened hands. 'You're familiar with normal office routines?'

'Yes, Mr Challoner.'

Of course, Mr Challoner. Call me a liar, Mr Challoner.

'Where did you gain your experience?'

'In Hobart.'

Check on that, Jason thought.

Another sigh. 'You will need to get out around the mine, pick up the loading dockets, sort out the drovers before they leave. They can be a burden. Have little notion of proper accounting records . . .'

The thin voice scratched on; the thought that he might be able to escape from the prison of the office made Jason happier.

'I can handle the drovers, Mr Challoner.'

Once again the accountant eyed Jason's sturdy

body, his determined and pugnacious jaw.

'Perhaps you can. I certainly hope so.' He reflected. 'Seven shillings and sixpence a week,' he said. 'Your hours are seven until seven, twenty minutes break at dinner time, you are required to live on the mine, no alcohol at any time permitted on the mine property. Start tomorrow.'

Seven and six. Stefan had told him some of the face workers earned as much as thirty shillings a shift. Learning about mining clearly came at a price.

'Where do I sleep tonight?'

Challoner eyed him coldly, dithering no longer. They were now employer and employee and he clearly welcomed the chance to show Jason that their relationship had changed.

'Tonight you sleep where you like. Your employment, I repeat, starts at seven tomorrow morning. Do not be late.'

NINETEEN

Asta had known for years that life was not intended to be easy. She had not wanted to leave Norway—surrounded by the sun-burned expanse of the peninsula, as different from her homeland as it was possible to be, she saw that clearly now—she had never wanted to come to Australia, she had not wanted to come to Whitby Downs. She had done all these things. She had had children and lost them, a husband and lost him, a foster son and lost him, too.

She made her way around the run, attending mechanically to the things that had to be done. For days the shock of Jason's going dragged like chains at her heels.

All her plans. All her hopes.

Gradually her will re-asserted itself. Two things remained: herself and the confidence she felt in herself and in Whitby Downs, the sheep run she and Gavin had carved out of the wilderness.

Herself and the land.

She would never permit herself to lose either of them, would never share them with another human, would guard them with her life.

Ian went to see her again, trying to reason with her. He smiled into her eyes, tried to place his hands on her. She rejected him, not trying to hide her contempt. He stormed out of Whitby Downs and rode home, burning with frustration and anger.

'There is nothing worse,' he told the surrounding bush, 'than trying to reason with a woman who won't see sense.'

It was difficult to see what he could do about it. He would have to be patient—something that always came hard in Ian's life—but it was the only way. She'd run things pretty well up to now but one of these days she would be sure to trip over her own feet; then she might welcome his offer of help.

He had been home less than an hour when Blake came riding furiously up to the house.

Ian went out to meet him. 'What's up?'

Blake did not dismount. 'Fire is what's up!'

'Where?'

'In the north paddocks.'

'Damnation!'

It was the worst possible news. Ian ran for his own mount. A hot north wind had been blowing for several days. All the paddocks were tinder-dry. A fire up in the northern paddocks would threaten the whole run.

He swung himself up into the saddle.

'Who's up there?' he shouted.

'Asta's there with Cato Brown.'

'How did she get there so fast?'

'Said she smelt it.'

They rode fast to the north. It wasn't long before they could smell it themselves. It certainly wasn't hard to spot. A dense black cloud of smoke came rolling towards them, heavy with the stench of burning, and as they grew nearer they could see the red of the fire reflecting off the underside of the cloud.

With Cato helping, Asta was lighting a back burn down wind from the main blaze. She ran frantically along the line of fire, lighting fires and damping them down, expending energy like a lunatic. The others went running to join her.

Her face was rosy with heat and exertion, her skin smudged with soot. 'Spread out,' she shouted above the roar of the fire. 'If it gets past us we're done for.'

Even fighting a bush fire came down to routine: lighting the back burn, letting it spread far enough to prevent the main blaze from jumping the burnt ground, keeping it under control so that it could not itself run away and join the main blaze. It was hard, dangerous, frightening work and the wind did not help. Showers of sparks exploded skywards as a bush vomited flame, a gum tree that had been guarding a slope for a hundred or a thousand years burst into a tower of fire, the heat carried on the wind dried their skins until they, too, felt like exploding into flame.

Through the roiling smoke the sun blinked and vanished, just one more ball of fire in a world encompassed by fire. Yellow flame, red flame, sparks, heat and black smoke: their only universe, like the first days of the world.

They controlled the flames only to have them spring up again somewhere else, ran cursing to control the new blaze, the ashes so hot that their feet blistered inside their boots. Lashed by heat, the wind eddied, carrying sparks swarming across the cleared area, setting a hundred new fires blazing in the open ground beyond.

Asta was everywhere, energy flowing from her in a seemingly endless tide. At one point, when the flames died momentarily, she stood with her boots touching a smouldering log, the remains of the grass spiralling smoke and fumes all about her, and screamed her defiance at the rampaging flames.

'You shall not win!'

She challenged the fire in English, in Norwegian, with her tongue, her mind, her heart.

'You shall not destroy me!'

Again she summoned the ancient gods to her aid. Odin and Thor fought on her side and slowly, inch by reluctant inch, the fire drew back, contained within the circle of cleared ground that she had built around it.

Ian, Blake and the rest watched her, awed and overwhelmed by the intensity of her will that outshone the flames themselves.

At last it was out but no-one would be able to leave it for hours yet, not daring to turn their backs in case the fire seized the opportunity to burst out again.

They sat on the ground, the burnt earth all about them, the air acrid with fumes.

Asta laughed. 'Flame and heat everywhere,' she said, 'but we do not have any fire to make tea.'

At that moment it was the most important thing she could think of.

'You did well,' she complimented the others. 'Thank you for what you did.'

They all knew they would not have overcome the fire without the inspiration that Asta herself had given them.

'You are a real man,' Asta told Blake. 'You did the work of ten.'

She neither liked nor trusted him nor ever would, perhaps, but respect was something else. Respect— for his strength, his will, his sheer basic ability—she was prepared to give him in full measure. No-one, man or woman, could hope to run Whitby Downs completely on their own. Ian was right in that, at least. Blake would never be Jason, of course, but Jason was gone. Provided Blake was willing to accept orders from a woman she thought he would do.

Asta stood at the paddock rail, one hand on the neck of her favourite gelding, and watched as the distant rider drew slowly nearer. Both man and horse had their heads down as though weary to death or perhaps dispirited, but they came on anyway. There was something about the man that triggered a chord of recognition in her. She studied him thoughtfully as he came down the last slope and started up the hill towards the house.

She had no reason to suppose the new arrival meant trouble. Nonetheless, she went indoors to fetch her rifle. This was frontier living. It did not pay to take too much for granted. She came back. The figure was much nearer now. He was no horseman, that was plain. He sat his mount like a sack of potatoes and, suddenly, she knew him.

'Joshua Penrose from Kapunda. That's who you are.'

Penrose halted a dozen yards from her.

'Mrs Matlock,' he greeted her, raised hat, smiling eyes. 'Good morning.'

Asta held the gun, not pointing it, but making a statement with it all the same. It said, *I am free. I may be a widow but I run my own life. Do not mess with me.*

Just in case he had any ideas.

'Mr Penrose,' she said. 'This is a pleasant surprise. Perhaps you had better get off before you fall off.'

'Ma'am, I shall be very pleased to do so,' he said frankly.

Did so with difficulty, nonetheless.

'You have ridden a long way.'

'And fear I may have wasted my journey. But had to speak to someone. We are partners, after all.'

They went indoors. She went to pour them both a glass of cordial, paused with the neck of the bottle over his glass. 'Unless you would sooner have whisky?'

'I would indeed, ma'am, if it's no trouble.'

She fetched his drink.

'Come, Mr Penrose,' she said. 'Sit down. Tell me why you are here.'

He cleared his throat. 'I'm in trouble, ma'am, that's the size of it, but I'm not sure there's anything you or anyone else can do about it.'

'Perhaps I should be the judge of that.'

It took a long time to squeeze the story out of him but in the end she managed it.

'There's a hill north of Kapunda. Some of it came up for sale. The main line of the lode seemed to head that way, I decided to go to the auction and see what sort of price it fetched.' He cleared his throat. 'I suppose I got carried away. I bought two hundred acres.'

'How much did you pay?' Asta asked.

Joshua's voice was so low she thought she had misunderstood him. '*How* much?'

'Sixty-five pounds an acre.'

'So much!'

'The worst thing is, the lode pinched out before it reached my land. It seems I am the proud owner of two hundred acres of prime grazing land.'

'At sixty-five pounds an acre.'

'As you say.'

324

Thirteen thousand pounds.

'It has created certain financial strains.'

She could well imagine it.

'But why are you here, Mr Penrose? I do not have surplus money to lend you.'

Or to invest in failed mines.

'I shall have to realise some investments to ease the financial pressures on me. Part of my interest in Neu Preussen will be among them.'

'How much of your interest?'

'I thought one third?'

'At what price?'

Penrose frowned at his empty glass, turning it in his hands. 'Three thousand pounds?'

'For one third of your interest. You are valuing it at nine thousand pounds, then, this one quarter interest.'

'It is a fair price—'

Gavin had bought his own quarter interest for five thousand pounds. Now Penrose was asking almost twice as much.

'No,' Asta said.

Silence. Penrose looked at her, eyes unfriendly. 'Naturally I expected to negotiate—'

'No negotiations. No talk. What I am willing to do is buy out your whole interest in Neu Preussen for the price my husband paid for his own share.'

'Five thousand pounds?' Penrose puffed indignantly. 'There has been a considerable amount of development since your husband bought into the mine. A very considerable amount. Forgive me, ma'am, but I fear that as a woman you may not understand the implications of such an investment—'

'Take it or leave it.'

A pause. Penrose took a deep breath. 'You force me to leave it, ma'am.'

Asta smiled at him. 'Tell me, Mr Penrose, why have you come such a long way to see me?'

'To offer you my shares—'

'Which Mr Lang would no doubt have been pleased to take from you without need for such a journey. Did you ask him for three thousand pounds?'

'No, ma'am, I did not. There are others who might be interested. Captain Bagot—'

'But our agreement requires, does it not, that any shareholder wishing to sell must first offer his shares to his partners?'

Impasse. They stared at each other.

'I shall tell you what I think,' Asta told him, 'I think you are using me as a stalking horse. I do not think you will sell me your shares for any reasonable price I might be prepared to offer for them.'

Penrose fumbled awkwardly with the brocaded collar of his shirt. 'Why do you say that?'

'Two reasons, Mr Penrose. Because Mr Lang already owns fifty percent of the mine and you believe that he will always outbid me in order to obtain control. One share, Mr Penrose, that is all it takes. He might well be prepared to pay three thousand pounds for that share. I would, myself, if it gave me control, but it does not. All your shares will give me is fifty percent, equal with Lang. That I might be interested in. But not one share less. And not for nine thousand pounds.'

Pause.

'You mentioned two reasons, Mrs Matlock.'

'The second reason is that I am a woman.'

'Why should that matter to me?'

'It is how gentlemen think.'

'Then why should I have come all this way? If I was not prepared to sell to you because you are a woman?'

'I did not say you would not be prepared to sell at any price. But at a *reasonable* price: I do not think so.'

Penrose eyed her with growing respect.

'You are a clever woman, Mrs Matlock.'

'This is a man's world, Mr Penrose. If a woman is not clever she gets nowhere.'

Over supper that night he asked her about Jason.

'Jason has gone, Mr Penrose. God willing, he will one day return. In the meantime, we go on living our lives.'

They walked the run, she showed him the view from the cliffs; he probed, ever so delicately, into how she had learned to manage as a grazier in what she herself had described as a man's world.

Asta laughed. 'I do what I suppose everybody does. I survive: or try to.'

'I have to sell,' Penrose told her frankly, 'but would like to keep an interest. Would you not be prepared to take less than fifty percent, perhaps?'

She liked him but this was business. She would not be swayed. 'All or nothing, Mr Penrose.'

'You are a hard woman,' he complained.

She took it as a compliment. Eventually, to her own surprise and perhaps to his, she bought his shares for six thousand pounds, to take account of the development that had taken place at the mine since Gavin had acquired his shares.

'You drive a hard bargain, ma'am. I doubt Mr Matlock himself could have done better.'

More than ever Asta needed an agent to look after her interests in Kapunda. She had thought to offer Penrose the job but did not. She needed someone able to stand up to Walter Lang, and Penrose, she saw, was not the man. Oh Jason, she grieved, why did you abandon me?

Nevertheless she liked the Cornishman. He was not the man Gavin had been, would never dominate his personal landscape as her husband had, but there was comfort in that. She knew she could handle him, had done so over the question of his shares, yet he was not so weak that she despised him.

Red face and lively eye, Joshua Penrose was as different from Gavin in body as he was in personality, yet there was a spark between them. She saw that he felt it, too. A sense of mutual awareness drew their eyes to each other.

She hesitated, wondering whether to encourage that awareness or not. On balance, she thought, they would make a good pair, she with the advantage, to be sure, but that was necessary. Never again would she settle for being the chattel of a man.

It had been so long since she had had a man. She had thought she would never have one again, accepting that Gavin's death had closed that particular door forever. Now she was not so sure. She watched the powerful shoulders, the strong column of Joshua's neck, and wanted him with an animal lust that startled her with its intensity.

She waited for him to make the first move but he did not. She was sure he shared the same feelings. Perhaps she should take the initiative. Supposedly it was something that no woman did but it was a long time since she had allowed herself to be governed by such prejudices. Since Gavin's death she had spent her life doing things that no woman did and, so far at least, the sky had not fallen.

She thought she might take him to the grotto on the cliffs, see what might develop when they got there, yet at the last minute drew back. Penrose was paying only a brief visit to Whitby Downs. His base was Kapunda and she would spend little time in the mining town. Whatever her feelings, she was not interested in a fleeting relationship with Joshua or any man.

The timing is wrong, she thought. I will wait.

Then, after he had gone, riding northwards on the first leg of his long journey home, she missed him. Now that it was too late, she regretted having done nothing.

By an effort of will she put regrets behind her. She would not allow herself to miss anyone, neither Penrose nor Jason. Her life was here, with demands of its own. It permitted no room for weaknesses of any kind.

Blake Gallagher was another for whom weakness had no place. Since his father had put the idea into his head, he had thought of little else but the land. To begin with he had doubted. It seemed impossible that anyone would be willing to hand over what was theirs to another person. Within the family, perhaps, although even that seemed barely possible, but to an absolute outsider ... It was against every dictate of nature. If he had owned it he would have seen the land in ruins before he allowed one inch of it to fall into the hands of another person, would kill anyone who laid claim to what was his own.

He thought, I am not even the overseer. I am the son of the overseer. Is it possible that ...?

It was possible. The love of the land, the determination to have and to hold: that he had. But was his will strong enough to do whatever had to be done to win it?

His father evidently thought so. 'You got to sweet-talk the girl, if that's what it takes. Do what you got to do.'

Blake walked the land, knelt upon it, allowed the soil to sift through his fingers. Desire ran through him, a lust more intense than he would ever feel for a woman. A woman you could possess, conquer, whereas the land ... It could be his but only so long as he was worthy of it.

Blake raised his face to the sky, clenched fists raised. A vow. This would all be his, for himself, his children, his children's children. His by virtue of work, of opportunity, of lust of ownership. If he married Alison, if anything happened to Ian Matlock, this would be his.

First, Alison.

'Eagles,' he said. 'Down at the dam.'

She stared at him as though she did not understand what he was saying.

'I thought you might want to see them.'

'Why?'

Her immediate reaction: if she let him see she had any interest in the eagles he would shoot them. She had never forgotten the kittens.

'Why should I want to see them?'

'Because they're free.'

She had not known what she had expected him to say; not that, certainly. It made her doubly suspicious.

'How do you know about eagles?'

He knew nothing about them, had mentioned them only because he had thought she would be interested. Now he was at a loss how to answer her, his campaign running into snags almost before it had started.

He thought, How can I please her if I don't understand her?

'They're birds, ain't they?'

'Birds? Of course they are birds.' Contempt edged her voice. 'It isn't likely they'd be sheep, is it?'

He flushed. 'Nobody's talkin' 'bout sheep! You wants to see 'em, they're there, that's all.'

And stalked away.

It was the best thing he could have done. Alison thought about it that day, and the next. He had considered her likes and dislikes enough to tell her about the eagles, to realise she might be interested.

Her response had been to tell him that eagles weren't sheep.

She could have gone to look for them herself but would not do that. It would be the sort of victory she did not want him to have, the satisfaction of knowing that she *was* interested but lacked the courage or graciousness to permit him to show them to her. If now she allowed him to show her the birds it would also be a victory for him yet somehow that seemed less bad.

Alison had done no hunting; lacked Blake's instinct for stalking and capture. She went looking for him.

'I am sorry.'

He stared at her, his hard-eyed glare.

'About what?'

'The eagles.'

'Oh, *them*.' He laughed dismissively and she thought she had lost her chance. Then he said, 'They're still there, I reckon.'

He was right. They were there, free and beautiful in their freedom.

Alison watched them, entranced, two large birds that had come to them from nowhere, their unconscious grace giving them control over the skies with effortless, barely perceptible movements of the great wings.

Beautiful, indeed.

'Thank you for showing them to me.'

Blake seemed as uncomfortable with her gratitude as he had been affronted by her rejection.

She felt the need to repay him by sharing something of her own with him but had nothing. The lack made her uncomfortable, too.

'It was very kind of you,' she said.

He muttered something, at sea in this new environment, left her as soon as he could. He retained a lasting impression of a smile he had not seen before, a look in her face that told him he was on the right lines.

Slowly, inch by inch, with the passing of the weeks, the months, he drew closer.

She no longer thought of Blake as the bullying boy who had murdered the kitten. Now he was Blake, a man at one with his surroundings.

Asta dominated what was about her, humans included, by effort of will rather than by natural instinct. What she could not dominate at once she fought into submission: humans, animals, the land. Only the sea did she not seek to control, although Alison wondered whether she would not have done that, too, had she been able.

She also missed nothing of what went on around her.

'You like Blake a little better than you did, I think?'

'Perhaps a little,' Alison admitted cautiously.

'Blake is a very determined man.'

Asta did not condemn him for it; in this environment determination was a quality necessary for survival.

After a childhood with her father Alison knew all about determination. Blake shared with Ian Matlock one fundamental characteristic: if there was something you wanted in life you took it. It was an attitude Alison understood and respected. It occurred to her that she herself might be what Blake wanted but that was unimportant. She told herself she remained as committed to Jason as she had always been although she would have been more confident of it had she ever heard from him.

There had been information of a sort. Walter Lang had written to say that Jason had been at Kapunda and had then travelled north to take a job at Burra Burra. After that: nothing. He could still be at Burra Burra. He could have travelled into the interior. He could have gone back to sea. He could be dead. There was no way of knowing. The vast land had swallowed him up.

Her memories still warmed her, especially of *that* time that would be forever embedded in her consciousness, but for how long, she wondered, would she have to make do with memories?

Half the problem was that there was no way she could communicate with him. The only way was to send a message with one of the drovers who passed increasingly regularly through the peninsula but this she dared not do, fearing her father. Why should it be necessary? she thought resentfully. Surely, if Jason wanted to contact her, he should be able to get a message to her?

So she waited but no message ever came and gradually she began to doubt. Perhaps she had been a fool to let her feelings overwhelm her in the way they had. Had he really cared for her? Had she for him? Even her memory of his face began to blur. She had thought their act of love had been a declaration both to him and to herself of the depth and sincerity of her feelings. She had assumed it had meant the same to Jason but now was unsure. What if he had been interested only in the physical act and now had no further use for her?

She did not want to believe it yet supposed it was possible. She knew nothing about men. In the meantime Blake was here, attentive, not at all as he had been, making no secret of his admiration for her. With the arrogance of youth she took his attentions for granted, found herself watching him in turn: the sun-bronzed arms, the strong shoulders, the way he walked like a king through their shared world.

He was strong, and strength, like determination, was necessary. He would protect her, if it came to it, in the same way her father protected her. Blake, she told herself, had not run away.

It was not something that needed an urgent decision; then, one day, it did.

One of her mother's horses, a young stallion with a hard mouth and vicious temper, had split its hind off-hoof. This was something her mother would normally have dealt with herself but a foaling mare took her attention. Her father agreed to deal with the stallion for her. Alison came out of the house and saw it happen.

Blake and her father had the stallion tied by a head stall to the paddock railing. The afternoon sun varnished the little tableau: the animal, coat liquid chestnut with the light on it, tossing its head and bugling furiously against the restraint, Blake on the far side of the horse and partly concealed by its restlessly surging body, Ian gentling it, stooping to one side of the beast, reaching for the damaged hoof.

Her father had never been as good with horses as her mother. He lacked the instinct or the patience but Alison saw that the stallion, half-wild though it was, was at least under reasonable control. What made her pause and watch the scene she never afterwards knew but she saw her father take the hoof, leaning his head towards it, the horse twist suddenly, screaming, and try to rear. Its lashing hoof was plucked straight from her father's hands and sent with full force into his head. She heard the thud, like an axe in rotten wood, and was running, running, mouth wide, voice keening, a furious burst of energy even as her mind said *too late, too late*.

Blake said, 'Dunno what happened. One minute everything was under control, the next it was going mad. Damn near pulled my arms out of their sockets.'

Mary said, 'I blame myself. I should never have let him near an animal like that.'

Asta said, 'There is no point talking about blame. The man is dead. What we have to consider now is what is to be done.'

Alison running, running, as she had run towards the scene of the accident, knowing that what had happened could not be undone yet hoping that somehow, if she ran far enough, fast enough, it might still be possible to turn time back to how it had been in the instant before . . .

Running from the thought that the horse *had* been reasonably calm, that something had happened to turn it into a killer, that there had been blood on its flank as from a knife jab, that . . .

Running.

*

'Your aunt's right,' Blake said. 'I don't like to talk about these things neither, not now, but they got to be discussed. Someone's got to run Bungaree.' A pause. 'I got to think about me own future. I needs to know where I'm placed.'

'You aren't thinking of leaving?' Alison was shocked. 'Not when we need you so much?'

A smile: apologetic but with steel in it. 'Depends how much you needs me, don't it?'

Alison's eyes—she could not control them—strayed to the knife hanging in its sheath on Blake's belt.

'Sunburst had a gash on his shoulder,' she said. 'Any idea how that could have happened?'

'Must have bin while he were jerking about,' Blake said easily. 'These things 'appen so fast.'

Asta's words: *Blake is a very determined man.*

Asta raged, barely coherent. 'How can you? How *can* you?'

Jason will be back, she warned. All you have to do is wait.

But Alison had long given up hope of any such thing.

They were married by the Reverend Laubsch on the last day of June after a long and mostly incomprehensible sermon. The day was clear but cold. An icy wind scythed across the peninsula to set the women's clothing fluttering and cause the men to clutch their unaccustomed tall hats. The happy couple stood outside the little hut that Mr Laubsch had persuaded Asta to set aside as a chapel, the bridegroom smiling, his bride demure beside him.

Who could blame Blake for his smile, with such a beautiful and compliant bride?

Stiff-faced, Asta had watched at snivelling Mary's side throughout the drawn-out ceremony. She knew, they all knew, the story of Ian's fatal accident, how Blake had been holding the stallion's head at the time. She thought, I must make sure he never has anything to do with horses around me.

She thought Alison was lunatic to throw herself away on a man like Blake Gallagher but after her initial outburst had made no attempt to influence Alison's decision. The world was full of fools.

TWENTY

'The biggest bastards ever walked the earth.'

Silas Tregloam swilled beer, banged his empty pot on the counter for a refill. Red nose, red eyes, but Silas knew his way around mining and Jason listened to him, as did the half-dozen others gathered in the Miners Arms. Outside a winter gale battered the walls of the building; somewhere a loose shutter slapped and crashed against the stonework.

Silas swilled from his refilled pot, wiped a hand the size of a shovel across his mouth and returned to his perennial evening topic: the iniquities of the management of the Burra Burra mine.

'That feller John Graham. They d' say he take ten thousand a year out of the mine an' 'e never even been yur! Never once set foot in the town! An' see 'ow they was when they had that there labour trouble last year. Talked 'bout gettin' in the militia to deal with poor miners what hadn't hardly the price of a crust of bread to their names. I tell ee, brothers, them Frenchies had the right idea when they 'anged the bastards.'

'They di'n hang no-one.' Eli Pentewan knew Silas better than his own wife, saw a lot more of him, after all. He had been listening to him put the world to rights for twenty years: which didn't stop him slipping his spoke in from time to time. 'What I 'eard, they cut their 'eads off.'

Robert Noakes, an older man with a reputation for being politically conservative, said, 'Di'n do too well in that there latest effort, did they now? They Commune fellers didn't get nowheres, from what I did 'ear.'

'More the pity,' Silas said. 'I tell ee sumen, though. Commune or no Commune, there be trouble comin' yur if the management don' watch its step.'

'Why?' Jason asked.

It had taken three months for Silas Tregloam and his cronies to accept him into their circle; another three before they had been willing to talk openly in front of him.

Silas tapped his red nose. 'I d' smell it,' he said with an expression of indescribable cunning. 'Tes comin', brother, aren't no doubt 'bout that.'

'Why?' Jason asked again.

Silas said ominously, 'If they starts their tricks with the assayin' over agen ...' Bloodshot eyes looked at Jason through the smoke-fumed air. 'Tell me agen what 'e were sayin' 'bout that.'

'Only what I heard in the office. They're going to use company surveyors in Adelaide to recheck the assays carried out here at the mine.'

'So's they can claim the copper content be lower 'n what tes and they can cut wages agen! Twill be like 'forty-eight all over agen!'

'You don' know that,' Robert protested. 'Mebbe the company's learned its lesson.'

Silas laughed derisively. 'Henry Ayers? When did

'e learn anything except how to turn a bigger profit for the shareholders?'

'Tesn' in their interests to cause another strike,' Eli said. 'There'll be no profits at all, that road.'

'No wages, neither.' Once again Silas addressed his beer pot, wiped his moustache. 'I tell ee, brothers, profits or no profits, a strike be what they'll get if they start messin' 'bout with the assays!'

'I've a notion they mean it,' Jason told Mura.

Jason had used his position to get Mura a job labouring above ground at the sorting tables. Accommodation had been a different matter. Jason had known Challoner would never have given permission for that. A black living in the company's accommodation? He would have been more likely to approve a herd of pigs. In any case, Mura did not want to stay there. He preferred to camp out in the open with a handful of other aborigines who had also been drawn to the Burra Burra in hope of wages. It was primitive but Mura was used to that. There was liquor, which he was not used to at all but was seemingly beginning to like.

Now they sat before the glowing coals of a small fire, coat collars pulled up, while the wind brought a splatter of cold rain about their ears. Mura clutched a tin pannikin of spirits that he replenished periodically from the bottle at his side.

'You want to go easy with that stuff,' Jason said.

Mura ignored him. 'If there's a strike,' he said, 'what'll it mean to us?'

'Depends if we join them or not.'

'Will we?'

'Dunno.'

He had thought about it, certainly. These days

340

that was all he was good for, he thought, thinking about things. Always thought, never action. Quite different from how he'd been in the old days. Then he would have made up his mind, one way or the other, and done it. Now . . .

He was adrift. Had been for months, since he got the news.

Not a day he would forget. A day of bright sunshine, he remembered, after weeks of rain. A day of hope. For the first time in a long time he had allowed his thoughts to turn back to the run.

He remembered the vast, grassy expanse of Whitby Downs, the waves pounding the base of the cliffs. He thought, without letting himself think too closely, of Alison, what had happened between them, his hopes for the future. He knew a lot about mining now, about the business of mining. He had a notion that this might be more important in the long run than knowledge of geology or metallurgy: the ability to turn what lay beneath the ground, copper or tin or lead, into gold. It was the secret of Henry Ayers' success and Henry Ayers, avaricious and meticulous, was a man whom Jason both hated and admired. Hated for his penny-pinching ways, admired for the way he held every aspect of the Burra Burra operation in his hand. Given half a chance it was the way he would have been himself although Henry Ayers, unlike Jason, had no reputation as a fighting man.

Another reason for remembering that day, special as it was in so many ways.

'Fine strong lad like you,' Silas had said. 'Just the man we bin lookin' for.'

'There's a thousand miners in town,' Jason protested, 'what's special about me?'

Jason had been involved in a punch-up with an

obstreperous drunk a week earlier, had put him away in no time.

Silas cackled. 'Got the name fer un, see? Got the name.'

One of the muleteers, one Silvio Fernandez from Valparaiso, had also been making a name for himself. Big rowelled spurs, ferocious moustache, he had been terrorising the local hotels and—far worse—drawing the eyes of the few unattached local women. The time had come for him to be taught a lesson and Jason, it seemed, had been chosen for the task.

'Championship of Burra Burra,' Silas said, 'think of the honour!'

'A thousand Cornishmen and you're leaving it to one Australian and a bloke from Chile to decide who's champion? Where's your pride?'

Another cackle. 'Don' ee worry, my son. We'll all be in your corner, never fear.'

A fat lot of good that would do.

It was a well-organised affair. There might be few prepared to climb into the ring themselves but no shortage of those willing to arrange for someone else to do so.

Bunting was strung gaily in the Kooringa square. An area was roped off. The union flag was much in evidence. A milling crowd in holiday mood, excited voices, bright shirts, in one corner a silver band playing suitably martial airs. Everyone eager to see blood spilt as long as it wasn't their own.

No sign of the Chilean contingent.

'Perhaps he won't turn up,' Jason said hopefully.

'No chance of that,' said Eli, self-appointed second. He massaged Jason's shoulders, took a swig from a bottle taken from his jacket pocket. Jason reached for it, had his hand slapped away. 'Later,' Eli said, swigging again.

By the time the Chilean arrived Jason's second, plus half the crowd, were in a very cheerful mood. Jason was cold and scared but at least he was sober.

He sat in one corner of the square, a coat around his shoulders, and waited.

A murmur, swelling. A blast of unfamiliar sound. The trampling of horses' hooves. He looked up, heart beating furiously. The Chilean party rode into the square. First came the outriders, sombrero hats in tune with their huge moustaches, silver harness shining in the sun. Then a dray decked with flowers containing half a dozen smiling women, all black hair, flashing eyes, scarlet shawls. Two buglers in a cart. Finally, in an open carriage drawn by four matched mules, Silvio Fernandez himself, standing upright and throwing kisses to the crowd.

'Jeez,' Eli said, seeking consolation in the bottle.

'Nothing to worry 'bout there, my son,' said Silas. 'A fighter throwing kisses ... Take un on meself, I would, only twould be too one-sided, I reckon.'

Jason had seen the muscles in Fernandez's arms and shoulders and was not so sure.

They would soon find out.

He waited while Silas Tregloam, well to the fore as always, made the announcement in a stentorian voice blurred only slightly by drink.

'Ladies and gentlemen ...'

Wild cheers.

'For the championship of the world ...'

Even wilder cheers.

'From Chile in South America ...'

Boos.

'Silvio Fernandez!'

'Silvio,' someone yelled.

From the carriage Fernandez bowed, beaming and waving.

Silas cared nothing for such niceties. 'And from South Australia . . .'

'Van Diemen's Land!'

'Our very own Jason Hallam!'

The square erupted, the band, well liquored by now, attempted to play the national anthem.

'Go and kill him,' Eli said.

They toed the line. A bell clanged. The fight was on.

After all the jocularity it was a grim business. The muleteer might throw kisses but he threw punches, too, and a number of them landed. Some of Jason's landed, as well, but it was hard to tell what effect they were having. He swung, missed, swung, connected, sweat ran into his eyes, a violent blow made him stagger and he felt an eyebrow split. Now it was more than sweat in his eyes, the target blurred with red. Twenty minutes into the fight he was knocked down for the first time.

Ears ringing, eye swollen shut, he mumbled through a mouth gaping for breath, 'Too long in the office.'

'What?' Eli worked furiously on the eye.

'Got soft, see? You should have used one of the miners.'

'Weren't none of 'em fool enough to try it,' Eli said.

The bell clanged. The fight resumed.

Five minutes more, Jason caught Fernandez on the side of his head, sent him flying. The jar ran all the way up Jason's arm into his shoulder. He stood there, flexing his knuckles, while the other side battled to revive their man.

Fernandez toed the line, swaying and staggering, and Jason heard the tortured breath whistling in his throat.

No kisses for the ladies now, he thought and hit him again, savagely, and again felt the satisfying jar as the Chilean's feet left the ground.

He relaxed, knowing it was impossible for Fernandez to come up to the mark a second time, but he did, swaying but still dangerous, and unleashed a powerhouse swing that would have taken Jason's head off had he not seen it in time.

He ducked under it, felt it whistle through his hair, unleashed a cracking reply of his own and it was over. Great consternation and activity from the Chilean's corner but there was no response from the fallen man and when the bell rang for the last time Jason toed the line alone.

Silas raised his arm amid a mixture of cheers and boos, Eli flung his arms first in the air and next around Jason's sweating shoulders, a bottle was thrust into his hand and over in a corner of the square Jason made out the figure of Mura, hovering uncertainly.

After his victory Jason was filled with energy. If he'd wanted he could have pushed the whole world over. Now was not the time for shyness, hanging back. He shouted to Mura, gesturing hugely.

'Come over here! Join the party!'

Cautiously Mura approached. One of the onlookers grabbed his arm.

'Piss off, you black bastard!'

Jason was there in a second. He took the man by the nose, twisting.

'You were saying?'

He backed him through the crowd, the man

whimpering and pawing ineffectually at the hand gripping his nose, his mates hovering. Black looks but no-one with the guts to have a go. There was a horse trough. Jason backed the man into it; the back of his knees caught the edge of the trough; he fell in an explosion of scummy water.

Spluttering and shaking himself, black oaths choked by slime, the man staggered to his feet. Jason gestured to Mura to join him. Smiling, all teeth, he said, 'Let me introduce you to my mate. Shake his hand, why don't you?'

Stood over him until he had done so.

'Made an enemy there,' Eli said.

'I wouldn't want him as a friend.'

'Watch out for him. Regular troublemaker, John Davey,' Eli told him. 'Got the ear of management, see? Some nice wife, mind. Beautiful wife. Young, too.'

'Lucky for him.' He slapped Mura on the shoulder and said, 'What do you think? Reckon I'll make a champion?'

Mura said, 'A friend of mine is come. Walpannina. You remember him?'

'Of course I remember. What's he doing here?'

'Like me. Come here to work. The old life all gone now. People must work if they want food. Or drink, eh,' gesturing at the bottle in Eli's hand. He giggled foolishly, staring about him with bloodshot, wandering eyes.

'Dunno what I'm going to do about you,' Jason said. 'Carry on the way you are you'll kill yourself.'

'Walpannina bring messages,' Mura said.

'Yeah? How they all doing?'

'I told you. Everything is changed. The clan is broken up.'

Jason stared at him. 'Where have they gone?'

Mura shrugged. 'Some here, some there. Walpannina come here. Others go to Port Wakefield, work the barges.'

'Nantariltarra?'

Mura shook his head, scowling.

'Don't tell me something happened to him.'

'There is no-one of that name.'

'What do you mean?'

'His name,' Mura said, 'may not be spoken.'

Meaning he, too, was dead.

'How?'

'A fight.'

'With a white?'

Mura shook his head. 'A man of the Warree clan. My people tried to move on to land that was not theirs, to get away from the white men. The man of the Warree killed him.' Mura shrugged. 'If the Warree people had come on to our land, we would have done the same.'

White men had killed him as surely as if they had directed the spear or club that slew him.

'I'm sorry,' Jason said and was, unprepared for the intensity of the pang that twisted him. At one time, after his brother's death, he had wanted to kill him. Now all that was forgotten. It was not simply his personal loss; Nantariltarra had seemed the only member of the clan who had come close to understanding what the white arrival meant. Even with his guidance there had been a good chance that the clan was doomed; without it, there was no hope. It saddened him. They had taken him in, he had lived with them. Their ways had not been his but had suited them, enabled them to live at one with their world. Now it was all over, as he had known it would be. He remembered how Nantariltarra—no, he corrected himself, how He Whose Name Could

Not Be Spoken—had asked him despairingly what he should do, how at the time he had come so close to telling him that there was nothing he could do, that the clan and its age-old ways were doomed. He had lacked the courage to say it but that had not prevented it from happening.

'There was more news,' Mura said.

'Yes?'

'Ian Matlock.'

'What about him?'

'Got kicked in the head by his wife's horse.'

'Is he badly hurt?'

Mura shrugged. 'He is dead.'

So both the Matlock men were gone. Such vital men. It was hard to believe.

'Who is running Bungaree?'

'Blake Gallagher.'

He supposed it made sense but did not like to hear it.

'There is more news,' Mura said, troubled.

'You're not telling me he's dead, too?'

Mura did not smile. 'He is well. But he and Alison ... There is news about them, also.'

IMPOSSIBLE.

The thought hammered inside his head, over and over. The thought, the rejection, the utter and absolute incredulity. It was not true. It must not be true. It could not be true.

It was.

As soon as he had heard it he had known with a sickening sense of certainty that it was so.

Why? *Why*?

She had hated Blake and feared him. Not only that: she was Jason's, they belonged to each other.

348

How could she have married anyone else, least of all Blake Gallagher?

I shall go there, he thought. I shall take her away from him.

He knew it was impossible. She had made her choice. She—and he—would have to live with it.

A day to remember, indeed.

There had been other days, arising from the first. Drifting days, while he came to terms with a life suddenly, achingly, without future.

It had advantages. He could drink, if he chose: who cared, so long as he was at work the next morning? He could hate his work: who cared? He still had the evenings, still had Sundays.

For those who did not work below ground Sundays were sometimes special.

The man he had put in the horse trough: John Davey, the miner with Gwyneth, the lovely wife. With the lovely and, as it turned out, restless wife. John Davey worked for tribute. The more ore he raised, the more he earned. John Davey spent hours below ground. Days. There were times when it seemed he must live there, weeks when he came up to grass only to eat, drink, sleep briefly and go back down again. A lovely wife going to waste: in her own estimation, too.

Jason, foot-loose and resentful of the world, had focused on her very quickly.

A Sunday afternoon tea, sponsored by the Methodists, attended by a miscellany of adults and children: chapelgoers, parents, teachers, a handful of others.

'Your husband not here?'

A shake of the cartwheel hat as she turned towards him, a Welsh accent to cut bread. 'On shift, he is.'

'Pity.'

Eyes slanted, sparkling. 'Lucky for you, you mean.'

'Lucky?'

'Got it in for you, no error. No wonder, after what happened.'

'He should learn not to mess around with my friends.' Jason very confident; he was the champion, after all.

A pause as she sized him up. Jason returned the compliment. Eli had been right, she *was* a lovely creature.

'Is it true what they say?' she asked.

'What's that?'

'That you lived with the cannibals?'

He laughed. 'Don't know about cannibals. I lived with the blacks when I was a kid: that much is true.'

'Don't they eat people?'

'Not that I saw.'

'My husband says they do.'

'Your husband talks rubbish.'

Later:

'You ever go strolling along the creek?'

Eyes watching from beneath her hat brim. 'Why?'

'Very pretty up there. In the ranges.'

'Is that so?'

'I go up there often.'

'It's one thing for a man to go wandering. Wouldn't be right for a married woman, though, would it now?'

'Married,' he said. 'You could have fooled me.'

'I am, though. And a husband who thinks so, too.'

'It's a pleasant walk,' he said, 'with a friend. Very quiet. If you know where to go.'

Their eyes watched each other.

'I often go up there on a Sunday afternoon,' he said.

And slipped away before anyone could note them talking together.

The timber had been stripped from the hillsides to fuel the smelter's furnaces but along the creek, beyond the line of dugout homes, it still grew thick. There were waterfalls and deep pools with grassy banks overhung by the green branches of trees. Magpies and currawongs burbled and there was an occasional glimpse of a wallaby staring startled from the undergrowth. As Jason had said, it was beautiful and very quiet if you knew where to go.

The next Sunday he was up the hill early, well away, he hoped, from prying eyes, wagging tongues. It wasn't easy. There were children as well as sun-dappled leaves, men off-duty chancing their luck with a line thrown into isolated pools, no way of knowing when a watchful eye was not spying on you from the shadows.

Jason risked it, strolled nonchalantly in a green-gladed world, met no-one who counted, returned out of sorts with himself and everyone. Not a sign of the wretched woman.

To hell with this.

Instead went looking along the creek bank, found Gwyneth at home in the dugout, as he had hoped. He knocked on the door that led into a home like a rabbit hole in the creek bank, one of more than a hundred. Everywhere noise, children, pigs, rubbish along the banks, floating in the polluted creek. Rubbish you could see, more you could imagine.

'How do you live like this?'

'We can't all afford three bob a week for rent,' she told him. Her eyes were frightened, imagining scandal. 'What are you doing here?'

'Husband home?'

She shook her head. 'Down below.'

'Is he ever anywhere else?'

'Not often.'

'Next week,' he told her under his breath, as mindful of gossip as she was. He left, shouting for the benefit of neighbours, 'When you see him tell him I called.'

Knowing that the husband was sure to hear of his visit, whatever he said. There was never any shortage of malicious tongues willing to hurt a friend. He wondered if John Davey would come looking for him, if only to find out what Jason had wanted, but he did not.

The following Sunday was not like the previous one. It was a close day, too close for the time of year, with a humidity that promised rain, the clouds bruised and heavy, darkening above the livid hills. At intervals a drum-roll of thunder growled, drawing steadily nearer. Lines of sudden lightning drew cracks in an indigo sky. Between the thunder claps, the hills held their breath.

The creek cascaded noisily. Gusts of wind rattled the uneasy leaves, raised flurries on the surface of the pools. No sign of birds, of animals. Only Gwyneth, edging nervously through the afternoon, eyes fearful of watchers.

'I shouldn't have come.'

'There's no-one to see us,' Jason reckless, buoyed by her presence, at that moment not giving a damn whether anyone saw them or not. 'All we're doing is taking a stroll.'

'It's enough.'

It was more than enough and both of them knew it.

Apart from the rushing creek there was no sound,

no birds. Even the burble of the magpies was still.

'If he finds out I've met you . . .'

'Anyone can take a walk.'

They walked further but it was not safe and they knew that, too. He embraced her quickly, both of them gasping and eager, terrified of what was overwhelming them but unwilling, unable to stop. Shuddering, gasping, skin pale as chalk in the darkening air.

'Oh God . . .'

Kissing breasts like alabaster, body writhing beneath him. Feverishly she snatched at him, guiding. There. There. The thunder roared, drowning her cries. He felt release, little pleasure, above all a sense of corrosive anger at Gwyneth, at himself, for cheapening what he had lost.

Afterwards, a sprinkle of raindrops as heavy as stone, she dragging clothes together, combing leaves and twigs from her hair, searching frantically for her boots.

'He'll kill me . . .'

More than a figure of speech if he heard about it, but who was here to tell him?

'It'll be fine.'

Jason tried to embrace her again but she, panicking, avoided him.

'Don't you follow me!'

And was gone.

Obediently, he strolled on up the hill, the rain heavier now, came back to the town another way in what had become a drenching downpour.

Silas said, 'We needs to put up a deputation, see.'

Jason wanted nothing to do with it but Jason worked in the office, Jason could write.

'You don' 'ave to say you agree. All you got to do is write to the management on be'alf o' we and say we wants another assay of copper values. We needs somen to do it for us, tes all.'

'They won't like it. Could cost me my job.'

But did it, nonetheless.

Challoner summoned him, face white, hands trembling. He held the offending petition.

'Who wrote this?'

Jason looked him in the eye. 'Who knows?'

'It is your hand!'

'Copperplate's copperplate. Could be anyone.' Greatly daring, decided to gamble. 'Could even be yours, Mr Challoner.'

The turkey neck swelled red. '*Mine*?'

'Not saying it was,' Jason assured him. 'That would be ridiculous, we all know that. I'm just saying it could have been you or anyone. By the writing, I mean.'

'Are you saying you had nothing to do with this ... petition?' Holding it between fastidious fingers like so much dung.

'Absolutely nothing,' Jason lied cheerfully.

'I shall report it to Mr Ayers,' Challoner threatened but Jason was deputy accountant now and thought he was safe.

It rained for a week, heavier and heavier, without let-up. Cakes of yellow foam carpeted the surface of the water. Eddies swirled, sucked, bringing down tree trunks, drowning pigs, breaking away clumps of earth that fell with a lurch and roar into the gushing torrent as banks caved in under the relentless pressure of the water. The creek level rose: an inch, a foot, three feet. It lapped the footpath, already inundated beneath the weight of the rain, slopped into dugout doorways, threatening the inhabitants with tongues of moisture that probed and ran and spread.

Men and women banded together to build earth barriers against the water, using baulks of wood, large pieces of rock, barriers of earth and branches and leaves to hold back the rising flood.

Still the rain fell. Still the creek levels rose.

In the office, rain thundering on the roof, Jason said, 'Shouldn't the mine give them a hand?'

Challoner was astounded by the suggestion. 'Mr Ayers would never countenance such a thing.'

'If it keeps raining—'

Challoner's white fingers played with a cylindrical ebony ruler. 'It is no concern of ours.'

'But common humanity—'

'That is enough. They should have thought of the dangers before they built there.' The accountant did not sound angry but Jason would have found anger easier to bear than his evident indifference.

'They may drown.'

'Unlikely, I would say. In any case, that is not our concern.'

'I think—'

Challoner interrupted. 'Hallam, I said that's enough. The dockets for the shipments to the foundry ... Do you have them there?'

That night, somewhere up in the range, some natural barrier to the floodwater gave way. Even from his room Jason heard the roar of the creek. He learned later that the level rose three feet in ten minutes, sweeping away all the puny barriers that had been raised in its path. That was how long it took for every dugout to be under water. Sticks of furniture, crates of chickens, livestock of various kinds, were swept away in the flood. Babies, too: at least three. The burrows dug out of the creek banks collapsed. People who owned nothing suddenly found themselves with even less as their homes disappeared.

Morning shed grey light on a scene of devastation: swirling waters as brown as chocolate washed-out banks, saturated scarecrows picking over banks of mud in search of anything that might be salvaged. Destitution, misery, despair under the leaden weight of the rain.

First thing Jason was there, too, along with a maintenance team from the mine. They salvaged what there was to save. It wasn't much.

'What shall we do?' Gwyneth wept.

'Start again,' he said uncomfortably. It was useless advice but what else was there?

John Davey was up from the mine, grumbling about lost time, lost production, lost wages.

Saw Jason talking to his wife. His face darkened.

'You get away from her,' he shouted.

Sixteen hours non-stop, fingernails ripped, hands raw from picking over debris in the pelting rain, seeing scenes of misery that no man should have to see, Jason had had enough.

He bunched his fists, moved closer to Davey, crowding him. He stared down at him. 'Take my advice. You want to keep your wife, look after her. Another thing. *Don't raise your voice at me.*'

He was out of line, of course he was. A man's dealings with his wife were his business and Davey was the sort to prove it.

The next day Gwyneth, face bruised, lip cut.

'An accident, that's what it was!'

Jason did not believe her. He went looking for her husband, found him in the pub, picked a fight. John

Davey was tough but little whereas Jason was now six feet tall and big with it. He was also mad with rage. Three minutes of one-sided warfare and he had to be dragged off the Welsh miner before he killed him, ended up in the Redruth lock-up with the drunks.

He stared out at the still-pouring rain. Talk your way out of this, he thought.

'When do I get out of here?' he asked the gaoler.

'Got an appointment?'

'I've got a job.'

'Not any more you haven't. The Secretary sent word from Adelaide. You're fired.'

Even in the gaol, everyone knew everyone else's business.

'Why?'

The gaoler shrugged. 'Fighting?'

Jason knew better. Henry Ayers had obviously not believed his lies about the petition. John Davey, friend of management, might have had something to do with it, too.

'The magistrate will be here in a couple of weeks,' the gaoler said. 'In the meantime you can stay where you are.'

'The *magistrate*? But—'

'Who did you expect? The Queen, maybe?'

This was serious. A magistrate meant the possibility of a gaol sentence. For affray? Six months, probably more.

One of the drunks, sore but sober, was on his way.

'Find Michael,' Jason said to him. 'Find the black boy. Tell him what's happened.'

He had no hope that Mura could do anything,

could not even be sure that the drunk would find him, but at least had done what he could. Mura, if he was sober enough to understand, would have been told what had happened. What he would do with the knowledge, if anything, would be another story but at least he would know.

How do I get out of here? Jason wondered. The idea of six months was unthinkable but the walls of the gaol were sixteen feet high, crowned with broken glass, and the gate was of studded oak. There was no way out.

Two nights later, another drunk, yelling and singing, was brought in: Mark Mitchell, friend of Silas Tregloam, not much given to booze.

'What happened to you?' Jason asked.

'Brought a message,' Mark whispered, suddenly sober. 'You got to get out of yur.'

'How do I do that?'

'There'll be a rope over the wall tonight.'

'If they see me they'll shoot me.'

'You must get out. The way you went for Davey, they'll be after you for attempted murder. They convict you of that, it'll mean ten years.'

Jason could not believe it. *'Ten years?'*

'Or more. People know 'bout his wife, see. Don' like it.'

'What about his wife?'

'Don't treat me like a fool.'

There were cells along the back wall of the exercise yard, each with its door and lock. Jason prayed that the gaoler, confident in the security of his walls, would follow his usual practice of leaving the cells unlocked. A rope over the wall would not help if he was locked away in a cell.

His heart sank when at dusk the gaoler said, 'Inside . . .'

For a wild moment Jason thought of resisting but it was pointless. With bad grace he shuffled into the cell, small, with a tiny barred window not more than a foot square and a heavy wooden door. The door slammed behind him. The steel bolt securing the door shot home. Footsteps crunched, withdrawing across the yard. Silence but for the almost inaudible cawing of crows in the gum trees on the far side of the wall.

He sat, head in hands, on the edge of the wooden plank that projected from the white-washed wall. Despair settled on him in the silence.

Slowly the daylight faded. Occasional clangs and shouts came from the rest of the building. He welcomed them. They showed that even in here he was not entirely alone but eventually they died and silence settled over the prison.

Jason went to the door, tested it cautiously. It did not budge. The closely barred window, steel bars set firmly into the stonework, was as impassable as the door. Even without the bars it would have been too narrow to crawl through. In his mind's eye he could see the outer wall, smooth and high, its crown of jagged glass shining in the moonlight. Absolutely impossible.

He was here until someone decided to let him out.

A whisper of sound, barely audible.

The prison had been silent for what seemed hours. For a moment Jason thought he had imagined it. A tiny mouse of sound, the barest shift and scuttle of sound, followed by silence. The gaol's previous noises had all been assertive, whereas now . . . It was its very furtiveness that drew this particular sound to his attention.

He waited but it did not come again.

After a few minutes he stood, went to the door and pressed on it with the flat of his hand, so cautiously that he could barely feel the smooth wooden planks against his palm. The door quivered. He pressed again, a shade harder. It shifted, opened a fraction of an inch. The hinges screeched. Blood flooded his head. He froze. After a minute tried again. Again the screech of rusted hinges. Someone, somehow, had drawn the bolt on the far side of the cell door but how was he to open it without the rest of the world hearing?

Outside the window he could see the white glare of moonlight but inside the cell everything was dark. His fingers felt for the hinges secured by iron straps to the walls of the cell. He spat on his fingers, used the spittle to lubricate the hinges, tried, oh so cautiously, once again. Another creak, not so loud this time. Did it again, mouth rapidly drying, what spittle remained now rust-tasting, but this time when he tested it the door shifted with barely a whisper. Heart hammering, he slid the door open a foot, eeled through the gap into the yard.

On this side of the yard the gaol was in darkness but beyond the shade cast by the buildings the moonlight glared on the bare ground, the blank whiteness of the wall. Anyone glancing out of a window would have seen a fly, had one moved on it. Jason looked about him. The building lay in darkness, silent under the brilliant glare of the moon. Nothing moved.

He studied the wall. It looked utterly smooth, not a crevice anywhere to give the slightest hope of scaling it without a rope. He was as helpless here in the yard as he had been in the cell.

Yet the door would not have been unlocked without reason.

He waited in the shadow of the building, watching the wall in the pitiless white glare.

Time passed. The moon climbed higher, the area of moonlight advancing inch by inch across the yard. Somewhere in the trees beyond the wall an owl called. Along the top of the wall the crusting of broken glass glistened frostily. Time passed.

When something did happen it was so quick, so furtive, that he almost missed it: a flicker of movement like an eye-blink, an uncoiling thread of darkness as something flew through the moon-bright air.

In the corner of the yard a rope had been flung over the wall and now hung motionless in the silent moonlight.

This was it.

His head turned slowly, cautiously. Nothing moved. He took a step. Waited. Still nothing. Another step. Waited. Absolute stillness. His heart had settled down during the long wait; now it beat as wildly as ever. He took a deep breath, ran on tiptoe across the yard, seized the rope and yanked it as hard as he could. It held firm. Far above his head the cruel glitter of glass waited. He got a good grip, took one final breath, leant backwards and set the soles of his boots against the face of the wall. Slowly, step by step, inch by inch, he began to climb.

Hand over hand he rose, breath gusting audibly. Below him the empty yard sucked at him as he climbed higher. If he slipped, if he fell . . .

He told himself not to think about it but that was hard to do. Every foot was hard-won, now. The rough texture of the rope was harsh against his burning palms, the muscles of his upper arms quivered under the strain.

If anyone looked out of the window, if anyone heard the noise he was making . . .

An inch, another inch. One by one, the stone slabs of the wall receded beneath him. He dared not look up, had no idea how far he still had to climb, but could feel the glass waiting for him. Now the muscles of his hands were threatening to cramp.

One more pull, he told himself. Just one. He made himself do it, face contorted, shoulders on fire. He was almost crying with effort and frustration. One more pull. On and on.

He reached the top. The glass gleamed like green ice in the moonlight. He clung to the top of the wall, drawing deep breaths into tortured lungs. He felt glass fragments puncture the skin of his palms, blood run down his arms. He hooked one leg up and over. The jagged edges of the glass snagged in the cloth of his breeches.

At least now he was in no immediate danger of falling back into the yard but up here, on top of the wall, he could hardly have been more exposed.

Teetering on top of the foot-wide wall, he tried with only partial success to use his boots to chip away some of the worst pieces of glass. It made so much noise he was afraid it would waken the township, never mind the gaol.

I shall never do it, he told himself with mounting panic. Or if I do I shall geld myself on this goddamned glass.

Another piece of glass cracked and fell away, the sound as loud as a pistol shot in the silence. A sudden yell from below him.

'What's going on up there?'

That was it. Gelded or not, he couldn't risk staying up here a moment longer. In this light, a rifle shot would knock him off the wall as easy as winking. Recklessly he drew up his other leg, gathered himself precariously on top of the wall for a second. He stared down wildly but could see nothing of what lay below. The thought of ten years in prison steeled his nerve. He took a deep breath, launched himself forward into the void. As he did so there came the sharp concussion of a rifle shot.

He landed in a heap, unsure in the general pain of landing if he had been shot or not. A rush of footsteps. Hands helped him to his feet.

'You all right? Run, can ee?'

He didn't know if he was all right or not. Bruised and shaken by the fall, the stealthy slither of blood from a dozen gashes, he could barely speak. He stood, swaying.

'Don' want to hurry you none,' Silas said, 'but if we don' get movin' there's a good chance we may all end up inside. Always assumin' they don' shoot us first.'

Lurching and staggering, helping hand on either elbow, Jason crossed the open ground in front of the gaol into the shelter of the trees.

''nother 'undred yards,' Silas urged him. 'Tes all. Then we got 'osses.'

Somehow he made it. There were three rescuers—Silas, Eli and Mura—and two horses.

'Git movin',' Silas urged him. 'Fast as ee can. Get a couple miles away ee can afford to rest up a while. Not yur. Go on: git!'

'What about you?'

'Don' ee worry 'bout us! We'll be fine. Haven't stirred outa bed all night, 'as us?' and nudged Eli in the ribs.

'Never a step,' Eli agreed.

Jason needed no further urging, climbed up painfully into the saddle, put heels to the horse's flanks and took off through the scrub, Mura riding along-side him.

For all his cuts and bruises his heart was singing. Free!

He galloped on through the moonlight.

They didn't get far. Within half an hour Jason was swaying with exhaustion, the pain of the lacerations rapidly becoming more than he could bear.

He turned in the saddle.

'We're going to have to find somewhere to lie up,' he said.

Until now he had barely taken note of where they had been heading. Now he looked about him. In the dazzle and glare of moonlight it was hard to tell where they were but from the shape of the ground around them he could see that they had climbed out of the valley and were now crossing the range that overlooked the cluster of settle-ments—Kooringa, Redruth and the rest—with the mine itself on the far slope. Ahead of them, to the west, a dense stand of timber stood black in the moonlight.

Jason gestured. 'We'll rest up there.'

It could not have been more than half a mile ahead yet he scarcely made it, slipping semi-conscious from the saddle when they were no more than twenty yards into cover.

They hobbled the horses and turned them loose. Jason stretched himself full length on the ground and went immediately to sleep.

It was daylight when he woke, Mura shaking him out of an exhausted slumber.

'What is it?'

A black finger counselled silence. 'Listen . . .'

He did so, heard at once the distant baying of hounds.

'We can outride them,' Jason said hopefully.

Mura shook his head. 'Once we're out of this timber they'll see us as we cross the slope. They're bound to have horses themselves. They'll ride us down.'

'What, then?'

'We look for water.'

'What do we do with the horses?'

'Take them with us. If we don't, they'll find them and know we can't be far away.'

A hundred yards further on, in the densest part of the forest, they found water. There was a mere rimmed with reeds from which the creek flowed down the hill. Mura urged his horse forward into the water, dismounted and slid into the hissing reeds until both horse and rider were completely hidden. Jason followed. Bubbles of foul-smelling gas, disturbed by the hooves, burst on the surface around them.

Beneath the trees the water stretched away amid dappled pools of sunlight. Through the dense scrub nothing was visible; neither movement nor sound marred the stillness. Then Jason heard again the baying of the hounds and shivered. Slowly he urged his mount forward. The reeds closed about them. All he could see now was the wall of greenery, a blue patch of sky overhead.

He waited. Water lapped. Insects buzzed.

He might have been alone in the world. The green light changed to gold as the sun climbed higher, the horse pricked its ears and shook its head.

A voice, shouting.

Jason strained his ears.

'Nothing,' the voice called. 'Nothing over here at all.'

Over where?

Another voice, so close that it could not have been more than a few yards away.

'If he's got into this lot we'll never find him.'

'The dogs . . .'

'Them dogs is useless.'

The sound of bodies forcing their way through the crackling undergrowth.

Further away now, the first voice asked, 'Why are we bothering with him, anyway? He was only some bloke worked in the office, wasn't he? You'd think he'd stolen the crown jewels, the way everyone's going on.'

'Politics,' the second man explained. 'Challoner reckoned he was the bloke wrote the miners' petition. They want to get rid of him before he causes any more trouble.'

'He's on the run, ain't he? What trouble's he going to cause?'

The voices faded.

Still Jason waited, looking for a lead from Mura. At last, after what seemed hours, the black man stirred.

'Let's get on,' he said.

Mud sucking beneath the hooves, they waded slowly through the edges of the mere until they arrived once again at dry ground. They rode up the bank and between the trees until they reached the woodland fringe. Once again they paused, eyes and ears alert, but nothing stirred.

'Where are we going?' Mura asked.

Jason hesitated. After he had heard the news of Alison's marriage he had thought never to go back to Whitby Downs. Now, however, it seemed the only refuge.

'We're going home,' he said.

They rode out into the yellow afternoon sunlight and headed south-west.

BOOK THREE

EAGLES

*Eagles are the largest and most powerful
of raptors and ruthlessly dominate their
territories. The females are usually much larger
than the males.*

TWENTY-ONE

Asta Matlock watched as Hector Gallagher brought the bleating, jostling mob off the hill towards the homestead. Around him the dogs circled, driving the sheep towards the shearing shed that had replaced the ramshackle framework of sawn boughs that Gavin and Ian had erected when they first set up the two runs.

Hector trotted up. 'We'll be ready to start shearing in the morning.'

'Yes.'

' 'Bout time. Blake started two days ago.'

'So you have already told me.'

You have told me twice, she thought, but would not give Hector the satisfaction of saying so.

'This rate 'e'll finish afore us.'

Blake would certainly do his best. Two days either way would make no difference but Blake would always want to be first, determined to prove that a good man would always beat a woman.

Asta saw no reason to give him that satisfaction if she could avoid it. 'Then it is up to us to stop him, is it not?'

Hector grinned. 'We can try.'

He would, too. After the wedding Hector had made the mistake of telling his son how to run Bungaree and Blake, fired up by a lifetime of beatings, had told him to go to hell. The two men had not spoken since.

She went into the house. That was another change she had made, replacing the slab-built shack with this cottage. Hector had disapproved but Asta cared nothing for that.

I am going to live the rest of my life here, she thought. I intend to do it in comfort.

Or in as much comfort as was possible in this place.

She poured water into a tin bath, stripped off her shirt and began to rinse the dust from her upper body. There was no water for baths; it was part of the price she had to pay for living here. She paid it willingly. Her attitude to the land had changed. She was determined that in this place she would build something of enduring value. It would give purpose to what would otherwise have been without purpose, the deaths of Edward and Gavin, the loss of Jason, if lost he were. Nothing else mattered.

She towelled herself until her skin glowed, shook her sweaty shirt to free as much dust from it as possible, put it on again and began to cook her evening meal.

At Bungaree, too, Alison was cooking supper. On the far side of the yard Blake was still working but would be coming in shortly. He would come in heavy-booted, he would sit at the rough table while she waited on him, he would shovel the food down. When he was finished he would go back outside to carry on working until he could work no longer, working with a passion that was frightening in its intensity. When at last he was finished he would blow out the lamp and come in, shutting the door on the swirling bugs, the darkness. He would sit for a while before collapsing into bed, he would sleep.

Sometimes she slept, too. Even as she slept she would be conscious of him watching her.

Waking or sleeping, it was the condition of her life. To Blake, marriage meant ownership. Even while he was working she knew he watched her. It seemed he wanted her to have no separate existence at all.

Alison had relied on her father all her life; even, to a lesser degree, on her mother. Now her father was dead and Mary Matlock, daughter safely married, had fled back to the country outside Adelaide where she now owned a horse stud. Without either of them, Alison needed Blake's strength to compensate for her own lack of confidence but she also needed room to breathe and this Blake denied her.

Not until after the wedding did she realise how bitterly Blake had resented her friendship with Jason. He never knew—thank God—how far that friendship had gone but remained convinced she had married him only because Jason had gone away.

It was foolishness. Whatever Alison might have done had Jason stayed, the fact remained that he had not. She had made her marriage willingly and wanted it to be a success yet even in their moments of passion Jason always stood between them. In Blake's mind it was Jason's body she embraced and not his own; his jealousy imprisoned her like a cage. She was frightened by its ferocity. All her life she had believed that indifference was the one thing she could not bear. Now there were times when she longed for it.

There was nothing she could do. Jason had gone; she would probably never see him again. She told herself it was better so. I shall endure, she told herself. Each day, each night, hoping for better things.

She finished the supper and walked across to the door. 'Blake . . .' she called into the darkness, 'tea's ready.'

Next day Alison decided to ride over to Whitby Downs. Nowadays it was something she seldom did. In the months after her father's death she had made the journey often, the visits helping to carry her through that bad time, but gradually they had dwindled away.

Asta is always so sure of everything, she had told herself.

Too sure, was what she had meant. It was a quality she resented, desiring it so unavailingly in herself, but that was not the reason she had stopped going. Asta detested Blake and the knowledge created an awkward atmosphere between the two women, not because Asta was wrong to hate Blake but because in her heart Alison knew she was right. She had married a truculent bully who frightened her. That was the truth but it was something she would never admit: not to Asta, not to herself.

Today, however, something had made her decide to go. We are neighbours, she told herself. We should see more of each other.

As she rode she remembered the grotto on the cliffs where Asta had taken her the day Jason had saved them from the black warriors. She had never been back. It had merged into all the other memories that made up the lost paradise of childhood. Today was a day for fancies and she decided to revisit the place.

It was not as she remembered it. There had been little rain recently and the trickle of water had been reduced to a patch of dampness, shielded beneath the canopy of rock. Lichen and a few straggly ferns still grew in the crevices of the cliff face but of the garlands Asta had laid on the stone altar not even the dried-up fragments remained; wind and time had swept them away long ago.

There was nothing here. Alison stared about her. She had been happy in this place yet now loneliness oppressed her. She was alone, caught between a husband she feared and a woman she had thought would be her friend but was no longer. Yet needed to make a gesture, at least, to the past. Self-consciously she picked ferns from the crevice and laid them on the altar. She stood for a minute listening to the silence, to the barely comprehensible feelings of her heart, then turned and retraced her steps to the cliff top.

When she arrived at Whitby Downs she rode up past the creek towards the cluster of buildings. There were strange horses in the paddock. Asta came running to meet her, the lines about her eyes and mouth clearly visible in the morning sunlight. Her eyes were red. Alison stared.

'I was going to send word to you,' Asta said, 'I wanted you to be the first to know.'

'Know what?'

'Jason.'

Alarm: her hand flew to her lips, a pulse thumped in her body. She thought, Jason is dead. 'What about him?'

'He is here. Jason has come home.'

TWENTY-TWO

Her first impression was that he was older. Dirty, too, as though he had ridden a long way without rest. Michael the black boy was with him, dressed in rough shirt and breeches as Jason was, but after the first smiling greeting her eyes were all for Jason.

He has come home, her heart said, and the apprehension she had felt at the idea that he might one day come back was gone.

He came across to her, took her hands in his. His touch made her feel faint. 'A long time,' he said.

'Yes.' There were scars that were new, an eyebrow bisected by a vertical line, some fresh gashes on his hands.

'I hear that a lot has happened while I've been away.' Smiling but with a shadow darkening his eyes. The life they faced, how different it was from the life that might have been.

'Jason has been telling me his adventures.'

There was an indulgent note in Asta's voice that Alison had not heard for a long time.

'You must tell me about them.'

The barest nod. 'How is ... Blake?'

'He is well.'

Her husband's shadow lay between them like a reproach: a threat, too, perhaps.

'I was sorry to hear about your father.'

They were so polite with each other, like strangers. She remembered the peaceful movements of horses beyond the wooden partition as the straw sighed beneath her. She remembered lamp light flowing like golden oil over naked limbs, the soft brilliance of eyes and teeth, the smells and textures of love.

I shall scream, she thought.

Jason's expression told her that he felt the same.

She said to Asta, 'Now Jason is back he will be able to help you at Whitby Downs.'

'We have not discussed what Jason will do now he is back. Perhaps he is just paying us a visit before he disappears a second time.' Now the note of indulgence was gone. In its place there was an edge in Asta's voice; she had obviously not completely forgiven him for going off the first time.

'That depends whether there's a place for us here,' he said.

'Why should there not be?'

'Things are different now. Alison is married and Blake is running Bungaree. Maybe he won't want me around.'

'Blake does not decide what happens at Whitby Downs,' Asta told him. 'There is a place for you here as long as you want it.'

'What's he come back for?' Blake asked.

'It's his home,' Alison said. 'Where else should he come?'

'Why leave, then? If it's his home?'

'Because of Michael.'

He glared suspiciously. 'You seem to know a lot about it.'

Quickly she shook her head. 'I know nothing.'

'Make sure you don't.' He took her arm, smiling. Her skin crawled. 'I wouldn't like to think you wasn't tellin' me everything.'

She tried to laugh. 'What could I know? I've had no more contact with him than you have.'

His fingers moved over her skin: a caress or possibly a threat. 'Keep it that way.' He laughed and released her; she breathed more easily. 'Though what Asta's goin' to do with him now he's here God only knows.'

'She said he'll help her on the run.'

Blake's lip curled. 'For all he knows about sheep.'

Three months passed without trouble. Blake and Jason saw little of each other and when they did the meetings passed without incident. For the most part Mura kept out of the way, disappearing for days into the bush to re-establish contact with what was left of his people.

'It's no good,' he told Jason after one of these episodes. 'When I talk to them about the things I've seen and done, they don't even try to understand. We've nothing in common any more.'

Without a proper job Jason, too, felt out of place but did what he could to make the best of things; he took wool to Adelaide, sold it for a good price. On the return trip he delivered a load of mining equipment to Kapunda.

The town had grown. The number of stone buildings had increased and there were several hotels where before there had been only the Miners Arms.

Jason had hoped to see Stefan Lang but the Langs were away. Instead he saw Joshua Penrose. They went for a drink at the Sir John Franklin, one of the new hotels.

'Haven't found no copper over your part of the world yet?' The Cornishman emptied his glass.

'Far as I know no-one's looked.'

'Never know what you might find if you don't look.' Penrose eyed Jason keenly. 'You find copper, I'm the man'll get her out of the ground for you.'

'I would have thought you had your hands full here.'

Penrose looked wistful. 'Be out of here like a shot if I could. Things aren't what they used to be. Finding copper and developing the seam, that's what I d' like about mining. In Kapunda I'd say we've found just about everything there is to find. Nowadays tes a case of digging her out and selling her. Tes just business now and I've never had no interest in that. Not too keen about the people I got to do business with, either,' he added. 'Mrs Matlock tell you I come over to see her?'

'She mentioned it,' Jason said.

'Handsome woman, Mrs Matlock,' Penrose said approvingly, a man who appreciated a good-looking woman. 'I got a lot of admiration for her.'

'Well, she's unattached,' Jason said. 'Except to her sheep run. She's pretty attached to that.'

'I don't have no interest in sheep. You find copper and I'll be over,' Penrose told him. 'Then we'll see.'

When he got back to Whitby Downs Jason told Asta what Penrose had said. 'Sounds like he may have fallen out with the Langs,' he said.

'Mr Lang is a very hard man,' Asta told him. 'I would not be at all surprised if Joshua had fallen out with him.'

Joshua, Jason noted. Well, well.

'He spoke well of you, though. Maybe you'll find him turning up here, one of these days.'

Asta laughed. 'I don't think so. Joshua Penrose is like you, he's no farmer.'

'He said he'll come if we find copper. But you're right. I'm no farmer, never will be. I've been thinking about it. Maybe it would be better if I moved on, too.'

The idea of his going so soon troubled Asta. 'Why should you do that?'

Jason looked evasive. 'You said it yourself. Running sheep isn't something I want to do for the rest of my life and there's not much else to do around here.'

'We are not talking about the rest of your life.' Asta looked at him, knowing that he was hiding something. 'What is the real reason you want to leave?'

'I think there'll be trouble if I don't.'

'Between you and Blake?'

'Between Blake and Alison.'

'Blake is a jealous man, that is true. But if you give him no cause . . .'

He was silent.

'But where would you go?'

'Mining's what I fancy,' he said. 'I'll go anywhere there's a mine.'

'Back to Burra Burra?'

'Maybe not there.'

'You never told me why you left in the first place.'

'There was trouble.'

'Tell me about it.'

He hesitated but did so, in the end.

'Attempted murder?' She was horrified.

'That's what they called it. It was just a fight, really.'

'With a man over his wife. You certainly choose your women.' But was more concerned about another aspect of his story. 'Burra Burra is not far away. Do they know you come from this part of the world?'

'They don't know anything about me.'

'You never told the woman?'

'I never told anyone.'

Her eyes probed his; satisfied, she nodded. 'I suppose that is why no-one has come looking for you.'

'Why should they bother? All her husband wanted was to get rid of me. He won't care what happens to me now I'm gone.'

'You broke out of gaol. That means the troopers are also involved. Make sure Blake doesn't find out what happened,' she instructed him. 'You have said nothing to Alison?'

'You surely don't think Alison—'

'Alison has also changed.'

'She would never betray me.'

'Why not? You betrayed her.'

Jason was indignant. 'I'd have said it was the other way round. We had an understanding, then she went off and married Blake.'

'An understanding?' Asta's mouth was filled with contempt. 'You expect her to wait for you forever? Without a word? Over a year she waited. I watched her. I saw the hope die. After her father was killed, she needed someone and you weren't here for her any more.'

He didn't want to hear about it; didn't want to believe that he might have been the cause of what had happened. 'That doesn't mean she'd say anything to Blake, of all people.'

'Blake is her husband. Now you are back, perhaps she feels guilty about her old feelings.' She stared at

him. 'You knew Alison was married. You knew that
Ian was dead and Blake was running Bungaree. You
are not a man of the land and never will be. Why
come back at all? You said yourself it may cause
trouble.'

'It is home,' he said, not looking at her.

They both knew the real reason. He might talk
about leaving but as long as he had breath he would
never give up hope of Alison, married or not.

She smiled. 'Good. Then stay here, at least for a
time.'

She will hold him here, she thought, if I arrange
things right.

'The thing I'd like to know,' Blake said for the hundredth time, 'is why he's come back at all.'

At Bungaree night had descended over the silent
countryside. In the fireplace the flames flared as the
booming wind drew them up the chimney.

'It is his home,' Alison said.

'Home?' Blake repeated derisively. 'This place
ain't never bin his home.' For a minute he did not
speak. 'Why do *you* reckon he's here?' he asked
eventually.

It was a dangerous question. 'Where else should
he go after he left the mine?'

'Why leave the mine at all? He's a lot more interested in mining than he is in sheep. He's running
away from somen, that's what. Or else he's come
back here to look for somen, or someone.' The
leaping flames dazzled her eyes as he took her chin
in strong fingers and twisted her face to look
upwards at him. 'Which do you think it is?'

His voice was still soft but she could sense danger
in his glaring eyes. She had always known he was a

violent man yet too much subservience might be as dangerous as too little. She risked a straight answer. 'I'm not responsible for what Jason does.'

His body went rigid. Too late, she knew she had guessed wrong. With a sudden, scything movement he slapped her, very hard, across the face. Lights exploded in her head. She staggered back, ears ringing, stumbled and fell full length upon the floor.

'Don' tell me what you're responsible for!'

He kicked her; she took the blow on the thigh and her leg went numb. Frantically she twisted her body away from him, knees raised protectively to her chest, eyes squeezed tight. 'Why?' she screamed. 'Why are you doing this?'

No answer. Instead, he kicked her again and the flesh over her ribs took fire. She tried to scramble away from him. He bent, lifted her effortlessly until her face almost touched his own. Her tears—how she hated them, despising herself for shedding them—dazzled her so that she could no longer see his anger but sensed it, oh yes.

'Don' get smart wi' me.' Rage in his hands, his heart. He threw her down. She lay on the floor like a broken doll.

Jealous ... The word sang in her head. That's what it was. Jason hadn't been back five minutes and Blake was jealous. The word shone golden through the terror, the pain. Blake was jealous. With reason. There was glory in knowing it, the confirmation of what in her heart she had always known. But for the moment there was danger. She could do nothing about that; knowing the reason for his rage did not help.

'Get my tea,' he said.

She could barely move. Somehow she dragged herself upright, went to the fire, lifted the lid from the pot. Through the gush of steam she peered down at its contents. A stew of meat and vegetables. It looked done. Thank God. She doubted she could have managed to do more, not tonight. Slowly she fetched a plate, ladled stew, took it to the table, put it in front of her husband.

He stared at it. 'What's this?'

'Stew.'

His lip curled. '*Stew.*'

She might have said garbage. She stood, head hanging. She was conscious of his hot eyes crawling on her, looking for a residue of defiance, perhaps, but she had no defiance left in her.

'Get me somen to eat it with, then. Or do you expect me to *drink* it?'

She fetched knife and spoon, gave them to him.

'Bread,' he said.

She fetched that, too.

'Alison,' he said.

She felt herself swaying. 'Yes?'

'Got anythin' to say to me?'

'No, Blake,' she said. The tears ran unimpeded down her face.

'Be sure you keep it that way.'

TWENTY-THREE

In the middle of the winter a motley group of travellers and their carts arrived at Whitby Downs.

Asta greeted them without enthusiasm. They were a rough-looking bunch, half a dozen coarsely dressed men escorted by three armed troopers: two black, one white, with a sergeant's stripes on his sleeve.

'What brings you to this part of the world?' she asked their leader, a scraggy-bearded man named Benson.

'We're looking for the abos,' Benson told her.

'What do you want them for?'

He grinned brown-toothed. 'I suppose you could say we're a kind of mission.'

Asta didn't like the look of the men at all.

'We already have the Reverend Julius Laubsch of the Lutheran Mission. He lives among them, not far from here. He caters for their spiritual needs.'

Benson's grin became derisive. 'Not that sort of mission.'

'What, then?'

'All sorts. We find work for them as wants it. We

trade with 'em, too, when they got money or anything to sell.'

'And the troopers?'

'As much for our protection as anything.'

Benson and his men were bristling with arms; they did not look as though they needed protection.

'Protect you against what?'

'Some of the blacks don't take kindly to strangers coming into what used to be their territory. The troopers are there to make sure they don't try nuthin. They're on the lookout for criminals, too, o' course.'

'What crimes do the natives commit?'

Benson heard the disbelief in her voice. 'Murder, robbery: you'd be amazed.'

'What do you sell them?'

'Anything they fancies.'

'They have no money.'

'Quite a lot of 'em finds work o' one sort or another. Money works its way back. Nowadays most of 'em can lay their hands on enough to buy the things they need.'

'Such as?'

'The ones who've worked for white men pick up white men's tastes. We're here to give 'em what they want.'

'You are here to sell them whisky,' Asta said contemptuously.

Benson's eyes narrowed at her tone. 'Nobody makes 'em buy.'

'Have you seen what the blacks are like when they drink too much?' She gestured impatiently at her own words. 'Of course you have. You must see it all the time. It is the devil's trade, I think.'

'They want liquor, they'll find it somehow,' Benson said. 'If we don' do it there's plenty will.'

Two days later Julius Laubsch came riding into Whitby Downs.

'That man Benson,' he said angrily, 'I have complained to him about what he is doing but he takes no notice. And Dawkins, the white sergeant, is even worse.'

'What are they doing? Apart from selling them whisky, I mean?' Asta asked.

'Is that not enough?' Experience had dulled some of the innocence with which Laubsch had left Kapunda but such blatant wrong-doing was still capable of arousing his anger. 'The natives,' he said despairingly. 'Men like that reduce them to the level of animals.'

Asta nodded vigorously. 'I told Benson it is the devil's trade.'

'Not only that. When they have drink taken they do not know what they are doing. Trouble we may expect later, I think.'

'What sort of trouble?'

'Who knows? Attacks on the whites, killing sheep. Anything is possible.'

'Has anyone threatened you?'

'Not yet. When they do anything—if they do—it will be action first, I think, not threats. But so far there has been nothing.'

'I shall go and see for myself what is happening,' Asta decided.

'That might be unwise. A woman by herself—'

'I shall not be by myself. I shall take Jason with me.'

Benson came to meet Asta and Jason on the edge of the native camp. A tangle of bush surrounded it so they could see little but they could make out the

387

shapes of one or two sleeping shelters, a smear of smoke from cooking fires.

Benson addressed Asta, smiling ingratiatingly. 'You don' want to go in there, ma'am.'

Asta bristled, hating this scruffy intruder and what he represented. 'It is my land. Why should I not go there?'

She dismounted but Benson still barred her way. 'Ain't no place for a lady,' he said.

Jason was at her side. She stared at the unshaven face confronting her. 'We are going in there, Mr Benson. Make up your mind about that.'

He must have realised she meant it; he glowered sullenly as he stood to one side. 'Don' say I didn' warn you, that's all.'

They walked down the slope to the camp site. Off to one side she saw the trader's waggons, neatly parked, with an armed black trooper standing beside them. In front of her . . .

She stared in appalled silence.

'They're rubbish,' Benson said at her side, 'not human beings at all.'

Filth lay everywhere. Over the whole area was a pervasive stench of corruption. Asta looked at the blacks who lived in this squalid place. There were about twenty of them. Some of them were naked, others wore rags and tatters of European clothing—an old shirt, a ripped frock—that they had gleaned from somewhere. The partially clad women, in particular, looked more naked than the ones who wore no clothes at all. All of them, no exceptions anywhere that she could see, were drunk. Many had fallen and now lay snoring, their faces in the dirt. There were plenty of bottles in evidence, most of them empty. The few natives who remained conscious brandished ones that were still partially full.

'No better'n cattle,' Benson said.

'They are human beings, Mr Benson,' Asta said. 'If they have been reduced to behaving like animals we know who is to blame.'

She was horrified by what she was seeing but did her best not to show it. For the moment this group of natives was beyond causing trouble but she thought that later Laubsch's words might prove prophetic. Anything would be possible, then, but by that time the whisky traders would have moved on.

At her side Jason stood looking about him at the drunken scene, his face rigid with shock and horror.

'Is there anyone here you know?' Asta asked.

'I know them all.'

It was only partially true. They were all from his old clan but he had known them as they were, never like this. He remembered them as they had been and compared the memory with what he saw in front of him now.

'What have these bastards done to them?'

He remembered what Mura had said at Burra Burra after Jason's fight with Silvio Fernandez.

Everything is changed. The clan is broken up.

Here was the reality behind Mura's words.

Jason had foreseen the destruction of the old way of life and had tried to warn Nantariltarra about it. He had never visualised anything as bad as this.

'It is degrading,' Asta said.

Jason stared about him, frowning.

'What are you looking for?' Asta asked.

'I thought Michael might be here but I don't see him.'

He was relieved. Perhaps things were not as bad as they seemed. If even one of the clan had managed to resist the blandishments of Benson and his mates . . .

Asta said, 'There must be other groups. Perhaps he is with them.'

She was probably right. There was no sign of the old sealer, either, yet Mura had told him that he had elected to stay with the clan, or what remained of it. Perhaps Mura was with him. But Jason remembered how easily Mura had taken to drink back at Burra Burra and remained uneasy.

'Where is Sergeant Dawkins?' Asta asked Benson.

He was someone else Jason had been looking out for. Asta had told him that the liquor party, troopers included, had come here straight from Adelaide but he would not be easy until he had satisfied himself that Dawkins was not from Burra Burra. For weeks at a time he forgot how he had broken out of gaol but doubted that the authorities would be as forgetful as he was.

'He's around some place,' Benson said.

A sudden commotion in one of the shelters drew their eyes.

'If the lady's seen enough,' Benson said, 'perhaps I can escort her back to her horse?'

Asta raised a gloved hand. 'What is going on there?'

'Two of 'em havin' a scrap, I'd say,' Benson said. 'This lot, they hack each other to bits when they're in the mood.'

'And we all know why they get in the mood,' Asta told him. 'I wish to see what is happening.'

'Beggin' your pardon, ma'am,' Benson said, 'but I can't allow that. It might not be safe.'

Asta raised her chin. 'I shall be the judge of that.'

She went to push her way forward but at that moment the figure of a man emerged from the shelter from which the sound of fighting had come.

'Sergeant Dawkins,' Asta said. 'Perhaps you can tell me what is going on here?'

Jason's first thought: the man was a stranger, after all. He breathed more easily, confident he could not be mistaken. Sergeant Dawkins was not a man easily forgotten. He was tall and powerfully built, as big as Jason himself, shoulders tight with muscle and heavy fists. His closely cropped black hair topped a head as round as a cannonball from which small dark eyes glared belligerently at the world.

He stared at Asta as he considered her question. 'Sortin' out a problem,' he said. 'No sweat.'

His knuckles were broken and bleeding. He raised one of his hands to his lips and sucked it, his dark eyes daring her to say anything.

Asta rose to the unspoken challenge. 'With your fists?'

'Sometimes it's the best way.'

She walked past him as though he did not exist; Jason followed her. They bowed their heads almost to the ground to get into the low brushwood shelter.

Jason's first thought was that the man was dead. From his breeches and long-sleeved shirt he might have been a European but the dark head and hands gave lie to that. Jason bent over him, hearing the breath wheezing laboriously in his chest. It was dark in the shelter but Jason could see that the man's shirt was dark with blood. He turned the black face up to inspect it and then realised who it was.

From the shelter's opening Asta asked, 'Is he . . .?'

'Dead? No.' He was numb with shock but the beginnings of fury were not far away. 'He's been badly beaten, though. It's Mura,' he said.

'Who?'

'You call him Michael. Mura's his real name.'

'*Michael*? But he is one of us. I am sure—'

What else Asta had been going to say Jason never knew. He shoved his way past her into the light.

A red wave was rising in his head. His breath came short. Fists clenched, he glared about him, saw what he was looking for. From the other side of the clearing Dawkins, tall as a tower, stared back.

Jason walked across to him, taking his time, feeling the blood pulsing in his temples. Dawkins came to meet him. His fists, big and dangerous, lay quiet at his side, the bloodied knuckles showing like pebbles through the skin. He seemed amused by something but his dark eyes were watchful.

'Somethin' on your mind, sonny?'

'You half-killed him,' Jason said.

'Sorry about that.' Dawkins grinned at him. They were the same height but, to Jason, Dawkins seemed a good deal bigger and very dangerous. 'You people must've turned up before I finished the job. Don't worry. I'll get back to him later.'

Fury flared. Jason swung at the sergeant with all his strength. His clenched fist landed flush on Dawkins' jaw and Jason felt the pain of the blow lance up his arm to his elbow. It was like hitting the side of a mountain. Jason had given him his best shot, right on target, and Dawkins had not even staggered.

The sergeant shook his head and his mean eyes gleamed. 'Well, now,' he said, and started forward. The big fists were cocked, the left high near his chin, the right low and ready for an opening. 'Time I taught you a lesson, sonny.'

He obviously expected Jason to back off but Jason did not. The rage hammering in his head made him cool, not wild, and his thoughts flowed fast, as clear as crystal. This was a fight they were in, not a boxing match. He lowered his head and ran straight into

Dawkins, catching him off balance before the big man could throw a punch or move out of his way. Dawkins staggered, arms flailing. Jason butted him as hard as he could, slamming the top of his head into the big face, feeling the crunch and hot wetness as blood exploded from the smashed nose. Dawkins took two steps back, looking for room, but Jason gave him no time to recover. He was on him at once, hitting him twice, as hard as he could, once on the shattered nose and again on the jaw in the same place as before. Dawkins slipped, trying desperately to hang on to Jason while his head cleared but Jason, inflicting pain and enjoying it, would not let him. A heavy wooden billet was lying in the dust. Jason snatched it up and hit Dawkins with a roundhouse swing to the side of the head. The billet broke like matchwood. Dawkins was badly hurt now, the big fists nowhere, but still he hadn't gone down. Jason walked right up to him and sank his right fist as hard as he could into Dawkins' gut. The blow went in almost to the elbow and he felt the whoosh in his face as the breath came out of Dawkins' straining mouth. He was going down this time, all right, but now Jason prevented him. He remembered how Silvio Fernandez had recovered when he had thought it was all over; he wasn't about to let the same thing happen here. He supported the big man's sagging weight and kneed him viciously between the swaying, staggering legs. That did it. Dawkins' face curdled. Jason opened his hands and let him drop.

Suddenly he was very tired. He looked at the crumpled body lying at his feet, wondering whether he should round off the job by kicking him in the head, but was too tired to do it. Not tired physically—he realised suddenly that Dawkins had not landed a single blow on him—but emotionally he was exhausted. He remembered the pleasure he had felt in beating the other man to a pulp, how the red rage and racing thoughts had helped him destroy the sergeant. At the beginning of the fight he would have killed him with pleasure but no longer felt sufficiently interested to do it. Instead he felt wounded, as though Dawkins had managed to hit him after all. He stood for a few moments to catch his breath, then turned away, leaving Dawkins lying there.

For the first time he became aware of other people around him. The drunken natives gave no sign of being conscious of anything but the two black troopers were watching him from the waggons, eyes wide, faces incredulous. Benson, too, was staring at him in stunned amazement. For some reason Jason felt he owed him an explanation.

'The man in the hut is my friend,' he said.

Asta's face was ashen. She looked as though she had witnessed something she would rather not have seen. She turned to the whisky trader. I think you should pack up and move along, Mr Benson, before someone gets killed. And we,' she said to Jason, 'shall take Michael back to Whitby Downs until he's had a chance to recover.'

'If they'll let us,' Jason said, but none of the natives made any move to stop him as he went into the shelter, lifted Mura in his arms and carried him to where they had tethered their horses. Mura was semi-conscious now but incapable of sitting a horse unaided. Jason hoisted him onto his saddle and lashed him so that he could not fall, then mounted behind him. Mura was not a heavy man and Tommy, the horse he had brought from Burra Burra, gave no sign of noticing anything unusual about its load. Asta mounted also.

'Mr Benson,' she said imperiously, 'remember what I said, please. 'I think it would be best if you moved on.'

Benson was beginning to recover from the shock of seeing his colleague trashed. He scowled. 'We come 'ere legal,' he said. 'We won't be movin' nowhere until Sergeant Dawkins recovers. If he does. If he don't I suppose you'll be hearing from us.'

Jason stirred in the saddle, not too exhausted to sort out this problem, too, if needs be, but Asta raised her hand to still him. 'I saw very clearly what happened here,' she said. 'I shall inform the authorities accordingly, if I have to. About *everything* I have seen.' She looked meaningfully at the sprawling group of natives, some now staring vacantly up at them. 'I recommend you move on as soon as the sergeant is able to ride.'

She clicked her tongue at her mount and rode away up the slope, Jason following. As soon as they were clear of the trees she dropped back to ride beside him. 'I hope you know how lucky you are.'

'Lucky?' Jason felt anything but lucky. 'Why?'

'To have me there. If you had been alone they might have killed you.'

'Dawkins did his best. And if it hadn't been for you I wouldn't have been there at all.'

'As well for your friend's sake I was, then.'

Asta always had to have the last word, he thought, but she was right. If they hadn't turned up when they did Mura might have died. He still might.

'I hope he doesn't die on us,' he said.

'Who? Michael or the sergeant?'

Jason had not been thinking of Dawkins but realised he had probably meant both. 'There'll be trouble if the sergeant dies, that's for sure.'

'We must just hope Sergeant Dawkins makes a good recovery,' Asta said.

They made good time back to Whitby Downs. They eased Mura to the ground and carried him into the house.

'I'll put him to bed here,' Asta said, 'where I can keep an eye on him. I want you to ride to Bungaree.'

'Why?' Jason was dubious about his reception at Bungaree.

'We must warn them that Benson is selling drink to the natives.'

'Blake won't care if Benson poisons every black in the colony.'

'Then he should. If the drink drives them mad he is in as much danger as we are.'

'They aren't in a state to be a danger to anyone.'

But went anyway. Blake, as he had suspected, surly in his greeting. He stood between Jason and the house and made no attempt to invite him indoors.

'What do you want?'

Jason explained about the whisky men.

'Damn mongrels stirring up trouble,' Blake said. He stared angrily at Jason as though blaming him for Benson and his activities. 'All right, so you've told me. I'll keep an eye out.'

Jason remounted. 'Alison well?'

Blake glared. 'What's it got to do with you?'

'Just asking,' Jason said. 'No need to get in a state about it.'

'A friend of yours was here,' Blake said.

I have no friends, Alison thought. I am alone in this place, with this man. But said nothing, trying to avoid trouble. For two days, since the beating, she had done and said only those things she thought would be acceptable to her husband.

'Who was it?' Since he obviously wanted her to ask.

'Guess.'

'I suppose it must have been Jason.'

'Why d'you think that?'

'You asked me to guess,' she said desperately. 'I guessed. That's all.'

'Mebbe you wanted it to be Jason?'

She was close to tears. 'I didn't want it to be anyone. I didn't even know he was here.'

'Don't you care who it was?'

'No!'

A dangerous pause.

'I don't believe you.'

Tears pricked like needles at the back of her eyes. 'I don't know what you want me to say.'

'I want the truth!'

Very well, she thought, I will give you the truth. God help us both if you don't like it. 'I married you from choice. I haven't looked at another man since. Not Jason, not anyone. You wrong me with these ... suspicions.'

Blake scowled. 'What d'you mean, suspicions?'

'Asking questions—'

'I told you a friend had been here. Nothing suspicious in that. Or are you sayin' Jason isn't a friend?'

'I hardly ever see him—'

'You sayin' he's never been a friend?'

'Of course not—'

'What suspicions?' Shouting.

'You seem to think ... The way you spoke ...' Coherence fragmenting before the juggernaut of his anger.

'Maybe I was right to think it,' he said.

'No!'

He took her by the hair. Slowly he tightened his grip, lifting her to her toes. Her eyes were squeezed shut. In the blackness she felt despairing tears running down her face.

He slapped her, not hard, but the fact that he could do it at all was a humiliation beyond blows.

'Don' tell me what I think,' he said. He held her, crucified upon her web of hair. He said, 'Look at me.'

She whimpered.

'*Look at me!*'

She forced her eyes open, willing herself to give him no grounds for punishing her further. Splintered by tears, his face loomed close, jaw outthrust. He tightened his grip on her hair until fire ran through her scalp.

Please . . .

The word screamed in her head but she made no sound. That much of her independence remained, at least.

'I would love you if you let me,' Blake said.

The notion of Blake loving anyone . . . Yet it was her only hope.

'I want you to love me.' Her lips were stiff. Somehow she managed to utter the words. 'I want it more than anything.'

He released her hair. The sudden easing of pain made her cry out. More tears flooded her eyes, riming every image with frost.

'Show me,' he said.

For the moment she was at a loss. 'Show you what?'

'How much you love me.'

She stared at him. Was that what he wanted? To

move, within seconds, from the intimacy of torture to the intimacy of the bed? She could not believe he meant it.

'I am your husband,' he said.

She was lost, totally. 'I can't . . .'

'*Can't*?' Teeth bared in the congested face.

She shook her head, weeping, hand groping imploringly at his shirt front. 'Please . . . I can't . . .'

Futilely hoping that by repetition she might somehow appeal to the better nature that it seemed he did not have.

He backhanded her again, much harder, and threw her backwards across the bed. He followed, hands ripping at her bodice. It tore open. Her breasts lolled. She sensed him delving at his breeches, her mouth opened to scream, he hit her again. She felt him wrench at her garments, open her to him, followed by a ripping agony as he filled her.

Pain and humiliation overwhelmed her. As he spasmed between her thighs she thought, He thinks I am nothing. Through the pain she felt a different sensation: the steady glow of mounting anger. All her life she had relied upon a man for protection, had believed that was a man's function, but there was no protection here. Very well, she thought, I will rely on myself, if I can. And felt stronger for the thought.

Deception was the first rule. Teeth clenched, body sick with pain, she held him close.

'I don't like it,' Jason told Asta. 'He didn't ask me into the house and Alison didn't come out.'

It was unheard of for anyone to visit another run and be offered no hospitality. Asta frowned. 'Did you ask after her?'

'I did. He said she was well but he didn't like me asking.'

'It means nothing,' Asta said. 'He is jealous, that is all.'

'He'd better have done nothing to her—'

She interrupted him at once. 'I will not allow you to interfere between husband and wife.' She smiled secretly. 'Besides, it is not necessary.'

Jason's lips tightened. *Husband*. It was still hard to accept, would always be hard. 'What do you mean?'

'A man's way is to seek confrontation, conflict. A woman learns to think around corners. You must think like a woman.' She could see he had no idea what she meant. 'There is no need to create a crisis between Alison and her husband, it already exists. Wait, say nothing, and in time things will resolve themselves.'

Jason did not believe in letting things resolve themselves. 'How much time have we got? All we know, he may be beating her to a pulp this minute.'

'I shall ask Mr Laubsch to call on them,' Asta said. 'He will tell us if anything is wrong.'

When Ian Matlock died Laubsch had called on Alison with his commiserations and Blake had sent him away. This time things were different.

'My dear,' Blake said, 'we got the missionary come to see us.'

Perhaps Laubsch had come to spy on them. His eyes warned her: guard your tongue. She needed no telling.

'Mr Laubsch,' she smiled at the sombre-coated minister, 'what a pleasant surprise.'

Casually Blake walked to her, put his arm around

her waist. 'Maybe we can offer the minister some refreshment?' he suggested.

'There is no need for that,' Laubsch protested.

'Not offer you something when you've taken the trouble to call on us?' said Alison. 'We wouldn't think of it.'

She fetched tea; they exchanged small talk while they drank it.

'There are some liquor dealings in the area,' Laubsch said in his stilted English. 'They are selling the spirits to the natives.'

Blake grinned sardonically. 'Selling the spirits, eh? I thought that was your job.'

It was difficult to know if Laubsch understood the joke or not. 'These people cause trouble when they have drink taken,' he said.

'We can look after ourselves,' Blake told him. 'They come here, they'll find more trouble than they can handle, I promise you that.'

Laubsch finished his tea. 'None of us can look after ourselves,' he said. 'We are all in need of the loving kindness of God.'

Blake scowled. 'Them abos come sniffin' round here, it's them that'll need loving kindness, not us. And not likely to find too much of it, either.'

Laubsch observed how Alison Gallagher stood close to her husband, never moving out of the shelter of his arm. 'And you, Mrs Gallagher? What do you think?'

'I agree with my husband,' Alison said, and smiled. 'In everything.'

When Laubsch got back to Whitby Downs he reported that Alison was not only well but seemed very loving to her husband, too.

'I don't believe it,' Jason said.

'I am glad, if it is true,' Asta said, but was not.

Alison was her best hope for keeping Jason at Whitby Downs. If he believed she was happy with Blake he might give up and move away. She would do everything she could to stop that.

'Showing affection in public does not seem in Blake's line,' she said thoughtfully.

'An act, that's what it was,' Jason said savagely. 'Laubsch has got it wrong.'

'We shall have to keep our eye on things,' she told him. 'If we wait, we shall find out the truth.'

Two days later Jason was riding through a patch of woodland when he met Blake.

'Had any trouble from them savages?' Blake asked.

'I reckon it was a false alarm,' Jason said. 'Doesn't do any harm to be prepared, though.'

'Damn right,' Blake said. 'I always said we should have got rid of 'em at the beginning.'

They eyed each other with dislike.

'You did a fair job.'

'Not good enough or we wouldn't be talkin' trouble now.'

'You were going to shoot me, too, as I remember.'

'Damn right. Come to think of it, there ain't nuthin to stop me finishin' the job now.'

Jason eyed him, hostility very near the surface. 'The natives, you mean, or me?'

'Take your pick,' Blake said.

'Alison well?' Jason asked.

Blake's expression darkened. 'A word of advice,' he said. 'Keep away from her.'

'I'll not lay a finger on her—'

'Make sure you don't.'

Jason ignored the interruption. 'Just so long as you treat her right.'

A dangerous pause.

'And what's that supposed to mean?'

'Like I said. Treat her right and you'll have no trouble from me. Treat her bad, you'll have more trouble than you can handle.'

'That so?' Blake urged his horse closer; the two men's legs pressed against each other. 'Alison is my *wife*, mate. What goes on between us ain't none o' your business.'

'I ever hear you've harmed her I'll make it my business,' Jason said, 'and don't you forget it.'

Blake's teeth shone in his red mouth. 'The day you do that is the day I kill you.'

TWENTY-FOUR

As soon as Asta was able to find the time she rode to Bungaree to visit Alison at home.

'We are the only white women for a hundred miles,' she said, 'but for all we see of each other we might as well be at opposite ends of the earth.'

Alison hurried to clear piles of clothes from a rough stool so that Asta could sit down. She smoothed the front of her dress with nervous hands and smiled at her unexpected visitor. 'I'll get us something to drink,' she said.

Left alone, Asta looked about her. The sun's rays, slanting through the open doorway, varnished the earth floor with golden light; unlike herself, Blake had done nothing to replace the slab-walled house that Ian had built when he first took up his run.

A pigsty, Asta thought. How does Alison bear it? She should make Blake do something about it. But knew there was small chance of that.

Alison returned carrying a bottle of cordial and two glasses.

At least she has glasses, Asta thought.

Asta was wearing her usual breeches and shirt;

Alison's skirt, stained and dusty, with a tear in the hem, trailed along the ground.

'I'm a mess,' she said apologetically, 'but I've been out dealing with the lambs and I haven't had a chance to tidy up.'

'A skirt is not the easiest of clothes for that sort of work,' Asta agreed.

'Blake prefers it,' Alison said.

He would. 'It is you I have come to see,' Asta said. 'Not your clothes.'

Alison sat on the other stool and poured cordial for them both; her hand shook and the glasses chimed uneasily. 'It is good to see you,' she said but seemed unsure of it.

Asta's eyes stripped her bare. 'Is anything the matter?'

'Of course not.'

'Are you happy?'

An uneasy smile. 'Why shouldn't I be happy?'

Which was an answer, of sorts.

'I have come to ask you to visit me more often,' Asta said.

'That would be nice,' Alison said formally.

Asta saw that she had no intention of accepting the invitation. 'I mean it. We have always been such good friends. I want us to go on seeing each other whenever we can.'

Again the formal smile, promising nothing.

'If you don't come I shall send Jason to fetch you.'

Alison's hands flew like wings to her mouth. 'You mustn't—'

Asta would never have done such a thing but Alison's reaction told her what she wanted to know. 'Promise me you will come, then.'

Still Alison tried to evade commitment. 'When I can.'

'That is not good enough.' Asta laughed, making a game of something that was not a game at all. 'We must set a date and a time.'

'It is very difficult,' Alison protested. 'There is a lot of work here.'

'Work?' Asta laughed again. 'I have been wedded to a sheep run for enough years to know about work. That is why we must have a break from time to time.' Sharp as knives, her eyes studied Alison's face. 'Unless you think that Blake will not allow it.'

Alison would admit nothing, even managed a light laugh. 'Why shouldn't he allow it?'

'Some husbands do not like their wives going out of the house.'

'Blake is not one of them.'

'Then you have no excuse.' Asta had set her teeth into the argument and would not let go. At last, reluctantly, Alison agreed a date when she would visit Whitby Downs.

'A week today. I shall ride to meet you,' Asta told her gaily. 'It will be like old times.'

Asta was sure that Alison would think of an excuse not to come but by the time she rode out to meet her she had heard nothing. Deliberately she was early and had almost reached Bungaree when she met Alison riding towards her.

'You see?' she greeted her. 'It is a lovely day, just for us.'

For the time of year it certainly was: cool but cloudless, with no wind. They rode along the edge of the cliffs. The sea creamed peacefully against the rocks beneath them and overhead the blue sky arched to meet the darker blue of the sea on the far side of the gulf.

'We shall go to the grotto,' Asta said.

They followed the path down the cliff face until they came to the level stretch of turf, the vertical cliff on one side, the drop plunging to the waves on the other. The spring seeped audibly, the rock wall cast a shadow over the altar stone. The ferns still grew in the crevice in the rocks. Asta cut fronds and laid them on the altar.

'Father Odin, god of battles,' she said, 'Loki, god of fire, take care of us all.'

It was a game yet not a game.

Alison watched. 'Do you believe?'

Asta did not know what she believed. 'This place reminds me of my childhood. The cliffs are different, the sea is blue instead of grey, but something here calls to me out of the past.'

'And Odin? And the other one?'

'Loki?' Asta laughed. 'Mr Laubsch would not be pleased, would he? But God has many names. Does it matter which one we call Him?'

'Will they really take care of us, do you think?'

Asking questions like a child. I could make her believe, Asta thought, if only I believed myself, and for a moment wished she did. It would be good to believe in something other than oneself. I could lie to her about it and she would believe me but faith is too important for lies.

'I hope someone will,' she said. 'We all need it. You, especially, I think.'

The two women stared at each other. Asta's face was alert; Alison merely looked sad. 'Why do you say that?' she asked.

'It is what I believe. Only you know if I am right.'

She had said enough. She had been determined to raise the subject; now she had done so. The rest was up to Alison.

But Alison said nothing. Asta watched her desolate expression. She doesn't know where she is going or why, she thought, and felt sad, too, and full of feeling for the girl.

'It is warm here out of the wind,' she said. 'We can sit for a while and look at the sea.'

For Alison's benefit she had put on a dress; she had thought Alison would prefer it, compelled to wear women's clothing herself. The way it restricted her movements was a nuisance but now she was glad she had done it; Alison needed all the consideration she could get. Asta arranged her skirts primly and sat down on a level rock. In a minute Alison joined her.

'In some lights you can see Adelaide from here,' Asta said. 'I sometimes wonder what my life would have been if I had never left it.'

'Would you have been happy?'

'At the time I didn't think so. Now, I'm not so sure. I like to think I would have managed quite well, wherever I was.'

'If I had gone back to Adelaide with my mother I wouldn't be married now,' Alison said. It was impossible to tell whether she regretted it or not.

'You can't tell. You might have met some handsome city man and married him. Now you'd be driving up and down Hindley Street in a carriage, looking at the people.'

'And the buildings. I wouldn't want to live surrounded by buildings.'

'There are no buildings at your mother's place.'

'She never wanted me there,' Alison said without bitterness, 'any more than I wanted to go.'

'Is that why you married Blake? So as not to have to go with your mother?'

'All I ever wanted was to have someone to look

after me,' Alison said. 'My father did, in his lifetime. He made the decisions and I relied on him.
When he went . . .' She lifted her shoulders, smiling
wanly.

'There was Jason.'

'But he went, too, and then there was no-one.'

Asta thought to ask her what she would have
done had Jason written but decided against it.
Talking about what might have been solved nothing.
'If your husband ever ill-treats you,' she said, careful
to avoid any suggestion that Blake might already be
ill-treating her, 'will you promise to tell me?'

Alison turned to watch the sea and Asta could not
see her expression. 'You have the wrong idea about
Blake.'

'Perhaps,' Asta said. There was no hint of apology
in her voice. She remembered the Blake she had
known for so many years and did not believe she
had the wrong idea at all. Blake was bad through
and through, always had been, always would be.
The question was, what could she or anyone else do
about it?

She knew there was nothing she could do and
was angry with Alison for doing so little to help
herself. 'We all have to learn to stand up for ourselves,' she said.

Still Alison watched the sea. 'I told myself that,
not long ago, but it is not easy.'

'You must learn,' said Asta, impatient with
human frailty.

Alison said no more and for the moment Asta
gave up trying. She stood up. 'We had better get on,'
she said, 'unless you want to spend all day staring
at the sea.'

When they reached the house they had something
to eat and chatted a little about nothing at all. Alison

never let her get too close and Asta was glad when at last she said she must go home.

'I will get Jason to ride with you,' she said.

Alison looked alarmed. 'There is no need for that.'

But Asta was determined. To bring Jason and Alison together had been one of the main reasons for inviting her; she was not about to let her slip away now. 'I am sure that Blake would not like it if I sent you home without an escort.'

Blake would not like the idea of Jason accompanying his wife, either, but Asta was beyond caring what Blake thought.

They rode side by side without speaking until the weight of the silence grew too much for Jason to bear.

'How have you been keeping?' he asked.

'Good.'

Five minutes passed.

'Been a nice day,' he offered.

'Great.'

He was irritated that she should so ignore his overtures. 'If you'd sooner I went back—'

She said nothing. He did not know what she wanted him to do. She seemed angry with him without reason and the idea made him stubborn. 'Forget I said that,' he said, angry himself now. 'I promised Asta I'd take you back and I'm going to do it.'

More silence; he might have been talking to the sea.

'We haven't had a proper conversation since I got back,' he said. 'Why waste the chance now we've got it?'

'What do you want to talk about?'

'Anything,' he said, exasperated, but in truth could think of no subject that was safe. The fact of her husband's existence stood like a wall between them.

She turned in the saddle to stare at him. 'You want to talk about what you did at the Burra Burra?' she asked. 'You want to tell me why you never bothered to write?'

'You *knew* I was going,' he said angrily. 'You helped me. We had an arrangement.'

The idea of writing had never occurred to him but now, seeing the expression on Alison's face, he understood he had done something terrible. Worse than terrible: something that could never be put right. He could think of no words to express the regret he now felt so said nothing.

Alison, who had been silent for the whole ride, suddenly had plenty to say. 'You might have been dead. You might have changed your mind. Anything. What was I supposed to think, hearing nothing for so long?' Anger surfaced. 'Not just months, Jason. *Years.*'

'Is that why you married him?' He had his own hurt, too.

'Why should you care?' she asked. 'You had your chance and threw it away.'

'I do care.' It was all he could think to say.

The reply seemed to vex her more than ever. 'It doesn't matter whether you care or not. I'm a married woman, Jason. Can't you understand that? It's too late to talk about caring.'

'Are you happy?' he asked, not looking at her.

'That's none of your business.'

'You aren't happy,' he said. 'I know it.'

'You know nothing about it.'

'I feel it.'

'Jason, can't you get it through your head? I'm married! There's nothing for us to talk about any more.'

And rode on more quickly, face turned away from him.

She had been right in everything she had said and Jason knew he had no business saying anything more to her at all. He knew too that if he went on badgering her he ran the risk of losing her forever yet could not remain silent. He trotted after her until once again they were riding side by side.

'You didn't answer my question,' he said. 'You never said if you were happy or not.'

She did not answer. He did not know whether she was still angry with him or not.

'You say it's none of my business, what happens to you,' he said, 'but I can't just switch off my feelings.'

He turned in the saddle to look at her. Her expression no longer seemed angry, only sad, and she said nothing to interrupt him. Emboldened, he went on, 'I cared for you. You know that. I still care. You can't tell me you're none of my business because you are.'

She shook her head. 'Words change nothing. Even if I agreed with you it would make no difference.'

'*Do* you agree with me?'

Silence. Suddenly resolute, he took his heart and placed it in her hands. 'A week today I shall be at the grotto,' he said. 'If you want to come—'

'Can't you see that's impossible?'

'Just to talk. Nothing else. I'll wait.'

'You'll be wasting your time,' she said.

'Perhaps. But I'll go anyway. Just in case.'

They rode the rest of the way without speaking, their minds filled with a multitude of thoughts and memories. Jason remembered how things had been

412

between them before he had gone away. Now everything had changed; yet he could not escape the feeling that nothing between them had really changed at all. Even the fact of her marriage meant nothing. He still felt the same about things and was certain she did, too. If he could only find the right words he believed he would somehow break through to her. I shall go to the grotto, he told himself. She will come or not, as she chooses, but at least I will have tried.

Alison was afraid of Blake's anger should he discover that Jason had escorted her home, so half a mile from the house she sent him back and rode the rest of the way alone.

She was glad to have a few minutes to herself. Her day out had unsettled her. In some ways she wished she had not gone yet at the same time was glad that she had. It was dangerous to compare what she had now with how things might have been but she was pleased that Jason still cared for her. It did no good and might indeed be dangerous but all the same it gave her a warm feeling and she was glad of it.

As to her own feelings . . . She would not examine them too closely, fearing what she might find.

You are married, she told herself as fiercely as she had told Jason. There is nothing you can do about it. Nothing you would do, even if you could.

She reached the house, put her horse in the paddock, went indoors and began to cook the supper. Routine enfolded her.

Blake came home earlier than she had expected. He fetched a bottle from the cupboard and drank from it as he sat watching her finish cooking their meal. It was something he had never done before and the change of routine made her uneasy. She had learned to tread cautiously around her husband so said nothing while she tried to gauge his mood.

'Enjoy your outing?' he asked eventually.

'It was all right.' She spoke indifferently, having learnt never to sound too enthusiastic about anything in which Blake had not been involved. Oh, it was so difficult, always having to be careful what she said and the tone in which she said it.

'Asta didn' have no business lettin' you ride back alone.' Blake tipped the bottle, gulped noisily. 'She sends that mate of yours to warn us how dangerous the bloody blacks are, then lets you come back by yourself.'

So that was what he thought. Let him go on thinking it, she thought. It might help her to avoid trouble, if he was in the mood for trouble.

'I didn't see any natives,' she told him.

He grunted. 'No thanks to Asta Matlock.'

She put the food out. He thrust it into his mouth, chewed and gulped, washed it down with grog. He did not go back to work, as he had always done, but sat brooding, red-veined eyes watching her as she finished her chores. His watchful presence was like a scream in the silent room. She hoped the liquor would put him to sleep but it did not. She thought nothing could be worse than the last time but feared, all the same. She moved silently about the room, trying to do everything she could to avert his anger, trying to still the terror inside her.

He waited until she had finished tidying up. 'Bed,' he said, rising. He swayed a little, unused to the liquor. He went to the bed and sprawled on it.

The lamp cast shadows across his face so that Alison could not see his eyes. He neither moved nor spoke but she was frightened to take too long. She made everything ready for the morning. She drew her dress over her head, quenched the lamp, walked silently to the bed, praying that he slept. She finished undressing in the darkness, slid inch by inch beneath the covers, holding her breath, willing her body not to disturb him.

She lay for a minute, eyes staring up at the darkness. He did not move and she had a few seconds in which to feel the first stirrings of hope before he turned and fell upon her, using her with such brutality that she thought he meant to destroy her. At the last, ravaged and sore, sick with despair, she heard him say, 'You lying bitch. I saw you riding with him,' and knew that her punishment had only just begun.

Six days later Blake and Asta met as they were riding through the thin bush that bordered the two runs. They nodded stiffly; they had never liked each other and saw no reason for pretence, but they were neighbours in what might be a hostile land and the courtesies had to be observed.

Sitting side by side on their horses, they talked for a few minutes about the condition of the sheep, the prospects for rain, the likely wool price at Adelaide later in the year.

'I so enjoyed Alison's company the other day,' Asta told him eventually. 'I hope you will allow her to visit me more often.'

Blake had already decided there would be no more outings. 'She's got things to do about the house,' he said.

'They must have priority, of course, I understand that. But perhaps it might still be possible for us to meet from time to time?'

He pretended to consider. 'You'd best forget about it,' he said eventually.

'I could always come to her if she has no time to come to Whitby Downs.'

'Not a question of time. Ain't safe, ridin' around the country without an escort. Not for you, neither.'

'Why? Have you had any trouble from the blacks?'

He laughed harshly. 'They knows better than mess wi' me.'

'With us too, it seems. We've seen no sign of them. It's a miracle, with those whisky traders in the district. Those men should not be allowed to do what they do.'

'Free country, ain't it?'

'But look how the natives are when they've been drinking. It destroys them completely.'

He didn't see what the fuss was about. 'Nobody makes 'em drink. Anyway, drunk or sober, they don' scare me. Them whisky blokes don' 'ave no trouble, do they?'

'They are armed to the teeth. Besides, they have troopers with them.'

He was interested. 'Who told you that?'

'I visited the camp and saw them for myself.'

'They'll keep the abos in line. They're tough blokes, from what I've heard.'

'Brutal,' Asta conceded. 'Perhaps not so tough, from what I saw.'

'Oh?'

'Jason was with me. He and the sergeant, a man called Dawkins, had a disagreement. It led to a scuffle.'

'A real fight? Wi' fists?'

'Of course with fists.'

'That right?' Blake was intrigued. 'Who won?'

416

'Jason won. For a minute I was afraid he was going to kill the man.'

'I'm surprised he dared, eh.'

Asta's eyes questioned him. 'What's that supposed to mean?'

'The day he come back,' Blake said. 'I heard that horse of his had just about had it. I wondered then what he'd done to be in such a hurry.'

Immediately Asta was on the defensive. 'The troopers weren't after him, if that's what you mean.'

'You don' know that no more than I do.' He watched her, eyes scavenging for any shred of information.

Asta's expression gave nothing away. 'I know.'

'Told you, did he?' Making no attempt to conceal derision.

'He has no reason to conceal anything from me.'

'Then you won' mind if I mention it to the troopers, eh?' He grinned slyly, enjoying what he thought was his power over her.

Carefully Asta inspected the threads of one of her riding gloves. Eventually she raised her head and stared at him coldly. 'There is something you should remember. It is Mary Matlock who owns Bungaree, not Alison.'

Blake eyed her, truculent but unsure. 'What about it?'

'Mary Matlock is the widow of my late husband's cousin. How long do you think it would take me to get a power of attorney from her if I wanted to?'

'Power o' what?' Blake was uncomfortable, conscious of unfamiliar waters.

'A power of attorney is a piece of paper drawn up by a lawyer. It would give me as much power over Bungaree as if I owned it myself.'

He still did not fully understand. 'What you getting at?'

'We are alone in this country. We have to work together or we cannot survive. If you do anything against Jason or the rest of us I shall obtain that power of attorney from Mary Matlock and you will be finished at Bungaree.'

He jeered. 'You couldn't run Bungaree without me and you know it. And what about Alison? Don' tell me you'd chuck her out, too?'

'You rate yourself too highly,' she told him. 'I would run Bungaree somehow, make no mistake about that. As for Alison, she chose her road when she was foolish enough to marry you. Now she will have to follow it to the end.'

TWENTY-FIVE

It had taken Alison almost a week to recover from the trauma of that night yet recover from it she had. Not entirely, that she would never do, but at least she felt able to get on with her life again. What had happened had come as no great surprise, after all. She had known for a long time that Blake was the boy who stamped on the heads of kittens, not the pleasant fellow he had been in the months before she married him, yet had continued to delude herself that she was immune to his violence. No room for delusions, now.

'I was a fool,' she told herself.

There was nothing she could do about it. It would be nice if one of these days he got so angry with her that he just walked out but she knew there was no chance of that. Being married to her represented Blake's only chance of owning Bungaree. Her mother might live another fifty years; on the other hand a horse might kick her head in any day, as had happened to her father, and Blake would certainly want to be on hand if it did. After he had got his hands on the property he might get rid of her, even kill her, but never before. The prospect of violent death did not trouble her. Spending the rest of her life with Blake was more dreadful than the thought that he might kill her once Bungaree was his.

'By then I'll be happy to die,' she told herself.

Tomorrow was the day that Jason had said he would be at the grotto but she had already decided she would not go. Alison knew that even if Blake had allowed it, a platonic friendship between her and Jason would be impossible because in their hearts neither of them wanted it. But the real reason she would not go was her fear of what Blake would do if he found out.

For the time being I must go on as I am, she thought, living from day to day, hoping for better things. God knows there is plenty of room for them.

That afternoon the weather changed. Clouds swept in threatening battalions across the peninsula and hung low over Bungaree's paddocks. Out at sea lightning slashed spasmodically at the dark horizon, thunder muttered and gusts of cold wind brought freezing rain to drench the land.

Riding home from his encounter with Asta, Blake's mood matched the weather.

He had done more than anyone to set up the two runs. He had been the best woodsman, had understood better than anyone else the needs of the land and the animals, yet it made no difference. The bitch had been dead set against him from the first. Now, to protect her damned pet Jason, she was threatening to turn him off the run altogether. He wouldn't let her get away with it, by God. This was his place. No-one was going to take it from him.

He reached the cluster of buildings and turned into the yard.

My run.

Blake took his horse into the stable and unsaddled him. He rubbed the animal down, fed and watered him. The storm slammed about the building, its commotion adding fuel to his mounting fury. When he was finished he extinguished the lantern and headed for the house through rain that had now become continuous.

My house.

Inside the house, his wife.

The bitch would steal her, too, if she could, just as she wanted to steal the land. And why? Because she had never thought he was good enough, that was why. Did she really think he didn't know what she was up to with her invitations?

He opened the door. The wind tore it from his grasp and sent it crashing against the wooden wall. Alison, bent over the fire, had not heard him in the din of the storm and straightened with a startled cry.

My wife.

For what she's worth.

She came towards him, carrying a towel that had been warming in front of the fire. 'Here,' she said, 'dry yourself with this.'

He wiped his face. He knew she was watching him, assessing his mood, and it exasperated him. 'I saw that bitch mate of yours today.' He threw the towel down and warmed his hands at the fire. 'You know what she said? Threatened to chuck us off Bungaree, that's what.'

'Can she do that?'

The question angered him. 'How do I know what she can do? Said something about getting a piece of paper from a lawyer. It ain't right,' he burst out.

'Here's me putting everything I got into the place and she talks of throwing me off.'

On the fire a pot began to bubble, the lid flapping in the steam. Alison took the lid off, stirred the contents.

'I doubt she meant it. You probably annoyed her about something.'

Her calmness bruised him. He wanted her to rant and rage, to share his own sense of outrage, but she didn't seem to care. For the hundredth time he thought how little his wife understood him. Always she was out of his reach. It aggravated him. He needed to feel in control of everything that happened in his life but Asta's threat and Alison's reaction to it made him realise how far he was from achieving that.

He went to the cupboard and yanked out a fresh bottle; he had finished the other one when he had got drunk a week ago. He pulled the cork, threw his head back and took a good swallow. He walked to the door and stared moodily out into the darkness, the bottle hanging from his fist.

'Bloody bitch . . .'

He felt sorry for himself, angry at the whole world. Worse, he felt frightened. From time to time he swallowed a mouthful of whisky and the liquor did not improve his mood. It was Alison's fault, he thought. Her and Jason. If it hadn't been for them, none of this would have happened.

Jason Hallam, her one-time lover. He drank again, whisky spilling down his shirt. There was an image branded deep and forever in his brain. The night they had the black boy penned in the shed, Blake on guard to make sure he didn't escape. Sounds from the hay shed behind the stable. Whispers. A muffled cry, dying to a moan.

Did they really think he hadn't heard?

Perhaps they hadn't cared, didn't think his feelings mattered.

Jason Hallam and the woman who became Blake's wife. Jason, a nothing from nowhere who had never had one tenth of his ability to work the run, who did not even *care* for it as he did.

Alison, whom he had thought to capture by marriage, always managing to evade him. As now it seemed the land itself might evade him.

Never, by God.

When the meal was ready he came to the table and ate without pleasure. Alison said nothing.

Blake scraped his plate. 'Cat got your tongue?'

'I don't have anything to say.'

'You never do.' His eyes were hot. 'Not to me, anyway. Dunno why I married you.'

Not for conversation, she thought, but dared not say so. Instead she concentrated on her food, chewing each mouthful as small as she could and saying nothing.

'At least you could tell me what you think o' this business,' Blake said.

'I told you, I doubt Asta meant it.'

She wondered what had happened between them for Asta to say such a thing but did not ask. Blake would not like it if she did. When he was ready he would probably tell her, anyway.

'She meant it, right enough.' Anger spurted in a sudden rush of words. 'Spend all your life workin' a place, puttin' everything you got into it, and some cow thinks she can chuck you off at a moment's notice.' He bruised the table with his clenched fist, glaring at her. 'I ain't goin' to put up with it!'

He shoved his chair back, picked up the bottle and walked out through the doorway. The rain had stopped and Alison, watching, saw him cross slowly to the shearing shed and go inside.

She was glad to see him go. Blake in this mood might erupt at any time. She'd be lucky to get through the rest of the evening without trouble but, in any case, even a few minutes' respite was welcome.

He didn't come back until late. He was drunk. He stumbled over the doorstep, holding out the almost-empty bottle to her. ''Ave a drink.'

'I don't want one,' she said.

'Sometimes I wonder whether I can give you anythin' you do want,' he said. 'Maybe only Jason can do that.' His expression changed. Before she knew it tears were running down his face. 'My wife. My run. People trying to take 'em both away from me.' Anger shone through the tears. 'I ain't goin' to put up with it, you hear me?'

She did not speak. Saying anything would probably only make things worse. She had never seen Blake cry before—had never thought he *could* cry—and his tears alarmed her far more than anger would have done. She was afraid that his rage, when it came, would be worse than anything she had experienced before and the idea terrified her.

'I know I don' always treat you right.' Tears again, maudlin. He swayed, eyes trying to focus on her. 'But you won' ever leave me, will you?'

'You know I won't.' Thinking, if only I could.

He led her to the bed. Stinking breath, hot eyes; her skin cringed but she knew better than to argue or resist. He pushed her down and sprawled on top of her. They were both fully clothed; she lay there doing nothing either to help or hinder him, letting him do whatever he wanted. Somehow he wrestled her drawers off and crushed himself up against her but the drink had taken its toll and he could manage nothing.

The last thing she wanted was to have sex with him; even so, her heart sank. Another humiliation piled on top of everything else might be enough to tip him into violence. She lay still, eyes staring at the ceiling, waiting in dread for whatever might happen next.

His head rested against her breast. 'I'm goin' to make 'em pay,' he mumbled.

His weight settled more heavily on her. Presently he began to snore. For the first time she allowed herself to hope that, just this once, she had got away with it. She waited another ten minutes, just to make sure, then wriggled out from under him and went to the door. She was relieved but still frightened and desperately unhappy. Softly she opened the door and walked out into the darkness. After the frowsty room the night air was wonderfully fresh. The clouds had gone. Overhead the stars blazed in splendour.

She thought of what she had left behind her in the house, of what her life had become since she had married Blake.

'I have to do something,' she informed the night. 'This is becoming impossible.'

As soon as it was light Blake set out for the north-western border of the run to check on the flocks there. Cato Brown was looking after them and Cato knew what he was doing but Blake, like Ian before him, always liked to keep an eye on things for himself.

'I'll be back before dark,' he told Alison. His eyes were red; otherwise the previous night might never have been.

Alison watched him go then went back into the house. She dressed carefully in her best clothes, went out to the paddock and saddled her mare Star.

'You are going for a good run today,' she told her.

Again and again she had told herself she would not go to meet Jason but last night had changed her mind. It was conversation and friendship she wanted, nothing more, but what had happened had made her realise how short of both these things she was.

She rode north along the coast. She did not hurry but her heart was beating fast. When she reached the head of the track there was no sign of Jason. Perhaps he was not coming, after all. She tethered Star in a cluster of gum trees a hundred yards from the cliff and walked down the track to the grotto. No-one was there.

She sat on a boulder and waited, gloved hands tap-tapping against each other.

I told him he'd be wasting his time, she thought. He will not come. But waited, nonetheless.

'He could have been delayed,' she told the rocks about her, taking courage from the sound of her own voice. On a sheep run unexpected things were always cropping up. She would give him an hour.

As the minutes passed she began to wish she had not come at all, not because she didn't want to see Jason but because she did. If he did not arrive she knew she would never have the courage to try again. In which case she would be more alone than ever.

The sound of sliding stones came from the path above her head and an instant later Jason appeared. He had been hurrying and was out of breath.

'Thank God you're here,' he said. 'When I didn't see your horse I thought you must have decided not to come after all.'

Her heart had leapt at sight of him. Now she did

not seem able to stop smiling. Her eyes devoured him, seeing his lips, his eyes, the way his teeth gleamed when he smiled back at her. She remembered how things had been between them the night he went away. So many things had happened since, important things, yet now she felt as though that night—our only night, she thought—had been yesterday. It will not do, she told herself. You are a married woman, she told herself. It is not why you came here, she told herself. Carried on smiling at him, all the same.

'I was held up,' Jason said. 'I came as fast as I could.'

'I thought you must have had second thoughts.'

'Never.'

She did not tell him how she very nearly had not come at all. They were here, together, and that was all that mattered. Yet now they were here they were as formal as strangers.

'Have you been well?' she asked.

'Fine. And you?'

'The same.'

'I'm glad you were able to make it,' Jason managed. 'It can't have been easy.'

If Blake had not chosen today to ride to the far side of the run it would have been impossible but did not say so. She did not want to think of Blake or even mention his name. Instead she continued to smile at Jason, drinking him in, watching the way his throat moved as he spoke, the grain of his skin as the sun caught it.

'Tell me how your week has been,' Jason said.

Alison did not answer. There was nothing she could tell him that did not involve Blake and she was sure he wanted to hear about Blake's doings as little as she wanted to talk about them.

Instead she looked across the gulf. 'Asta showed me how you can see Adelaide from here,' she said. 'Strange, isn't it? Like another world. Yet here we are, looking at it.'

He was wounded that she should want to keep her life secret from him. Why are we here, he wondered, if not to talk?

He watched where she was looking. You could indeed see the distant huddle of buildings but so far away that only the tops of the tallest ones were visible above the horizon. 'Can't see much from here,' he said.

'But at least what we see shows us it's still there.'

It struck Jason as an extraordinary remark. Where else should the city be but where it had always been?

'Do you ever wish you lived in a city?' Alison asked him.

He had never thought about it. 'Don't know that I would,' he said. 'Too many people. I lived in Hobart Town when I was a kid. I hated it.'

'Why?'

'Where I lived was a dreadful, stinking place. I couldn't wait to get away from it.'

'Then you went to sea and got shipwrecked,' Alison remembered. She put her hand on his. 'You've had so many adventures.'

He grinned, resentment ebbing. 'Could have done without the shipwreck. I nearly drowned.'

'You lived with the natives. Then with us. Then you went to Burra Burra. Now you're home again.' She watched him out of the corner of her eye. 'It makes me wonder where you'll be off to next.'

She still had not removed her hand from his; now his fingers curled to enclose it. 'I'm not planning to go anywhere.'

She was very conscious of his warm hand holding her own. 'Truly?'

For a minute he studied her gravely, then turned and looked out at the sea. He muttered something so softly that she could not hear him.

'What did you say?'

He cleared his throat. 'I said everything I want is here.'

It was wonderful to hear him say it but she did not answer. She could not be sure what he meant. Perhaps he was talking only about the run and Asta Matlock and didn't mean her at all. She could hardly ask him to explain. She waited for him to continue but he had apparently said all he wanted to say, sitting on the rock beside her with her hand still clasped in his, his eyes contemplating the sea. For a time she was content to sit there as well, but there were too many things she needed to know. Eventually she said, 'Tell me what you did when you were at Burra Burra.'

He turned and stared at her. 'Why do you ask?'

He sounded angry and suspicious; it startled her. 'Because I'm interested,' she said.

'Your husband's been talking to Asta. He's been trying to find that out, too.'

The shock made her blink. Her feelings, until that moment so warm, tightened and grew cold. She withdrew her hand from his. 'You really think I came here to spy for him?'

Anguish crossed his face. 'Of course I don't! It's just that I wouldn't want Blake to hear about it, that's all.'

It would take more than that to soothe her feelings. 'If you think I'm not to be trusted—'

'I broke out of gaol,' he said. 'If they find me I suppose they'll put me back.'

'Gaol?' She would never have thought of such a thing. 'What did you do?'

'I beat someone up.'

'Why?'

'Over a woman.'

'I see.' Coldly.

'No, you don't see! It happened just after I heard you'd got married. For a time I didn't know what I was doing. Didn't care, either.'

His words pierced her. She thought about it for a while. 'What was her name?' she asked eventually. It was a peace-offering, whether he recognised it or not.

'What difference does it make what her name was?'

'I need to know,' she told him. Hearing Jason say her name would tell her if he cared for this woman still. She did not want to believe but had to be sure.

'It matters to me,' she said. And waited.

'Gwyneth,' he said sulkily.

She wanted to question further: what Gwyneth had looked like, what their relationship had been, whether Jason told her he loved her. But did not. Her name was enough.

'Gwyneth,' she repeated. 'It is a pretty name.' Sure now that Jason's affair with this woman—if that was what it had been—was well over, she smiled, putting her hand on his arm. 'I was curious, that's all.'

'Tell me about Blake,' he asked.

Blake was the last person she wanted to talk about. She shook her head. 'Nothing to tell.'

He stood abruptly, walked to the cliff edge, looked down at the sea tumbling beneath them. When he turned his face was flushed with anger. 'Don't mess with me, Alison.'

She threw open her hands. 'Blake works the run. He works very hard, very well.' For some reason it was important to be fair. 'I look after the house, cook the meals. Just what you'd expect.'

Telling him everything and nothing.

Jason watched her steadily. 'If you won't even talk to me I don't know why you came.'

She remembered how she had told herself she would not do so but knew now it had been inevitable, part of the fate that linked them. 'To see you,' she said.

Her words unlocked his body. He came eagerly towards her.

'As a friend,' she said hastily.

Jason's arms had been open. Now his expression changed. He stopped in mid-stride and his arms fell to his side. 'As a friend?'

'I am married,' she reminded him.

'You didn't come here out of friendship.' His voice was harsh with pain and anger. 'You wanted to make use of me, that's all.'

'How can you say that?' Anguish tore her voice.

'You're lonely and unhappy,' he accused her. 'You thought that seeing me would make you feel better but now you won't even let me get close to you.'

'I daren't.' Her voice was desperate.

'Why? Because you're afraid what I might do to you?'

'Afraid what I might do to myself.'

She had not intended to say such a thing; knew, as soon as the words had escaped her, that she should never have done so if she wanted to keep him at a distance. Too late. His hands were on her shoulders. Their touch was like fire but filled her not with pain but peace. He held her close. She felt his strong heart beating against her breast. Her body and spirit surrendered themselves to him, letting his enfolding arms press her tightly against him. Peace flooded her. It was like a calm blue day, not too hot, the lush paddocks dreaming, the tranquil sea rumbling softly as it met the land. There was serenity there, a sense of rectitude. After months of tribulation and loneliness Alison had come home. He held her close.

She craned her head to look up at him. His face was dark against the brilliant sky but she could see his eyes as he bent to kiss her. Her own eyes closed.

His hand was on her breast. Even as her body responded she said, 'No.'

The hand continued to mould, to coax.

'No!' she repeated more emphatically, her own hand moving to stop him.

A murmur of protest in his throat but he stopped, nonetheless. His eyes questioned her.

'We mustn't,' she told him. 'It's not right.' It was true and she knew it, even as her rejection of him pained her.

'It is absolutely right.'

And that was true, too.

Jason sensed her indecision. His hand moved again, seeking to penetrate her fragile defences.

'Please don't,' she said, face anguished.

'You want me to stop?'

She breathed deeply through her mouth. 'It's not a question of what I want but what we must do. Must not do.' She seized his hand, guiding it away from her. She stared at him, willing him to understand, not to be hurt or angry. 'If I let you do what you want—'

'You want it, too.'

She did not deny it but what either of them

wanted was irrelevant. 'I will not betray my husband,' she said, knowing that she had already betrayed him by coming here but knowing, too, that there were matters of degree in all things. She would have to face Blake on her return. As it was she would be able to put this meeting behind her but anything more and she could not. Blake would sense her guilt. Often he had beaten her for nothing; what he might do with such provocation she dared not contemplate.

Alison stood a little apart from Jason now, tidying her clothing, composing her racing heart. When her breathing had calmed she said, 'I must get back.'

'What will you say if he wants to know where you've been?'

'I'll tell him I've been out riding.'

'Rather say you've been with Asta.'

'What if he checks?'

'He'll never check, it would make him look bad. But I'll warn Asta, anyway.'

'Then she will know.'

Jason laughed. 'She knows already.'

'But—'

But nothing has happened. She had been about to say it but did not, knowing that much indeed had happened.

'Next week,' he said.

'If I can.'

He shook his head. 'No ifs. Be here.'

They parted, she mounted Star and rode home. She had been far longer than she had intended. For all her confident words, her heart beat nervously as she entered the house but Blake had not returned. This time, at least, she was safe.

TWENTY-SIX

'Glad you come by,' Cato Brown said to Blake. 'Somen here I want to show you.' The shepherd took something from his saddlebag and held it out. 'Look at this.'

For a moment Blake did not understand what he was seeing. 'Green pebbles?'

Cato touched a grimy finger to the side of his nose. 'Question is, what sort of pebbles, eh?'

Slowly Blake said, 'At Kapunda Dutton found green rock, too. That mine of his bin goin' ever since.' He took a piece of the rock and weighed it in his palm. 'It's heavy, right enough. Where d'you find it?'

'A mile north of here. Just over the border with Whitby Downs.'

'Let's take a look.'

There wasn't much to see: a shallow scrape in the sandy soil where wombats had been digging, the mouth of a burrow, a scattering of earth and stones. Blake knelt, sifting the loose material through his hands.

'There.' Cato pointed at a tiny green fragment

amid the earth. 'That look like copper to you?'

Blake had no idea. 'Only one way to find out,' he said. 'We got to get it assayed. First thing, though, we must file a claim for the mineral rights. This whole area could be solid copper an' it won't do us no good if we ain't got the rights.'

'How can we do that?' Cato asked. 'It ain't our land.'

'The government issued grazing leases,' Blake said. 'Mineral rights is somen else.'

Cato scratched his head. 'I don' follow.'

'Don' matter who owns the grazing. Anyone can make a claim for the minerals.' He grinned slyly at the shepherd. 'You should've kept quiet about it. If you'd staked the claim yourself you might've been rich.'

Cato knew very well what Blake's reaction would have been if he had done that. 'I ain't got the money to set up no mine.'

'If this is what I think it is,' Blake told him, 'we could be sittin' on enough money to set up half a dozen mines.' He smiled vindictively. 'Then we'll see what Asta Matlock has to say about her bits o' paper.'

Cato did not follow. 'Eh?'

'Never mind. One of us must get to Adelaide, that's the first thing. Best be you, I reckon. If I go Asta Matlock will be sure to find out about it.'

'Go where?'

'To the Lands Office. Register a claim for the mineral rights to this whole area. Then we'll see who owns what around here.' He rubbed his hands gleefully. 'I can't wait to see her face.'

'What about the sheep?' Cato asked.

'Let me worry about the sheep. Jest get down there, quick as you can, and make the claim.' He stared at the shepherd with eyes that were suddenly cold. 'Don' try nuthin smart, will you?'

'Like what?'

'Like puttin' the claim in your own name.'

'I wouldn't do that.' Virtuously.

'Be sure you don't.'

Heavy rains had flooded the countryside and it was over a week before Cato Brown returned. He brought bad news.

'No title?' Blake was furious. 'Why the hell not?'

'They said they got to have a survey of the whole area or they can't register no claim.'

Blake needed to blame someone and Cato was the obvious target. 'Didn't occur to you to fix up a surveyor, I suppose?'

'Yeh, well I did, didn' I?' Cato said, aggrieved. 'Fellow called Hargreaves, operates in Wild Horse Plains. Said he'll come through and measure up for us.'

'You should have brought him with you.'

'He were too busy. But he said he'll be here directly.'

Peddlers came and went with increasing regularity but a stranger in a tall hat was a rare sight on the peninsula. Asta eyed the angular figure with curiosity. The man was obviously uncomfortable to be here. When Jason had come across him he was on his way south and anxious to continue his journey. However, it had been almost dark, more rain was threatening and curiosity, like hospitality, had rules of its own. Jason had escorted the man to Whitby Downs, Asta had given him a good meal and was now determined to find out what she could about him.

'What brings you to this lonely place, Mr Hargreaves?'

'I have been retained to act for a grazier south of here.'

'What is your line of business?'

'I'm a surveyor.'

Blake Gallagher was the only grazier south of Whitby Downs. What was Blake doing with a surveyor?

'Bungaree is owned by my sister-in-law,' Asta said. 'She has not asked for a survey.'

Hargreaves smiled politely, clasping large-knuckled hands around his knee, and said nothing.

'Let me offer you a drink before you go to bed.'

The surveyor was by no means averse to enjoying a drink with Mrs Matlock but he had a hard head for liquor and people had tried to get information out of him before this. When he left the next morning Asta was no wiser than she had been when he arrived.

Blake took the surveyor to the site and left him to get on with it. He had expected that Hargreaves would be finished within an hour or two but it was not until evening that he arrived back at the run.

'I'd thought you'd have bin on your way to Adelaide by now,' Blake said crossly, impatience eating him.

Hargreaves smiled. 'The deposits won't go away, Mr Gallagher.'

'The deposits don' worry me, it's other folks gettin' there first.'

'I'll be away first thing in the morning.'

'How long before the claim's registered?'

'Directly I get there. Say a week.'

Blake scowled. 'That the best you can do?'

Hargreaves seemed to find Blake's impatience amusing. 'My dear sir, those deposits have been lying there for millions of years. What's another week?'

'Listen to me,' Blake said. 'For all either of us knows this might be the richest copper deposit in the colony. If you can't get to Adelaide in three days I'll send someone else. Or mebbe go myself.'

Hargreaves did not take kindly to being harried. 'Do whatever you think is right,' he said huffily.

'Damn right I will.' Blake considered. 'What's to this business of filin' a claim?'

'You go to the Land Registry Office, give the Registrar these drawings I've prepared, register your claim. It will take you half an hour—less—once you're there.'

'In that case I won't be botherin' you no further, Mr Hargreaves. I'll send one of my men.'

'As you wish.' Stiffly.

'Your fee,' Blake said.

'Twenty pounds. As we agreed.'

'That included filing the claim in Adelaide.'

'Which I am still willing to do.'

'Mebbe, but I ain't willing to have you do it. I'll give you twelve pounds for yon piece of paper and we'll call it a day.'

Hargreaves was indignant. 'Twenty pounds was what we agreed and twenty pounds is what I expect. I'm afraid twelve would be completely unacceptable.'

'That right?' Blake fetched a small sack of coins, tossed them on the table in front of the surveyor. 'Count 'em.'

Hargreaves smirked, spilt coins on the table, counted them rapidly. He looked up in mounting indignation. 'There's only ten pounds here.'

Blake nodded, grinning. 'I offered you twelve but you turned me down.'

'Outrageous.' Hargreaves stood. His lips were white with fury. 'You'll regret this.'

'Word of advice. Don't threaten me.' With a swift gesture Blake scooped up the coins and jingled them beneath the nose of the indignant surveyor. 'What's it to be?' he asked contemptuously. 'Ten pound? Or eight?'

'Ride like the wind,' Blake told Cato Brown. 'When the claim's registered get back here, quick as you can. Everything goes according to plan I'll cut you in for a share of the mine.'

''Andsome.' Cato wiped his mouth at the thought of riches.

'If it don't,' Blake cautioned, 'you'd best not be coming back at all.'

'When do you want me to go?'

Blake's big frame vibrated with energy and determination. 'Now. This minute. Ride all night. Don't rest 'til you get there. There could be millions dependin' on this. Remember, there ain't no room for second place. You got to get there first.'

Hargreaves said, 'I don't make a habit of disclosing confidential information to third parties but Mr Gallagher's behaviour was unconscionable. Quite unconscionable.'

'What exactly are you telling me, Mr Hargreaves?' Asta asked.

'I am telling you there is a copper deposit on your land.'

'How can you be sure of this?'

'I have seen a good many deposits in my time, ma'am. As you know, copper has been found in the colony for some years now.' He laughed deprecatingly. 'At one time people seemed to be falling over it every week. Not all the claims proved of value but in some cases, as in Kapunda and Burra Burra, they did. Extremely valuable. The only way to find out the richness of a deposit is to develop it, of course.'

'And these deposits? The ones on my land?'

'I would say they appear promising, ma'am. Very promising.'

'And how does one go about registering a claim?'

'I was going to explain that, ma'am.' The lanky surveyor coughed delicately. 'There is one consideration we should perhaps discuss first.'

'How much?' Asta said.

'Shall we say twenty pounds?'

'You've got to get there first,' Asta instructed Jason. 'Hargreaves thinks that Blake will already have sent someone. Cato Brown, most probably.'

'What's the rush? It's your land.'

'I own the grazing rights, not the mineral rights. Anyone who registers a mining claim can develop a mine.'

Jason stared at the drawings that Asta had given him. 'And we can register a claim with these?'

'Certainly. Mr Hargreaves has marked the relevant areas on the map. He has also given me a letter for the Registrar. Don't lose it,' she cautioned him. 'He said it might be important.'

'What's in the letter?'

'He didn't say. But he told me the Registrar is a friend of his.'

'Why did he do it? If he's supposed to be working for Blake?'

Asta laughed. 'Blake tried to cheat him.' She clapped her hands. 'No more talk! On your way, quick as you can! It could be worth a fortune to us but only if you get to Adelaide first!'

Cato had Blake's best horse and covered the ground so quickly that by daylight he was already well on his way to Port Wakefield. He had seen nobody on the trail but that was to be expected. It was in daylight that he would be likely to meet war parties, if there were any about, and he kept his eyes alert as he rode furiously along the mud flats fringing the northern edge of the gulf. Beyond the fringe of mangroves the mud-brown waters stretched away towards the eastern shore. He could just make out the shapes of two barges moored off the mouth of the invisible Wakefield River.

Cato's mount was strong but there was a long way to go and, with daylight, Cato eased him to a steady trot. There was nothing to be gained by running the horse into the ground before he reached his destination and Adelaide was still a hundred miles distant. Not for all the copper in Australia could he hope to get there until late the following day, however fast he rode.

The blacks were what worried him. At Bungaree they'd had no trouble from them for a long time but he'd heard there were still wild groups scattered throughout the peninsula and was frightened he might ride into them. One meeting was all it would take if they were looking for trouble. He looked back over his shoulder but could see no sign of pursuit. He should be safe enough here, he thought. He had a good horse under him and the first signs of civilisation were already visible a few miles away on the far side of the gulf. All the same, he rode as briskly as he could, knowing he wouldn't feel really safe until he was south of Port Wakefield.

Wild Horse Plains was a tide of yellow grass. Every hour or two Jason passed a cluster of buildings where some enterprising settler was attempting to put down roots but the only other landmark was a range of hills, thirty miles distant, running north and south along the eastern horizon.

Jason had left Port Wakefield far behind, with its dust and creaking drays loaded with copper ore. Ahead of him the plain stretched empty and seemingly eternal. Twenty miles after rounding the head of the gulf he broke his helter-skelter journey at an inn that had been built on the banks of a slowly moving creek. There was a livery stable at the rear and it was here that he picked up his first news of Cato Brown.

'Come through earlier. Ridin' like hell, he was,' the ostler said.

'When was this?'

The man scratched his head. ''Bout seven hour gone.'

Seven hours. Before he left Whitby Downs Asta had calculated that Cato was nine hours ahead. He was catching him, then, but not quickly enough to beat him to Adelaide.

'How far from here to the city?'

''Bout seventy mile, I reckon.'

He had to catch up seven hours in seventy miles. There'd be no sleep for him tonight, then.

'Where's the next place I can change my horse?'

'Twenty miles ahead.'

After the fast ride from Whitby Downs Tommy was already tiring. He would never last another twenty miles.

'I'd best change here, then. I'll pick him up on my way back.'

Through the long hours of darkness Jason rode on. The replacement horse was not a patch on Tommy but maybe it was as well; he was tired himself now, beginning to sway in the saddle, and the last thing he needed was a highly spirited animal under him. In truth he would have preferred to ride a lot slower than he was but with seven hours to catch up he could not afford to do that. His only hope of getting to Adelaide first was to push on as fast as the hired horse and his own tired body would permit. He rode all night in a daze of mounting weariness and seventy miles had never seemed so far.

When daylight came he looked about him, hoping to see some sign of progress, but from the appearance of the countryside he might not have moved at all. To his left the plain still extended to a distant line of hills blocking the horizon, while far away to his right Jason could just make out the dark line of mangroves that bordered the gulf. Here there were no buildings, no people or animals, nothing but the unending plain. And then, emerging it seemed from nowhere, came a band of black, spear-carrying warriors who moved swiftly through the yellow grass to intercept him and into whose arms, helplessly, he rode.

Close to exhaustion, Cato broke his journey at a tumble-down inn thirty miles north of Adelaide. The next morning, after a night plagued by fleas, he set out wearily on what he hoped fervently would be the last leg of his journey. Now there were settlements everywhere. Farms and vegetable gardens bordered the road, he overtook carts and drays at regular intervals, groups of children waved to him as he passed. He took it more easily, now. There was no longer any danger from marauding blacks and he could see no point in killing himself when he was so close to his destination.

At last, shortly after midday, he crested the final hill and rode slowly down the slope and across the river into the city. He went straight to the Registrar's office.

The scrawny clerk eyed him with a supercilious eye. 'The Registrar is at lunch.'

'What time will he be back?'

'Three o'clock.'

Cato looked at the clock ticking ponderously in the corner of the office. A quarter to two. 'Might as well eat myself, then.'

He went to a local pie shop, ate and drank, returned at a quarter to three. The office was as empty as before. He sat down to wait while the minute hand of the big clock ticked its slow way around the brass dial.

At three there was a whirr of mechanism and the clock struck the hour, measured, sonorous strokes in the silent room, but nothing else happened. Behind his tall desk the clerk's pen scratched in the silence. The Registrar did not appear.

Cato turned to the clerk. 'I thought you said he'd be back at three?'

The clerk stared down his nose. 'The Registrar will see you when he is ready and not before.'

Cato grunted. 'Wonderful lives you fellows lead.'

He went back to his chair and sat down, trying to control his impatience. At ten past three the door was thrown open and a figure hurried in.

The black men surrounded Jason as he reined in the hired horse.

After so long away from the clan his tongue was rusty but he greeted them as best he could, using the Narungga dialect Mura had taught him so long ago.

They stared, astonished to find a white man who spoke a tribal language. A moment's hesitation, then one of them replied in a tongue that was not dissimilar to the one he spoke himself.

'Where are you from?' the man asked him.

'The peninsula.'

'How is it you speak the Narungga dialect?'

'I lived with the clan for a long time. Nantariltarra?' he asked. 'Mura?' But the names meant nothing to them.

The spokesman tapped himself on the chest, laughing. 'Kaurna,' he said. Kaurna was the name of the people who inhabited the plains between the head of the gulf and Adelaide. They spoke a language similar to the Narungga and had much in common with them. The two peoples had not always been friendly but for the moment at least Jason sensed no hostility.

'Where are you going?' the spokesman asked.

'To the city.' A thought occurred to him. 'I am trying to catch another man, also white, riding a brown horse like mine. He is a bad man,' Jason said, making it up as he went along, 'I have to catch him before he gets to the city. Have you perhaps seen such a man ahead of me?'

They turned and talked to each other, speaking too fast in their Kaurna language for him to understand clearly what they were saying. Then the man who had spoken before turned back to him.

'We saw such a man,' he agreed.

'When?'

But time meant nothing to them and they could not tell him.

'Will he have reached the city by now?'

They thought not.

'How far is the city?'

Distances meant nothing to them, either.

'I must go on,' he told them. 'I have to catch the man if I can.'

'What will you do when you catch him?' they asked. 'Will you kill him?'

It was the answer they wanted so Jason gave it to them. He slapped the rifle in its holster behind his saddle. 'Kill him,' he agreed. 'Kill him dead!'

They grinned cheerfully, approvingly. 'Kill him,' they agreed.

Jason edged his horse through them. They made no attempt to stop him but stood waving at him as he rode away. He thought that if he rode flat out he might still have a chance of catching Cato Brown before he reached Adelaide. He put heels to his hired mount and headed south towards the invisible city.

Every mile was a penance of heat, dust and flies. Every mile he hoped to see Cato ahead of him. Every mile he was disappointed. By the time he reached the top of the hill overlooking the city and saw Adelaide spread out below him Jason knew that, after all his efforts, he had failed. Cato Brown had got there first.

He almost gave up but some inherent stubbornness would not let him.

'At least let me get there,' he told himself and rode on down the hill.

The river slid silently beneath its new-looking bridge as he crossed it, numbers of people—mounted, in carriages and on foot—passed to and fro through the streets. There were many buildings. Jason did not know where to go. He hailed a passer-by, obtained directions and rode his weary horse in the direction indicated.

He found the building without difficulty, tethered his horse and went inside. In an office adjoining the hallway a clerk, thin and squinch-faced, worked at a sloping desk. The hands of a tall clock pointed to ten past three. In a corner of the room and sitting on a hard wooden chair, Cato Brown.

Jason walked over to him. The shepherd eyed him cautiously.

'You're a long way from home,' Jason said.

'What you doin' 'ere?' Cato asked.

'Same as you, I reckon. Come to register a mining claim.'

'Weren't no-one supposed to know about it.'

'That Hargreaves tipped Mrs Matlock off.'

'How come?'

'Seems he reckoned Blake cheated him.'

'Wouldn't put it past 'im. When did you leave?'

'First light yesterday.'

Cato's eyebrows rose. 'You made good time.'

'I haven't stopped since I left.'

'Pity you wasted your effort.'

'Your claim's not registered yet.'

'Will be, though.' Cato grinned complacently. 'First come first served, mate.'

'We'll see,' Jason told him.

I'm damned if I've ridden all this way for nothing, he thought. He walked over to the clerk seated behind his tall desk.

'The Registrar is out,' the man said before Jason could speak.

'When he comes in, I wonder if you would give him this?' Politely he proffered Hargreaves' letter.

'What is it?'

'A letter from Mr Hargreaves.'

The clerk eyed it suspiciously. 'Mr Hargreaves is a friend of the Registrar. How did you come by it?'

'He gave it to me. Mr Hargreaves was very insistent that the Registrar should see it as soon as he came in.'

'Give it to me.'

Jason handed it over; the clerk turned it once or twice in his hands, staring at it dubiously, then went through a doorway into a back room.

'What's goin' on?' Cato demanded suspiciously.

'A letter for the Registrar,' Jason explained.

Cato relaxed, thrusting out booted feet. 'A letter won't do no good,' he declared. 'You come in second and that's an end to it.'

At the back of the room the door opened. The clerk returned. 'The Registrar will see you now.'

In an instant Cato was on his feet and pushing past Jason towards the door.

'Not you,' the clerk said. 'The other man.'

'But I got here first,' Cato protested angrily.

'The Registrar,' the clerk said, enunciating each word clearly, 'will see the other gentleman. You will wait your turn.'

'Looks like you came in second after all,' Jason said, and passed through the open doorway into the Registrar's office beyond.

TWENTY-SEVEN

Asta wrote to Penrose and a week later, taking Luke Hennessy with her as an escort, she set out to ride to Kapunda.

The town had grown considerably since she was last here. Stone buildings stood where before there had been bare ground. There were several hotels and shops. There was even a dressmaker, a Mrs Owen, whom Asta visited after she had left her bag at the hotel. For what she had in mind, a new dress was likely to be a useful weapon.

'I may live in the middle of nowhere,' she told Mrs Owen, 'but that is no reason not to be up to date in matters of clothing.' But raised her eyes, nonetheless, at the pictures Mrs Owen showed her of the latest dress style that, it seemed, had just arrived in the colony.

'It is all the rage in Melbourne,' the dressmaker assured her.

'It looks so outlandish,' Asta said. 'Not at all practical.'

The dressmaker would not agree. 'It is extremely smart. I believe it will suit madam very well.'

'If you have some material that I like ...' Asta suggested, and spent a happy twenty minutes poring over various bolts of cloth before making her choice: a silk upon which the light played like blue fire. 'I congratulate you on the range of material you have in stock,' she said.

'There is plenty of money in Kapunda with all the mines working,' Mrs Owen told her, hands busy with her tape measure, mouth full of pins. 'We must just hope it continues.'

'Is there any doubt about it?'

'There are always rumours.'

'Such as?'

'People are saying that Wheal Sennen may be in trouble.'

Asta was alarmed. If Wheal Sennen was in trouble perhaps Neu Preussen was, too, and she had a lot of money tied up in that mine. She had never found anyone to represent her in Kapunda but in truth it had not mattered. Lang, meticulous as always, sent her regular statements of income and expenditure, he wrote letters discussing future developments, the price of metal, the state of the workings and the labour force. There had never been any hint of difficulties but she supposed he could have concealed them from her.

'What about Neu Preussen?' she asked.

Mrs Owen was able to reassure her. As far as she knew, Neu Preussen was still doing very well.

Asta was relieved. Apart from her investment, her plans depended upon Neu Preussen continuing in profit.

After arranging to come in next day for a fitting, Asta left the shop and rode over to the Wheal Sennen mine to meet Joshua Penrose at his house. The miner had obviously been on the lookout for her; he came out to meet her before she had even dismounted.

'Mrs Matlock,' he exclaimed, rubbing his hands, his florid face beaming. 'Well, well.'

If he was surprised that she should visit him unescorted he did not show it; protocol had never been as strict in the colony as in Europe. He led the way to the living room. Asta looked about her with pleasure. The house was much smaller than Lang's place but a lot more comfortable and she felt at home in it at once. At home, too, with its owner, a feeling that it seemed he shared.

He served madeira in crystal glasses, raised his own in a toast. 'Welcome back to Kapunda.'

She sensed they still had feelings for each other. The last time they had met she had not wanted to take things further but now circumstances had changed.

'I was delighted to get your letter,' he told her. 'Absolutely delighted. To think that you've found copper on your own land! Tes a miracle, dear Mrs Matlock! A miracle!' He topped up their glasses. 'In your letter you talked about wanting my help. It goes without saying that I shall be glad to do anything I can. Of course! But in what way, eh? In what way?'

Asta decided the direct approach was the best. 'I want you to come to Whitby Downs and develop the Matlock mine for me.'

'Ah.' He raised his glass, squinted through it at the colour of the wine, put the glass down on a side table, all the time without looking at her. 'Ah.' He got to his feet, walked to the large bay window that filled most of one wall and looked out of it at the countryside extending into the distance.

Asta watched him, waiting patiently while he pondered.

Eventually he returned to his chair. He sat down and stared at her, eyes anxious. 'It wouldn't do,' he said. ''Tes a temptation, I don't deny it. Oh yes! A compliment, too, and I thank you for it. But entirely out of the question, don't you see?'

'Why?'

He gestured at the room with its large, shabby, comfortable furniture, the oil paintings, their images barely visible in the dim light, hanging on the walls, the samples of rock crystals displayed upon a side table. 'Look about you, ma'am. This is my home. My place is here.'

'You are a miner, Mr Penrose. Your place is wherever there is a good mine to develop.'

'I already have a mine.'

Her eyes met his. 'There is talk in the town that Wheal Sennen is in trouble,' she said.

He sighed. 'I see you are well informed. Unhappily 'tes true enough. Our present ore reserves are running out. But there is more there, I know it.'

'How can you tell?'

'You said it yourself, I'm a miner, born and bred. I come from a long line of miners. I can smell it, ma'am, smell it.'

'Then surely you have no problem?'

'The problem is getting to it. Knowing 'tes there is one thing, putting your hand on it quite another. It means further exploration, you see. Excavation.' He sighed. 'It all costs money.'

Asta frowned. 'But surely if the mine has been in profit up to now ...?'

'Barely, ma'am, barely. Enough to carry on, to pay the wages, but not enough to put anything aside.'

'And the money I paid you for your interest in Neu Preussen?'

Penrose looked troubled. 'There were debts,' he confessed.

'From that land purchase you told me about?'

'In part, ma'am. That was what brought things to a head. But there were other matters, too. The fact is, ma'am, I'm a fair enough miner, though I say it myself, but when it comes to business I somehow never seem to put my feet right.'

'And now? Do you still owe money?'

'Some. Not a great deal,' he hastened to assure her, 'but some.'

'Beyond your present capacity to pay?'

His head hung. 'I fear so.'

It was Asta's turn to consider. 'I have no money to spare,' she said. 'I need everything I have to develop Matlock. But I may be able to help you, all the same.'

He raised his head to look at her and for the first time there was a flicker of hope in his eyes. 'How can you do that?'

'You will have to trust me. Tell me,' she asked, 'have you spoken to Walter Lang about this?'

Penrose laughed bitterly. 'He was the first person I went to. We were partners once, after all. It was no use. He refused to advance me any money at all.'

'Of course he wouldn't advance you any money.' Asta was surprised that Penrose had even thought of such a thing.

'But he knows the copper's there! His money would be safe!'

'That is why he won't do it. If the mine closes he will be able to pick it up himself for next to nothing. Then all the copper you say is there will be his.'

Penrose's red face fell. 'I fear I am a lost soul in such matters, ma'am. A lost soul.' He beat his clenched fist softly on the arm of his chair. 'Tell you the truth, ma'am, there are times I wish I'd never heard of Wheal Sennen.'

'I can help you,' Asta said, 'but only if you're willing to come and help me develop the Matlock mine.'

He stared at her dubiously. ''Tes a great deal to ask.'

'I need a miner. I know nothing about mining but I seem to have a feel for business. We would make a good team.'

He shook his head. 'I don't rightly know—'

'That is my price, Mr Penrose,' she said crisply. 'I will help you if you help me. Otherwise, no.'

'How do you know there is copper there?'

She explained how the copper had been found. 'Mr Hargreaves said it looked very promising.'

'Hargreaves is a surveyor, not a miner.' But was tempted, Asta saw.

She stood. 'I hope you will accept my offer,' she told him. 'I am not the expert you are but I believe the copper is there. I am willing to invest money to extract it but I must have an expert and I would like it to be you.'

'I have the mining skills—' he began grudgingly.

She interrupted him, looking him in the eyes. 'Not only for your mining skills,' she told him softly. She saw his expression change but before he could speak she had turned and walked across to the door. 'I am staying at the Sir John Franklin hotel,' she said. 'When you've made up your mind perhaps you will send me word.'

I have baited the trap, she thought as she rode back through the town. Now it is up to him.

That evening Joshua Penrose waited on her at the Sir John Franklin hotel. They talked in a small but smartly furnished private drawing room with windows overlooking the main street.

Asta looked at the miner's troubled face. 'You have come to a decision,' she said.

'I have, ma'am, I have, but I doubt you will like it.'

'You are not coming.' A statement, not a question.

'I would like to come very much.' He stole a sideways glance at her. 'For a number of reasons. But tes impossible, you see.'

Asta had rung the bell for wine; now she gestured towards the tray. 'Please pour us both a glass. Come, Mr Penrose, sit down and tell me what's troubling you.'

He did so, sitting close to her, resting his elbows on his knees and leaning forward with his eyes fixed on hers. 'I can't afford to turn my back on Wheal Sennen,' he explained. 'The moment I do that my creditors will pounce. I can feel their breath on my neck even now.'

'Matlock will make up for anything you might lose here.'

'With respect, ma'am, we can't be sure of that. The mine is unproven. Besides, tes not in my nature to run away from trouble. I cannot do it, simply cannot.'

She liked him for that; found that on renewed acquaintance she was liking him very well indeed.

'If you were to receive a good offer for Wheal Sennen, what then?'

'It would put a different complexion on things, of course.' Momentarily his eyes brightened, then his face fell again. 'What's the point of talking about it? Tes not going to happen.'

Asta had no patience with defeatism. 'I want you to give me a clear undertaking,' she told him briskly.

'If I can solve your problems with Wheal Sennen, will you promise to come and help me develop Matlock?'

He looked dubious. 'I'll come and *inspect* Matlock, mebbe—'

She cut him off. 'Not good enough. Anyone can inspect. I need someone to develop it.'

'What if there's no ore?'

Asta did not reply. She was determined he should yield to her, ore or no ore. She fixed her eyes on him and waited for the promise she was certain would come.

'I don' see what you can do about Wheal Sennen,' he said eventually, 'but if you can, then all right, I'll do it. I'll help you develop the Matlock mine.'

It was too soon for triumph. 'I shall just have to make sure I can do something about it, shan't I?'

Lang greeted her in the living room of his house. The room was as stiff as ever, the furniture lined the walls like guardsmen, Lang himself courteous but totally without warmth.

'I heard you had arrived in town. I had thought you might have written to tell me you were coming.'

'I intended to do so,' Asta said, 'then decided against it. You are often away from home. I did not want to cause you to change your plans.'

Lang raised his eyebrows at the idea that anyone, least of all Asta Matlock, might cause him to change his plans. 'You received last quarter's reports?' he asked.

'They were very informative. Thank you.'

'As you see, the mine continues to prosper.' He smiled maliciously. 'Unlike some. As a friend I must warn you against investing in Wheal Sennen.'

It was to be expected that he already knew of her visit to Joshua Penrose. 'I hear there are considerable reserves still undeveloped,' she said.

'Perhaps.' His tone discarded the suggestion. 'I warned your husband at our first meeting, mining is a risky business. It is best left to the experts.'

'You may be right.'

'I am right.' He sat four square in his chair and stared at her. 'Are you here on a social visit,' he asked, 'or do you wish to talk business?'

'I have some business to discuss.'

Lang inclined his head an inch. 'Then I am at your service,' he said.

On her way back to the hotel Asta stopped at Mrs Owen's dress shop and had her fitting.

She stared dubiously at her reflection in the looking glass. 'The material is lovely but the dress itself . . .'

'It is something new,' Mrs Owen said. Briskly she adjusted one shoulder, her fingers busy with pins. 'That is all it is. Madam is not used to seeing herself in such a fashion.'

That was certainly true. 'But it feels so awkward.' Asta tried a few experimental steps about the room, the skirt swaying about her legs, the tight waist gripping her firmly.

'It is quite the rage in Europe,' Mrs Owen said.

'How does one sit down?' Asta asked.

Mrs Owen laughed. 'There is no difficulty in practice. It is just a question of getting used to it.'

Asta made up her mind. She was a modern woman; it was right that she should dress in the modern way. 'Very well,' she said. 'I shall take it.'

When she reached the hotel she sent out a boy

with a message for Mr Penrose. Twenty minutes later he came back with a note inviting her to dine with Joshua that evening.

Asta arranged with the owner of the hotel to hire a carriage; with her new dress it was impossible to ride and she lacked the courage to walk through the town wearing it.

As before Penrose came out to greet her. She went ahead of him through the front door. Her skirts were so wide that she could barely manoeuvre her way through the opening, neither could she sit in the narrow chair she had used before. As Mrs Owen had promised, sitting down was no problem but the width of the skirts forced her to choose a low-backed settee where there was room to accommodate her dress.

'A handsome dress, ma'am,' Penrose said. 'Very striking.'

'It is the latest fashion,' she told him.

When she had met him two days earlier Asta had known that Joshua Penrose was as attracted to her as ever. She was determined to take full advantage of the fact. It was why she had bought the dress, as part of her campaign to lure him to Whitby Downs, but now she suspected there had been a great deal more to it than that. The fact was that she was attracted to him too, much more so than she had thought, and wanted him to admire her, not as the owner of a promising mine but as a woman.

'Your note said you had news,' he said, mind on matters other than dresses.

'I have indeed.' She smiled coquettishly at him. 'You remember your promise? If I can solve your problems here you will help me develop Matlock?'

'I remember.' His face was tense. 'But only if we can sort out Wheal Sennen first.'

She had planned to tease him a little, keep him waiting for her news, but seeing his expression she remembered how much he had hanging on this business and decided to put him out of his misery. 'Walter Lang has agreed to make you an offer for Wheal Sennen,' she said.

'An offer.' He was cautious; weeks of anxiety would not be disposed of so easily. 'How much?'

It was the moment she had been waiting for. 'Eight thousand pounds,' she told him, and smiled as his mouth fell open.

'Eight thousand . . . I can't believe it. Tes true?' he asked, suddenly anxious. 'You're not just saying it?'

Asta's nose went up. 'Do you think I would lie to you?'

'Of course not. Forgive me. But eight thousand—'

'It seems that Mr Lang also believes there are additional reserves at Wheal Sennen,' she said.

'Oh yes, the mine is worth it. If I had enough capital I would never think of selling. But for Lang to make such an offer . . .' He seized her hands. 'It is beyond my wildest dreams,' he told her. 'I shall never be able to thank you for what you've done.' Suddenly diffident, he asked, 'I suppose you wouldn't be willing to tell me how you managed it?'

She laughed, delighted by his reaction. 'Our conversation was very interesting,' she conceded.

It had been a lot more than that. For a long time she had thought she was getting nowhere. Lang drove a hard bargain at the best of times; negotiating with a woman was a new experience and he had expected to browbeat her quickly into submission. He had been displeased and offended when he found he could not.

459

'But why should he agree to pay such a price?' Penrose wondered. 'You said yourself he'd only to wait and the mine would have dropped into his lap like a ripe plum. A ripe plum!' He shook his head, baffled as always by the mysteries of business negotiation.

Asta smiled but was not willing to slake his curiosity. She sensed that something was growing between them and was happy about it but would never again allow herself to answer to a man. Some secrets were best kept hidden; it would not do for him to know too much about her.

She let her mind dwell pleasurably upon the tactics she had used to win what she wanted from the formidable Walter Lang.

'I might decide to invest in Wheal Sennen myself,' she had said to Lang.

He had shrugged indifferently. 'I have already advised against it. If you wish to waste your money that is your affair.'

'So you had not thought of investing in Wheal Sennen yourself?'

'I do not believe in partnerships.'

'Yet you are in one. I own one half of Neu Preussen.'

He watched her carefully. 'What have you in mind?'

'I have copper on my land.'

'Perhaps,' he said. 'Perhaps not.'

'I have faith.'

'Then let us hope you are right.'

'If I am to develop the mine I shall need capital.'

He sat very still, his whole body watching, listening. 'So?'

'So I need capital and you say you do not like partnerships. Very well. I have the solution to both our problems. Buy me out.'

Walter Lang's face was utterly expressionless. 'And what price did you have in mind?'

'That is something we must discuss.'

Discuss it they had. The price she wanted for her shares; the fact that buying Wheal Sennen was going to be part of the deal. Lang had paced about the room. He had bawled, thrown his arms in the air, his face bright red as he had first mocked her, then threatened her, but Asta had stuck to her price and in the end she had won. Or had she? Perhaps she was as mad as Lang obviously thought her, to give up a half-share in a profitable mine for a venture that might prove as barren as the sea. But it was too late to think of that; resolutely she put the thought out of her mind.

'So,' she said now to Joshua Penrose. 'Eight thousand pounds. It is agreed, then?'

Now it had come to the decision itself he was uncertain. 'Tes a hard business,' he muttered, 'turning your back on your own creation . . .'

Asta had no time for sentiment, either. 'If things carry on as they are you will have to sell, anyway,' she said brutally, 'and for a lot less than eight thousand pounds.'

'You're right, of course.' But still dithered, reluctant to commit himself, until Asta, unable to bear the delay any longer, told him to make up his mind or she would drop the whole thing.

He sighed, capitulated. 'So be it, then.'

'And you will come to Whitby Downs?'

'Why not? There'll be nothing to keep me in Kapunda now.'

'I will tell Lang in the morning,' she said. 'Now we would both enjoy a drink, don't you think?'

While he fetched the wine she thought about what she was taking on. He was a good man, a decent man. He knew about mining yet she could not help wishing he were a little more forceful. It was ironic. All along she had been determined to be the one to make the decisions in whatever their relationship might become yet now she wondered if she would not in time grow tired of his amenability.

'God knows we humans are hard to please,' she said aloud.

Joshua heard the tail end of it as he came through the door. 'To please what?'

'Ourselves,' she said. Smiling, she extended her hand to him. 'That is what we have to do in life, is it not?'

He did not know what she meant. He took her hand gingerly, as though it might bite him. Deliberately he changed the subject. 'Your dress . . . Very becoming. I have seen nothing like it before. Does it have a name, this new fashion?'

'This?' She stroked the silk gently, feeling the thin steel hoops beneath the billowing skirts. 'It is called a crinoline.' She saw that she must once again take the initiative if she were to bind him to her, as she intended. She looked at him. He was so diffident. What she was about to do meant taking a great risk but she could see no other way of being sure of him. Ever since Gavin died she had spent her life taking risks. What was one more? It is not only for business, she told her conscience. I want him, too.

She took his hand and led it to the fastenings of the dress. 'And this,' she said, 'is how you take it off.'

TWENTY-EIGHT

Within three months of Asta's and Joshua Penrose's arrival back at Whitby Downs the Matlock mine was well into development. A confusion of gantries and pulley-driven lines led to the shaft. Twenty yards away three drays were lined up, waiting to load. These apart, there were as yet few signs to show that the mine existed at all. There were no huge mounds of broken rock, no horse-driven whims turning. It had proved a rich find with little to do but shovel the ore straight from the ground into the waggons, and the main shaft, although driving deeper by the day, had not yet reached a depth where de-watering was necessary.

Jason Hallam emerged from the small hut used as an office and crossed to the headworks of the new mine.

At the head of the shaft he came face to face with the sturdy figure of Joshua Penrose, just returned to the surface after his daily inspection of the mine workings.

'All well?'

They usually went below together but today Jason

463

had been busy preparing production figures for Asta.

'All very well,' Penrose said. 'The ore body's still heading straight down. No sign of any fractures at all.'

The two men walked together to the loading area where heaps of dressed ore waited for the carriers.

'See there,' Penrose said, pointing, 'tes about a hundred percent pure, what we're lifting at present. That won't last, of course. When we get deeper we'll have to start blasting to get at the ore, but for the moment tes like picking plums out of a pudding.' He rubbed his hands. 'Does a man's heart good to come across a patch o' ground as rich as this.'

'Not everyone's as pleased as you are,' Jason said. 'Blake Gallagher's as sore as a bull over missing out on it. I expect he's still hoping it'll come to nothing. That way he won't have missed so much.'

'Can't say I blame him,' Penrose said. 'I'd have been mortal sick myself, missing out on a strike like this. Richest ground I ever saw. They tribute workers be coining a pretty penny,' he added ruefully.

It was a sore point. Tribute workers received a percentage of the value of the ore they lifted: the richer the ore, the richer the tribute. As was traditional in the mining industry, rates had been fixed when the mine opened and had only the previous month been renewed for a further period of two months. They would be adjusted downwards at the next fixing but for the moment the men were making a killing. It was a source of grievance to Asta.

'You set the rate too high,' she had complained.

'No choice with a new mine,' Penrose had told her. 'If the miners hadn't seen the chance of a good return I wouldn't have been able to get them here.'

She knew he was right but it frustrated her, nonetheless, and she wasn't slow to say so.

The two men walked together to the office. For an hour they went over the figures in detail until Jason was satisfied that he had all the answers to the questions that he knew Asta would throw at him.

'Though I daresay she'll think of something I've missed,' he said.

'Getting downright pernickety,' Joshua agreed comfortably. It didn't seem to worry him. Nothing did; he had settled into his relationship with Whitby Downs and its owner with as little disturbance as a fish in a pool.

'The only way to make a fortune, I suppose,' Jason said. Unlike Joshua, he found the new Asta hard to take. She insisted on knowing everything, repeating the same questions over and over again until she was satisfied with the answers. If she noticed his frustration she did not care.

'Copper is down again. Why don't we stockpile the ore until prices go up?'

'Because we don't know if it will go up. Burra Burra is flooding the market. Kapunda, too.'

'Everything is so expensive.'

'We watch every penny.'

'Watch closer, then.'

It wasn't just the mine; her control over Whitby Downs was just as tight, perhaps more so. She was more at home with sheep, had a better idea of what questions to ask. She demanded estimates: the number of animals, the expected rate of lambing, the current price of wool, the *future* price of wool. The fact that it was impossible to produce such figures did not deter her. She would accept no excuses for failure to give her the information she wanted. She drove Jason mad.

When Cato Brown had returned to tell Blake that he had won the race to Adelaide yet had still lost the mine Blake had been so angry that he could not think straight. Without pausing to consider he had thrown a saddle across Sceptre's back and ridden furiously to Whitby Downs to confront Asta Matlock.

'Robbery,' he raged. 'I wonder you got the nerve to make the claim.'

'It's your own fault. You cheated Hargreaves out of his fee and he paid you out by backing me instead. If you'd kept in with him I would have known nothing about it.'

Being told what he already knew did not improve Blake's temper. He thrust furious fingers through his long blond hair. 'I found the ore,' he said. 'But for me there wouldn't 'a' bin no mine. At the very least I deserve a share.'

'Cato Brown found the mine,' Asta said, tart as an apple, 'on my land. You tried to cheat me out of it. Be thankful you've still got a job, never mind a share in a mine that was never yours in the first place.'

Blake glared at her, incoherent with rage. Whitby Downs was hers by right of inheritance. Because of the legal paper she could get from Mary she was in a position to control Bungaree, too, if she wanted. Now, on top of everything else, she had the Matlock mine.

The unfairness infuriated him, but fury didn't help. 'There are no prizes in coming second,' Asta told him. 'You should remember that.'

Small chance he would forget it.

When he married Alison he had thought that everything in his world would fall into place; now it was all coming apart and he didn't know why.

There seemed nothing he could do about it. His temper suffered as a consequence and Alison, as always, bore the brunt of it.

'That woman won't never rest 'til she owns the whole damn country,' he stormed at her.

His need for violence, almost sexual in its intensity, became more urgent. Alison knew it was only a matter of time before it engulfed her once again. She sought consolation in the only place she knew to find it.

The days were warming as summer approached. Along the cliffs the grass had dried and turned brown. Even at the grotto the turf between cliff face and precipice was dry. It crunched beneath Alison's shoulders as she looked up at Jason, his face anxious as he bent over her.

'I am afraid for you,' he said.

'No,' she said, smiling softly at him.

'Blake—'

She raised her fingers to his lips. 'Don't let's talk about Blake here. This is our place.' Her eyes caressed the rock crevice with the ferns still green inside it, the black stone of the altar, the emptiness of the softly murmuring sea. 'I never want Blake to come here. I don't even want to hear his name. Having you with me is too precious for that.' She smiled up him. 'You mustn't worry.'

No use saying it. He did worry. Shutting Blake out did not alter the fact that he was still at Bungaree, that she would still have to return to him when they left here. If Blake found out what was going on he was likely to kill her. Try to kill Jason too, perhaps, but Jason could look after himself. Alison was a different story. There were nights when he lay awake, frantic with worry for her and for his hopes of future happiness. His feelings for her had intensified, become absolute. He had loved her before but it seemed nothing compared with how he felt about her now.

'If anything happened to you I wouldn't want to live.'

'Hush.' Once again her fingers caressed his lips. 'Don't talk like that.'

'I can't help it.'

'I love you with my whole heart,' she said. 'I think I always did. I just began to deny it after a while. I should have trusted you. Everything that's happened is my fault.'

'Fault's got nothing to do with it,' he told her. 'We're here now and that's all that matters.'

It was not true. The fact was that she *had* married Blake, that her husband had claims on her he would not otherwise have had, that if he found out about their relationship there would be hell to pay.

Yet there was no complete relationship between them at all. They met here, they talked softly and lovingly together, they bared their hearts to each other; they had not, in a dozen meetings, made love. They both knew it was inevitable, both wanted and yet did not want it. Without that final commitment they could still pretend that being here together meant nothing, although both knew that such distinctions would not protect them if Blake found out.

Every time they rode to the grotto they asked themselves whether perhaps today would be the day but so far that day had not come. For all their eagerness to be with each other they still drew back from that final step. Perhaps today . . .

Now Jason bent over her, his expression grave,

concentrating as he undid the buttons of her dress.

She watched his face. 'You mustn't do that,' she said, 'you don't know what it does to me.' But did nothing to stop him, feeling the warm breeze on her skin as finally her dress fell open.

He kissed her warm flesh. His tongue explored her, he breathed the scent of her body. She moaned a little, body writhing.

'God, Jason . . .'

He drew back. They looked at each other, panting. He kissed her again, mouth, eyes, throat, breasts, her arms were round his neck, holding him close, his hand explored her, found her.

'Oh God . . .' Voice dying, senses drowning as sensation overwhelmed them.

Now, perhaps, was the time. After all the uncertainties, all the business of saying to themselves this and not this, so far and no further, perhaps now was the time.

He became bolder, explored further. She did not stop him.

Now.

And then, lying naked together on the grass, he touched her face and found it wet with tears.

He drew back a little and she opened her eyes.

'What's the matter?' he asked her.

'Nothing.'

'There is something.'

Silently she shook her head.

'We don't need to go further if you don't want to?'

'No!' Passionate denial. 'Never that!'

'What, then?'

So quietly that he could barely hear her she said, 'Blake . . .'

'Are you afraid of him?'

'I didn't mean that. I meant . . .' And was silent.

He waited, saying nothing, holding her closer to him, feeling the length of her body against his.

'I married him,' she said, her voice very small. 'I was afraid you would never come back and then my father was killed and I . . .' The tears choked her voice and ran down her cheeks.

'You were alone,' he said. 'It doesn't matter.' Knowing that it mattered very much.

'It matters to me. If I had been braver,' clutching him, speaking into his hair, 'we could be together now, properly. There would be none of this.'

'We are together now,' he told her.

She twisted in his arms so she could see his face. 'And do you love me? In spite of Blake?'

'I love you with my life.'

She looked at him wonderingly and he saw her heart in her eyes. 'And I you,' she said.

'Then nothing else matters.' He stroked the side of her face. 'But I am still afraid for you.'

'Don't be.'

'If Blake finds out—'

'I told you not to mention him. Not here. Here there is just the two of us.'

'But if—'

'If there is going to be trouble there will be trouble,' she said, 'whatever we do.'

Which was true, certainly.

'I hope there won't be trouble,' she told him, a smile forming in her eyes, 'but if there is it will seem a hundred times worse if we've done nothing to deserve it.'

He looked down at her, feeling her heart beating, the swells and hollows of her body pressed against his. A great peace, a great joy and exultation, rose within him. 'You mean . . .?'

Her smile widened, her fingers moving, the nails running gently over him.

'Yes,' she said. Then, fiercely, 'Yes.'

When Alison rode home she wondered if the joy and fulfilment she felt would show in her face but Blake was out and, when he came home, seemed to notice nothing. He was surly but these days he was always surly. It did not matter. She wondered if he might want her tonight. She hated the idea of it but if it happened that wouldn't matter, either. Nothing mattered except seeing Jason again as soon as possible.

It wouldn't be easy.

'You an' that Asta,' Blake said that night. 'Seems like you got a regular love affair goin'.'

'Hardly that.' She laughed. 'But it is nice to see another woman.'

Blake did not know what to make of it at all. 'She threatened to put us off,' he said, 'yet still you goes an' sees 'er.'

He did nothing to stop her; if his wife and Asta became close friends, as it seemed they had, it might serve to protect him if Asta ever turned nasty. For the same reason he managed to control himself when he felt the urge to lash out physically at Alison. It wouldn't do to cross her now she had Asta on her side.

So twice every week Alison rode off, twice a week she met Jason at the grotto, twice a week they made love. No thought now of doing nothing; as the summer wore on they could scarcely wait to get their clothes off when they reached the ledge. They both knew it was foolhardy but neither of them spoke any more of danger. They were committed. Alison in particular barely thought about what she was doing. Nothing could happen to her while she felt like this. Jason felt something of the same and he, too, went his heedless way without regard for prudence or his earlier fears. Now, now, now: it was the only imperative either of them acknowledged.

Until, one day, much like all the other summer days, they rode separately to the grotto, as usual, they met, as usual, they made love, as usual, and when it was over she looked up at him and told him she was pregnant.

Eyes anxious, she spoke as though it were a calamity. 'I'm sorry,' she said.

'Don't ever say that!' He seized her hands and shook them sharply to repudiate her words. Then he smiled at her, emotion spilling into his eyes, his voice, his heart. 'It's wonderful news, wonderful!' He hesitated. 'You're sure?'

She did not know if he meant was she sure she was pregnant or was she sure the child was his. Both, perhaps. She had missed for the second month so at least that was certain. As for the other, there was no way of knowing. Blake came to her far less often than he had but still he came so anything was possible, but every instinct told her that the child was Jason's. It might be wishful thinking but she willed it to be so, was determined it was so. Another Blake? She would not contemplate it. She lied, as though lying could make it so. 'I am sure. Sure I'm pregnant. Sure it's yours.'

He did not question her certainty, did not wish to question it, perhaps. He stared down at her, delight like a flame in his face. He scrambled to his feet, went and stood at the very edge of the cliff and stared out at the rippled expanse of the gulf. He was naked. From where she lay Alison watched the play of muscles across his broad back, the narrow waist, the way his backbone tucked in above the taut flare of his buttocks. His hands and neck were burnt dark by the sun, the rest of him milk white. Sunlight lay in a golden pool on him. She thought she had never seen anything more beautiful in her life but her face remained sombre. He turned and came quickly back to her, arms outstretched, his whole body suffused with such energy that it seemed he could not remain still even for a moment.

He said, 'It's the most wonderful news I ever heard.'

'Isn't it?' Voice flat, face unsmiling.

He looked wonderingly at her wand-slim body stretched full length upon the turf. 'No-one would ever know.'

'Give it time, everyone will know.'

Her tone penetrated his consciousness at last. His smile died. He stared at her, perplexed. 'Aren't you glad?'

A little boy, she thought, hurt because no-one likes his toys.

'It will be brought up as Blake's child,' she pointed out.

The thought shook him. 'Never!'

'Of course. It must be.'

'No!' His expression was savage with determination. 'I shan't allow it!'

Men, Alison thought, when would they learn to face reality?

'How do you plan to stop it?' she asked him.

For a minute he stared at her without replying. 'We'll go away,' he said at length.

'Where?'

'East. To Sydney. Or Melbourne. I don't care. All I know is I'm not having my child brought up as Blake Gallagher's kid!'

'What do we do in the city?'

'I'll find work.'

'What sort of work?'

'How do I know what sort of work?'

'I'm not traipsing off to the city if I don't know what I'm going to.'

He stared at her, exasperated by her insistence upon details that he had no way of supplying. 'You don't seem to want to go away with me at all.'

The knowledge that she was pregnant had given Alison a determination she had never had before. 'I don't know if I can say it but I'll try. I can't help seeing the problems. I won't be able to hide it from Blake, not for long, but I can't just get up and go away if I don't know where we're going. If it was just me I'd do it. I'd have done it a dozen times already if you'd ever asked me but you never did and now I can't.'

'Why not?'

'Because I've got the baby to think of.'

'I won't have it brought up as Blake's child,' he said again. He crouched beside her, took her hands in his. 'You're sure it's not his?'

She did not hesitate. 'Yes.'

'How can you be sure? I never asked you about it, I don't want to ask now, but there must've been times when Blake ... When you and him—' He floundered, unable to say it.

'It is your child,' she told him clearly. 'Don't ask me how I know. I just know, that's all.' It had become an article of faith.

Her utter confidence must have convinced him because she felt his hands relax in hers. 'What else can we do but go?' he asked.

'You go,' she told him. 'Find somewhere that'll be

right for the baby. Then send word and I'll come.'

'The last time I went away you got married,' he said. 'Sure you won't change your mind again?'

At one time such a question would have devastated Alison; now she did not blink. 'You'll just have to take that chance.'

'Maybe I should kill Blake,' he said savagely. 'That would solve all our problems.'

'And make a heap of new ones,' she said. 'There's no point talking like that. You know you're not going to do it.'

Jason walked back to the cliff edge, moving more slowly this time. 'Where would you want to go?' he asked her over his shoulder.

'It doesn't matter,' she said. 'Anywhere nice where we can bring up a baby.'

'I often thought I'd like to try my luck at the goldfields,' he said. 'Lots of people made money there. A dozen times I almost went.'

'No.' She was definite. 'From what I've heard the goldfields are too rough.'

Jason told Asta; she received the news gravely. She too had changed since Joshua Penrose had arrived. In matters of business she was as tough as ever but in other ways her personality had grown more mellow. Jason never had, never would, ask her anything about her private feelings but she seemed more comfortable and fulfilled than ever before. It looked as though the experiment—which was how Jason had always thought of it—was working.

She asked the same question that Jason himself had asked. 'Is it yours?'

'She says so.'

'How can she be sure?'

'I don't know but that's what she says.' He looked at her. 'Seems to me we'll have to go away.'

Asta shook her head slightly. 'You are sure that is a good idea?'

'What else can we do?'

'You can wait. Let us see this baby first. Then you can make up your mind.'

'I reckon we should go now,' he said.

'Because you are worried about Blake bringing up your child. Have you thought that if you go away you may end up rearing Blake's child?'

He shook his head stubbornly. 'She would never have told me it was mine unless she was sure.'

'If you wait you will know.'

'Not to be certain.'

'Of course. Look at you. You are big, dark.'

'Blake is big, too.'

'But blond as the sun. How can there be any doubt, with the fathers looking so different?'

'It might favour Alison.'

'You have nothing to lose by waiting.'

'I'll think about it,' he said.

'That is right,' she said. 'Think about it. Wait and see for yourself. Then, if you still want to go, good. At least that way you'll be as sure as possible. That is all I ask. You owe it to yourself.'

At Bungaree Alison said nothing, Blake seemed to notice nothing. At this stage there was little to see. Her body was as slim as ever and the few signs that existed—the infinitesimally increased weight of her breasts, the darkening and enlargement of her nipples—were too faint to be noticed by any man who had no reason to be on the lookout for such things. Yet there was a change in her that had nothing to do with the shape of her body. She walked in a slightly different way, she held her head back proudly, at times she smiled secretly to herself, at times without even being aware of it she ran the palm of one hand caressingly over her belly, and these things Blake noticed.

At first he thought nothing of it; then he was puzzled; finally, when Alison continued to say nothing to him, he grew suspicious. He did not speak but began to think, and his thoughts made him angry. He began to watch. Finally, he decided to act.

Asta stood with her arms folded, her back to the door, and stared up at Blake sitting relaxed and seemingly jovial in the saddle. 'We don't see much of you these days,' she said. 'What brings you to Whitby Downs?'

'I thought I would come.'

She knew he would never try to trade words with her, he was not quick enough to do that, but his eyes were everywhere. He looked particularly at the yard where the horses were penned, then shifted his glance back to Asta and smiled, but the smile did not reach his eyes. 'I came to ride home with my wife but it looks like she's already gone.'

Damn, Asta thought. 'You just missed her.'

'Then if I go now I'll catch up with her along the way.'

Asta made her voice casual. 'Unless she decided to ride around a different way.'

His eyes did not shift from her face. 'Why should she do that?'

'For a change. Who knows?'

'Did she say she was going a different way?'

She smiled. 'Alison doesn't have to account to me for what she does.'

He continued to stare at her. She would not look away but stared straight back at him. Their mutual dislike was heavy between them.

Blake nodded. 'I'll be on my way, then.'

He clicked his tongue at the horse and cantered off, dust rising in a filmy brown cloud behind him.

Asta watched until he was out of sight then ran for her own horse. I must warn them, she thought as she ran, but with luck they may already have left.

They had not; she found the two horses tethered in the strip of bush that ran parallel with the cliff. Thank God, she thought. At least they had not grown careless, as she had feared. She tethered her own horse with the others and hurried down the path.

God knows what I will find when I get there, she thought, but did not slow her steps. There was no time to think about such things now.

Jason and Alison looked up, startled, as they heard her steps on the path.

At least they are clothed, she thought. That is something, at least.

Jason was on his feet before she reached them. 'What's up?'

'Blake,' she panted. 'He came to Whitby Downs looking for Alison.' She turned to the girl who was scrambling white-faced to her feet. 'Get home as quickly as you can. I told him he had just missed you but you might have decided to go for a ride rather than head straight home. As long as you don't take too long it'll be all right.'

Pray God, she thought.

They hurried up the path as quickly as they could. Asta stood beside her as Alison swung herself up into the saddle. 'Go steadily,' she instructed. 'Don't get home in a fluster. And think what you're going to tell him.'

She and Jason watched as Alison rode away southwards.

'You think she'll be able to manage it?' she asked him.

'Of course she will.'

Asta heard the uncertainty in his voice. Alison had better manage it, she thought. She did not dare think what Blake might do to her otherwise.

Alison rode through the last of the scrub that surrounded the Bungaree homestead.

All the way home she had been lecturing herself. Be calm; be relaxed; be surprised when he tells you he has been out looking for you. Laugh with him a little, if he will let you. You can do it. You must. What if he hits you? a part of her mind screamed. What if he knocks you down and kicks you? Kicks you in the stomach? What will that do to the baby?

Stop it, she told herself fiercely. That won't happen. He has been much better lately. Hasn't laid a finger on you for—what?—months. Why should he start again now?

Because now he is suspicious, she thought. You were careless and now he suspects. Now he *knows*. He will look at you with those dead eyes and his fist—

Stop it, she told herself. *Stop it!*

She rode into the sunlight, her head up proudly, drawing the air deep into her lungs as she tried to steady herself. Her eyes slanted nervously in every direction, seeking danger. Finding . . .

Nothing.

The palms of her hands were wet. Despite all her efforts, the nerves were vibrating in her stomach. She dismounted, opened the door of the harness shed, took off the saddle and went inside, hung it in its place. When she came out Blake was standing by her horse. His shirt sleeves were rolled over arms bulging with muscle. His head was thrust forward belligerently. He did not smile or speak.

Her nerves screamed. Somehow she managed to smile at him. 'Hello.'

'I rode out to meet you,' he said. 'I couldn't find you.'

'I'm sorry. Where did you go?'

'I went to Whitby Downs. That Matlock woman said you'd just left.'

'I went for a ride through the bush,' she said.

'Best be careful.'

She frowned. 'Careful?'

He eyed her, jaw still belligerent, and she held her breath. 'Them blacks is still about,' he said eventually.

'They won't harm me.' There had been a time when Alison, like her mother, had been terrified of the natives, their spears and savage appearance. Now she was more frightened of her husband than she had ever been of them.

'Be careful, that's all I'm sayin'.'

'I will,' she promised him. 'I really will.'

He studied her a moment longer, then turned and stamped away. Relief made her weak. Once more she had survived. It couldn't go on, though, she knew that. Jason was right. They would have to go away.

TWENTY-NINE

Three days later Jason left the Matlock mine to ride back to the Whitby Downs homestead. He had travelled about a mile when he saw a shadow move in the dense bush bordering the track ahead of him. He hauled in on the reins, reaching for the rifle he carried in his saddle holster, and Mura stepped out into the daylight. The last time he had seen him Mura had been wearing European clothes; now he was naked and carried a bundle of spears in his hand and Jason had to look at him twice to make sure it really was his friend.

'My God, Mura,' he said, 'you want me to shoot you, you're going the right way about it.'

Mura did not smile and when he spoke it was not in English but in the Narungga dialect that was the only language either of them had spoken in the days before the Matlocks and all the other white settlers had arrived on the peninsula. 'We are going away,' he said.

After so long a time Jason had to think out his words before he could reply. 'Going where?'

Mura shrugged. 'I don't know.'

'If you go into another clan's area there'll be trouble.'

'What choice do we have?'

'You can stay here. No-one bothers you.'

Mura drew his lips back over his teeth. 'Benson and Sergeant Dawkins, you think they don't bother us?'

'They're long gone.'

Mura shook his head. 'They are on their way back again. They will be here within two days. They will keep on coming back, them and all the other white men who think like them. They will never stop until they have destroyed us.'

'You said yourself that the white ways were the ways of the future,' Jason reminded him. 'You wanted to be a part of them.'

'And was I allowed to be a part of them?'

'Takes time, I suppose.'

'Men like that will never allow it. They force us to remain as we were, yet that is impossible. The old ways are gone but we have nothing to put in their place. It will be even worse when there is no more game. What will we do, then?'

'We've always allowed you to take a sheep or two.'

Mura gestured angrily at the landscape around them. 'This land is mother and father to us. Now it is all taken by the whites. You think we should stay here forever, living on the white man's charity?'

'I don't see what else you can do.'

'We can do what we are doing. Go away and keep moving until we find another place.'

'The whites will keep coming after you,' Jason warned him. 'I don't reckon they'll ever stop.'

'They will stop at the desert,' Mura said. 'You cannot feed sheep in the desert.'

'The desert is not your place.'

Mura turned. His eyes, shadowed beneath their heavy brows, dwelt once again on the land he was leaving. 'This is not our place, either,' he said. 'Not any more.'

'What about Reverend Laubsch? And Karinja?'

'They are coming with us.' Mura shrugged. 'Laubsch likes to think he leads us. We allow it; it does no harm. As for Karinja, he is an old man. I think he will die before we get where we are going but we are the only home he has.'

They looked at each other, two friends who would almost certainly never see each other again.

'We have far to travel,' Mura said. 'I must go.'

To Jason it didn't seem right that such a casual meeting should end years of friendship. Words of farewell and regret struggled in his mind but he found he could put his tongue to none of them. Instead he raised his hand. 'See you.'

Mura raised his hand in return. A second later he had turned and vanished into the bush. For an instant there was a black shadow gliding, then nothing. Jason watched after him for a minute, then rode on.

'Some ways I envies you,' Blake said.

'How come?' Dawkins asked.

'You come and go. We're stuck here but you see the country.'

'What there is to see.' Dawkins belched.

The two men sat in Blake's house with glasses and a bottle placed conveniently on the floor between them. Dawkins topped up his glass and drank appreciatively. He had a waggon load of whisky parked under the trees a mile away but had no objection to drinking Blake's liquor, if that was what Blake wanted.

'What brings you back so soon?' Blake asked.

'Thought we'd get rid of some more of our grog to the abos but it looks like they've moved out.'

'Wasted your journey, then.'

'Maybe not. I got a bone to pick with a bloke. Get half a chance, I'll settle with him while I'm here.'

'Jason Hallam,' Blake said.

Dawkins scowled. 'Know about it, do you?'

'Heard somen,' Blake admitted.

'Friend of yours?'

'Friend?' Derisively. 'That'll be the day.'

Dawkins glanced at Alison, busy at the fire. He leant forward, voice confidential. 'Lots of blokes got somethin' in their past,' he said. 'Things a man like me might be interested in knowing. You wouldn't happen to know if Hallam's got anything like that?'

Blake hesitated but for the moment the tradition of saying nothing to the authorities was too strong. 'Don' know nuthin about that,' he said.

Dawkins watched him. 'Might be a reward for the right information.'

'Tole you. Don' know nuthin.' Blake tipped the remains of his drink down his throat and stood. 'I got to get back to work.'

'If you ever hear—'

'I'll tell you. Yeah.'

Blake watched as Dawkins limped away. One of the black troopers had told Cato Brown that Jason had smashed Dawkins' balls for him. Looked like he still hadn't got over it.

Somen happened at Burra Burra to bring Jason back so fast, he thought. I'd swear to it. But if I breathe a word to Dawkins and Asta finds out I'll be out of a job. Best leave it. He smiled. They weren't *my* balls he smashed.

'I shan't see you for a few days,' Jason said. A hundred feet below them the surf creamed peacefully. 'We're starting shearing tomorrow and I won't be able to get away.'

'I think you should leave altogether. Get right away from here.'

'Not before we finish shearing. I can't just walk out on Asta after everything she's done for me.'

'I've got bad feelings about it,' Alison said.

'Soon as it's over I'll go,' he told her. 'Ballarat should be far enough.'

'No mining,' she warned him.

'It's all big companies now. No room for little blokes like us. I ought to be able to get a job in a mine office, maybe. I was good at that. When I'm settled I'll send for you.'

'We can get a little house,' Alison said. 'Somewhere for the baby. With fruit trees, maybe. I always fancied the idea of fruit trees.'

Jason looked about him. 'I'll miss this place.'

'Maybe one day we'll come back for a visit. Anyway, we won't really be leaving it.'

He looked at her. 'If we go, of course we'll be leaving it.'

She shook her head. 'A part of us will always be here. And this place will always be a part of us.' She looked at the rocks about them, the trickling thread of water, the sea's expanse. 'Wherever we go, it'll go with us.'

'You got some funny ideas,' Jason said.

'I must get back,' she told him.

'We've only just got here,' he objected. 'Why, we haven't even—'

She stood, brushing shreds of grass off her skirt. 'I told you. I've got a bad feeling about things, today.'

'Hang on a minute.' He put his hands on her shoulders and looked down at her. 'If I go, you will come, won't you? Later, I mean? You won't let me down?'

'You're my life,' she said.

They walked up the path to the tethered horses. Jason watched her as she rode away. Just a little while and we'll be together, he thought. For always.

He mounted Tommy and rode north. A minute passed, then another horse and rider rode out of the undergrowth.

Blake looked along the track from which Jason had now disappeared. 'I were right, then.' His voice, tight with rage, broke the silence. 'Right all the time, by God!'

He wheeled his horse and took off southwards, riding fast.

I'll teach the pair of 'em. By God I will.

The hooves echoed his thundering heart.

'Got somen to tell you.'

'What is it?'

At Dawkins' back two loaded waggons stood, ready to leave.

'Jason Hallam.'

The trooper's eyes lit up. He smiled maliciously. 'Thought o' something?'

'He were up at Burra Burra, see? When he come back here he were in a hell of a rush. Like the law were after him, mebbe.'

Dawkins waited for Blake to continue but he did not. 'So?' he asked impatiently.

'What you was saying about people havin' secret things in their lives ... Maybe that's 'is secret.'

'You reckon he did something at Burra Burra?'

'Could've done.'

Dawkins' expression was sour. 'Ain't much,' he said.

'Why don' you check up? All we know, he maybe killed a man.'

'And maybe he didn't.' He thought about it a minute. 'We're pulling out of here, heading north. I could always check up at the mine, seein' we're goin' that way. Wouldn't hold your breath, mind,' he warned. 'Probably ain't nuthin to it.'

'When will you be back?' Blake asked. 'If you find anything?'

''Bout three days, give or take.'

A flicker of movement, that was all it was. A patch of light in the shade, a few yards from Dawkins' tent. Walking back through the bush Blake's eyes were drawn to it. He watched it without turning his head. It vanished but he knew he had not imagined it. More, he knew what it was.

When he got back to the house Alison was busy at the stove. Blake had long got out of the habit of looking at his wife but did so now. It was stinking hot inside the house and her face was flushed. No doubt because of the heat, she had hitched up her skirt to her knees. He thought she looked very pretty. He wasn't sure what love was, wasn't sure it existed, but certainly there had been a time, shortly after their marriage, when he had felt tender towards her. He had never told her, of course; no man worth the name would talk about such things, but he had felt it, all the same. Not for a long time now, though. Least of all today.

'Bin anywhere?' he demanded.

She did not look at him. 'No.'

Liar, he thought.

Slowly he walked across the room towards her. 'Look at me.'

She had just lifted a heavy pot from the fire, the steam gushing around the iron lid. She stood and looked expressionlessly at him.

All their married life he had tried to find her, to seize hold of the very essence of Alison. He had failed. Now that sense of failure came back with a rush. He remembered what he had seen earlier on the cliffs and his frustration turned to blood-red rage.

'Bitch!' he shouted. 'Bloody whorin' bitch!'

One step, steadying himself. He hit her once with his clenched fist full on her left breast. She dropped the pot. The boiling contents exploded down her legs.

A clang as the iron pot struck the hearthstone. It fell on its side, spewing scalding liquid and steam. A sudden, excruciating agony savaged her. A high, shrilling sound that only later Alison identified as herself, screaming. She was running, frantic. The air was like a branding iron on her scalded skin. She fell, lay writhing, mouth agape. Merciful darkness washed away the pain.

When she came to, a single thought was beating in her head. The baby ... She lay on her back, eyes still closed, not daring to move. Cautiously she sent out little tendrils of consciousness, checking, testing. Her breast throbbed painfully. Her legs were on fire. Anything else? She held her breath, still checking, but nothing else seemed damaged.

Cautiously she opened her eyes. Memory returned, as painful as the throbbing in her breast.

Blake's fist. The rage and calculation in his eyes as he hit her. It had been deliberate, hitting her where he had. He had intended damage, perhaps even to kill.

He knows, she thought. Nothing else could explain that expression of hatred.

She could remember little after the pot had slipped from her hands. There had been the pain, of course. She seemed to recall tearing at herself, throwing herself on the floor. Her hand explored. She was not on the floor now. She turned her head. She was lying on the bed. Of Blake there was no sign.

She tried to get up but was too weak to move. As for her breast, that was nothing. At one time the thought that he could strike her on the very spot that had given them both such pleasure would have devastated her. Now, apart from the bruise itself, she felt nothing. She no longer had any feelings for Blake, neither love nor hatred. At last she was free of him.

I shall go away with Jason. We shall find somewhere together. She tested herself again, trying gingerly to raise her legs and failing. A few days, she thought, that is all it will take. A few days and we shall go.

By now night had fallen and Alison, unable to move, lay in darkness until, an hour later, Blake returned.

After he had lit the lamp he came and stared down at her. 'All right?'

'My legs are burning,' she said. Her voice sounded stronger than she had expected. She had thought she would never be able to speak to him again but it was easy; indifference had unlocked her tongue.

'You burned yourself with that there pot. I put some grease on 'em. They'll be better soon.' He turned away and went out into the main room. She heard him say, 'Christ, this place stinks.'

It did indeed; some of the contents of the pot must have fallen in the fire and the smell of burning hung acrid in the air.

Blake came back. 'Any food?'

'There's some cold mutton in the meat safe.'

He grunted and went out again. He did not offer her any, not that it mattered. The thought of food made her sick.

She slept. When she woke it was still dark. At her side Blake breathed in his sleep. She remembered what until now she had forgotten: she had followed Blake through the bush to his meeting with Dawkins and hidden from him as he walked back. A sergeant of troopers, she thought. The few snippets of conversation that she had managed to overhear floated in her mind. She could make nothing of them. What had Blake wanted with him?

The next morning, somewhat stronger, she managed to walk unaided to the outhouse. When she got back Blake was just going out. 'What did you talk to Dawkins about?' she asked.

He stared down at her. 'None o' your business what we talked about.' An unpleasant grin. 'But I don' mind tellin' you. Sortin' out a few problems, tha's what we was doin'.' He nodded significantly and walked out into the sunlight.

She had no idea what he meant.

The soreness in her legs lingered. The skin, bright red where the liquid had scalded it, blistered. For a day she ran a fever. She spent it in bed, hugging herself to keep warm, shaking with repeated bouts of ague, then it passed, leaving her drained but with her brain as clear as water. She inspected herself. Her breast was black but that was nothing. The legs were the problem. The blisters had joined together to cover large patches of skin. One or two had broken and oozed a clear liquid but at least there was no sign of infection.

Another night. In the middle of it she awoke. Her brain, suddenly alert, was alive with memories: of Jason telling her of his escape from prison; of Blake talking furtively with Dawkins. Fragments of conversation came back to her. She mulled over them, trying to discover ...

Jason's name had been mentioned. Then Dawkins had said that something would take him three days. She had heard the name Burra Burra. And now Dawkins was gone.

The fragments fell into place. Dawkins had gone to Burra Burra to check up on Jason. In three days, he had said, he could be back. And today was the third day. Wasn't it? She tried to work it out. The day she was scalded. The day of fever. The day after. Today. Three days.

Terror flooded through her. She had to warn Jason before it was too late but knew that as long as Blake stayed close to the buildings she could do nothing. Even if he left her it would be difficult. With her legs the way they were it didn't seem possible for her to ride, yet there was no other way.

It was still dark when Blake woke her. She could not bear the weight of the covers upon her legs so was lying outside them. He brought the lamp close so that he could inspect her legs. He looked up and caught her watching him.

'How you feeling?'

She was surprised he was interested enough to ask but still did not trust him. 'Bad,' she said.

'Then you won't be goin' nowhere, will you?'

It was frightening, the way he had apparently read her mind. 'Where should I go?'

His bared teeth threatened her. 'Time we got a few things sorted out, my girl.' He leant closer and she smelt his body. 'Any more fun an' games an' I'll kill you, 'ear me? And anyone else who's stupid enough to get in my way.' At the door he turned. 'I'm goin' to the other side of the run,' he said. 'Make sure you're still 'ere when I get back, eh.'

He went out; the door closed behind him. A few minutes and Alison heard the sound of Sceptre's hooves, diminishing in the dawn's faint light. She got up at once. She massaged cooking fat into her legs, tore up some cloths and bound them as tightly as she could. The burns were agonising. When she touched them the pain brought tears to her eyes. '*Never mind,*' she told herself, 'you can put up with that,' knowing that it would be worse when she was riding but knowing, too, that she had no choice.

She went out to the paddock, somehow managed to saddle her mare, somehow managed to haul herself into the saddle. The pain lacerated her, bringing sweat to her forehead. She clicked her tongue and slowly, very slowly, she rode north.

THIRTY

Nightmare. She had never imagined such agony.
With every mile it grew worse. It wrenched at her,
driving every thought and emotion out of her head.
Before she was halfway she was sobbing helplessly
but still she rode on. It never occurred to her to do
anything else; she knew that, once dismounted, she
would be unable to get back into the saddle.

By the time she reached Whitby Downs she was
reeling, barely conscious, broken words and phrases
emerging meaninglessly from lips bitten until they
bled.

From the shearing shed Asta saw Alison arrive,
realised that something was amiss, came to her at a
run.

'My God, Alison, what is the matter with you?'

'My legs,' Alison managed to say before half-
slipping, half-falling from the saddle.

Frightened, Asta helped her indoors, got her to lie
down and with care unwound the cloths covering
her legs. What she saw drained the blood from her
face.

Alison looked at her through half-closed eyes.

Somehow she managed a tremulous smile. 'A mess?'

The legs were indeed a mess, of blood and broken skin. Asta was frightened even to touch them. Where Alison had found the courage to ride here with legs like this she could not imagine.

She took a hold of herself. 'Nothing we can't cure,' she promised her robustly. 'But why are you here? What's happened?'

'Jason,' Alison whispered.

'What about him?'

'He must get away. Blake has been plotting something with Sergeant Dawkins. I don't know what, exactly, but Blake is fit to kill Jason, he's so jealous, and somehow I think he's found out we've been meeting.'

'But what happened to you?'

'Dropped a pot with broth in it.' The ghost of a smile. 'Don't worry, I'll live.'

Asta was not so sure of that. If infection set in . . . But that would have to wait. Her first concern was for Jason.

'What did Blake arrange with Dawkins?'

'They said something about the Burra Burra mine and Dawkins going to check up.'

Asta took a deep breath, her face grim. If Dawkins checked at Burra Burra he would be sure to learn of Jason's escape. He would be back with a troop of men to arrest him.

'When did this happen?'

'Three days ago. That's why I'm here. Dawkins said he could be back in three days and with these legs I couldn't get here any earlier.'

Three days. Swiftly Asta calculated times, distances. Dawkins was right. If he had ridden straight to Burra Burra he could be almost here by now. Alison was right, too. Jason must get away at once.

'Jason is at the mine,' she said. 'Joshua needed him. He should be back soon. We'll have to wait.'

It was no good but it would have to do. If she went to look for him she might miss him on the way.

Alison struggled to sit up. 'You must tell him,' she said, 'I'm not going to be able to wait.'

Asta stared at her. 'You're not going anywhere. Not with legs like that.'

'I've got to. If Blake finds out I've come here he'll be right behind me. The mood he's in, he'll be looking to kill the lot of us.'

'I can take care of Blake,' Asta said contemptuously.

Alison shook her head impatiently. 'No, you can't. The way he is at the moment, no-one can handle him. I must get back before he finds out.'

Asta looked at the ruined legs. 'You can't.'

Alison smiled. 'I can do a lot of things I used to think I couldn't.'

Asta was awed by the girl's courage. She had always seemed weak; now she was like steel, tempered in the fire. Asta knew that she would not be able to stop this new Alison from riding back to Bungaree.

'Let me at least bind your legs,' she said.

Half an hour later she stood at the door of the house, watching as Alison clawed her way painfully into the saddle. God knows how she'll manage the ride back, she thought.

'Are you sure you wouldn't be better to stay?' she asked.

'I would only hold Jason up if he sees me,' Alison said. 'It's better this way. Besides, you never know what you can do 'til you try.' She looked at Asta. 'Tell Jason to find somewhere for us,' she said. 'As soon as he lets me know I'll come to him. Tell him that. And tell him I love him.'

Asta nodded, her throat tight with tears.

She watched as Alison rode slowly away. She was not sure she had done the right thing in letting her go but Alison had been determined and her arguments made sense, of a sort. Above all, Asta had finally met someone with a will to match her own; that the person was Alison made her immensely proud.

'Blake has made you grow up,' she said softly as the departing figure disappeared from view. 'Let us hope the experience does not kill you.'

She went back to the shearing shed. Now she could do nothing but wait.

It was almost midday by the time Jason arrived.

She heard him come clattering into the yard and hurried out to meet him. 'You must get away at once,' she told him.

'What's happened?'

She explained as quickly as she could. 'If Dawkins has been asking questions at Burra Burra—'

Impatiently Jason interrupted her. 'What about Alison?'

'She came to warn you but her legs are very bad. She shouldn't have been riding at all.'

'What's wrong with her legs?'

She explained, watching his face darken as she spoke.

'And you let her ride back again?'

'She was afraid what Blake might do if she didn't.'

'Why should he?'

'Alison thinks he's found out about the two of you.'

'Then I must go after her and get her away from him before he does anything else.'

'Jason, listen to me,' Asta said. 'That girl rode all this way to save you. Her legs are in ribbons. How she managed it I shall never know. And then to go all the way back again ... You know why she did it, don't you? Out of love of you! And you intend to repay her by going back there? You think she will thank you?'

'You should never have let her go back.'

'She was afraid she'd be a burden to you if she stayed. That was all she was thinking about, getting you away before the troopers came.'

'Blake,' Jason said through clenched teeth. 'It's time for a reckoning with Blake.'

'No! You must get away before Dawkins gets back!'

He glared at her. 'I told you ... I won't leave her there with that animal.' He ran towards his horse, then hesitated and turned back. He took her hands in his. 'I've never told you what you've meant to me. I know I should have managed it but somehow I never had the words. I haven't got them now but I wanted you to know, that's all.'

Asta needed all her willpower to keep her voice steady. 'You get along. Find Alison if you must. Get her away from here as quick as you can.' She hesitated. 'Goodbye,' she said.

'Not goodbye yet. We'll pass through here on our way north. We'll stop and see you then.'

More than anything she wanted it but could not allow him to do it. 'Don't do that. Ride around. You don't know who may be here by then.'

He thought about it, then nodded. 'Right. We'll let you know where we are.'

Her eyes were blurred with tears. All she could see was his outline. 'Of course you will,' she said.

He ran and swung up into the saddle.

'Don't kill him,' she called to him, 'not unless you have to.'

He nodded, face grim, and put heels to his horse.

Asta watched him go. The sound of the galloping hooves died. The dust drifted slowly down. She went back into the shed.

Two hours later Asta heard the sound of horses. She straightened, hands on her aching back.

Hector Gallagher looked at her. 'Who is it this time?'

'Troopers,' she said and went out into the sunlight.

She was right. Sergeant Dawkins and four black troopers, all well mounted, all very smart and military-looking. In the saddle holsters the butts of the rifles shone with oil. Each man carried a pistol with cross-belts of ammunition strapped across his body.

She eyed the sergeant in unfriendly fashion. 'Have you come back to sell us more whisky?'

'We have come to arrest Jason Hallam,' Dawkins said.

'What do you want him for?'

'That is none of your concern—' Dawkins began pompously.

Asta interrupted him. 'It is if you want my co-operation. Not that I am promising anything, mind you.'

'We have reason to believe he escaped from the Burra Burra prison.'

'On what charge?' Every minute she could delay them would help Jason to get clear.

'Attempted murder.'

'He's not here.'

'It is a very serious crime—'

'I do not care if he has killed the Pope,' Asta said. 'He is not here.'

'We shall search the buildings,' Dawkins threatened.

'Please go ahead.'

They searched, found nothing.

'Where is he?'

'At the mine.'

'Why didn't you say so?'

'You didn't ask.'

Dawkins gave sharp orders to his men, turned to Asta again. 'If he ain't there we'll be back.'

They cantered away, dust puffing behind their horses' hooves. Asta waited until they were out of sight, then ran into the shearing shed.

Hector Gallagher threw a fleece on the table while the freed animal clattered awkwardly away down the chute. 'What did they want?'

'Jason. He had some trouble at Burra Burra. They had him in the gaol but he escaped.'

His eyes were pools of shadow. 'How'd they know to find 'im 'ere?'

'Blake told them.'

'Blake?' His face winced.

'I am going to Bungaree to warn him.'

Hector did not ask what Jason was doing at Bungaree, knew without asking, perhaps. 'I'm comin' with you.'

'There's nothing you can do. You stay here, get on with the shearing. I'll be back as soon as possible.'

She ran to the paddock to fetch her horse. Within minutes she was on her way.

Dawkins rode at the head of his troop through the scrub. He thought, This is all too easy. I thought I'd have to beat it out of her and she came right out and said it.

At the mine.

I reckon she's lying.

He raised his hand and the troop came to a halt.

'You three go on,' he ordered. 'If he's there arrest him and bring him back.' He turned to the fourth trooper. 'You come wi' me.'

They retraced their steps, pausing at the edge of the bush that surrounded the Whitby Downs buildings.

'We ain't bin more'n a few minutes,' Dawkins said, 'I don' reckon she's had time to get away yet.'

Almost immediately they saw Asta come out of the shearing shed and hurry across to the paddock where the horses were. She quickly saddled a horse, mounted and headed south.

'Bungaree,' Dawkins said with satisfaction. 'That's where 'e is. Bungaree.'

They followed her, keeping to the bush. When they caught sight of her dust they settled down to trail her.

From the way Asta had spoken of Alison's condition Jason had half-expected to catch up with her along the way but by the time the Bungaree buildings came in sight he had still not found her. He reined in, checked that his rifle was primed and loaded, then rode slowly forward through the last of the trees.

The buildings baked in the hot sun. On the slope of the hill sheep grazed but down here nothing moved. He rode on, step by step. His spine itched between his shoulders and he twisted in the saddle to look behind him, but there was nothing. The door of the barn stood open. He swung himself down from his saddle. Three quick steps. He peered inside. Nothing. His eyes went to the horse paddock behind the house. Sure enough, Alison's horse was there, the saddle still on its back. She was home, then.

Once again he looked carefully about him. No sign of Blake. No sign of anyone at all. He crossed to the house and went in.

'Alison?'

He went into the inner room. Alison lay on the bed. Her eyes were closed. She was so still he thought she was dead and for a moment his heart froze in his chest. He bent over her, saw the faint rise and fall of her breathing. She was sleeping or unconscious but he could not wait until she woke naturally. He put his hand on her shoulder and shook her gently. 'Alison . . .'

It took some time but eventually her eyes opened and he saw pain flood into them. 'What are you doing here? The troopers—'

'I came to take you away.'

'I can't. My legs—'

'I won't go without you.'

'But I'll hold you up.'

'Can't help that. When's Blake due back?'

'Before dark.'

'We haven't got long, then.'

She shook her head weakly. 'I can't.' Tears were running down her face.

Jason saw that she had indeed reached the end of her strength but for either of them to stay now was unthinkable. 'We won't go far tonight, just enough to stop him finding us. In the morning we'll push on. Perhaps I'll be able to get a cart or something from Whitby Downs. That'll make things easier for you until your legs are better. The important thing is to get away from here now.'

He helped her, taking off the cloths that Asta had used. Alison's legs were terrible. He tried to bathe them but she could not bear him to touch them and he had to stop. If the legs became infected it would be very serious. She might die but if Blake came back and caught them here they were also likely to die. There was no help for it; they had to get out of here as fast as they could.

'As soon as we can find a doctor we'll get him to look at those legs,' he told her. 'Then you'll be right.'

She told him where he could find more cloths. He wrapped her legs in them, tightening them as much as she could bear. She tried to stand but could not.

'It's no use. I can't do it.'

'Is there any kind of cart we can use?'

'A cart will slow you down too much,' she protested. 'Leave me and get away while you can.'

'I've already said I'm not going to leave you,' he told her, 'so you might as well save your breath.'

Moving like an old woman she sat down again on the edge of the bed. 'There's a small cart in the barn,' she said.

He went out to the barn. Sure enough, there was a cart. He fetched Tommy. 'Sorry, mate,' he told the horse, 'you'll have to pull something for a change.'

With the horse between the shafts he went back to the house. He filled the largest container he could find with water, stowed it in the cart. He took a side of mutton from the meat safe and put that in, too, with some stale damper from the kitchen. He went back for Alison. She was sitting where he had left her. Her eyes were shut; she seemed barely conscious. He picked her up carefully and carried her outside.

The sun was far down in the sky as he carried Alison to the cart and laid her inside it. He looked down at her drawn face, black rings around her eyes. 'I'm sorry for hurting you,' he said.

'Don't worry about it.'

'I'll drive as carefully as I can but I can't promise not to jar you at all.'

She smiled faintly without replying. He climbed on the driver's bench, put his rifle beside him and flapped the reins. 'Walk on,' he said to the horse.

Until the last he had been afraid that Blake would come back and catch them but once they were among the trees he began to breathe more easily. In an hour it would be dark. They had managed to give him the slip, after all.

He spoke over his shoulder. 'We'll keep going as long as we can, then rest up 'til morning. A good rest and we'll both feel better.'

She did not answer. He glanced back at her. She seemed to be asleep.

He kept the cart moving as long as he could, stopping only when it was too dark to see the way between the trees. He turned to check on Alison. She was still asleep but her forehead was hot to the touch and she was shaking with fever. Gingerly he felt her legs through the bandages. They too were hot, burning.

He was sick with worry. He was alone in the bush, far from any possibility of help, with a sick woman in urgent need of treatment. There was a very real danger of her dying yet he could not even light a fire to warm her for fear the flames might draw Blake to them. He thought of climbing into the cart and cradling her in his arms but did not do that either, afraid of waking her, of adding to her pain. He loved her and was frightened for her and could do nothing to help her. He sat on the ground, his back against the wheel of the cart, and the time passed very slowly. He needed sleep if they were to make good time in the morning but did not dare sleep in case Alison woke and needed him.

After an hour he got up to check on her. She seemed the same. He was about to sit down again when her eyes opened.

She looked up at him. 'Hello, my love.'

'How are you feeling?'

'Thirsty.'

He fetched the container and helped her drink. 'How are your legs?'

A wry smile. 'I know they're there, all right.'

'Would you like me to put water on the bandages?'

'Do we have enough?'

'Plenty.'

With dry country ahead they most certainly did not have plenty but he was determined to make her as comfortable as he could. He poured water carefully over the bandages. 'How does that feel?'

'Wonderful.'

'Still sore?'

'I'll live.'

'Make sure you do. I brought some mutton,' he said. 'Want any?'

'No, thanks.'

'You must keep up your strength.'

'I'll have some tomorrow.'

'Do you want to sleep some more?' he asked.

'I want to lie here and talk to you. Unless you want to sleep?'

'We'll talk,' he said.

For a while she lay silently, then said, 'Tell me where we're going.'

He had no idea where they were going but now was not the time to say so. He said, 'We're going up the peninsula to the head of the gulf with the sea on our right and the hills on our left.' He carried on talking, drawing a picture of the route they would take to Melbourne, a route that he had never travelled but telling her about it all the same, using his imagination to describe the lakes they would pass, the green and golden hills, the flocks of multi-coloured birds living in the trees. She listened to him like an obedient child, eyes fixed on his lips, and he went on inventing stories of their journey that he knew would never happen and not caring until at last she said, 'What house shall we have when we get there?'

So he told her about that as well, how it would be large and comfortable with a garden full of flowers and a thatched roof to keep them warm and safe in winter.

'And fruit trees,' she told him. 'Don't forget the fruit trees.'

He was still talking when, at last, she closed her eyes and was at once asleep. Carefully he disentangled his fingers from hers. He touched her forehead with the back of his hand and was relieved to find her temperature was down. He returned to his place by the wheel of the cart, leant back with the rifle across his knees and fell asleep also.

The horse woke him, whickering softly. Jason opened his eyes to the grey light of early dawn. He stood, rifle loose in his hands, and looked about him. The horse whickered again and Blake stepped out of the trees twenty yards away, his rifle already raised to his shoulder, the muzzle pointing at Jason. Too late, Jason remembered how good Blake had always been in the bush.

'Gotcha, you bastard,' Blake said. Without lowering the rifle he walked slowly forward. When he was ten yards away he stopped again. He lowered the rifle to his waist but the muzzle was still on target, Blake's finger was on the trigger and Jason knew that he would not be able to move even an inch without Blake killing him.

'Put your gun down,' Blake said. 'Very carefully.'

He did so, leaning it against the wheel of the cart.

'Now move away from it.'

He did that, too. There was a loose piece of rock lying three yards away. If he could get to it, if he could throw it, if it was on target ... He knew he had no chance of reaching it.

'Stop.'

He stopped.

'Why shouldn't I kill you?' Blake asked.

So they were going to play games. Rage was building. At himself for letting Blake catch him off-guard. At what would certainly happen to Alison if Blake got her back again. At the fact that he could see no way out of the situation.

'If you're going to kill me, get on with it,' he said. 'Don't just talk about it.'

'I ain't goin' to kill you,' Blake told him. 'The troopers are on their way. They're going to lock you up for the rest of your life. I reckon that'll be a better punishment than killing you. Try to steal my wife?' His voice grew shrill. 'I'll see you rot in gaol a hundred years!'

'Is that so?' Jason took two steps to his left, forcing Blake to turn to keep him covered.

'Sit down,' Blake ordered. 'Put your hands on your head.'

'Why?'

Two more steps. If he provoked Blake too far he might shoot him anyway, but if he could draw him close enough . . .

Blake moved swiftly, not towards Jason but to the cart. He yanked a pistol from his belt and cocked it, aiming down into the cart. 'I said sit down.'

Jason stood motionless, fists clenched at his side.

'I'll shoot her if you don't.'

'Then you'll hang.'

Blake shook his head, grinning. 'You went for me, I defended myself, she got in the way of a bullet. No-one will know the difference.'

'I'll tell them the difference.'

Blake's grin widened. 'Who's goin' to believe a gaolbird like you?' His voice sharpened to a lash. 'Now: *sit down*!'

Jason could not risk Blake carrying out his threat. He sat as ordered.

Blake prowled closer, the pistol still ready. Jason knew he was as helpless as ever yet had to do *something*.

He took a deep breath, feeling his heart hammering in his chest. Now.

'Alison!' he shouted in mock alarm. 'Don't!'

For the second he needed Blake's eyes wavered. Quick as thought Jason yanked off one of his boots and flung it. The boot hit Blake in the face and he staggered. The pistol was no longer on target. Jason's legs bunched beneath him and he flung himself after the boot, crashing with full force into Blake's chest. Blake staggered backwards, he dropped the gun, but his arms seized Jason in a bear hug and Jason winced at the power in Blake's shoulders. He twisted sideways and thrust out a leg, trying to throw him, but Blake moved with him without breaking his hold and forced Jason back until his spine creaked. Jason tried to knee him but Blake blocked the blow with a thigh like a tree trunk and applied greater pressure, forcing Jason back another inch. The breath sobbed in Jason's throat as he strove to break the hold before his spine snapped. He clenched his right fist and lashed out blindly, using it like a hammer, and felt Blake's nose crunch as he struck home. For a second the deadly pressure eased. A second was all Jason needed. He twisted again and slammed the side of his hand with full force into Blake's neck. The hold was broken. Blake staggered back, gasping for breath, and Jason flung himself at him again. Off balance, both men fell, grappling and lashing at each other. Jason's strength was going now but Blake must be tiring, too. He made a supreme effort, rolling over so that Blake was beneath him, and sank both hands into Blake's thick neck. Got you, he thought, but Blake jackknifed, catching him by surprise and throwing him clear. Before Jason could recover Blake was on him. A fist like a hammer stunned him, knees pinned his arms and Blake grinned triumphantly as he snatched his knife from its sheath and lifted it, blade gleaming in the early sunlight. Frantically Jason tried to throw him off but it seemed nothing could move Blake's massive bulk.

There was a sharp sound. Looking up into Blake's face, Jason saw his eyes widen in astonishment. He coughed. A trickle of blood appeared between his lips and ran down his chin. The knife dropped. Strength gone from his suddenly flaccid body, Blake slid slowly away from Jason and fell to the ground. He lay on his side, his legs straightened convulsively, he was still. An open eye stared sightlessly at the dust. Unable to understand what had happened Jason staggered to his feet and saw Alison, his rifle in her hands, the smoke still fuming from its muzzle.

He ran to her. Her face was white as bone; she swayed as he gathered her in his arms. 'He was going to kill you,' she said, 'so I shot him.'

She was shaking uncontrollably. Jason held her tight. 'You saved my life,' he said into her hair. 'Again.'

'Is he dead?' she asked presently.

'He's dead, all right.'

'I didn't want to kill him,' she wept into his chest. 'I wanted to stop him, that was all.'

'It was the only way you could stop him. He'd have killed us both, otherwise.' He helped her to sit down. 'How are you?'

'I'm a lot better,' she said, 'but I wish I hadn't killed him.'

Jason looked down at her, feeling strength flowing back into his body. 'I don't want to rush you but we should move on,' he said. 'Those troopers may be on their way. If they are they'll have heard the shot.'

'Blake must have his horse somewhere,' she said. 'It can't be far. I'll ride. That way we'll make better time.'

He was doubtful. 'It's too soon—'

'They're my legs and I tell you they're much better. I want us to get away from here as quickly as we can.' She smiled up at him and put her hand on his. 'Do you think I've gone to all this trouble just to have the troopers catch you?'

They found Blake's horse twenty yards into the bush. 'You're sure your legs will be up to it?' he asked her, still worried.

'Of course.'

He reloaded his rifle and returned it to its holster. He fetched Blake's two guns. The pistol he thrust into his belt, the rifle also into its holster. He cut up the meat and loaded it with the damper and water into their saddlebags. He helped Alison mount. Finally he took his own horse out of the shafts and mounted as well. He smiled at her. 'Let's go, then.'

They rode north through the thinning scrub.

Half an hour later they reached a wide patch of open land. Long ago there had been a fire here and the scorched remains of dead trees stuck like broken bones out of the grey soil. Ever since they had left the cart and Blake's dead body, Jason had been filled with the strangest of feelings. He could not get used to the idea that he was alive. Blake had been about to kill him, had had the power to do it. Jason, in those last seconds, had accepted its inevitability, and then it had not happened. Because of Alison, he told himself. Because she had killed Blake first. That was true, of course it was, but the sense of wonder and disorientation remained. He could not get away from the idea that he ought to be dead and the feeling was like living in a dream.

They had seen and heard nothing of the troopers. He did not even know if there were any troopers. They were acting as though the pursuit were hard behind them yet for all he knew Dawkins had not returned from Burra Burra.

He'll have come back, all right, he thought. He won't have forgotten the fight we had. He'll want to get even for that. But where he is, whether he is a mile behind or a hundred miles, that we have no means of knowing. Without the gunshot they would never find us, he thought, but it was too late to think of that. Without the gunshot he would have been dead.

Some instinct made him rein in at the edge of the burnt ground. There was no reason to suppose that Dawkins would be here rather than anywhere else but, if he *were* here, he would see them clearly as they crossed. He looked both ways but could see nothing. The open ground continued in both directions as far as he could see. He had a bad feeling but there was no help for it; if they wanted to continue north they would have to cross the open ground and hope there was no-one there to see them do it.

'Let's get it over with,' he said.

They rode out into the open. At this point the burnt area was half a mile across and they had not crossed more than a third of it when he heard the sound of shouts and, a moment later, the distant crack of a rifle.

'Go!' he shouted to Alison and put heels to his horse. Side by side, they galloped towards the far trees. There were more shots but they were far away and seemed to represent no immediate danger.

'We're going to make it,' he yelled to her, unsure whether she could hear him, 'we're leaving them behind.'

The persistent dream that had troubled him all morning had vanished. He could see the distant line of trees drawing steadily nearer, feel and hear the pounding of the horse between his thighs, sense the wind in his face. He was filled with exultation. They would escape and start afresh and perhaps, just perhaps, the dreams and stories he had dredged out of his imagination the previous night would come true.

Not perhaps, he told himself. They *will* happen. I know it.

The shelter of the trees was only two hundred

yards away. He looked towards them, full of triumph at their escape, and saw two blue-clad figures ride out of the bush ahead of them.

For an instant he could not believe what he was seeing, then swung his mount to the left, forcing Alison to do the same, and rode flat out for the trees with his body and his horse between her and the two troopers.

There was a shot. Another shot.

A hundred yards, now. Less.

A third shot and this time he heard the pluck of air as it whistled past. He lowered himself as flat as he could in the saddle, his head far down the horse's flank, hearing only the heaving gasp of the horse as it stretched itself over the final yards to safety. Then there was a sharp blow under his ribs and he was suddenly cartwheeling through the air to land with a crash on the ground.

For a moment he lay half-stunned, then his head cleared and the pain came, a terrible burning pain that stole his breath and threatened to stop his heart.

His eyes were shut against the pain but opened as Alison, who must have dismounted and come back for him, tried frantically and unavailingly to lift him, to carry him into the trees that were now so close.

'Leave me,' he said, 'you can't manage it.'

Tears were pouring down her face. 'I will,' she said through clenched teeth. 'I will!'

'I'm too heavy for you. Besides, it's no good.'

She stared at him, face working. 'You don't know that!'

'The bullet went up into my chest,' he told her. 'I can feel it. I'm all broken inside.' He knew he was finished; knew, too, that he had only a few moments before the troopers arrived. 'You must go back with

Asta,' he told Alison. 'Stay with her. She'll look after you.'

Her face was swimming before him as he spoke and his voice sounded strange in his ears.

'I don't want you to leave me,' she said.

He tried to smile. 'I love you. I'll never leave you.' He took a deep breath. His chest felt as though it were filling with blood. Now he had only a minute, perhaps less, but there was still something he wanted to say. 'You told me yourself,' he said. 'On the cliffs. You said a part of us would always be there. And that place would always be a part of us.' She was receding from him as he spoke. It was becoming more and more difficult for him to speak at all but he made a final effort, determined to say what he had to say to her. 'Go there,' he told her. 'And I . . . will be there for you. Always.'

Now she was no more than a pinpoint of light, shining still but diminishing swiftly as he watched. He tried convulsively to grasp her hand but could no longer feel it. He tried to speak but there was nothing left to say. He took a deep breath. His head fell back.

Alison looked down at him. To the end, despite his terrible hurt, he had been there, as he had promised. There for her. There for their future.

Gone.

She saw him with devastating, blinding clarity. A sheen of dust across one cheek, a few specks sullying the fixed and open eye. She was filled with a choking flood of terror, rage, denial.

Gone.

She sat quietly while the rage and pain devoured

her. 'I will be there for you,' he had said. There for you.

She heard a sound behind her and looked up. The troopers had come up and were staring down at them, their black faces expressionless. She should hate them for what they had done but did not. The surge of rage had passed as quickly as it had come, leaving behind it an emptiness that filled the world.

I will be there for you.

She heard his voice, telling her again that he loved her. The remembered words filled her heart then slowly died, muffled by a distance too great to comprehend. He had been everything, her strength, consolation, laughter and passion, her hope for the future. Her love.

Gone.

Gently she laid down his head. She bent, kissed him. She stood. Her face was frozen, bereft of tears. She turned and walked away.

EPILOGUE

I

So, at last, we have come home. Alison, Alison's unborn child, Joshua and myself. We are content together. I say little to Alison about what has passed; it is beyond my ability to tell her how much I admire her courage, her determination to face the future.

Whitby Downs lies at peace, bathed in sunshine. I stand in the open doorway of the house, looking across the golden acres towards the invisible sea. This far country to which my husband brought me has become my life and from hatred I have come to know and love it well. It is peopled with my ghosts. Edward and Gavin, Ian and now Jason. Blake, too, is part of those memories. In his lifetime I hated him but now ... Let him rest. All of them striving to create a future from the raw materials of the earth, all now gone. Yet not gone, while I live. In my memories they are alive as I, too, shall be alive in the hearts of those who know me. Joshua, should he survive me, Alison, Alison's child.

It is a miracle that the last two survived.

Alison has told me what happened, of their night-mare journey, the battle with Blake, the renewed flight and its tragic end. What she did not know was how Dawkins was able to out-think them and lay the ambush into which they blundered. I knew. I was there.

II

I reached Bungaree shortly before sunset to find no-one there, neither Jason nor Alison nor Blake. Later I understood that Blake had been and gone by then, following Jason's trail while the light lasted, but at the time I did not know that. I had come to warn Jason and Alison that Dawkins and his troopers were in the district; now they were gone I could do nothing but return home.

Before I could set out for Whitby Downs Dawkins and his man arrived. He did not arrest me but neither did he allow me to leave. He sent the trooper to fetch his other men, keeping me with him at Bungaree, and at first light the next morning we all rode north.

I had refused to tell him why I had ridden to Bungaree but he knew, of course.

'They're somewhere close,' he said, 'I kin smell 'em.'

The sun was barely clear of the horizon when we

came across a strip of burnt land half a mile wide extending east and west across the peninsula. He sent his men to ride along it and when they returned to report no sign of tracks he rubbed his hands. 'If they ain't crossed they still got to be south of 'ere.'

He set his ambush, himself and two of the men at one point, the others a mile further on, and here it was that Jason and Alison, two hours later, arrived.

After Jason was dead Dawkins wanted no more to do with us. Even the discovery of Blake's body did not interest him. Jason he had sought and Jason he had found; now all he wanted was to go home. He would have taken the body with him but Alison talked him out of it.

'Let him lie here where he belongs.'

Dawkins, brute though he was, agreed. Less trouble than taking him, I suppose.

Hector Gallagher took Blake's death better than I had expected.

'He'd gone from me long ago,' he said, but aged overnight, no longer the violent man he had been.

We buried Jason and Blake with the rest of our dead and got on with our lives.

III

Alison often goes to the grotto and when she returns her face is that of one who has walked with the spirits. As for me . . .

Long ago I had a dream. Jason was that dream and Jason lives on in memory, in his unborn child. The future still beckons all of us, as the shores along this coast must have beckoned Jason when first he arrived here. I have arrived at the point of acceptance. Not of forgetfulness, never that, but acceptance of something that cannot be changed. The acceptance brings comfort, of a sort.

Joshua tells me we are rich, will be richer still, in time. There seems to be no limit to the wealth of the Matlock mine. I would have known that for myself, once, had my finger on every ounce of ore raised, every penny spent. For the last three months, since Jason died, I have taken less interest. It no longer matters to me. Still, it is better to be rich than poor.

Joshua has been pressing me to marry him. I think I shall say yes, not now but soon. It will provide a symmetry to my life that it currently lacks. I swore I would never again be answerable to a man but Joshua is not the type to take advantage of a husband's authority. Besides, I have come to love him. There is certainly great comfort in that.

Today is a bad day. Despite my acceptance, there are still times when my sense of loss becomes too strong to bear. Anguish returns. In the old days, after Edward died in the sea, I used to return often to the spot where it had happened. It is years since I last did this but now, once again, I shall go on pilgrimage to the place where Jason was gunned down.

I shall sit there, alone with my memories. The silence will soothe me and restore my strength. Finally, when my heart has grown quiet within me, I shall mount my horse and ride home.

AUTHOR'S NOTES

The Narungga people, or Narrunga as it is sometimes written, inhabited the Yorke Peninsula of
South Australia from ancient times until shortly after
the arrival of the first white settlers in the 1840s.
Their first contact with Europeans is generally
accepted to have been with mariners and sealers
shipwrecked on the peninsula. The Narungga had
no difficulty in absorbing such isolated individuals
but the arrival of organised groups of white people
proved fatal to tribal society as it did elsewhere in
Australia and, indeed, throughout the world. The
scattering of the Narungga was so complete that
few traces remain of their language or culture. The
ceremonies described are based on aboriginal ceremonies but no-one can say with certainty whether
the beliefs and customs I have attributed to the
Narungga people belonged to them or not.

Winda, or *winta*, as some sources would have it,
is the Narungga word both for a spear and a barn
owl. It features in the dreamtime legend that I have
recounted here.

As a result of white settlement alcohol became

available to indigenous people who had no previous experience of it. As in many other countries, the experience proved catastrophic and remains so to this day.

Although there were very many acts of sympathy and kindness between the races, atrocities of the type described undoubtedly took place from time to time. The hatreds created over the ensuing years, justified or unjustified but invariably counter-productive, are also with us to this day.

The reference to the island far to the north where the Narungga people obtained the flints used to tip their weapons is to South Molle in the Whitsundays where the remains of an old quarry are still being examined by archaeologists. Current belief is that, through trading, the stone from this quarry found its way throughout Australia.

The first white settlers bought pastoral leases from the government and in terms of their own society were legal owners of the land. Conditions were always harsh for the pioneers but the high price of wool enabled some of them to make large fortunes. The Matlock family is fictitious, as are all the main characters, but the way they lived is based on records of pioneer life. The murder of Gavin Matlock is based loosely on an actual incident where a relation of the pioneering Bowman family was killed at the Foresters Arms at Tarlee. The inn no longer exists but a heap of stones in a paddock outside the town shows where the inn once stood.

Coppermania was the term used to describe the frenzy that overcame the colony at the time of the great copper discoveries.

Kapunda was the first mining settlement in Australia. It was discovered more or less by chance by Francis Dutton, a local squatter who, with his neighbour Captain John Bagot, developed the mine. There were numerous German and Cornish immigrants in the area, although both Walter Lang and Joshua Penrose are fictional characters. Contemporary reports indicate that in its early years the town was much as described. Much of the rock in the area is soft in character and could often be worked without blasting. Occasionally, however, explosives were used. Mining ceased at Kapunda many years ago but the old mine workings still exist and form an important part of the town's heritage. As readers of my novel *The Burning Land* will know, the town later became an important centre for the sale of livestock driven down from the interior. The Sir John Franklin hotel where Asta Matlock stayed during her second visit to Kapunda still stands in the main street, although the earlier Miners Arms no longer exists.

Joshua Penrose's injudicious purchase of land with no payable ore deposits is based on an episode when Captain Bagot paid a huge sum for land that proved to have no mining value at all.

Whittaker, the man to whom Lang refers in his discussions with Gavin Mortlock, was one of pioneer Kapunda's most notable businessmen.

The Burra Burra mine, or Monster Mine as it was known, flourished in the 1840s and for many years afterwards. It was managed from Adelaide by the efficient but unscrupulous Henry Ayers, after whom Ayers Rock (now known as Uluru) was named.

The company charged a rent of three shillings a week for their miners' cottages. By the standards of the time this sum was exorbitant. Miners avoided the rent by digging homes for themselves along the creek bank. Conditions were as described and, after the dugouts had been flooded, the company required all miners to move into company cottages or face dismissal. Help to the stricken miners was initially provided by the mine captain until Ayers issued specific orders that no assistance was to be given.

Mine accountant Challoner existed, although was not necessarily as described. Many years later, in the dying stages of the mine, he became general manager.

Burra Burra mine's dishonest attempts to change the assayed weight of copper were engineered by Henry Ayers and caused serious labour troubles about this time.

The muleteers at Burra Burra were mostly from Chile.

Silas Tregloam's complaints about John Graham taking ten thousand pounds a year from a mine he never saw were in fact an understatement. Graham, an ironmonger from Hindley Street, Adelaide, was the largest shareholder in the Burra Burra mine. In its best years his annual dividends exceeded £16 000. But let's be fair about it. He risked every penny he had to take up his stake in the mine and the gamble came off. If it had not, he would have been destitute.

The gaol from which Jason escapes exists to this day as a tourist attraction.

The name Burra Burra, incidentally, is not an aboriginal name but is taken from the Hindi word *burra*, meaning great.

Port Wakefield, although never really suitable because of its offshore shallows, was opened up at this time as a means of avoiding the long overland route to Port Adelaide. Numerous small towns of South Australia's mid-north—Mintaro, Watervale and Leasingham among them—owe their existence to the route connecting the Monster Mine with the coast. Port Wakefield was originally named Port Henry.

The horse race to Adelaide was an historical event and took place when huge copper deposits were discovered at the northern end of the Yorke Peninsula. It ended much as described, the latecomer being granted title on the strength of personal connections; it is interesting how little the world has changed over the years. The mines at Wallaroo and Moonta on the Yorke Peninsula subsequently eclipsed the Monster Mine itself.

The Burning Land
John Fletcher

That land out there has been burning me as long as I can remember. All these years I've been getting ready for this moment. I'm going out there to take hold of it ...

Raised by struggling Scottish immigrants in the sparsely inhabited mountains of the Port Phillip District, Matthew Curtis dreams of the vast unexplored spaces of inland Australia.

Defying his stern foster-father, he leaves home—and the warm grey eyes of Catriona Simmons—at sixteen. His journey takes him first to the brawling life of the goldfields with the beautiful Janice Honeyman, then north into the burning wilderness of the unexplored outback.

An engrossing historical saga in the tradition of Evan Green and Wilbur Smith, *The Burning Land* bursts with life and the passion and daring of the Australian pioneers.

Extract from *The Burning Land*

Hot sunlight lay yellow upon the moored ships and the waters of the cove; the wharf thronged with bustling, shouting men. Lorna McLachlan stood on the deck of the three-masted barque *Mary*, one hundred and twenty-three days out of London, and watched as sweating longshoremen secured the hawsers connecting the ship to the shore at the end of its eleven thousand mile journey.

The waiting passengers surged forward. Lorna took her husband's arm, her full black skirt swaying about her legs as she did so. The skirt and matching black jacket, fitting snugly to her hips, and the high-necked white blouse in plain cotton were uncomfortable in a climate far hotter than that for which they had been designed. Her blonde hair, pulled back off her forehead in a tight bun, was partially concealed beneath a black bonnet with a deep crown and rounded brim set four-square on her head. Andrew McLahlan, a stiff, hard Presbyterian whose life had been ordered from birth by the Bible, or his own interpretation of it, was not one for frivolities and took it for granted that his wife would follow his lead in this as in all things.

Andrew turned at her touch. At thirty-one he was ten years older than she. They were of a height although she was not particularly tall. She did not need to raise her head for her blue eyes to look into his hazel ones but in every other way she looked up at him, with respect and some fear, for Andrew McLachlan was an intolerant man although not a violent one.

He smiled austerely. 'Landfall at last,' he said in his broad Scots accent. 'Praise the Lord. Now mebbe we can make a start.'

'Aye,' Lorna said. 'Mebbe we can.'

She looked past his shoulder. Moored ships raised a forest of spars against the blue sky. Buildings—brown wood, yellow stone—huddled along the water's edge or straggled up to the crest of the low hill that rose behind them. On the other side of the cove a large warehouse faced the water. Its cargo bays stood open, its interior hidden in shadow. Scurrying figures carried bales and barrels into the recesses of the building. The merchant's name was painted in large white letters on the iron roof. THORNTONS. The name meant nothing to her.

Lorna turned. Beyond the waters of the harbour the blue-grey land stretched away, enigmatic and silent. New South Wales, she thought without pleasure. She feared the prospect of life in this unknown place but took care not to let her husband see her fear. Nothing displeased Andrew McLachlan more than a lack of faith.

The waiting passengers inched forward again. The odour of impatience, of sweat, mingled with the smells of the waterfront brought to them on the light breeze—dust and dung, mud, weed and salt water. A seagull perched momentarily on the ship's rail and screeched once before rising and circling away across the sun-shot harbour.

Eventually, after much shuffling and grumbling, the McLachlans' turn came. Lorna took a deep breath as she stepped for the first time onto Australian soil, as though feeling it beneath her feet made irrevocable the move to which they had been committed since that time, almost a year ago, when Andrew had come into their granite-built house on the east coast of Scotland and told her he had decided to sell the business to Angus Ross and move to the other side of the world.

It was only now, stepping onto the uneven cobbles of the roadway, seeing the buildings, the strangeness of the hot and avid sky, the unknown emptiness of the land beyond the township, that she accepted the reality of this new place where it was her destiny to spend the remainder of her life.

I shall no' look back, she thought. I shall no' think about what might have been. Scotland is gone. The old life, the friends and family, all gone now. Here is where I am, in this new place.

My life begins now.

Claim the Kingdom
John Fletcher

A vast land lies open to those fearless enough and ruthless enough to claim it ...

The year is 1793. Cash and Jack Tremaine have arrived in Sydney Cove from Cornwall, summoned by their father to help him build an empire.

Daring and headstrong, a leader of men and lover of women, Cash is determined to make his fortune. But his efforts bring him into conflict with the colony's most powerful and corrupt men and soon he finds himself surrounded by enemies.

Deeply troubled and prone to sudden fits of violence, Jack moves out to Parramatta to farm his father's land. But Jack is a haunted man and his dreams are filled with a horror he can barely understand.

The Tremaine brothers can claim this Kingdom for their own ... but only if they are willing to pay a terrible price.

Extract from *Claim the Kingdom*

Cash Tremain stood at *Bellona*'s rail, watching the land rise up out of the dawn haze that lined the western horizon.

Five and a half months, he thought. Excitement frothed in his veins. Five and a half months from London Town and here we are. At Last.

It was a hot, humid morning—Tuesday, 12 February 1793.

The vessel steadied on its approach, barely rolling as it did through the water on the light morning breeze. The rays of the rising sun lay golden on the low olive-green cliffs that extended from one horizon to the other, foam gnashing white at their base. There was a shout behind him and a rush of bare feet as the crew ran to alter sail.

Cash felt his brother Jack come and stand at his shoulder. He did not turn his head. Jack was older by two years but in all things Cash took the lead and always had. Jack stood with his face turned towards the land, knuckles white as he grasped the sun-warmed rail.

Some yards away was gathered a group of the passengers with whom they had shared the cramped quarters of the ship for so long. They would all be glad to get ashore after the wet, interminable voyage but for now their expressions were uneasy as they looked out at the approaching land and wondered what lay ahead of them.

'Some strange,' Jack muttered, the Cornish accent strong in his voice. He, too, sounded troubled.

Cash had no such doubts. Exhilaration sang in him. His long black hair flew about his face. He was elegantly dressed in the pale green breeches, knee-length boots, a fawn frock coat with silver buttons and a white stock. He was five feet ten inches tall with good shoulders and an easy, athletic stride.

His feet tapped impatiently on the wooden deck. He felt he could shout, jump, run. 'Strange?' He shook his head. 'It's wonderful.'

Now he could hear the faint booming of the surf as it broke sullenly against the base of the cliffs.

The hull creaked and complained softly beneath their feet. Cash turned and squinted upwards, the sunlight warm on his face. Along the yards, sailors were silhouetted against the brilliant blue of the sky as they worked to reduce sail. Clouds of gulls screamed above the wake or rocketed shrieking past as the land approached.

Bellona slipped through the entrance into the vast harbour that lay within. After the space and movement of the open sea, the sudden hush was like entering a cathedral. The land lay all about them. Cash's eyes gloated on it. It had a dry, peppery smell, of smoke and soil and drought. He breathed deeply, drawing the smell deep into his lungs.

'There's nothing here,' Jack murmured, his voice still uneasy, striving to come to terms with the unfamiliar. 'Not a house, Not a living soul. Nothing.'

Cash laughed. 'That's why we've come, my handsome. To make something of it.' This strange land— ancient but new. His excitement threatened to boil over. He couldn't wait to get ashore.